JURY
TOWN

OTHER NOVELS BY STEPHEN FREY

The Takeover

The Vulture Fund

The Inner Sanctum

The Legacy

The Insider

Trust Fund

The Day Trader

Silent Partner

Shadow Account

The Chairman

The Protégé

The Power Broker

The Successor

The Fourth Order

Forced Out

Hell's Gate

Heaven's Fury

Arctic Fire

Red Cell Seven

Kodiak Sky

JURY TOWN

STEPHEN FREY

THOMAS & MERCER

This is a work of fiction. Names, characters, organizations, places, events, and incidents are either products of the author's imagination or are used fictitiously.

Published by Thomas & Mercer, Seattle

www.apub.com

Amazon, the Amazon logo, and Thomas & Mercer are trademarks of Amazon.com, Inc., or its affiliates.

ISBN-13: 9781477827697
ISBN-10: 1477827692

Cover design by Stewart Williams

Printed in the United States of America

For Lily. I love you very much.

PART ONE

PROLOGUE

1992

CHARLOTTESVILLE, VIRGINIA

The chill crawled up her spine like a black widow spider stalking her naïve mate—deliberately and purposefully.

Despite the midsummer heat of the Piedmont noon, Victoria shivered.

She and her mother had arrived seventy minutes ago—an hour early. But she'd been counting down to this day for five years. They were so close . . . but now he was ten minutes late. The anticipation was almost unbearable.

She took an exaggerated breath to calm herself down. Slowly and deeply in—then back out just as deliberately. Exactly as she had a month ago right before stepping onstage to make her eighth-grade valedictorian speech to the entire middle school.

She hadn't thought she'd be this nervous. But, as they'd driven over the mountains from their dairy farm in the Shenandoah Valley, her anxiety had built and built.

Standing by the passenger side of the old Chevy, she looked up once more at the dark brick wall rising forty feet above her like a huge, terrifying tsunami. The surveillance towers soared another sixty feet into the clear blue sky.

Shading her eyes from the sun, she could just make out a pair of silhouettes on the closest tower's observation deck. They wore Stetsons and aimed long-barreled guns down at the other side of the massive barrier. They looked like the Devil's angels up there, and she hated them without even knowing them.

"There he is!" her mother shouted excitedly from the driver's side of the Chevy, already sobbing. A figure had just emerged from a narrow steel door at the base of the wall. "Go, Victoria, go. I'm staying here. I'm not ready yet."

Victoria kicked off her flip-flops and covered the distance across the parking lot to her father in seconds, long blond hair streaming out behind her.

As she crossed from sunlight into shadow, she caught her breath. He was gaunt, stooped at the shoulders, and his dark hair had turned mostly gray. He'd always seemed younger than her friends' fathers. But, standing outside the Archer Prison wall, he seemed shockingly older—five years had aged him twenty.

"Hello, Victoria," he whispered as she flew into his arms. "I can't get over how pretty you are. You're a beautiful young woman."

"Thanks, Dad." His shirt smelled awful, like wet dirt. "I missed you so much."

"I was worried you wouldn't come."

She wanted to reach out and take his hand. She would have slipped her fingers into his without thinking when she was nine, before he'd gone away. At fourteen, that time had passed—whether he was innocent or not.

"Are you okay?" she asked as they headed for the Chevy. It was two hours back to the small town of Luray and their hundred-acre farm. She wanted to get home. They had his favorite meal waiting—fried chicken, mashed potatoes and gravy, biscuits, and corn.

"Yes."

"Are you sure?"

"What's on your mind, Victoria?"

"You're walking so slowly." Her father had always been a man on a mission, even with nowhere in particular to be. "It's like you're shuffling."

"You haven't lost your directness, I'm glad to see."

"I didn't mean it in a bad way, Dad."

"Maybe I have lost a step or two," he admitted. "Could be you're a few steps faster as well. Or maybe the shuffling is force of habit from the shackles."

"I'm sorry, I shouldn't have—"

"Or *maybe* I'm just taking time to reacquaint myself with everything I've been missing for five years. Always consider all sides of an issue," he counseled. "You'll need to do that when you're governor."

He was her biggest fan, and he'd been telling her she'd be governor ever since she could remember.

"I'm serious," he replied to her silence. "Virginia Governor Victoria Lewis. It's got a ring to it, doesn't it?"

She hesitated. "I . . . I guess." Superstition drove her caution. The Fates hated arrogance.

"It *definitely* does. After you're governor, you'll be president." He nodded confidently. "I had that vision the night you were born." As they cleared the wall's shadow and emerged into sunlight, he stopped and caught her arm. "Is there anything else?"

He never ducked or dodged anything. She got that from him and only from him, she knew. Her mother hated confrontation.

"Mom explained everything," she answered as she stole a glance at the observation deck. One of those death angels seemed to be watching. The long barrel was aimed outside the wall. "She told me you didn't steal money while you were county treasurer. She said you were framed, that Judge Hopkins fixed the jury. I didn't understand what 'framed' or 'fixed' meant when you went away. But we studied the judicial system in school this year. And Mom and I talked about it last night and again this morning coming over the mountain. It makes more sense now."

"*More* sense?"

"Why did Judge Hopkins do that to you?" It wasn't the question she needed to ask, but she was getting closer.

"He and I disagreed . . . about many things."

"But how could a jury find you guilty if you were innocent?"

"You know how small Luray is, Victoria. People find out things about people. And people in charge can use that knowledge. That's what Judge Hopkins did. He got a snitch to tell the jurors on my trial that if they didn't vote his way, they'd have real trouble." Her father paused. "Don't always count on the system to save you. But always do *whatever you must* to protect it. It isn't perfect, but it's the best system on earth." He smiled proudly. "You'll protect it one day, Victoria. Promise me you will."

She swallowed hard. What she was about to ask . . . well . . . this was just him coming out in her. He couldn't blame her. "Did you do it, Dad? Did you steal fifty thousand dollars from Page County?"

He smiled subtly, like a wisp of a summer breeze rippling across a freshly cut field of hay, as if he was relieved.

"No, I did not, Victoria. I've never stolen money in my life. Not a dime, not a nickel, not a penny."

Relief surged through her. He'd never be able to stare directly into her eyes and say that with such conviction if he was lying. He wasn't wired that way. She knew that for certain . . . because neither was she.

"Do you hate Judge Hopkins?"

He glanced across the parking lot toward the old Chevy. Her mother was standing by the open door, both hands over her mouth as the tears continued to flow. "I've got a score to settle."

"I'll help." Her father's eyes moved back to hers, and she was struck again by how old he seemed.

"If there's time, Victoria," he finally murmured, "if there's time." He took her hand in his and smiled. "Let's go. I'm dying for that home-cooked meal I know you two have waiting. I bet it's fried chicken and mashed potatoes."

CHAPTER 1

PRESENT DAY

NORTHERN VIRGINIA (FAIRFAX)

Wayne Bennett balanced the pizza box on one hand and texted his wife, Janie, with the other. *Home soon.*

Last pregnancy, it was Chinese. This time she was constantly craving pizza: extra cheese and pepperoni *every* time. Rather than wait two hours for Saturday night delivery, he'd driven three miles to the parlor and downed a tasty, tall Coors while he was waiting. Janie was all into sharing her pregnancies—every aspect of them. Including: if I can't drink, you can't drink.

Wayne winced as he placed the phone and the large pie down on the roof of his rusty old Honda. He'd forgotten gum to mask the beer breath. Hell with it.

As he dug for his keys, a silver Dodge Charger raced through the strip-mall parking lot and skidded to a stop, blocking him in.

"What do *you* want?" Wayne demanded when a slim young man with short blond hair and buckteeth climbed out of the Charger.

"Are you Wayne Bennett?"

"Who wants to know?"

"Are you Wayne Bennett?"

"Yeah. *So?"*

"So you just won the Publishers Clearing House Sweepstakes," the young man announced. He gestured over his shoulder at the dry cleaner, which was beside the pizza parlor. "I got a camera crew in there working this." He patted the Charger. "And I got one of those crazy-huge checks in the back of my ride made out to you."

It sounded way too good to be true. But why would someone lie about winning a sweepstakes? "Seriously?"

"You won ten thousand dollars a month for *life*. Can you believe it, Wayne? Smile for the crew."

"Holy—Oh my God!" Wayne shouted. He raised his arms and danced—badly—for the camera. "This couldn't have come at a better time. I'm jammed up against the limit on both my cards and I—"

The punk grinned. "I'm just messing, Wayne."

Giddiness boomeranged to anger. "Hey, pal, you better tell me what's going on or—"

"You're a UPS driver. You wear that bad brown uniform all day long while you deliver boxes from your bad brown truck, right?"

"Move your ride. *Now.*"

"Been driving that truck for six years," the young man continued, "and you're moving up. Just got a seven-percent raise last month, I understand."

"That's it," Wayne growled, striding forward, fists clenched.

"But you never mentioned that felony conviction to your supervisor, did you, Wayne? You never told UPS."

He froze two steps away. "What?"

"Your felony conviction for grand theft auto in California nine years ago under your real name. Charles Liggett. Does your wife know Wayne Bennett is just an alias? Does Janie know the name she took at your courthouse wedding here is just a figment of your imagination? Of course not," he answered himself.

"I . . . I wasn't guilty. I didn't steal that car. It was all a big misunderstanding."

"Oh, sure. Hey, I haven't met a guilty felon in my life, including me. But none of that matters, Wayne. All that matters is what's on your record. And that's the conviction."

Wayne stared into the distance as his world cratered. He felt like a doll, incapable of blinking. How would he ever explain this? "What do you want?"

"Your vote."

"My *what?*"

"You've been cooped up in that Fairfax County courthouse for weeks. You're a big shot, foreman of the jury. Big criminal trial. What's his name again? The senior executive for that defense contractor, Keystone Systems."

"Scott Tolbert." Wayne lowered his voice. "He's the chief financial officer of Keystone. So?"

"Tolbert's accused of bribing a Pentagon official."

The young man's buckteeth gave him an innocent, childlike look when he grinned. But the cold glitter in his eyes reminded Wayne of the criminals he'd run with in California. They didn't care who they hurt.

"In exchange for a briefcase full of cash, Tolbert wanted that DOD guy to help Keystone get a seventeen-billion-dollar contract to build attack helicopters. That's what the state of Virginia wants you to believe, anyway."

"*So?*"

"So . . ." The punk tapped his fingers on the Charger roof. "How are you feeling about the case?"

Wayne glanced around furtively. "I . . . I can't talk about it. We're only out for the weekend to see our families. The judge warned us not to talk about it with anyone."

"Have it your way. So I'm thinking I'll call UPS and have them look you up in the Sacramento courts. The names have changed, but the fingerprints haven't."

"How in God's name do you know so much—"

"Based on what you've heard so far, do you think Tolbert is guilty?"

Wayne hesitated. "Yes."

"Now we're getting somewhere."

His shoulders sagged with relief. "Whew. Man, I thought there was a problem because—"

"You will find Scott Tolbert innocent."

Wayne stiffened again. "But he's—"

"As foreman, you'll be the voice of reason and persuasion in the jury room. You and a few other jurors I've already had the pleasure of shocking today."

"But the man's guilty. It's just a question of how long a sentence we give him."

"You'll find Scott Tolbert innocent, Wayne. He'll do no time in a Virginia prison."

"I can't find him innocent. *We* can't find him innocent. The evidence is overwhelming. I'll look like an idiot if I start banging the innocent drum."

"How you gonna look when your boss finds out you're a convicted felon?" The kid didn't wait for an answer. "Out of work," he sang as he breezed past Wayne, grabbed the pizza off the Honda roof, and backtracked to the Charger, "and divorced. Innocent of all charges," he called over his shoulder as he opened the back door and placed the warm box on the seat. "Are we clear?"

"Yeah," Wayne muttered glumly. "What the hell do I care what happens to Keystone Systems . . . or Scott Tolbert?"

"You don't. You care about your job and your family. And all's well with both as long as Mr. Tolbert goes free. By the way, what's on the pizza?"

"Extra cheese and pepperoni."

"Excellent, Wayne, excellent." The young man waved as he slid behind the steering wheel. "Have a nice day and don't forget. Vote innocent or vote to be fired."

NORTHERN VIRGINIA (LOUDOUN)

"Colin! Hey, Colin, wait up!"

Colin O'Hara stopped short in the Costco parking lot when he heard his name, near a return area for the oversized carts that made shoppers feel Lilliputian. He was headed inside to buy four juicy rib eyes. His wife had delivered Colin Junior three months ago, and the in-laws were visiting from Ohio to see the baby boy for the first time. CJ, as everyone was calling him, was their first child and the first grandchild for the in-laws.

"Don't you remember me from college, Colin?" a slim, blond guy asked when Colin turned. "From Virginia Commonwealth?"

"Sorry," Colin apologized politely. "I . . . I really don't."

"We were econ majors together. Man, that was rough, you know? All that theory crap was ridiculous."

"Sorry," Colin muttered again, making an obvious impatient glance at his watch. "I still don't remember, and I'm in kind of a—"

"That's where you met Lydia."

Warning sirens screamed at Colin. The guy had a bucktoothed grin straight from Appalachia . . . but there was something sophisticated in those eyes.

"When the three of us were taking those econ classes together, remember? You and Lydia were always passing notes back and forth."

Colin felt the blood drain from his face in a single missed heartbeat. "Huh?"

"Lydia Crawford," the guy answered, his voice turning surly. "That redhead you had the horns for at VCU and had a kid with last year. She lives two hours from here down in Richmond. You and Lydia named the little girl Haley. You married Betsy two years ago, but you and Lydia haven't stopped seeing each other since VCU. Pharmaceutical sales keep you on the road, Colin, which is why Betsy never suspects." He shook his head. "Two families. That's a daring lifestyle. Unfortunately, it just tracked you down, Colin."

"You . . . you have the wrong person," Colin muttered, glancing around fearfully. What if one of Betsy's girlfriends overheard him talking to this guy? Everyone in town shopped here. "I . . . I must look like someone else you know."

"You're the man I'm looking for, Colin. For sure . . . and I know *everything* about you. Including how you're a juror on the Bailey Energy trial." The kid stepped forward and poked a finger into Colin's chest. "You vote for the corporation when it's time for the verdict. You vote to allow Bailey Energy to build that pipeline straight through Loudoun County or Betsy, that good little Catholic girl you're married to, finds out all about Lydia and Haley. Your in-laws find out, too. *Everyone* does."

Colin suddenly felt like he had to puke. "Get away from me!" he shouted, turning around and stumbling for his car. "Get the hell away from me!" he yelled over his shoulder.

"Yeah, hell's where you'll be if you don't vote innocent!" the young man shouted across the parking lot, turning heads everywhere. "You'll see, Colin! *You'll see!*"

LOS ANGELES, CALIFORNIA

"You're looking awesome, girlfriend."

"Thanks to what you do for my hair."

Brandy Bond signed the credit card receipt with a quick scribble and then checked herself in the salon mirror once more. She did look good. As she should for what she'd just paid.

"You're my most gorgeous customer, Brandy. KABC better put you on camera soon. No more of this associate producer, behind-the-scenes BS."

"Thanks, Lillian."

"Someone at another TV station is going to discover you, and then KABC will be sorry."

"You're so nice."

Lillian waved a red-taloned hand in dismissal, bejeweled bangles jangling. "Go find yourself a man at this wedding in Beverly Hills. Hey, maybe that's where you'll get discovered. And praise the Lord the judge let you out for the weekend so you could go to the wedding. Maybe this is all part of his plan."

Voices caught Brandy's ears. "Speak of the Devil," she murmured as her gaze shifted from the mirror to the TV mounted above and behind the reception counter.

"Hey, isn't that the trial you said you're a juror on?" Lillian pointed at the female reporter on the screen as she followed Brandy's gaze. "That's the price-fixing case—the two oil companies everybody's talking about."

"That's it, all right," Brandy answered, grabbing her purse off the counter. "I never should have mentioned it." She sighed. "That was dumb."

"That reporter isn't anywhere near as pretty as you," Lillian called. "You should be doing that report, not her."

"See you next time," Brandy called back as she headed out of the salon and into the late-afternoon sunshine, toward her fire-engine-red MINI Cooper.

As she reached for the driver's-side door, a wiry young man with closely cropped blond hair stepped in front of her. She shrieked and, stumbling on a heel, backed away several quick, terrified steps.

"Innocent," he hissed, leering at her. "That's how you'll vote on the verdict. Those two oil companies are *innocent*."

"They're *guilty*," she blurted. It was a gut reaction, one she quickly regretted.

"Uh uh uh," the man clucked. "We know about your fake sources. The ones you've been ginning up on your news stories so you can get on camera."

Brandy cringed as her heart began to race, and her mouth went dry.

"We know how bad you want to get in front of the lens. So bad, you've manufactured witnesses and paid for information. Major no-no's in the news world."

"No, I—"

"Don't even try. We have people ready to testify if we need them."

"But, I—"

"If we told your executive producers what you've done, you'd be out of broadcasting forever and on your ass for good. And believe me, we will tell them if you don't vote to acquit both companies." He opened the car door for her, gestured inside, and smiled politely. "Have a nice time at the wedding in Beverly Hills."

"My God," she whispered. "Who are you?"

He grinned thinly. "I'm the man who knows everything about you. And, Brandy, I do mean *everything*."

CHAPTER 2

RICHMOND, VIRGINIA

Victoria Lewis stepped to the podium and tapped the microphone three times as the three pennies hanging from her simple silver bracelet jingled. The move on the microphone was driven solely by superstition, not necessity. A hush had swept through the audience the instant she and Judge Eldridge began ascending the stairs to the dais, followed quickly by tomblike silence. There had been no need to request it.

She always tapped a microphone three times before giving a speech. She had ever since her eighth-grade valedictorian address. She'd done the same thing as a senior in high school, again at her graduation from the University of Virginia, and just before her inauguration speech as governor. Maybe it was irrational—but it worked. And she wasn't about to tempt the fates by fixing something that wasn't broken.

The temporary platform she and Judge Eldridge had just taken their places on was erected inside the spacious, marbled-lined lobby of Virginia's brand new Supreme Court Building, directly beneath its massive chandelier. Now that she was standing below the glistening glass and before this powerful audience that had gathered in downtown Richmond from all corners of the Commonwealth, she was pleased she'd chosen such an important site at which to make this announcement.

"Good afternoon, everyone." She was wearing her favorite red suit trimmed in black, along with her killer, four-inch, black suede pumps, which matched the suit perfectly. "I want to welcome Governor Falkner, Lieutenant Governor Paulson, Majority Leader Franz, distinguished senators and delegates of the General Assembly, Richmond Mayor Eleanor Bush, distinguished members of the Richmond City Council, as well as the assembled press corps." She turned and nodded to Eldridge. "Most of all I want to thank Virginia's Supreme Court Chief Justice Daniel Eldridge for taking time from his busy schedule to join me up here."

Victoria paused as she turned to gaze out over the crowd again, to drink in this moment. Ultimately, today could be more crucial to her career than the night five years ago she'd been elected governor of Virginia at the politically tender age of thirty-two. She wanted to remember everything about this afternoon in minute and intimate detail.

"Most of you haven't heard from me since my constitutionally imposed single term as governor of our great commonwealth ended last year. When I was forced, kicking and screaming, to vacate my lovely office in the Patrick Henry Building as well as my beautifully redecorated bedroom at the mansion."

Polite laughter rippled through the audience.

"It's nice to see so many familiar faces. I've missed you. Though, I'm sure some of you from the other side of the aisle haven't missed me." She shrugged and smiled innocently. "I don't know. Maybe some from my side haven't, either."

The laughter grew, though not as much as she'd expected. They wanted the announcement.

"Ladies and gentlemen," she continued, transitioning to her all-business tone, "I'm honored to lead one of the most important initiatives in Commonwealth history, potentially in the country's history. Let me say that again, in the *country's* history."

Victoria allowed her last few words to fade into the marble before continuing.

"Our example in Virginia shall set the stage for other states to follow in what I believe will be a groundbreaking and dramatically positive change to our judicial system."

All eyes were riveted on her. Even Judge Eldridge seemed transfixed when she glanced over at him.

She held his gaze for a moment, impressed by his courage and conviction. By appearing today, he was taking great personal risk. This was the one time, he'd told her, he would publicly endorse Project Archer.

Seventy-six, Eldridge still radiated charisma, confidence, and power. He was tall, lean, and distinguished looking in his long, black robe with his white hair, jutting chin, piercing gaze, and naturally stern expression. After twenty-two years as chief justice of Virginia's highest court, he was the Commonwealth's moral compass. Scandal and controversy had never as much as grazed him, personally or politically, and his influence over the other six justices on the court was absolute—which was *the* key to Project Archer. She would steer the ship, but Judge Eldridge would keep calm the ocean.

Victoria turned back to face the expectant crowd.

"Two hundred Virginia citizens are about to become full-time jurors. These men and women"—she raised her voice above the intensifying buzz suddenly racing around the lobby—"will sit in judgment of Virginia's most important criminal and civil trials."

Reporters scribbled frantically on pads or tapped keyboards as she paused to give them time to catch up.

"I'll now turn the microphone over to Chief Justice Eldridge."

"Thank you, Ms. Lewis," he said in his gravelly drawl as he moved to the podium. "I too want to thank our distinguished guests for attending today's historic announcement." He adjusted his natty, red-polka-dotted bow tie as he took his turn to drink in the moment. "In this country we constantly strive to improve ourselves at all levels and departments of government. We are a nation unafraid of new ideas, undaunted by new possibilities, even as we respect and revere long-standing traditions.

"Ms. Lewis' powerful initiative weaves seamlessly into that tradition. Like her famous ancestor, Meriwether Lewis, who led Thomas Jefferson's Corps of Discovery to glory through this country's wild northwest, Ms. Lewis will, I am confident, lead this remarkable project to great success as well." He gestured toward her. "Selfishly, I'm very glad Virginia's constitution does not allow governors to serve consecutive terms. It made her available to lead Project Archer after approaching me with the idea." He gestured again, this time at Tom Falkner, who sat in the front row of folding, wooden chairs. "Given Ms. Lewis' immense popularity at the end of her four years, I'm certain Governor Falkner is also glad she was constitutionally precluded from serving a second term."

Eldridge's remark evoked the afternoon's heartiest laugh as well as a demonstrative nod from Falkner.

"Ms. Lewis has the full and unanimous support of the Supreme Court as she leads Project Archer," Eldridge assured the audience when the laughter faded. "Thank you again for coming today."

He shook Victoria's hand, smiled at her, then moved across the stage and down the steps toward the lobby hallway and the elevator, surrounded by his darkly dressed, stern-faced bodyguards.

When he disappeared, she stepped back to the microphone. She and Eldridge had agreed that she would not engage the press—all of whom were still feverishly scribbling or tapping—until he was gone and inaccessible.

"I'll open this up to questions."

Fifty hands shot into the air. Some reporters standing against the back wall shouted her name.

She pointed at the senior correspondent from the *Richmond Times-Dispatch*, the city's most respected newspaper. He was an old-school gentleman who would give her a friendly first question. He always had during her press conferences as governor.

"Yes, Harry?"

The elderly man rose from his front-row seat and raised both bushy, gray eyebrows. "I'm not sure where to start," he remarked with a wry smile.

"It's quite an initiative."

"It certainly is. So what is the main objective of Project Archer?"

A perfect pitch, just as she'd anticipated, right down the middle. "Project Archer will address and solve several fundamental problems inherent to the current jury system, Harry."

"Which are?"

"First, many people try avoiding jury duty because they view it as a terrible, even risky, time-sink. They see being away from their offices for an extended period of days, weeks, and sometimes months as potentially disastrous to their careers or small businesses. They receive that letter from the state informing them of their selection for jury duty, and their first reactions are anger and aggravation. Their next impulse is to find a way out of the obligation. We must stop that.

"Second, seating impartial juries in this social-media-crazed, up-to-the-instant-on-everything age is nearly unachievable, particularly in high-profile cases. Over the last decade, the Internet has made it almost impossible for lawyers to identify and agree on twelve objective citizens to hear high-profile cases. That dynamic has provided people who are hiding agendas the opportunity to make it onto juries because, ultimately, the lawyers must throw up their hands and accept people they shouldn't since the trial has to start at some point. My research indicates that the average number of potential witnesses that judges allow attorneys to disqualify before they shake their heads is four. That's nothing in this day and age. We must fix that very pressing problem as well."

People were nodding in agreement she was pleased to see.

"Finally, professional jurors, for lack of a better term, won't require a 'learning process' for each trial. They'll become familiar with the system and therefore efficient in their execution of justice. As we expand the program, jury decisions will come faster, yet, at the same time, be more accurate and defensible. Verdicts will be far less vulnerable to reversal on appeal, and in most cases not subject to appeal *at all*. And the ultimate cost savings will be *dramatic*. Project Archer will be a tremendous win-win for everyone but criminals." She paused to let that unassailable assertion sink in. "And that's what we all want."

There was a fourth objective . . . which was *by far* the most crucial. The three she'd just described were important. But even more significant than their individual goals, they ran interference for that last objective, which had to remain confidential.

She pointed at a female reporter on the left side of the lobby. "Yes?"

"How will this work, Ms. Lewis? How will it be remotely possible to keep jurors completely impartial and objective in this day and age?"

"These two hundred individuals will live full-time at a facility that is very close to completion. And they will hear cases remotely from this facility. For all intents and purposes, they will exist in a bubble. They will have no contact *whatsoever* with the outside world."

"Is the facility you're talking about the old Archer Prison outside Charlottesville?" a reporter on the right shouted, out of turn.

"Yes," Victoria answered somberly, the mental image of her father taking his first few steps of freedom still vivid in her mind. "But the facility will look vastly different than it did the day it was mothballed seventeen years ago."

"When you say the facility is 'close to completion,' what exactly does that mean?"

"We're days from opening."

"Does that mean you've already selected the two hundred jurors?"

"Almost."

"How many people were initially screened?"

"Over seven thousand."

"How did you choose the pool?"

"That's confidential."

"How did you choose *from* the pool?"

"All I can say is that we conducted the entire process in a deliberate, statistically meaningful way, guided the entire time by our joint team of attorneys here in Richmond and in Washington, DC."

"How long will those who are selected serve?"

"Two years. Then more will come."

"How will you incent them?"

"The way all employees in our society are incented. We'll pay them."

"How much?"

"I can't comment on that. It wouldn't be fair to the jurors."

"I've heard it's a million dollars a year!" another reporter shouted.

The audience gasped.

Victoria rolled her eyes just enough, as if to imply that the reporter was suffering a bout of temporary insanity. "You can't believe everything you hear," she cautioned as she pointed at another reporter.

"How were you able to avoid taking this through the state legislature?" the man asked.

She glanced at Barney Franz, Majority Leader of the General Assembly. She knew him well from her days as governor and was quite familiar with how he was not one to hide his emotions. This afternoon his face was beet red, and his arms were folded tightly across his chest.

"The Supreme Court of Virginia has unilateral purview over all aspects of the Commonwealth's jury system," Victoria answered as Franz rose from his seat and stalked from the lobby, accompanied by whispered chatter from the audience and an aide. She'd been prepared for Franz's aggravation—not for him to walk out. "Chief Justice Eldridge and the other six justices on the Supreme Court have complete control over this process. It may surprise some people, but there is no constitutional requirement to involve the General Assembly. Our attorneys have assured us of that."

She gestured at a young man in the back who'd been raising one hand politely as he clutched his tablet with the other.

"Thank you for calling on me, Ms. Lewis."

She grinned ruefully at his tousled hair, jeans, and unironed, untucked shirt. Harry was wearing a neatly pressed, three-piece suit, and every hair on his head was in perfect position. Times had changed.

"In your opening remarks, you spoke of leaving your office kicking and screaming when your term was over."

"I loved serving the people of the Commonwealth as their governor," she said, looking out at the audience serenely. "It was my dream job."

"You also mentioned having to leave your bedroom in the Governor's Mansion."

Victoria's eyes flashed back to the young reporter. She'd caught something in his tone. "Yes?"

"Would you care to use this forum to clarify your sexual orientation?"

The room exploded with a collective groan.

"You're thirty-seven, and you've never been married, never been linked to anyone romantically in the last decade that I can find," he went on, undeterred by the intensifying protest around him. "I don't understand why you wouldn't want to clear up this issue. I don't understand why you'd hesitate to make the admission one way or the other. Are you heterosexual or lesbian?"

Victoria glared down from the dais. Judge Eldridge had warned her about this. No skeletal remains, real or imagined, would be off-limits from now on. Those nameless, faceless shadows Eldridge seemed so concerned with had made their first appearance. This question was proof.

"Today is not about me," she answered coolly. "Today is about Project Archer." She detested the way the young reporter was looking back at her, as though he was enjoying himself immensely. "Let's keep it that way."

"How about your rumored cocaine problem?"

"This is ridiculous," she answered to another even louder groan from the audience, simultaneously motioning to security.

"What about aspirations for higher office?" the young man continued as she tried calling on another reporter. "Is that on the table, too?"

"Walter," she said, pointing at another familiar reporter, "your question?"

"And how about your late father?" the kid yelled as four members of the high-court security team closed in on him. "Any concerns about his legal troubles affecting you going forward?"

"I was elected governor, wasn't I?" Victoria muttered—under her breath and away from the microphone.

"He was a thief! He stole money from his county in the Shenandoah—fifty thousand dollars!"

She was about to engage, about to go at the young man with everything she had, about to explain to everyone in the audience how her father had been railroaded by a corrupt, small-town judge and a jury the judge had intimidated—the sort of intimidation her sequestered juries would never fall prey to. But she forced another serene expression to her face as the high-court security force rushed the young man from the lobby, all while he continued to shout fading questions.

When he was gone and order had been restored, Victoria shook her head, gave the audience a smile that said, *Now that we've enjoyed a moment of levity . . .* and pointed again. "Next question, Walter."

CHAPTER 3

DARIEN, CONNECTICUT

JD Ware sank into his favorite wingback chair in the sprawling, beautifully furnished, and tastefully decorated study of Philip Rockwell's mansion. This was the lap of luxury he'd always been obsessed with. And he'd driven a strange and winding road to get here. One he never could have predicted—even imagined.

This luxury wasn't actually his yet. But he was getting closer. Even Rockwell had no idea *how* close.

He was exhausted but exhilarated. Virginia, then Los Angeles, and back here to Connecticut where everything always started. He'd sprinted almost seven thousand miles in the last few days.

But he was young; he could handle it. And besides, all the flights had been aboard Rockwell's personal G5, with a pretty female attendant at his beck and call. It wasn't as if he'd been stuck in the middle seat of a jammed commercial flight.

He'd come a long way from his mother's trailer park outside Macon, Georgia. He was twenty-three, traveling in style, and making real money. Life was good.

"Anything happen yet with the Keystone Systems trial?" he asked.

"It went to the jury this afternoon," Rockwell answered from behind his wide desk. He was smoking his favorite Cuban cigar—a

Monte Cristo his gardener had smuggled through JFK from cousins at home. "So did the Bailey Energy trial."

Philip Rockwell owned and ran a small investment bank, which, until recently, had been struggling. But in the last few months, Rockwell & Company had *exploded* on Wall Street.

"Keystone and Bailey went to their respective juries a few minutes after Victoria Lewis made her insidious announcement at the Supreme Court Building in Richmond," Rockwell continued. "The symmetry was beautiful."

JD wasn't sure how an announcement could be insidious or what "symmetry" even meant.

"Will Wayne Bennett and Colin O'Hara vote our way?" Rockwell asked. "That's the crucial question."

"We're good to go with Bennett and the Keystone trial. That's a lock."

"How do you know?"

"Bennett sang the magic words."

"Which were?"

"'What the hell do I care?'"

Rockwell blew a thick cloud of celebratory smoke into the upper reaches of the high-ceiling room. "I do so love those lyrics of indifference."

JD wasn't fond of Rockwell. The silver-haired, middle-aged WASP had an arrogant air of entitlement about him. And he was always using big words, which JD suspected he did on purpose, to make him feel stupid. But he appreciated using the man's toys, like the G5, and he *loved* the money they were paying him—thirty grand a month.

"Like I told you, I'm not sure about Colin O'Hara and Bailey Energy. O'Hara actually ran away from me in the parking lot when I told him what I had on him. It's the first time that's happened since I joined your team nine months ago. And I've probably gone at fifty jurors by now."

"If Colin O'Hara votes the wrong way, and the Bailey trial blows up on us," Rockwell said, "he'll pay the price. It's that simple. We're all agreed."

"Who's 'we'?"

"That's none of your concern."

Rockwell always stonewalled about anyone or anything up on the next rung of the ladder. Rockwell was all into controlling that link in the chain, with keeping that connection very hush-hush.

"Why go through all this, Mr. Rockwell?" JD asked.

"Through what?"

"Why bother blackmailing these people?"

"Why not?"

"Pulling all this information together takes time, and going at jurors like we do might attract attention someday. And you've got to keep the data around, so people might get their hands on it. Then they would have evidence."

"What's your solution?"

"I tell a guy like Colin O'Hara I'll put a bullet through his mother's head if he doesn't do exactly what I want." JD shrugged. "Seems like that'd be way simpler than blackmailing him for having a kid with another woman behind his wife's back—and more effective."

Rockwell gave JD a condescending grimace. "The challenge with making death threats," he replied, "is that sooner or later you must follow through on one."

"So you're scared to take the ultimate step. Hey, I'm just saying," JD added quickly when Rockwell leaned forward over the desk, frowning.

"I have no problem taking the ultimate step," Rockwell assured him. "But we don't want to be egregious in our use of murder."

"Hey, look, I can do anybody without causing a—"

"More importantly," Rockwell interrupted, "killing a family member isn't always effective in terms of achieving the desired result. Some people need the threat aimed squarely at them in order to be manipulated."

"Give me a break. I tell somebody I'm gonna kill a family member and that person's mine."

"Really?" Rockwell glanced into the early-evening darkness outside the window, then back at JD.

"Absolutely."

"I could have your father dead inside the hour."

"Big deal. That man never gave a rat's—"

"You're making my case."

"But I'm not like most—"

"Or I could send you back to prison, this time for life."

JD laughed like Rockwell was reaching with this one. "How?"

"I have a video of you murdering that young woman."

JD's eyes flashed wide as Rockwell paused.

"I doubt you'd be able to plead to manslaughter this time with the DA in possession of those seven minutes of riveting recording," Rockwell went on. "You obviously take such grotesque pleasure in strangling her. Imagine what the jury would think of you after seeing that."

Perspiration broke out on JD's forehead.

"No," Rockwell continued confidently, "I believe the charge this time will most certainly be murder in the first degree when we anonymously turn you and the video over to the authorities." He pursed his lips and shook his head, apparently discouraged. "And after all that effort we had to go through to arrange your release from prison. Such a pity." He lifted the cigar to his mouth and puffed. "Didn't know I had that video, did you? Thought that recording was still locked away in the safe that's buried in the dirt floor of that shed in Pennsylvania, huh?"

"Yeah," JD mumbled, defeated. "I did."

"Have I made my point?"

"Yes, sir."

The computer on Rockwell's desk dinged with an alert. He frowned at the screen. "You were correct."

"About?"

"The Bailey Energy trial," Rockwell growled, picking up his phone. "It didn't go our way. We must act. Hang on a second."

JD tapped the chair's arm as Rockwell made the call, thinking about how carefully Rockwell controlled access to the people who were up the ladder, who were running all this. Rockwell was a middleman. And, eventually, middlemen were always cut out.

"Next week," Rockwell said when he'd finished the call, "you'll fly to Chicago and Minneapolis to cement the votes of jurors in critical trials coming to a head in those cities. But, first, you're going back to Virginia. You're getting your wish."

JD sat up in the chair. "I'm finally getting to use my rifle?"

He'd been a sniper in the United States Marine Corps before going to prison. One reason Rockwell had sprung him from prison was because he'd seen the astonishing scores—thirty-two out of thirty-five rounds or better, consistently inside the black, from amazing distances. And JD wasn't just good on the range. He wasn't just a practice player. He had nine confirmed kills in the field.

"No. You'll execute this mission from close range." Rockwell took one last puff from the cigar and then snuffed it out in a big ashtray on the right side of his desk. "This one *must* look like an accident."

"Fine . . . as long as I get to kill."

"Yes . . . as long as you get to kill," Rockwell repeated softly and slowly before gesturing toward the study door. "Get me another cigar, boy."

"Huh?"

"Go on, hurry up."

"Prick," JD whispered as he headed out of the study and down the hall toward the humidor.

"Make sure it's another Monte Cristo," Rockwell called, "and don't leave the damn door open like you did last week. You almost ruined my entire stock, you little shit."

JD's eyes narrowed as he reached the humidor. "We've all got it coming one day," he whispered. "I just hope when your day comes, Mr. Rockwell, I'm the one who gives it to you."

NORTHERN VIRGINIA (LOUDOUN)

Colin O'Hara smiled as he leaned back on the couch, cradling his baby boy, who was feeding greedily from the bottle. He'd come straight home from the courtroom after the verdict had been announced. Reporters had shoved cameras and microphones in his face, but he'd dodged them and bolted away.

"Can you get that?" he called when the apartment doorbell rang. It was probably Mrs. Hardy, the apartment complex gossip, looking for inside details about the trial. He'd be lucky to get dinner by eight now. And Betsy was fixing his favorite—lasagna. "I'm still feeding CJ."

"Sure, honey," Betsy called back as she headed for the front door. "Love you."

"You're my little man," Colin murmured as he gazed down at his young son, who lay securely in his arms, wrapped in his blue hospital blanket. "It's crazy. You look just like me, just like everyone says you do. I didn't believe it until just now, but it's true. I missed you so much, but I won't stay away that long again. I promise."

"Colin."

He glanced up. Betsy was standing across the living room, dishtowel draped over her shoulder. Out of nowhere, she seemed on the brink of an emotional abyss. "Yes?"

She held up a large envelope, and Colin's heart began to jackhammer, as it had in the Costco parking lot. He knew—instantly—even before she tilted the envelope, even before the photographs cascaded out and scattered across the floor.

He didn't need to see the pictures of Lydia and Haley—or the explanatory note he assumed accompanied the damning evidence. He knew exactly what had happened. He'd been delusional enough to believe that the thin young man with the short blond hair and the buckteeth was only a bad dream.

So he'd voted his conscience in the jury deliberation room, convincing two other jurors who were on the fence with his impassioned speech. Bailey Energy should not be allowed to build the pipeline. It would be incredibly dangerous and provide little economic benefit to Loudoun County.

Why had he cared so much? He didn't live anywhere near the pipeline's intended path. If it blew, it wasn't going to kill him.

"Give me my son," Betsy hissed, rushing for the couch, tears of rage already spilling down her face. "You bastard!" she shrieked, taking the baby from him and heading for the bedrooms. "Get out of this house, Colin!" she screamed over her shoulder. "And don't ever come back! I'm calling my father. He'll get you out of here! He'll *kill* you!"

Colin had just made the worst mistake of his life. He'd never see his son again.

CHAPTER 4

GOOCHLAND, VIRGINIA

"Compelling performance this afternoon," Cameron Moore offered as he sat down before the big desk in Victoria's home study. Picture windows looked out on the thick forest surrounding the bungalow, a calming sight after the noise of the press conference. "You were convincing and seemingly precise without actually giving away anything sensitive. You were . . . coy."

Victoria gazed at Cameron fondly. He was short and slight, belying the lion heart filling his chest. He kept his head shaved; sported stylish, black, rectangular-frame glasses she was pretty sure weren't necessary; and always dressed sharply.

"I was elected governor of Virginia," she volleyed back, recognizing the sarcasm. His tone was usually laced with a hint of it—he was a bit of a twisted soul—but this time there'd been more than usual. "Why in God's name wouldn't I be political?"

"First of all, you are no longer elected. Secondly, I said 'coy' not 'political.'"

"What's the difference?" Twisted but very good at what he did and, most important of all, loyal beyond reproach. "You're jealous, Cam," she kidded. "It's not becoming."

"You shouldn't have all the fun. I want to be coy in front of all those hypocrites."

She smiled nostalgically. Five years ago, she and Cameron had shared a quiet, out-of-the-way dinner in Fredericksburg, arranged by mutual friends. She hadn't expected much going in, but she'd ended up offering him the post of campaign manager over dessert. She knew a good thing when she saw it.

The next day he'd resigned from his high-octane lobbyist job on K Street and guided her gubernatorial run to a landslide victory.

His personal transition from Washington to Richmond hadn't been smooth. The cities were only a hundred miles apart, but in this bastion of southern conservatism, his sexuality wasn't as readily accepted. So he'd gone celibate, ensuring that nothing tawdry that could be confirmed would ever appear in the press.

After the campaign he'd taken the reins of her administration and helped her achieve huge successes in office.

Now he was second in command on Project Archer.

"In fact," he continued, "I wouldn't be surprised if you got an Oscar nomination."

"You can accept for me if I win. There."

"I'd be more deserving, given my body of work."

"By 'anything sensitive,' I assume you were referring to how much jurors will make to be cut off from family and friends for two years?"

"That," he agreed, "and you didn't give away the real sizzle behind Project Archer."

"I couldn't admit that Project Archer started with Judge Eldridge." Victoria reached out and picked up a five-by-seven gold frame from amidst the battlefield-like clutter covering her desk. "That Eldridge was the one who approached me to start this project, not the other way around."

"No, but it would have been fun to see—"

"I couldn't admit to the jury tampering Eldridge believes has been going on for several years here in Virginia." She gazed at the photograph inside the frame. It was a picture of a headstone. She'd taken the photograph a few days before announcing her gubernatorial campaign. "Every high-profile case tried in Virginia during the last decade would go under a legal microscope. The probability of massive mistrials would be staggering if the chief justice of the Supreme Court made that admission."

For a few moments, Victoria pictured the bedlam that admission would have evoked.

"Are you sure I did all right up there today?" she asked, still gazing at the headstone inside the gold frame—a tall, broken column representing a life taken too early. "Did I look like a deer in the headlights when that one reporter shouted out about jurors earning a million dollars a year?"

Cameron waved a hand like she shouldn't give it another thought. "You played him perfectly, made everyone believe *he* was crazy."

"What would have happened if I'd admitted that we're paying jurors *two* million dollars a year?"

Cameron smiled like he wished he could have seen it. "Pandemonium. The situation would have been far worse than if you'd admitted to jury tampering as being the real impetus behind Project Archer. People would have been begging to throw their hats in the ring."

"The compensation level will come out sooner or later."

"Sooner, definitely, but it didn't come out today. And that's the important point. If reporters had heard two million a year, that's all they would have focused on."

"It's a lot of money."

"I'm still hoping you'll accept me into the program."

"I'm glad you're kidding."

"Mmm . . . you might be kidding yourself."

"If I offered you four million dollars, would you completely cut yourself off from the world for two years? Tell me the truth, Cameron."

He took his time answering. "I've thought a lot about that. It's a ton of money. But it's two years inside those walls, doing nothing but being a juror and having no contact with anyone but the other hundred and ninety-nine souls. I'd probably hang myself."

"Exactly."

"Still, Governor."

"You can't call me that anymore," Victoria reminded him good-naturedly as she tapped the gold frame three times. "Tom Falkner is governor now."

"Ah," he said, "you'll always be governor to me. What is that?" he asked, pointing at the frame.

"It's Meriwether Lewis' headstone," she answered, holding it out so he could take it. "I went to his grave in Tennessee before we announced the campaign. I needed inspiration."

"I remember you going there, to Tennessee. He was a Virginian."

"He was from Ivy, Virginia, which isn't too far from Archer Prison." She shook her head. "What he and William Clark did leading the Corps of Discovery was amazing."

"I've read."

"But he died at thirty-three."

"He was shot."

"He shot himself. He loved danger. Unfortunately, he loved whiskey, too. In the end, the whiskey won."

"It was his vice."

"Yes," Victoria agreed.

"We all have them," Cameron observed, raising one thin eyebrow, "don't we, Governor?"

They shared a moment of silent acknowledgment.

Perhaps, she thought to herself, they knew too much about each other.

"Everyone was impressed," Cameron finally said, taking a last look at the photograph before handing it back to Victoria, "everyone except Majority Leader Franz. Of course, his snit was to be expected."

"I didn't expect him to walk out."

"He was making a statement, obnoxious as it was. He's still bitter about you convincing so many members of his party to abandon him while you were governor. He doesn't like being ignored, either. And he's terrified that a huge piece of history is about to sail out of port into glory with him standing on the dock, looking like an idiot."

"He should look like an idiot. He's a complete narcissist."

"Yes, but you might have kissed the ring just once."

"Why? I don't need him. The Supreme Court of Virginia is it, in this case."

"We can never be too proud in the pursuit of good. Isn't that what you always say?"

"Can you believe that kid firing all those personal missiles at me today in the press conference?" she asked, dodging the question they both knew the answer to. "I have to get used to those kinds of questions. Eldridge warned me about that."

"Eldridge also warned you about getting security," Cameron reminded her. "It's time."

She moaned at that prospect as she rose and stepped out from behind her desk—she hated having bodyguards—catching a glimpse of herself in the mirror above the fireplace. She'd worn her long blond hair up at the announcement, but now it was down. As soon as she'd gotten home, she'd traded contact lenses for her round, wire-rim glasses. Still no crow's-feet at the corners of her eyes or mouth, she confirmed, checking her reflection again. Not bad for thirty-seven, she figured.

"Get yourself out of that mirror," Cameron chided. "You're still a sexy little minx. You still turn heads."

"I'll need to hear that more and more as forty closes in."

"Fine. *What about security?*"

"I hate having bodyguards. You know that. I hated it when I was governor. I still do."

"Eldridge has security. They were all around him today when he left the lobby."

"He's chief justice of Virginia's Supreme Court. He has to have security."

"Raul Acosta has done a tremendous job there."

"As Raul will do for us," she added, glancing in the mirror for one more reassurance.

"Have you told Wolf about Acosta yet?"

"No. I'll pick a time tomorrow when it seems to make sense."

"That'll be interesting. Wolf won't be happy."

"I don't care, Cam. It's the right decision. If he's too unhappy, I'll fire him."

"Another day, another battle." Cameron inhaled deeply. "I'll talk to Acosta about who he uses for Eldridge's security."

"You do that," she said, clasping Cameron gently by the elbow and guiding him out of the study, through the living room, and to the front door of her little house in the woods. "You talk to Acosta. By the way, did you arrange to get that envelope?"

"Yes."

"What's the pass—"

"Dominick," he interrupted as she opened the door for him. "What's in that envelope, Victoria?"

"Don't open it," she warned.

"I heard you the first of four times. I'm not deaf, and I don't have Alzheimer's."

"And I'll tell you a fifth time if I feel like it," she said, leaning forward to kiss him on the cheek. "Good night."

"What's in the envelope?"

"Go on, get out of—"

"Hey, listen to me."

"What?"

"You live in the middle of the woods by yourself," he said, waving into the darkness outside, "at the end of a long, lonely driveway. You *need* security."

"We'll talk."

"Go *right* to bed when I'm gone. Don't get sidetracked."

"What are you talking—"

"You know *exactly* what I'm talking about. We've got a lot going on tomorrow, and we're getting very close to launch. Get your sleep. I don't want to catch you grinding your teeth tomorrow on the tour."

"Good night."

"Promise me."

"Good night, Cameron."

When he was gone, she moved back to the study, slid open the top right drawer of the desk, and gazed down at the small cellophane bag full of white powder lying on the plate—beside a rolled-up Ben Franklin, an old credit card, and a little pile of already-prepared powder.

The pressure kept ratcheting higher and higher. She hadn't had time for a serious relationship in quite a while because there was always another mountain to climb, so she had no one to truly confide in. Cameron was her business partner, but she was also his superior. Despite their closeness, there was only so much weakness she could show him. And his twist didn't allow him to help her with matters of the heart.

She wasn't a robot, for God's sake. She deserved a private life, didn't she? She gazed down at the plate, longing for that exhilarating sensation, even if the freedom it provided was only fleeting. Fearing that sensation desperately, but loving it more. She must. Why else would she take the risk?

Risk versus reward—wasn't that always the curve that had to be drawn? Sometimes that curve could be oh so dangerous.

She reached for the plate as she sat behind her desk, fingers shaking with anticipation. She moved some clutter aside, and put the plate down in front of her.

She glanced at the blinds covering the window to the left, the only window in her study. Could anyone possibly see in here?

She tapped the desk three times, watching the random motion of the three pennies hanging from the silver bracelet. The action and the pennies would protect her. They always had.

She reached for the tightly rolled Benjamin. Cameron would hate her for this—and she understood why. But she couldn't resist.

She'd be fine.

CHAPTER 5

RICHMOND, VIRGINIA (SOUTH SIDE)

Raul Acosta took a drag from the Marlboro Black just as the front door of the three-story brick colonial opened. It was one o'clock in the morning and graveyard-dark inside the drizzle soaking the neighborhood's impressive homes. Acosta's eyes had grown semiaccustomed to the gloom beneath the rain-swollen clouds, which had scuttled into Richmond earlier tonight from the Shenandoah. But with no lights on inside or out, it was still difficult to see much.

He pulled his cell phone out when it vibrated. The text was from Cameron Moore: He wanted to speak. That was all Moore had written, but the discussion could only touch on one topic—Victoria Lewis' security. In Acosta's humble opinion, Ms. Lewis should have had security before the announcement at the Supreme Court Building. *Long* before.

Acosta slipped the phone back in his pocket when a dark silhouette emerged from the house and, one hand clutching the railing, negotiated the steps leading down from the porch to the rain-slickened walkway. Oddly, the individual hadn't illuminated any exterior lights to guide his way.

Nearly ten minutes had passed since Acosta had swung his Ford Explorer into the driveway. His arrival must have been observed from inside the home, and his boss was always punctual. But time had passed—which was troubling.

Everything about tonight was troubling . . . and had been ever since Acosta groggily answered the terse, midnight call demanding that he come immediately but wait outside—no knocking. Acosta assumed the ban against knocking was to avoid awakening Mitch's three young children. But he'd wanted more details before climbing out of his warm, comfortable bed to leave Sofia, who'd sexily offered intimacy if he would ignore the call. Eleven years and two pregnancies and Sofia was still the most beautiful woman he'd ever seen.

The line had gone dead before he could ask Mitch for details—Acosta knew better than to call back.

He watched Mitch's silhouette negotiate the shadows. He'd always wondered how his boss could afford this idyllic home set on three wooded acres, the Mercedes SLK55, the brand-new Denali, three private-school tuitions, and the exotic vacations. It had to be family money, because a state salary couldn't cut it.

But family money didn't jive with the tours in Afghanistan. There was another possibility—one Acosta hated to consider.

Maybe he should confront Mitch about that possibility rather than trying to trail him—unsuccessfully so far—each time Mitch ventured into the shadows of Richmond's sketchier commercial districts. Determining whom Mitch was secretly meeting in the back of a long, black limousine would go a long way toward assuaging or confirming Acosta's suspicions. Of course, if it confirmed them, what was he supposed to do? Mitch was Judge Eldridge's nephew.

For a moment Acosta wondered if it was an imposter approaching through the darkness. He was naturally suspicious, had been ever since his stint as a prison guard on Rikers Island in New York City—before he'd moved his family to Virginia to escape the downsides of Brooklyn. It was a perfect career attribute and a primary reason he was head of security for the Virginia Supreme Court. Standing six feet four inches and weighing 240 pounds didn't hurt, either. He was the youngest of seven boys, but far from the runt.

Acosta would have been perfectly happy to stay in this job for good—but the money Victoria Lewis was offering to transition to Project Archer was simply too good. And, behind closed doors, Judge Eldridge had urged him to go to Charlottesville with Ms. Lewis.

Acosta's moment of uncertainty about the silhouette's identity passed quickly. Ryan Mitchell's excruciating limp was unmistakable. During Mitch's second tour of duty in Afghanistan, a Taliban mortar had ripped through a chaotic firefight, tearing off everything below his right knee. His right hip and face had also been badly damaged on that rocky crag.

Acosta had never once heard Mitch complain about the deep scars on his face, the constant pain in his hip, or needing a prosthetic. Never once heard him express any bitterness about the terrible, life-altering hand he'd been dealt as a twenty-four-year-old serving his country. Mitch only ever expressed regret at the deaths of others under his command that night.

"Why the cloak-and-dagger crap?" Acosta demanded in his tough Brooklynese as he pulled the Yankees baseball cap from his curly hair to shake away moisture. Even heroes weren't exempt from a little aggravated cross-examination at one o'clock in the morning. "This is ridiculous, Mitch."

"Quiet, sport," Mitch answered in his deliberate drawl.

Mitch reminded Acosta of an Irish altar boy, with his red hair, turquoise eyes, and cherub face full of freckles. They were only ten years apart, Acosta knew, but an objective observer would have guessed twenty.

"I ain't your beck-and-call boy. Don't ever forget that."

"Quiet!"

Acosta raised both eyebrows. Usually his boss was unflappable, the essence of calm. But tonight Mitch's eyes were darting around like pinballs beneath glass. And his voice had an edge to it, like he couldn't quite catch his breath.

Acosta put his cap back on so it tilted slightly forward and to the right. "As my late grandmother used to say, you're nervous as a long-tailed cat in a room full of rocking chairs."

"With all due respect to your grandmother, take this and get going." Mitch held out an envelope he'd been keeping under one arm of his slicker. "Now."

"*Right* now?" Acosta asked, taking it.

"If not sooner, sport."

Acosta chuckled despite his aggravation. Mitch used that nickname with everyone in the offices of Virginia's Supreme Court, even the women—everyone except the seven justices, of course.

"Where exactly am I going?"

"Head for the West End," Mitch said, "toward the University of Richmond. You'll get a call in a few minutes with more specific information."

"From you?"

"Maybe . . . maybe not."

Acosta flicked his half-smoked cigarette onto the wet grass beside the driveway, then took the envelope and stowed it in an inside pocket of his knee-length raincoat. Mitch was speaking barely above a whisper, as if someone else might be listening.

"I'll run it up there tomorrow morning."

"You'll run it up there now."

The West End was in the opposite direction from Acosta's home east of Richmond, near the airport. "I won't get home until three this morning."

"So be it."

Acosta peered into the South-Side gloom, scanning for telltale shadows. He was already craving another cancer stick. But if he lit up in the Explorer, Sofia would detect the smoke trail. She'd ride him relentlessly if she found out he'd picked up the habit again.

"What's in here?" Acosta demanded, tapping his raincoat above the envelope. "What am I carrying, Mitch?"

"It's better that you don't know."

"Tell me or I don't go."

"Oh, you'll go. We both know that."

"Why doesn't your boss just e-mail it?"

Mitch leaned in close again. "There can be no trail to Chief Justice Eldridge. Now," he ordered, breaking into a good-natured smile as he leaned back again, "get your brown ass out of here. The faster you deliver it, the faster you get home to that beautiful bride of yours." His smile widened. "How you ever convinced a woman nine years your junior to marry you, I'll never know, especially one as beautiful as Sofia."

Acosta smothered the desire to let his fiery temper fly, even if Mitch was his boss, and even if Mitch's boss was the chief justice of the state's Supreme Court. But he deserved at least some information for getting out of bed. "What's in the envelope?" he demanded again.

"Don't stop for anyone," Mitch advised, blatantly ignoring the question this time. "Not even a state boy with his cherries on fire. And if you do, be ready for bear."

"Meaning?"

"You got your nine-millimeter, sport? First round chambered?"

"Always."

"Be careful," Mitch advised. "Eyes peeled the whole way. Judge Eldridge told me to tell you that several times, and he never repeats himself, Raul."

Now Acosta *needed* that cigarette. He couldn't remember the last time Mitch had called him anything but "sport." And Mitch was right. Eldridge never repeated himself.

Mitch moved to go, but turned back. Acosta spotted the Taliban-inflicted divots carving the silhouette of his cheek.

"Do you know what's in the envelope?" Mitch asked.

This night kept getting stranger and stranger. "How could I?"

"You and Judge Eldridge have gotten awfully chummy. You've been behind closed doors a lot lately with him."

Mitch's voice suddenly carried a grainy, uncertain tone Acosta had never heard before. Maybe the envelope involved Mitch's late-night meetings with whoever was in the back of that limousine. "You're getting paranoid, boss. It's not flattering." He couldn't tell Mitch what the closed-door discussions involved. Eldridge had warned him several times about keeping the move to Project Archer hush-hush.

"If I'd been more paranoid in Afghanistan that night, five of my men would have survived." Mitch tilted his head slightly to one side. "What has my uncle been telling you behind my back? Has he found out something about me?"

"Is there something to find, boss?"

Mitch grabbed Acosta violently by his raincoat lapels. "What do you mean by that?"

For a split second, Acosta considered asking Mitch about the limousine. "What's in the envelope that scares you so much?" he asked instead. Mitch was already agitated. Asking about the limousine might send him to the stratosphere.

"What did Judge Eldridge tell you?" Mitch hissed.

Now that they were so close, Acosta caught a strong whiff of whiskey on Mitch's breath. "Back off." This time he pushed Mitch away with a single burly arm. He just wanted to make the delivery and get home to Sofia. Maybe she'd still want to make love. "Go inside and have another drink."

The two men stared each other down through the dim light.

Finally, Mitch cleared his throat and forced a thin smile. "Yes, I think I will . . . go inside."

"Good."

"You call me as soon as you deliver the envelope," Mitch ordered, the edge in his voice still obvious even as he tried to seem himself again. "I want to know who picks it up."

"I'll call you."

Acosta watched Mitch limp a few paces toward the house, then turned and headed for the Explorer. Mitch's intense expression had included dread, perhaps the expression he'd worn when he'd first realized his leg had been blown off.

A chill snaked up Acosta's spine as he climbed into the SUV, grabbed the open pack of cigarettes off the dash, and lit one up as fast as he could. Like his late grandmother, he was prone to premonitions. This one was bad.

He fired up the SUV and backed hurriedly out of the driveway.

When his phone rang ten minutes later, he dropped the portfolio of pictures he'd been holding open—to a photo of Sofia on her side in the middle of a big, four-poster bed, gazing demurely back at him—and grabbed the cell off the dash. He'd been starting to think the call wasn't coming. He'd been wondering what to do with the envelope if no call came. Given how strangely Mitch was acting, he didn't want to take it home.

"Hello."

"Who is this?"

"Raul Acosta."

"Do you have it?"

"Yeah."

"Head for the University of Richmond. When you get there, go to the far corner of Crenshaw Field from the Modlin Center for the Arts. Your contact's name is Dominick."

"Okay, I—*look out!*"

Acosta wrenched the steering wheel left, barely avoiding a white-tailed buck standing statue-like in the middle of the wet road—then yanked the wheel right to miss the guardrail now hurtling toward the bumper.

"Damn deer," Acosta grumbled when he had the Explorer back in control. "Just good-for-nothing tick barges." Despite the near hit and the possibility of more deer ahead, he glanced at the passenger seat and

Sofia's photograph. "I can't keep my eyes off you, can I, baby?" he asked, holding the phone up before him.

Just as Acosta located Crenshaw Field on Google Maps, the heavens opened up and rain began pouring down in sheets. He dropped his phone on the seat beside the portfolio and flipped on his wipers as he sped out onto the long, graceful span of the Huguenot Memorial Bridge where it crossed the wide James River several miles west of downtown Richmond. The all-night lights of the skyline were barely visible through the downpour.

He was leaving the South Side and heading to the north bank of the James, the bank on which center city lay, as did his destination— the pricey West End.

Acosta checked the rearview mirror. That same pair of headlights had been back there for several miles.

It was probably nothing. But the instincts that made him good at his job, coupled with the other unsettling aspects of this evening, had his antennae up.

He glanced over at the envelope resting on the passenger seat as the pelting rain played a helter-skelter tune on the SUV's roof. What was Eldridge sending? Why was he sending it so covertly? Who was he sending it to? And why wasn't Mitch delivering it?

That last question wasn't really fair. If danger was lurking, Mitch didn't stand a snowball's chance in San Juan of surviving. And it wouldn't do for Judge Eldridge's nephew and chief of staff to be caught up in anything scandalous. The ramifications of that were far too risky for far too many important people around town.

Acosta checked the rearview mirror again as he passed the north end of the bridge. Those headlights were still back there.

He raced across the East Branch of Tuckahoe Creek, which paralleled the north bank of the James, and slowed as he approached the stoplight at River Road. Crenshaw Field was only half a mile from the light, and he should be taking a left here.

But a voice in the back of his head was urging him to go straight through the light. And he never ignored that voice.

He sped through the intersection, paralleling the golf course of the Country Club of Virginia to his left now, checking the rearview mirror every few seconds. Halfway between River Road and the next left turn, the trailing headlights flashed into view. They seemed nearer. The vehicle was closing in.

Acosta wheeled the Explorer hard-left and gunned the engine. He raced a quarter mile up Three Chopt, headed hard-right onto Grove, veered left onto Somerset, skidded to a stop behind a Mercedes sedan, cut the lights, and turned quickly to peer over his shoulder.

A vehicle flew by on Grove. That had to have been the trailer. But was the car chasing him?

And it hadn't just looked like your average car. It had looked like a limousine from here, though it was hard to tell for certain through the darkness. If it was a limousine, that would make all this even more strange.

Acosta jammed the accelerator down and made a quick left onto York after flipping the headlights on again.

Moments later he turned onto a narrow lane across College Road from the University of Richmond, pulled off to one side, and cut the engine. He climbed out and went to the back of the SUV, exchanging his long, tan raincoat for a shorter, dark-blue slicker, which would be easier to move in. The rain had eased to a mist; however, green echoes on the weather app covered his phone's screen. Any second it might start pouring again.

He pulled his 9 mm from his shoulder holster beneath the slicker, made certain the first round was chambered, and then moved to the passenger side of the SUV, where he picked up the portfolio and glanced at Sofia. He considered slipping the photo into his pocket, but finally decided against it. This shouldn't take long.

He put it back down, grabbed the envelope, locked the doors, and began jogging toward College Road.

Rising all around him were stately brick colonials, like Mitch's. Except these homes cost twice what Mitch's did on the South Side. This was the West End of Richmond, the city's highest-rent district.

He wasn't familiar with the university grounds, so he kept glancing down at his phone as he jogged, letting it lead him. He turned off the lane, cut through several wooded yards, passed behind a massive home overlooking College, and then waited until he was certain no cars were approaching in either direction before dashing across the two lanes of pavement and quickly heading into the cover of trees lining one end of a soccer field.

Now he was on university grounds.

He remained inside the tree line until he was forced to emerge to cross a large parking lot, which lay just west of Crenshaw Field. At the other end of the field, the Modlin Center for the Arts rose up into the gloom, lights gleaming despite the late hour. But he no longer needed physical landmarks or the phone to guide him, so he slipped it into his pocket. Through the gloom, he'd spotted someone standing near the far corner of the field from the building. Who else would be out here at this hour of a nasty morning?

He drew his gun, prepared to fire if the individual made a sudden move. If this became an incident, Judge Eldridge would protect him.

The subject wore a long, dark raincoat but that was all Acosta could discern as he approached from behind. He couldn't tell if the person was holding a gun, but he'd rather have surprise on his side than *anything* else.

"Hands up," Acosta called from ten feet away, pistol out and aimed.

The figure threw both arms in the air and whirled around. "Don't shoot!" he begged when he spotted the 9 mm. "I don't have a gun. *I swear to God I don't have a gun.*"

Acosta had been concerned that associates might be hiding in the area. But the overwhelming fear inscribed in the voice instantly convinced him otherwise. This young man was alone.

"What's your name?"

"Dominick."

This guy was no Dominick. He looked more like a Brendan or an Ian. In fact, he reminded Acosta of Mitch with his cherry-blond hair and boyish good looks.

Acosta reached below his slicker and pulled out the envelope, which was wedged into his belt. "Here, kid," he muttered, tossing it to the young man, who nearly dropped it. All he wanted to do now was get home to Sofia. "Peace out."

He backed off a few steps, keeping his pistol trained on the young man's chest. The kid looked harmless, but you could never be too careful. Finally, at fifty feet, he turned and jogged back the way he'd come, checking over his shoulder several times.

After recrossing College, Acosta emerged from the trees of a back lawn out onto the lane fifty feet east of where he'd parked the Explorer. For an instant, he didn't believe his eyes. The SUV doors were wide open, and two individuals were rooting through it.

"Hey!" he yelled, blasting a bullet into the air. "Get away from there!"

A retaliatory shot rang out from behind a car parked up and on the other side of the lane, directly across from the Explorer. The bullet caromed wickedly off something to Acosta's right.

He bolted back into the trees, dodging tall oaks and maples as he sprinted from the scene. Bullets tore through the low branches all around him, shredding leaves, as sharp voices shouted out to each other through the night.

As he closed in on the Explorer, Acosta hurled himself against the trunk of a huge oak, using the tree to steady his hand as he fired five shots in rapid succession.

A sprinting silhouette pitched forward and tumbled onto the lane; someone screamed, and car doors slammed. Acosta fired three more times as another shadow helped its fallen comrade. An engine fired up, another door slammed shut, and the car raced past. He ducked as more bullets raked the branches around him, and then everything went eerily silent, as if the battle had never occurred.

He sprinted to his SUV. Shattered glass covered both front seats, and the portfolio was missing. "Damn it!"

He lumbered around the front of the truck, and a wave of relief rushed through him when he spotted something familiar looking on the pavement. He snatched the portfolio off the wet blacktop and gently smoothed water from its surface.

Only then did he feel a searing pain in his gut. He glanced down as he yanked his shirt from his pants and lifted it high.

"Oh, God," he muttered.

Blood was pouring from a gaping bullet wound beside his navel. This was the last straw. Once he was out of surgery, he was going to call Judge Eldridge and tell him what was happening with Mitch—the odd behavior tonight, the visits to the limousine downtown, the limousine that had tailed Acosta tonight. He just wished he hadn't mentioned all of it to Sofia. Mitch was no idiot.

As Acosta eased down to his knees, he found the photo of Sofia inside the portfolio. "Get me through this, baby," he gasped. "Get me through this."

CHAPTER 6
CHARLOTTESVILLE, VIRGINIA

Victoria climbed from her Lexus and walked to the front of the car, all the while staring up at the dark brick wall. She'd just pulled in beside Cam's BMW, in almost exactly the same spot her mother had parked that July day twenty-three years ago, when they'd come here from the Shenandoah Valley to pick up her father.

How had Cameron known? They'd never parked in this lot before. They usually parked in the south lot, where the four big buses that would transport the jurors up from Richmond tomorrow—and away from the facility in case of emergency—were kept.

Cam parking here couldn't be a coincidence. She didn't believe in coincidences—which, she had to admit, was odd because she was completely superstitious. But life wasn't a cookie-cutter proposition.

"You okay?" he asked, rising from the 3 Series and moving beside her in front of the Lexus.

"Yeah."

"Ironic, huh?"

"What?" She knew what he meant. They had no secrets. No lasting ones.

"It's ironic that this would be the venue for Jury Town."

Cameron had created the name for the facility a few months ago, but neither of them had told anyone yet. They were waiting for the opening of the facility tomorrow to play it for the press. They'd waited so it'd have more of an impact. Everyone would be calling it that after tomorrow night.

"I'll give you credit, Victoria."

"Why?"

"You could have chosen Mecklenberg for this. That mothballed prison down on the North Carolina border. But you didn't."

She shrugged as if she didn't understand. "Archer was better suited for what we needed, more central and much less expensive to refurbish. It wasn't a difficult decision."

"If you'd chosen Mecklenberg, you wouldn't have had to deal with the ghosts . . . and the demons."

He hadn't mentioned any of this before today, and the project had been under way for a year. "Why have you waited until now to say this?" she asked.

"Every time we drove up here together, I'd see the stress building in your expression. You always stopped talking about ten miles out, and your posture would get as rigid as a piece of thick plywood. As soon as you saw the prison wall through the trees, your eyes would go down. You wouldn't look at it, not even while we were walking toward it to go inside." Cameron gestured at the wall. "But today's different. You're staring straight at it. You're drinking it in. The same way you did before you made the announcement at the Supreme Court Building."

Her gaze ran along the top of the tall, dark wall to the nearest surveillance tower and then up to the observation deck—no Devil's angels up there today. "My father died of lung cancer before he could go after Judge Hopkins and make things right."

Cameron nodded. "And Judge Hopkins died of a stroke before you could go after him, which I'm sure you would have."

"I promised my father on his deathbed I would. But you're right. Hopkins died before I had the chance. Before I could expose him for the criminal he was."

"But that doesn't explain why today is different, why you can look at the wall without all that bitterness."

"It's not a prison anymore, Cam. It's actually Jury Town."

"Thanks to you."

She reached out for his hand and squeezed his fingers. "Thanks to both of us." She took a deep breath. "Where's that envelope you got last night?"

He reached into his coat pocket and pulled it out.

She took it, ripped it open, and read.

"What is it?" he asked.

Her heart was suddenly racing. "Nothing."

"Come on, Victoria. What's going on?"

The door to Archer opened, and a man stepped out. Victoria shook her head at Cameron—now wasn't the time—and pulled him toward the wall. "Let's go."

Once the security guard had let them in, Victoria and Cameron hurried down the facility's long administrative corridor. One wall was cluttered with broken furniture and large cardboard boxes bursting at the seams with junk. These were the final, unusable remnants of Archer Prison, which would be hauled off later today. When the last of it was gone, the renovation would be complete and the facility ready for the nation's first professional jurors.

"Does all this clutter remind you of anything?" Cameron asked, pointing at the debris as they hustled toward Clint Wolf, who was standing outside his office.

"What are you talking about?" Victoria asked, waving to Wolf.

She'd hired Clint a year ago to oversee reconstruction of the prison—and then run the facility's day-to-day operation after the jurors arrived.

"It looks a lot like the top of your desk."

"Thank you very little," she retorted, laughing.

"Yeah, well, I'm surprised FEMA's never shown up at your door."

"Be glad they haven't," Wolf said loudly with a wry grin. He was a tall, thick, full-blooded Cherokee who wore his straight black hair in a tight ponytail that fell from beneath his wide, white Stetson all the way to his belt in the back. "Things usually get worse after they do. I know from experience." Wolf nodded at Cameron, then at Victoria. "She's disorganized?"

"Oh, yeah," Cameron confirmed.

"Really," Wolf murmured as if the revelation came as a surprise.

"That's the great thing about working for her. I'll always have a job because—"

"Never would have thought that," Wolf interrupted, motioning them to follow as he turned away. "Let's go. Things have changed quite a bit since you two were here last."

Clint Wolf had spent seventeen years at the Federal Bureau of Prisons. His last post had been assistant director in charge of the massive Correctional Programs Division—where he'd been responsible for over a hundred federal prisons and more than two hundred thousand inmates. During his three-year tenure as head of CPD, only seven prisoners had escaped. Six had been recaptured within four days, while one had been killed in a gun battle after just an hour of freedom.

As far as Victoria was concerned, Wolf was eminently qualified and completely capable of keeping two hundred jurors inside this facility . . . as well as keeping their enemies out.

She wasn't as convinced of Wolf's ability to keep influence out and, just as importantly, of his ability to maintain peace at the facility. She wasn't convinced anyone could maintain that on a permanent basis. The team of psychologists who'd advised her on the project had predicted that the "cabin fever syndrome" would erupt at Archer Prison at some point.

A few strides down the corridor, Wolf turned right into another hallway, which had a pungent, fresh-carpet odor.

"Welcome to Jury Room One," Wolf said, holding open the first door on the left. "There are fifteen more exactly like it. Remember, this entire wing is new. It was not here when Archer Prison was operational."

"I love it," Victoria said as she followed Wolf. "It's sharp looking and roomy."

"As we discussed at the start of all this a year ago," Wolf said, "I've tried hard to make everything at the facility as spacious as possible. We don't want people ever feeling claustrophobic if we can help it. We're doing everything possible to fight that cabin fever you're so worried about, Victoria. Fortunately, Archer Prison was designed for a thousand inmates, so we started from a good place in terms of space for two hundred." Wolf pointed at the jury box. "Have a seat, both of you."

Fourteen chairs were arranged stadium-style in two rows against the far wall. Seven chairs in front and seven behind, those in back offset with those in front and raised eighteen inches for maximum viewing capability with plenty of room to pass by to get food and drink or take a bio break without disturbing others. Fourteen seats—two extras for alternates in case of illness or emergency—with a solid-oak, waist-high partition in front and to the sides of the chairs, perfectly replicating an actual courtroom jury box.

Victoria pulled back the gate at one end of the back row, climbed the solitary step, and eased into the first chair. "Comfortable but not too comfortable," she said approvingly. "We don't want people nodding off while court's in session."

"We've got the climate control programmed so that temperatures in the sixteen jury rooms will vary automatically and constantly between sixty-eight and seventy-four degrees. Research indicates that if the temperature varies that way, people have a harder time dozing."

"This *is* nice," Cameron said, relaxing into a seat in the middle of the front row. "Hey, they spin," he said, rotating toward Victoria.

"That's so we can use these as deliberation rooms as well," Wolf explained. "So people can face each other like they would if they were sitting around a table after the two sides have rested."

"Any concern that jurors in the back are physically higher than those in front and therefore will have a psychological edge as they argue?" Cameron asked.

"Fair point," Victoria agreed. "Maybe we instruct the foreman to—*Oh God!*" she shrieked as the entire back row began to descend until it was level with the front.

"Thought of that," Wolf said with a satisfied smile. He gestured toward the wall opposite the jury box and the four huge screens affixed to it. "Ninety-five-inch Samsungs," he said as he picked up a remote and aimed it at a stack of electronic equipment in one corner, which was encased in thick, clear plastic. The screens quickly flashed to life and to a trial in session. "You're watching a video of a trial that ended last month in Petersburg. But you get the idea. The jurors will have constant views of the witness stand, the defense table, the prosecutor's table as well as a panoramic perspective of the entire proceeding."

"Those pictures are *really* nice."

"They should be for what the screens cost." Wolf pointed above the stack of electronic equipment to a large camera bolted into the wall. "Through a feed to their laptops, the judge, the attorneys, and the defendant will be able to see the jury at all times through that camera."

"Good."

"Audio will also be two-way. So jurors can hear everything said in the courtroom, and the judge can communicate at all times." Wolf held up the remote again and pushed several buttons. A moment later the trial disappeared and was replaced on all four screens by the movie *Avatar* as the lights in the room dimmed. "When juries aren't in session, this wing will turn into a multiplex. We'll have sixteen different movies playing. We have a library of five thousand films, and we'll publish a schedule every morning of what will be playing once court is over for the day."

"Any chance somebody clever could hook these screens up to outside programming?" Cameron asked. "We can't have that."

"The only outside programming available to them will be the trials themselves," Wolf answered. "Every morning our technical people will be required to make each connection to each courthouse individually. They will continue monitoring those connections all day from the control room. And, every afternoon, when court's over, the techies will cut each connection to each courthouse individually. But listen," he said somberly as he placed the remote down on the jury box banister and headed for the door, "I learned in my nearly two decades at FBP that people are very smart and very creative, especially people with time on their hands. We'll have to monitor everyone and everything very, very carefully."

Victoria and Cameron followed him out, hustling to keep up.

"As you know, your office is that way, past mine," Wolf called to Victoria, gesturing to the left as he came out of the jury-room hallway and turned right onto the administration wing corridor. "The office of the head of the guard corps is also up there."

"The guard facilities are in a different building, right?" Cameron asked.

"Their lockers and lounge are in that brick building on your left just as you come through the main entrance to the property." Wolf waved at several doors on the right. "These are the medical facilities."

"Wait," Victoria called, taking a moment to check the large infirmary. New equipment glistened beautifully. "Remind me about procedure here, Clint."

"All visits will be recorded and carefully reviewed by staff afterward *unless*," Wolf said loudly as Cameron began to object, "the visit involves something of an intimate nature. A gynecology exam, a colonoscopy, a breast X-ray," he said, ticking off examples. "In those cases, of course, no recording will be made. However, there will be two members of the medical staff present at all times, and which members of the medical staff are in attendance will be determined by a random-number system generated by computer just prior to the exam. When the exams are over, everyone will be thoroughly searched, and the medical staff debriefed by me personally as long as I'm on premises. If I'm not, it'll be my second in commands doing the interviewing." Wolf removed the Stetson for a moment to run his hand through his ponytail. "We'll limit contact between the jurors and staff as much as possible, whether it's cleaning people, guards, medical people, or administrators. But the reality is, some minimal amount of interaction is unavoidable." He put his hat back on. "The key to securing those interactions will be the random nature of the staff present and the duplication of staff involved. It will be very, very hard to sneak information to jurors, whether it's to bribe them or intimidate them, if the sender has no idea which staff member will be in attendance *and* there are always at least two staff members around. In addition," he continued, "no schedule for anyone will be consistent week to week, not even for the administrative assistants. And schedules won't come out far in advance, two days at most. Finally, even jurors will have a hybrid lottery system in terms of doctor and dental visits, unless it's an emergency, of course." He held up his hand. "And I'll be all over every emergency visit. It's the easiest and fastest way to gain separation from the general prisoner—sorry," he interrupted himself, "the general *juror* population. I'll personally review in detail every emergency situation."

"How will jurors notify you and your staff of an emergency?" Cameron asked.

"There's a button in each juror room. Right beside the small screen built into the desk through which we'll communicate with them. Tell them what jury room to show up in for a new trial, what dinner choices will be that night. Things like that."

"And through which I will send an inspirational message every morning," Victoria spoke up with a wide smile.

Wolf rolled his eyes. "Are you still planning on doing that, Victoria?"

"Yes, sir, every morning. It'll be my tradition. They'll love it."

"Governor Lewis," someone called out.

Victoria turned toward an elderly woman who was standing between two tall boxes, clasping a broom.

"Hello there," Victoria called back, cutting in front of Cameron to greet the woman. "What's your name?"

"Rose," the woman answered softly as she took Victoria's hand.

"That's such a beautiful name."

"I'm sorry to bother you, but I wanted to thank you for one of the programs you got approved while you were governor. It's the program that guarantees every fourth-grader in the public schools gets a laptop and Internet connection, even if they can't afford them."

"Complete Connection," Victoria said, recalling the fight she and Cameron had waged against Majority Leader Franz to win funding for the initiative. "And yes, we had quite a battle in the General Assembly getting that legislation approved and financed. More than a few tight-fisted senators and delegates believed there were better ways to spend money than on education. We went twelve rounds, but we got it done."

"It did my granddaughter a world of good," Rose said, her voice laden with emotion. "Alicia was way behind all the other kids in her class when she got to fourth grade. And then she got a computer because of you. All of a sudden, she was on the Internet all the time, looking up things and getting so smart." Rose wiped her eyes. "Alicia's in seventh grade now, and she's top of her class, getting straight As. She wants to be a doctor, a *doctor*. I hope I live to see that day."

"I have a good feeling you will," Victoria said, gently embracing the frail woman. "Thank you for telling me that," she said. "You made my day."

"You're welcome, Governor Lewis." Rose gestured around. "What you're doing here is really good, too. God bless you."

"Thank you."

"That reminds me of a tour I gave President Obama," Wolf remarked as they continued walking. The long, narrow corridor finally gave way to a sprawling, brightly lighted, circular area, which lay at the heart of the massive facility. "Everyone loved that man that day."

"She gets it constantly," Cameron said.

"I'm sure."

"This is amazing," Cameron exclaimed in a hushed voice as he gazed at the brand-new tables and chairs, which were perfectly arranged below the ceiling soaring fifty feet above them. "It's beautiful in here."

"It really is," Victoria agreed, pulling out a tissue to dab at her nose, which was running. She shot Cameron a quick look, but he hadn't seemed to notice.

"What we're looking out at now is called the Central Zone," Wolf explained. "This is where jurors will eat and socialize. They can also stretch their legs here in the winter if all fifty of the gym's treadmills are in use." Wolf motioned around toward the edge of the area. "Extending like points of a star from the Central Zone are five two-story wings of rooms, as well as the admin corridor we just came down. You'll see it more clearly in a few minutes when we climb to the observation deck."

Victoria's heart skipped a beat. *"Observation deck?"*

"Yes."

"Like at the top of one of those surveillance towers?" Cameron asked.

"Just like that."

"I'm not big on heights," Victoria said firmly.

"Me, neither," Cameron seconded.

"You'll both be fine," Wolf said with a chuckle. "The engineers assure me that the rust you'll see in the stairway doesn't affect the structural integrity of the tower."

Victoria held up both hands. "Hey, I'm not going up any—"

"Archer Prison was built seventy years ago, and the star design was typical back then," Wolf continued, pointing at one of the large, two-story openings, which led to the living quarters. "Each cell wing could handle two hundred prisoners. There were a hundred on each floor with two inmates each to the eight-by-ten rooms. We're using four wings for the jurors. We couldn't take the building out any further without massive construction costs, so the rooms are still just eight feet deep. But now they're fifteen feet long, which allowed us to put thirteen rooms on each side of each floor and still have plenty of room for showers on each wing. Every juror will have his or her own room along with a sink and a toilet."

"So there are a few extra rooms?" Victoria asked, distracted by her worry about climbing a surveillance tower. "Assuming we have two hundred jurors."

"Eight extras," Wolf answered. "Two hundred and eight rooms in total."

"What about the fifth wing?" Cameron asked as he and Victoria hustled to keep up with Wolf, who was striding ahead through the maze of tables and chairs. "Is that the workout area?"

"Yup. Kitchen over there behind that wall of slots to the right," Wolf said with a wave, "and inmates will order from the menu above the—"

"Jurors," Victoria reminded him loudly.

"Got to fix that habit," Wolf muttered under his breath. "*Jurors* will order from the menu above the slot and have their meal come through the slot on a tray. Breakfast and lunch will be fairly standard, still excellent quality, but dinner will be different each night, and they'll be apprised of their choices on the screens in the desks of their rooms. Right above Victoria's daily words of wisdom," he muttered. "There will be central condiment stations, and everything will be cleaned every night while the *jurors* are sleeping. We're doing everything we can to remove the possibility of information passing between jurors and staff, including having rooms and showers cleaned while jurors are out of the living quarters. Again we'll use random-number generators to figure out who goes where to clean. Candidly, this place will be a lot like Las Vegas in terms of staff observation."

"What do you mean?" Cameron asked.

"People will always be watching people," Wolf responded. "You know, like box men watching the dealers, floor men watching the box men, pit bosses watching the floor men. You get the idea. We'll be trying to catch anything being passed from a staff member to a juror on a tray, wrapped in a towel, or stuck inside a medicine vial. We'll be watching for hand signals as codes, too. And we'll have eyes in the sky out here watching everything."

"But no cameras in the rooms or the showers," Victoria said firmly.

Wolf shook his head. "No, but everywhere else."

They reached the athletic wing and moved from the hallway into the sprawling workout center.

"Hey, this is really nice," Victoria said, gazing at the huge room full of high-tech exercise equipment. "This room was empty last time I was here."

"Everything came last week," Wolf said, pointing to the ceiling. "Upstairs are four basketball hoops and several racquetball courts. There are enough machines in this room for all two hundred jurors to be working out at the same time."

"Beautiful."

"Let's check out one of the rooms," Wolf suggested.

"No need," Victoria responded quickly.

Wolf glanced at her. "Why not?"

"Just no need."

He stared at her for a few moments, then shrugged. "Okay, then let's climb the surveillance tower."

Victoria glanced at Cameron, who was gazing back knowingly. She shrugged. She'd conquered most of the demons she associated with this place—but not all. Not yet.

Wolf nodded to himself in a supremely satisfied way as he gazed into the afternoon from a hundred feet above the ground, casually leaning against a rusty vertical beam at the edge of the observation deck with one hand as he clutched his white Stetson with the other.

As if he were looking out over his kingdom, Victoria thought to herself.

"It's beautiful up here," he called over his shoulder.

From the top of the surveillance tower, they had a panoramic view of the world—which, outside the facility property, was filled by tree-covered foothills as far as the eye could see. Even the narrow ribbon of blacktop leading into the facility from the outside world was obscured by the dense canopy. It would be beautiful, Victoria figured as a stiff gust hit the tower, if she weren't terrified. It wasn't nearly this windy on the ground.

"It's peaceful up here when you don't have inmates down there in the yard obsessed with escaping, because what else is there for them to think about all day?" Wolf's expression turned steely and his tone bitter as he gestured down. "Especially the ones sentenced to life who don't care about killing you during a breakout, because, after all, what are they risking? More time on their sentence?"

Victoria stood in the middle of the tower's twelve-by-twelve-foot observation deck at the point where the steps emerged, knees flexed as she clutched the top of the stairway's rusty railing. They'd spent the last few minutes climbing what seemed like a thousand steps of a light-house-like, circular stairway to get up here. She was in excellent shape thanks to a demanding aerobics regimen she attacked four mornings a week. But her legs had turned to jelly on the last few steps as the world outside the enclosed stairway reappeared. Her brain was screaming at her to retreat to the ground *now*.

White-knuckled fingers still clutching the railing, she leaned toward the edge as far as possible. The top of the dark, brick wall was sixty feet below, encasing the old prison like a huge, square box. At each corner of the box, a surveillance tower soared skyward like turrets of a fort—they were atop the tower on the old prison's northeast corner.

Wolf was right, she realized. The facility did resemble a five-point star from up here, if she ignored the administration corridor, which led to another, much smaller building that had served as the inmate receiving and discharge center—and the new jury corridor.

"Foothills and valleys covered by trees," Wolf spoke up wistfully. "We're in the middle of nowhere out here."

As though he was thinking that this was how the landscape must have looked to his ancestors three hundred years ago all over the state of Virginia, Victoria figured.

"I love it up here. This is the fourth time I've made the climb." Wolf glanced over his shoulder and waved to Victoria. "Come here. You'll have a much better view. I want to point out some things."

Victoria glanced at Cameron, who was clutching the top of the railing on the other side of the stairs.

"Go on," he muttered.

"You scared?" she asked.

"Petrified," he admitted. "This tower is swaying."

"Come with me," she begged.

Cameron glanced at the thin, waist-high railing, which ringed the edge of the observation deck, then retightened his grip on the banister. "Not a chance. I can see just fine from right where I am."

"Baby."

"Like I was born ten minutes ago. In fact, I may need a diaper in a few seconds."

"I thought you were my rock."

"As long as my feet are planted on the ground, I'll do anything for you." Cameron checked the perimeter railing again. "Right now I feel like we're on top of a tower made of toothpicks."

Victoria was about to pry her fingers from the railing, but sensed the structure swaying, as Cameron had said. Perhaps the swaying was just her imagination, but it caused her to vividly consider the terrifying possibility of the structure toppling over—with all of them up here.

"Come on," Wolf called impatiently.

She gave Cameron one more what-in-God's-name-are-we-doing-up-here expression and finally let go. She staggered several steps to the outer railing, like she was walking on a boat deck in a raging storm, and clutched it with a two-hand death grip. She was already getting dizzy. The ground below seemed to be swirling like a giant whirlpool.

She *hated* heights—always had.

"What's wrong?" Wolf asked, with a knowing grin. "You scared of heights?"

"No. It's the fall that concerns me."

"Falling won't hurt. It's the impact you need to worry about."

"I'm glad I can bring a little amusement to your day, Clint. What do you want to show me?"

"The precautions we're taking to keep jurors in."

"And our enemies out," she reminded him as a fresh burst of air blew her long hair back and off her shoulders.

"Exactly." He pointed down at the open space between the end of the closest wing and the high brick wall surrounding the facility. "That's a twelve-foot razor-wire fence ten feet from the primary wall on the inside and twenty feet from the primary wall on the outside. So if you're going to try and make it in or out of Archer Prison that way, you'll have to negotiate a razor-wire fence twice your height, the brick wall, and then another razor-wire fence twice your height. Between both wire fences and the brick wall, we've installed pressure pads and motion sensors, which, if tripped, will immediately alert central command inside the facility as well as the eight guards—two on each deck—who will be up here at all times. Bottom line, getting in or out of Archer that brazenly will be damn hard. Like I said while we were touring the inside, I won't ever call anything impossible because I've seen too many crazy things in my time at FBP to ever use that word. But let me put it this way, I'd be *very* surprised if it happened."

"The shifts up here will be what . . . about two hours max?" she asked as she shut her eyes tightly against another gust. "Isn't that when concentration starts breaking down?"

"You've been reading up on your prison security."

"It seemed like the thing to do."

"Yes, two hours. And the guards up here will be armed."

"No," Victoria objected. "No guns. I've made that clear all along, Clint. I won't have jurors looking up here and seeing barrels pointed down at them while they're trying to relax a little and get a breath of fresh air. And I can't have any accidents."

"What if I said the guns won't be loaded?"

"It doesn't matter if they're loaded or not, from a psychological perspective. It's still stressful to see a barrel pointed down at you. Besides, it'll get around that the guns are empty."

"Maybe, but only the guards and I will know for sure. Guns will still be a very effective deterrent even if that rumor gets legs. Just the sight of a firearm is intimidating. Trust me on this."

"Let me think about it." She wasn't going to change her mind. But the discussion had distracted her from her predicament, which was interesting. Maybe she could control her fear of heights, at least for a little while. She gestured down. "What else?"

He pointed at several tall light towers. "All yard space between the brick wall and the facility will be lighted bright as day at night." He turned toward the outside. "Same for the cleared area beyond the brick wall, which, incidentally, is two hundred yards in every direction."

She nodded. "I'm very happy with what you've done inside and out."

"Thank you."

"What about major attacks?" she asked.

"Major attacks?"

"What if someone wanted to destroy this place? How could they do it?"

Wolf looked at her like she was crazy. "Why would anyone do that?"

"Just go with me on this for a minute. Help me think it through."

He gazed at her for several moments. "Is there something you're not telling me, Victoria?"

Judge Eldridge had posed this same possibility a year ago at the outset of Project Archer, when he'd first asked her to spearhead the program and take ultimate responsibility for it. She'd pushed him on what he was driving at, but he wouldn't give up any details. In fact, she'd had to push him incredibly hard just to get to the bottom of his most critical reason for initiating the project—to protect against jury tampering.

In the end, she'd given him an ultimatum: Tell her everything or she was out.

Even then it had taken him two weeks to finally admit that it seemed likely Virginia had been the victim of widespread jury tampering on high-profile cases for several years.

Six months ago Eldridge had become nearly impossible to reach—until she'd requested his presence at the press conference. He'd apologized for—though not explained—his radio silence just before they'd taken the stage together to make the project's official announcement.

Now she had the explanation for why Eldridge had suddenly gone silent half a year ago—and why the normally straightforward chief justice had gone cloak-and-dagger. The mysterious answer had been sealed inside the envelope, which had been delivered to Cameron at his penthouse condominium in downtown Richmond by an aide who'd received it from Eldridge's messenger. The envelope Cameron had given her in the parking lot a few minutes ago.

He'd asked her what was inside it, but she'd steadfastly refused to explain—for his own good.

The doomsday scenario Judge Eldridge had been focused on a year ago had always puzzled her. But now she understood—and needed Wolf's answer to the question.

"Don't worry about what I am or am not telling you. What are the scenarios? You must have dealt with this at FBP."

"Bombs, missiles, airliners, biological—"

"Or the *threat* of those things," she cut in, snapping her fingers as the realization hit her. "Maybe *that's* what he was worried about."

"He who?"

"If we had to get everyone out of the facility because of a bomb threat," she went on, ignoring Wolf's pointed query, "it might give someone the opportunity to influence the jurors."

"The threat would have to be extremely credible, and we would not exit everyone from the premises without my specific say-so."

"After contacting me," Victoria said firmly.

"Okay," he agreed, after a moment's hesitation, "if we have time."

"I just wanted to make sure it was on your radar."

"It already had been," he assured her. "Yes, we dealt with threats like that all the time at FBP, but never once had to fully evacuate a prison. We had fires and one bomb threat, which turned out to be bogus, during which we had to move people around. But the staff and I are fully prepared for that contingency, believe me, Victoria. And with what we have in mind, I don't believe it would pose a security issue in terms of getting information to or from jurors. Always a possibility, but I think we'd be okay."

"Good." She grasped the railing hard as another gust whipped through the observation deck. "Here's something else I want on your radar," she said, pushing several strands of wind-blown hair from her face. "A man named Raul Acosta is going to be the number-two guard at this facility. He'll be up here tomorrow morning first thing to meet with you and George Garrison."

A month ago Wolf had appointed George Garrison—a longtime friend of his—as head of the guards at the facility.

"Please let George know and make certain he's here," she continued. "I'll have Acosta call you this afternoon directly to set up a time for tomorrow."

"You've got to be kidding." Wolf rolled his eyes in exasperation. "It's awfully late in the game to be throwing someone that senior into the mix."

"I understand, but that's how it's going to be."

"Who is this guy?"

"Acosta is currently head of security for the Supreme Court of Virginia. I want him on board as the number-two guard. He has the full faith and confidence of Chief Justice Eldridge and me."

"Does he have any experience that would—"

"Rikers Island, Clint. Pretty damn good."

"How much money did you promise him?"

Victoria shot Cameron a glance. He seemed entirely focused on clutching the railing. "Two hundred thousand dollars," she replied.

"*Are you serious?* That's fifty thousand *more* than Garrison's going to make. It's only ten grand less than I'm making, for God's sake. How can I have Acosta making more than his boss at Archer Prison?"

"Don't tell his boss."

"George Garrison will find out, Victoria, believe me. He's a resourceful man."

"Then maybe I'm very glad to have Raul Acosta around."

"Hey, I'll vouch for George—"

"Figure it out, Clint. And do me one more favor while you're at it."

"What?"

"From now on, I want you and everyone around here to call this place Jury Town." She gazed down on the facility affectionately, which came as a shock to her system. "No more Archer Prison."

She understood Wolf's irritation. He was taking the interjection of Acosta as a tacit admission on her part that she wanted a mole. That she didn't completely trust everyone else involved—including Wolf.

Well, too bad. She wasn't in this to be friends with anyone. Far from it.

"Understood?"

Wolf's eyes narrowed with aggravation, but he nodded—finally. "Yeah, I got it."

"Good." She staggered toward the steps, grabbed Cameron and said, "Let's get out of here."

"Thank God," he said, his face ghostly white. "I thought you'd never say those words."

CHAPTER 7

NORTH WOODS OF MAINE

Philip Rockwell rapped three times on the heavy door, counted slowly to ten, and then knocked again, twice.

He glanced over his shoulder as the seconds ticked by maddeningly slowly. As they always ticked by while he was standing on the porch of this cabin, secluded deep in the dense forest of northern Maine. As they always did while he waited for one of the four Grays to identify him before opening the door and allowing him inside.

His Mercedes sedan was the lone vehicle parked at this end of the long, gravel driveway that snaked through the tall pines like a wind-blown ribbon. Where were the other vehicles, he wondered. The other men had to get here somehow, and there were no garages or barns on the property in which they could hide their vehicles. The old hunting cabin was the only structure on this half acre of cleared ground in the middle of a seemingly endless ocean of trees. They must have a helipad deeper in the forest that he wasn't privy to. That had to be the answer.

Maybe they'd tell him during this meeting why they called them-selves the Grays. If they didn't, maybe he'd ask—if he got his nerve up.

For a year he'd been acting as their touch-point to the outside world, at least with respect to decisions made here. And everything they'd tasked him with had gone exactly as planned—except yesterday's verdict in the Bailey Energy trial.

Colin O'Hara had paid the price for defying the Grays—with a speed that had astonished even Rockwell—but, despite the bad outcome, there was still a silver lining to the lost verdict, Rockwell figured. Colin's fate was essentially more proof of concept. The information the Grays were using on people was *that* powerful. It had caused the young man to lose his family. This morning, he'd committed suicide by blowing his brains out.

Everything else they'd ordered of Rockwell had gone off perfectly—he'd worked very hard to make certain of that. He deserved more from this relationship. He deserved answers. He deserved respect.

Especially given what would happen this afternoon. They'd tasked him with executing the murder, but he had given the actual order. When it was over, he would be as responsible as JD, at least in a court of law.

The long drive from Connecticut had provided him ample time to develop a serious case of resentment.

"Come in," a voice called out when the front door finally creaked open on its hinges. "Turn to the left."

Rockwell needed no instruction as he entered the pitch-dark cabin. He was quite familiar with the routine.

His jacket was removed from behind, and then a blindfold, which smelled strongly of furniture polish, was applied. When it was knotted tightly at the back of his head, he was led forward several steps before being guided down into an armless, wooden chair. It felt like the same one he sat in every time he came, which was at least twice a month.

At least they could have found something more comfortable for him to sit in during these meetings. A big leather easy chair would be nice, like the one in his study back in Connecticut. A chopper to get to and from the cabin would be even nicer.

"As always, we appreciate you making the drive, Mr. Rockwell."

"Of course," he answered stiffly.

"It's a long way to come. But we must be cautious. We must maintain our secrecy at all costs."

That was easy for them to say because they weren't driving eighteen hours round-trip. He was certain they weren't. Making the drive seemed more a means of them impressing upon him that they were superior—not so much them being worried about maintaining secrecy.

"I understand."

He was vaguely aware that a light had been turned on. Still, he couldn't see anything through the thick cloth. The blindfold hung down over his nose and mouth all the way to his chin, impeding his breathing and speech, enough to be acutely annoying. Everything about this routine was annoying. Well, almost everything.

"You seem aggravated, Mr. Rockwell," a second voice spoke up.

He was tempted to start asking all those questions he'd come up with on the long, black road. "I'm fine."

"Your efforts do not go unappreciated."

A therapist would have a field day with the double negatives that voice seemed prone to.

"Last week," a third man said, "your investment bank won the lead manager role in two extremely profitable equity underwritings. One involving a technology firm headquartered in Seattle. The other involving a blue-chip, consumer-products company based in Chicago. I'm sure you know which companies I'm speaking of."

"I do."

The financial industry had been expecting Goldman Sachs to win the lead manager roles for both high-profile transactions. But Rockwell & Company had secured the deals instead. The Grays had manipulated both outcomes from behind the scenes, Rockwell knew. They'd told him a month ago what was going to happen, and despite his significant doubts, both deals had come to his people.

So the long drive wasn't without significant reward. The two underwritings would net Rockwell's little firm tens of millions in fees. And, ultimately, the publicity of beating out Goldman was even more valuable than the money.

"Thank you," he murmured respectfully.

"You're welcome."

"The verdict in the Bailey Energy trial did not go as planned," the fourth Gray spoke up—ominously. "They did not win permission to build the pipeline."

Once Rockwell was inside the cabin, they never wasted time getting down to business.

"As the four of you are aware," he spoke up, "until yesterday all verdicts in all trials you sought to manipulate in the last year have gone exactly as you wanted. In other words, my messengers are doing an outstanding job of locating the targeted jury members, making those jury members aware of what we have on them, and then informing them, in no uncertain terms, of how you want them to vote on the verdict."

Rockwell wanted to ask the men how they were getting that information, how they could amass so many razor-sharp blades of extortion. He already had his suspicions. Only one entity he was aware of could obtain blackmail firepower like this. At least one of these men had to be a senior official at the National Security Administration.

Though the Grays had never given Rockwell specifics as to how they were benefitting from the verdicts, he believed it was in the stock markets or through direct investments in private companies. He'd kept a list of cases they'd ordered him to influence since he'd joined them. Oftentimes at least one large, publicly held corporation was involved in the trial, and the verdict they desired was always positive for the company, immediately boosting its stock price. In other cases, when it was a privately held corporation battling in court, the verdict had enabled that entity to move forward on a project that would ultimately deliver a huge cash windfall—like building a pipeline.

The reality that the defense department was also a priority for the Grays had also been made clear to Rockwell. So it would be logical to assume that the Grays would assist those entities as well. The Keystone Systems case was a perfect example. The "not guilty" verdict in the trial had been a seventeen-billion-dollar win for a top DOD contractor as well as the Pentagon. The stock price had shot up in after-hours trading.

"The Bailey Energy trial is the first and only setback we've had. But the juror in question committed suicide this morning. Apparently, his second family spurned him as well."

"Hear, hear!" one of the men shouted. The other three men echoed the first and stamped their shoes on the wooden floor in unison.

"What about our most important target?" asked another.

"JD is back in Virginia," Rockwell answered. The shouting and stamping had shocked him, as it always did. He couldn't see it coming with the blindfold on. "He's tracking Victoria Lewis as we speak."

"He must succeed."

"Especially after the announcement she made in Richmond."

"We cannot allow Ms. Lewis to insulate juries from us. Given its proximity to Washington, DC, Virginia is vital to our interests."

"And if she's successful in Virginia, other states will follow. I'm hearing that New York and California are monitoring Project Archer with great interest."

"JD's mission may not stop Project Archer," Rockwell warned.

"But it will most certainly throw a huge wrench into the project's momentum."

Rockwell couldn't argue with that.

"You have confidence in this . . . convicted felon, Mr. Rockwell?"

"We pried him out of prison, and we pay him well," Rockwell answered. "I remind him from time to time that I could send him back to prison whenever I want."

"Is JD loyal?"

"There's no such thing as loyalty among felons, only short leashes."

"But they aren't all convicted *murderers*. They aren't all convicted of torturing a young woman to death over a period of days."

Rockwell shrugged. "True," he agreed. "But JD possesses another talent which we may require at some point."

"What *talent* are you speaking of?"

"Before his conviction, he was a Marine sniper. According to his records"—this piece of data had not come from the Grays—"he's one of the most accurate snipers in the world."

"I don't know," one of the men grumbled. "We want those who are malleable, Mr. Rockwell . . . not necessarily psychopathic."

"In this endeavor," Rockwell replied deliberately, "we must accept evil with good. We must use angels from behind all fences if we are to achieve our overall objective of social, business, and military control. Does anyone disagree?" When no one did, he continued. "Good, because given how quickly you want me to expand this effort, I'll need more individuals like JD."

The room went silent for several moments.

"Do we know when Project Archer will go operational?" one of the Grays asked. "Ms. Lewis made it sound as if it would be soon."

"Tomorrow," another answered.

"*That* soon? How do you know?"

"I have information coming from the Virginia Supreme Court. Chief Justice Eldridge seems to know as much as Victoria Lewis about this project." The man chuckled. "Though Eldridge has no idea that we know exactly what he knows."

No wonder, Rockwell thought to himself. *That* was how they were so informed about Project Archer. They had a Deep Throat inside the Virginia Supreme Court. And why did that surprise him? It shouldn't. It seemed like they could get past any door they wanted to.

"Let's get to the Angela Gaynor situation," another of the Grays suggested.

"Who's Angela Gaynor?" Rockwell asked.

"No need for so many questions, Mr. Rockwell," one of the men snapped. "We'll make sure you know what you need to know."

"We don't like questions," another piped up. "We've told you that from the beginning, Mr. Rockwell. We will ask questions. You will give answers. Don't make us remind you of that again."

CHAPTER 8

VIRGINIA BEACH, VIRGINIA

Angela Gaynor walked barefoot beside Trent Tucker through the afternoon mist. As her gaze shifted to the sea from the edge of the dry sand, tall swells appeared from the fog just before they crested, rolled, and crashed in a chaos of foam. She hadn't seen Trent in months, and the intimacy of the mist created a perfect setting for their reunion.

She was the Commonwealth senator from the state's Fifth District, and she worked tirelessly for her constituents, as she was this afternoon—potentially compromising a treasured personal relationship for their benefit. At least it was a nice place for the meeting.

"Have I told you yet how great you look, Angie?" Trent asked. "You're so thin these days."

Angela had been in a dogfight with her weight ever since she could remember, and as a child, had hated the season of swimming suits and bare skin. The name-calling and teasing had been relentless during summers, even from her cousins who were nice to her the rest of the year. Just the memory of it still made her wince.

She'd been overweight as a child. No, she'd been fat, *very* fat. A year from celebrating her fortieth birthday, Angela could finally admit that to herself.

It wasn't as if she was really skinny now. She wasn't and never would be. Trent was being nice. But at five six and 135 pounds, she was doing just fine, thank you very much. Keeping the weight off, especially from her hips, was a constant struggle, and chocolate was her archenemy. She hadn't had a single scrumptious taste of it in seventeen years.

"You must be sticking to that lifetime chocolate ban."

Angela put her head back and laughed as warm salt water from a dying wave washed over her feet. "How can you read my mind?" she asked as the wave hissed, hesitated, and then receded into the ocean. "How do you always know exactly what to say?"

"Because we've been best friends ever since we could see over the hoods of the tricked-out Lincolns in the ghetto. And we still are."

She glanced up as if looking at a seagull. Until two years ago, Trent had been a star power forward with the NBA's Washington Wizards. He was six ten, almost a foot and a half taller than her.

"Are we really?"

"Of course. Who knows me like you? And who knows you like me?"

"I suppose."

"When we get together, it's like we saw each other yesterday, even if it's been awhile, like it has been this time. As soon as I saw you coming down the beach, everything came rushing back."

"I'm sorry I haven't been better about keeping in touch," she apologized guiltily.

Getting away for an afternoon was a rare treat these days. He'd reached out to her several times in the last few weeks, but she hadn't found time to call him back until yesterday. And now she had a favor to ask him.

"It's okay. It used to be me who took forever to call back, flying all over to play ball. Now it's you because of this big political gig you got. Hey, that's the way it goes. It's the ebb and flow of life."

"You're so cool."

He smiled his huge, infectious smile and spread his long arms. "Thanks, gorgeous."

She loved him dearly, always had. The only thing she regretted about their relationship was that, in all the years they'd known each other, he'd never once asked her out on a real date. She would have said no immediately, of course, because ultimately, he would have dropped her to move on to his next conquest. That was simply the way it went for a man as coveted by women as Trent Tucker. Then they wouldn't have been friends anymore. Her pride would have precluded friendship after that. And not being close to him was too terrible a prospect for her to consider.

She muted a soft laugh. She would have liked one chance to turn him down, just to see his reaction, just to see his shock. And to find out if she actually could, to find out if she had the same willpower when it came to him as she did with sweets.

She wondered if any woman had ever turned Trent down. At least since he'd become a national sensation in college at the University of North Carolina where he'd led the Tar Heels to an NCAA basketball title. Those sharp, handsome facial features and wide shoulders way up there in the clouds had broken more than a few hearts around the country, his teammates had told her over the years, when she'd gone to his games. And, occasionally, the parties afterward—for a little while, until she couldn't take watching the girls throw themselves at him anymore.

She'd always wanted him. There. She could finally admit that, too, now that she was almost forty. The thing was, she'd want him for good if it ever got started.

"So, what young hip-hop sensation are you woo-wooing these days?" she asked.

Trent grimaced. "First off, I don't woo-woo anybody."

"Okay, then what hip-hop babe is woo-wooing you?"

"I'm done with singers," he answered flatly. "I'm tired of having to tell them how good they sound even when they don't. Nobody ever told me my shot looked good when I missed."

"Then it must be some hot, young actress."

"No more starlets, either. Man, talk about mentally fragile."

"Well, it has to be someone like that."

"Why?"

"You're always dating some young, gorgeous celebrity. I read about you in the magazines while I'm slaving away on my treadmill. I see the pictures. I know who you're with. Give me a break. Everyone does."

"Well, I'm on hiatus right now. And I'm definitely done with girls in their twenties. Guess I'm finally feeling my age, Angie. The drama's not worth it anymore."

"That just dawning on you?"

"I'm sticking with women my own age from now on," he said, as if he'd just reached a monumental decision.

"Bull. I'll open *People* next week, and there she'll be, on your arm. Some bombshell who's still getting carded. Even after all your talk."

"Nah."

"It's amazing that none of those women could ever pin you down."

Trent grinned. "They all turn off like a switch the second I say, 'pre-nup.'" He reached out and touched her gently on the shoulder. "You never got married, either. Why not?"

That brief touch had felt so good. It had sent waves all around her body. "My situation's different. I don't have men throwing themselves at me all the time."

"I don't have—"

"Don't even try," she interrupted good-naturedly. "Hey, I get it. It goes with the turf. You're an NBA star."

"Was," he reminded her. "And, hey, you're a celebrity, too."

"Maybe in my little local world. But not on the national stage like you. Besides, I don't have time for a private life."

"Yeah, I've heard about all the stuff you do, how hard you're working. And the people here love you."

"I hope so."

"You know you're the only black state senator Virginia's got. Other than you, it's a pretty pale slate in the General Assembly."

She slipped her fingers into his and pulled him to a stop. It always amazed her how long those fingers were. A basketball in his hand must have felt like a tennis ball did for most people.

"I gotta ask you a question."

"Uh-oh," he muttered, turning to face her. "There's that tone. What did I do?"

"Nothing, stop."

"I've heard it too many times. Come on."

"Will you marry me?" She laughed loudly when his eyes went wide, like he'd stuck his finger in a socket.

"Um . . . Angie, I'm probably a permanent bach—"

"I'm messing with you, Trent. Chill out."

He broke into that light-the-world-up smile. "I knew that."

"Sure you did. You should have seen your face just then. You've been worried I was gonna ask you that question ever since we were teenagers, and don't even try telling me you haven't."

"Maybe I was worried I'd say yes if you asked. You ever think of that? If I was ever gonna marry someone, it would be you."

"You just had your chance to say it, and I'm not asking again."

She dug a little trench in the sand with her toe. She didn't know how to start this.

He slipped a fingertip beneath her chin and lifted it slowly so she was forced to look up at him. "You're stressed, Angie. A woman who grew a construction company from nothing into the biggest outfit in the city, and then beat a good old boy out of his state senate seat should never feel stress. What's wrong?"

"You don't know what you're talking about," she whispered.

"When it comes to you, I know *exactly* what I'm talking about."

She hated how right he was. "Okay, here's the deal. Last week some very senior people in the party paid me a visit."

Grave concern swept across Trent's face. "Are you getting run out of your senate seat? People in Richmond don't like a black woman taking a white man's spot? Is that what's going on?" He shook his head. "You know, we start to think we're making progress in this country, and then something like this happens. Well, that—"

"They weren't from Richmond. They were national people."

"Even worse. I get the Richmond crew still fighting the Civil War, still thinking they'll rise again. They'll never let that die in a thousand years. But people from headquarters shouldn't be hassling you like that. They should be damn glad you're doing what you're doing. They should be kissing your feet for all the sacrifices you're making."

"Trent."

"Don't let them get to you like that. Don't back down. Hell, you've never backed down from anything in your life, Angie."

"*Trent.*"

"I remember you shooting that crackhead who broke into your apartment that night, looking for money to buy drugs when your mother was gone working. You shot him right through the chest. You took care of business that night, you didn't back down then. Don't let these people—"

"*Trent!*" Sometimes he got on these rolls that were almost impossible to stop. He had since he was a kid.

"What?"

"They didn't come to hassle me. They came to ask me to run for the big one, for the *United States* Senate. They want me to take on Chuck Lehman."

For a few moments, Trent gazed down at her as if he couldn't grasp what she'd said, as if she'd been speaking a foreign language. Finally he grabbed her, picked her up off the wet sand, and twirled her round and round.

"Put me down!" she screamed. God, he was strong. She already knew that, of course. But she'd never felt it before, not like this. No wonder they called his position on the court *power* forward. "*Put me down!*"

"United States Senator Angela Gaynor!" Trent shouted into the mist as he eased her feet back to the sand. "Can you believe it? You're going to Washington."

"Whoa, whoa," she cautioned, dizzy from spinning. She'd felt like a doll in his huge arms. "Senator Lehman is finishing his third term. He's the senate majority leader. He's an institution in Washington." She hated getting dizzy. Still, she wanted him to pick her up and do it again. It was so good to feel petite. "The odds of me beating the man are very small."

"When have you ever paid attention to the odds, Angie? You've been beating them all your life, longer ones than this, too. Don't give me that."

"I'm gonna need a lot of luck and a lot of help."

"What can I do?" Trent asked immediately. "Sign me up. I'll do whatever's necessary to get you to Washington."

She gazed up at him. "Seriously?"

"Absolutely."

"I . . . I . . ." She glanced out to sea again. The fog was closing in around them. The waves had already broken and were nothing but foam when they churned into view now.

"What is it, Angie? What's wrong?"

"I don't want you to feel like I'm imposing."

"I'd say if you were. No one's ever accused me of not speaking my mind."

"Still."

"Is it money? Is that what you need?" A curious look came to his expression. "It can't be. I see your Gaynor Construction signs all over the sites in the area." His shoulders slumped. "Oh, no, is your company having problems? Is that CEO you hired to run the place for you screwing up? Is Jack Hoffman taking you down?"

"Trent, I—"

"You had to hire an outsider when you went into politics, right? So there wouldn't be any conflict of interest, no chance for any appearance of impropriety when your company did work in this area?"

"Yeah, but—"

"So Jack Hoffman messed the company up, and now you need a loan to bail you out. That's what this is all—"

"*This is not about money,*" she interrupted, laughing this time. His loyalty bowled her over. "My company's fine. Jack Hoffman is doing a great job as my CEO. Earnings are higher than ever."

Trent spread his arms. "Then what is it? What do you need?"

Angela glanced down at the wet sand as the end of another wave approached. "I need you. I need your reputation. I need your time. Yes, I'm a big fish down here in Virginia Beach and Norfolk. Everybody knows me. But it's a little pond. Nobody in Richmond or northern Virginia, or any other part of the state, for that matter, has any clue who I am. And that's going to be a big problem when it comes to beating Chuck Lehman. All the money in the world might not be enough to raise my awareness factor among Virginia voters fast enough when I'm going up against the Lehman machine."

She glanced up at him as warm water washed over their toes. "But *you* are a national celebrity. Everyone in the country who's even remotely a basketball fan knows who Trent Tucker is. Heck, a lot of people who aren't basketball fans know who you are. You could be a huge help to me in Richmond and Washington."

"You got it," Trent agreed without hesitation. "Anything you want from me you got. You want me to do appearances, promotions, or anything else, you name it. I'm yours."

She gazed up at him as the mist closed in around them. "I was nervous about asking you."

"Why?"

"It could take a lot of your time."

Trent ran his fingers down her soft cheek.

And her heart jumped several beats. She had to fight these urges hard because she was *so* tempted. He'd make all the right promises, standing here on the beach in the heat of this moment. Men like Trent were experts at making promises—but not at keeping them, especially to women. Her father was proof of that, wherever he was.

"Life's a wild ride, isn't it, Angie?"

She nodded as he pressed his warm palm to her cheek, and his heat surged into her body. "Yeah," she whispered, shutting her eyes as she allowed her face to rest against his big hand.

"When we were kids in the ghetto, nothing was more important than money."

"Nothing."

"We were so poor. My mother served my brothers and me Spam and grits four nights a week. The other three she didn't serve us anything. She told us to mooch off friends."

"So that's why you were over every Tuesday night." Angela laughed softly. "How did you ever grow to six ten?"

"I don't know," he admitted, pulling her against him. "I really don't."

She slipped her arms around his large frame. She could get used to this. And he'd claimed he was giving up younger women . . .

"But that's the point," he continued. "We both beat the odds, and now money's not the issue anymore. Now it's about making the world a better place." He leaned back, slipped both of his large palms to her face, and gazed down at her intensely. "You're gonna win that senate seat in Washington, you hear me? You're gonna be a United States senator. And I'm gonna do everything in my power to make that happen. Okay?"

"Okay."

A thrill rushed through her chest as he leaned down toward her. She wanted him so much; she always had. Why was it that everything she wanted in the worst way could end up being so bad for her? Couldn't anything in life be simple?

"I've got another favor to ask of you, Trent. It's a little more immediate."

"Anything," he murmured, "anything at all, Angie."

CHAPTER 9

JURY TOWN

"Glad we're off that damn tower," Cameron muttered, his voice overflowing with relief as he riffled through the long list of e-mails, texts, and calls that had accumulated on his phone during their time inside Jury Town. "Ever noticed how it looks farther to the ground when you're up on a tower than it does to the top of the tower when you're back on the ground?"

"Sure," she answered as they neared their cars.

She wasn't really listening. She'd been focused on how good she was going to feel after she grabbed the small bag of joy that was tucked beneath the driver's seat of her Lexus, stuck a straw into it, and sniffed twice, *hard*. Once in a while, the stress of leading Project Archer combined with those demons and ghosts Cameron had mentioned required an antidote. This was one of those times—as last night in her study had been. Though, that need had been driven by loneliness, not the demons.

She was worried that those times were coming more often as Jury Town's opening grew imminent. Not less, as she'd anticipated—and hoped. The pressure was mounting instead of receding, especially after reading what was inside that envelope Cameron had passed along earlier.

"Wolf wasn't happy to hear about Raul Acosta coming to Jury Town to be the second-ranking guard," Cameron spoke up. "His expression was classic. I got a good chuckle. You were brave to do it up there."

"Why?"

"He could have tossed you off the tower."

"He's not going to toss me off any tower. He likes what I'm paying him, and he doesn't want to jeopardize it. That's why I wouldn't sign contracts with him . . . or anyone else, for that matter. They work at will . . . my will."

"It's an excellent idea to have your own mole inside the walls, *especially* inside the corps of guards. Wolf knows that, even though he'd never admit it." They stopped in front of the cars. "What was in that envelope from Judge Eldridge?"

"Again with the envelope?"

"You bet."

"What makes you think it was from Eldridge?"

"Who else would it be from? Come on, Victoria, this is me."

"He was congratulating me on my performance at the announcement."

Cameron groaned, exasperated. "Then why the dead-of-night pickup? My aide, I might add, had a very relieved expression on his face after he handed it to me and ran off. Give me a break, Victoria. What was Eldridge telling you?"

"You don't want to know."

"You're damn right I do. I'm gonna get pissed at you in a second."

"You want plausible deniability in this instance," she said, glancing over at him. "I'm serious."

He hesitated.

He'd heard the code loud and clear. She saw that in his expression. She was giving him a chance here *not* to know.

"No," he finally answered, shaking his head. "I've come too far on this project to start ducking now. I want to know. I have a *right* to know."

"You've been warned."

"Whatever."

"It turns out Project Archer didn't start with Judge Eldridge," she began quietly, glancing around the area.

"Who then?"

"Michael Delgado."

Cameron's eyes gleamed. *The attorney general of the United States?*"

"According to Eldridge, Delgado approached him eighteen months ago about initiating the program in Virginia because he knew he could trust the judge to handle it right and keep the Justice Department out of it. Delgado suspects that juries in high-profile cases all around the nation—not just in Virginia—are being blackmailed. There have been too many irrational verdicts coming down. And those bad verdicts are still coming. At some point"—she gestured back at the facility—"Delgado may ask to use Jury Town."

"For federal cases?"

"And Delgado is keen on this catching on around the country with other states when it's successful here so he can *completely* insulate the system, federal and states. That's the grand plan."

"Which puts even more pressure on us to make it work here in Virginia."

That little bag of white powder beneath the Lexus' seat was *screaming* at her. The pressure was rocketing toward the heavens. "Exactly."

"Why is Eldridge telling you all this now?"

"In case he turns up dead." She pulled the note from her pocket and held it out so Cameron could read it for himself. "So I know to contact Delgado for help. The note says Delgado called last week to tell him he was more convinced than ever that someone or some group is blackmailing jurors around the country. Do you get what that means? The power, the ruthlessness—the hubris—it takes to execute something like that. They won't be easily deterred by Jury Town. They'll fight it with everything they have. Eldridge is concerned for his physical safety." She pointed at the paper. "It's all there."

"That sure looks like Judge Eldridge's handwriting," Cameron murmured as he scanned the page. "He didn't sign it for obvious reasons, to maintain his own plausible deniability. But this is almost certainly his chicken scratch. I recognize it from other notes he sent you before he went off the grid six months ago." Cameron glanced up as she took the paper back and headed for the driver's side of the Lexus. "Where are you going?" he called.

"I've got an errand to run."

"I'll run it with you. Then we'll go to dinner when we get back to Richmond. We've got a big day tomorrow, everything we've been pointing to for a year, and I've got a punch list a mile long to cover with you."

"Can't," she called back, reaching for the door handle. "We'll meet tomorrow morning for breakfast."

"Victoria."

"What?"

"Where are you really going? Tell me."

"To see my father."

"To Stony Man?"

She nodded. He knew her so well. "I need inspiration."

"I'll go to the mountain with you."

"I want to go alone." If Cameron was tagging along, she wouldn't be able to enjoy her distraction. In fact, he'd physically take the bag from her if he saw it. "I want to *be* alone."

"Are you crazy? Did you not just read that note from Judge Eldridge?"

"Of course, I—"

"Of course you did because you told me yourself that he wrote in it about being worried for his safety—for his *life*. In case you didn't read the entire note—which I'm sure you did, but I'll give you the benefit of the doubt—he also told you in no uncertain terms to get security for yourself."

She sighed. "I won't be intimidated."

"Or is there another reason you don't want people like that around all the time?"

"Don't go there," she warned like he was way off . . . even though he couldn't have been more right.

"I'll take care of everything for you. You know that," he promised as his phone pinged with a new e-mail. *"Oh, Lord."*

"What is it?" she demanded.

He looked like he'd just seen an execution. *"What happened?"*

"Raul Acosta died last night," Cameron murmured, looking over the BMW roof at her. "It says here he was murdered."

"Murdered?"

"He was shot."

"Do the police have a suspect?"

Cameron shook his head. "Victoria, don't go to Stony Man."

"How do the police know he was murdered?"

"He showed up at a hospital last night with a bullet hole in his gut and died on the operating table. A hospital in the *West End*," Cameron said, pointing at his phone. "Maybe he was the one who delivered that envelope to my aide." He tapped the phone again. "It says here they've increased the judge's security as a result, even though they don't know if Acosta's death is related to the Supreme Court." Cameron stared over the roof at her. "It's time for you to get security. Victoria, you've got to listen—"

She slammed the door as she dropped in behind the steering wheel and fired up the Lexus. She had to get out of here.

CHAPTER 10

SKYLINE DRIVE OF VIRGINIA

Hiking up from the small, secluded parking area off Skyline Drive to Stony Man Mountain Overlook wasn't that challenging. It was less than a mile in distance and slightly shy of nine hundred feet in elevation gain to the summit's cliff, which was four thousand feet above sea level.

Victoria had taken just twenty minutes to reach the last hard turn in the trail. She was only a few hundred yards shy of emerging from the dense woods and onto the spectacular overlook, and she was barely breathing hard.

The path was steep in certain stretches, but technical climbing wasn't involved. No clinging to cliffs or creeping along tightrope-thin ledges, nothing that would ignite her intense fear of heights.

The overlook was another story altogether in terms of her phobia. But she would stay far enough away from the sheer cliff to control it. She always made sure to.

A hundred miles northwest of Richmond, she was hiking up the Appalachian Mountains' easternmost wave. When she reached the overlook, she'd have a magnificent view of the wide, deep Shenandoah Valley. From the cliff, she'd be able to make out the farm she'd grown up on. The house and barns would be just specks on the valley floor, but she'd be able to pick them out.

She'd be able to spot Judge Hopkins' house as well. She knew exactly where he used to live.

The trail up through the thick woods was well marked. Had it not been, she still would have had no problem finding her way. She was quite familiar with the route. Her father had first brought her to this peak when she was four years old, and she'd hiked up Stony Man Mountain no less than sixty times since.

She'd done the math in her head as she'd climbed today—twice a year for more than three decades, even during her term as governor, even during her father's prison sentence. It was like seeing an old friend each time she visited because she and her father had climbed this same trail together at least fifteen times before he'd been framed and sent away.

During those trips she'd had him all to herself. She'd had every bit of his attention, and adored every moment.

A few hundred feet from the overlook, Victoria stopped short and whipped around. The eerie feeling of being followed had been gnawing at her since the halfway point of the trek. This was the third time she'd cut her progress short to check.

No other cars were parked in the small lot when she'd arrived. But she hadn't pushed herself during the climb. So it was conceivable that someone had arrived soon after her and caught up.

However, no one was back there when she peered down the slope into the lengthening shadows. No one she could see, anyway. Of course, there were plenty of boulders and trees to hide behind, and the afternoon light was fading.

If she didn't hurry, she'd miss a gorgeous sunset. And, if she stayed for the entire show, the hike back down the mountain would be through darkness—which didn't bother her. She'd done it before.

She'd never had this feeling of being stalked, either. And Cameron's warning about the need for security kept ringing in her ears.

"It's just your imagination," she muttered to herself as she turned and headed for the summit. "It's his fault for getting me started on this bodyguard thing. And don't forget the selfie," she reminded herself, patting the phone that was wedged deeply into the front pocket of her jeans. He'd asked her to send a picture of herself on top of the mountain when she made the summit, just so he could feel okay about where she was. "If you don't send it, he'll go crazy."

Fifty feet from the overlook, she paused at a towering oak tree, and moved off the trail to the far side of its massive trunk. Despite the fading light, she paused to stare at the two sets of vaguely legible initials. Higher on the trunk than when her father had carved them that summer she was seven, but still there. She touched her letters and then her father's, and heat rose to her eyes as she remembered watching him carve.

She touched the initials once more, wiped her eyes clear of moisture, then retook the trail, and climbed the last few yards to the summit.

Her pace slowed to a deliberate shuffle when she emerged from the tree line and moved out onto the wide, flat rock. She was acutely aware of the rock disappearing in front of her, turning ninety degrees and plunging a thousand feet as it gave way to the incredible view and the solitude she'd climbed up here to enjoy.

She inched forward until she stood on the spot she always stood on when she came up here, identifiable by three parallel gouges in the flat boulder, each an inch deep and a foot long. The spot where her father had let go of her that first time, when she was four years old, and made her stand close to the edge on her own. At this point she was five feet from the sheer drop-off that had been left completely natural by the Park Service, open and unprotected by railings or banisters.

The height still bothered her intensely, but she was on firm ground here. Not wavering around in the wind on a flimsy, shaky surveillance tower. This was solid rock beneath her feet. Still, she would go no closer to the edge. This was far enough, as far as she'd ever gone.

She shielded her eyes against the orange fireball grazing the soaring mountaintops of the wide valley's western side. Amazed at how quickly the sun descended at the end of the day. You could never recognize that speed when the fireball was high in the sky, never get a perspective on how quickly it raced across the sky. But that was obvious now as it dropped to the valley's far wall.

Victoria made certain she was alone up here on top of the world before digging into her pocket for the small bag of cocaine. She'd done some in the Lexus a mile out from Jury Town, after pulling over to the side of the narrow, winding road in a secluded spot.

Now that she was on top of the world, she wanted to feel wonderful—again.

Four hard sniffs through the straw and ecstasy quickly caught up to her—again.

She glanced around as she retied the tiny knot at the top of the cellophane bag, then replaced it and the straw in her pocket as she gazed down at Judge Hopkins' house—bastard.

Her gaze flashed right at the disconcerting sound of a twig snapping, at a spot she'd been looking.

A slender young man with closely cropped, blond hair stood thirty feet away, just outside the tree line. He hadn't emerged at the trailhead, but out of the underbrush on the far side of the opening in the trees and bushes. Why?

The tiny hairs on the back of her neck stood straight up the instant she recognized him as a predator.

He was physically average, nonthreatening in every way save for his hungry, one-eye-closed stare, which made her feel as if he were looking at her through the crosshairs of a rifle scope. There was a cold indifference to that expression. As if he understood very well that he was about to cause her horrible pain, but had no sympathy for her plight. Like he was a wolf—and she was a deer.

It was now or never, Victoria realized. To hesitate at this moment would be to accept death. Somehow she knew that with every fiber of her being.

She bolted left.

Why hadn't she listened to Cameron, especially after the news that Raul Acosta had been killed?

Thank God she'd done the coke, she thought as she sprinted, and the rush of the drug surged through her. Without it, she'd be helpless against this predator.

CHAPTER 11

NORTH WOODS OF MAINE

"We've need to talk about the Commonwealth Electric Power situation," one of the Grays spoke up, "for obvious reasons."

Rockwell groaned softly from beneath the thick, low-hanging blindfold as he shifted in his seat. He had a bad back from a skiing accident in Deer Valley. After what had been hours of sitting in this wooden, armless chair, the bulging disc was beginning to act up. Soon, the pain would become acute. He was longing for that comfortable, warmed seat in his Mercedes. He was actually looking forward to the nine-hour drive back to Connecticut.

"What's wrong, Mr. Rockwell?"

"Nothing, I'm fine. Why do we need to talk about Commonwealth Electric Power?"

"I thought we told you about asking so many—"

"It's all right," another of the Grays interrupted. "We may need Mr. Rockwell's assistance with this."

"CEP," a third voice spoke up, "is by far Virginia's largest public utility, Mr. Rockwell. It provides electricity to over ninety-seven percent of the state's population, mostly using coal at its many plants to fire the generators, which produce the power. Spent coal from the burners also produces mountains of ash, which contain high levels of arsenic, selenium, mercury, and lead. All very nasty stuff, so, of course, the ash is supposed to be disposed of carefully. But that can be a time-consuming and costly process. And the ash accumulates quickly. So, if you don't keep up with disposal, the mountain can quickly become unmanageable and spill outside property lines."

"Or worse, as in this case."

"One of Commonwealth's plants in the extreme southwestern corner of the state has been accused by Virginia's Department of Environmental Quality of dumping large amounts of that toxic ash into a river, which runs beside the plant and then flows into North Carolina. The DEQ and the citizens in the area are claiming that gray sludge has coated the riverbed for miles and miles downstream, destroying the ecosystem, killing significant amounts of fish and other wildlife, and basically making the river unusable for anything. Plant managers claim a flood is responsible. The DEQ says no way."

"And if the DEQ can prove that plant managers dumped ash into the river knowingly and are, therefore, guilty of gross negligence, Commonwealth Electric could have a major problem on its hands. A cleanup of that magnitude could cost hundreds of millions of dollars, possibly more, especially if North Carolina jumps on the bandwagon. And then there is the whole criminal element to this, which is what we're concerned about."

Rockwell sneered. "It's a *public* utility regulated by a *public* utilities commission. At the end of the day, even if the cleanup costs *billions*, the citizens of Virginia end up footing the bill by paying for it in the rate base. Translated, the commission will let CEP raise rates on all its customers. In the end, the same people who had their river destroyed will pay for the cleanup." He shrugged. "Too bad, but that's how it works. A few catfish died. What's the big deal? Seems like what we ought to do is invest in the companies that will perform the cleanup."

"The big deal is that someone we're close to is very involved with Commonwealth Electric Power."

"Yeah," another of them snapped loudly, "my brother's the damn CEO, and he could face—"

"Hey, hey, no details!"

"Damn it!"

"What were you thinking?" someone hissed.

"Sorry."

Clearly, Rockwell realized, that exchange wasn't to have erupted in front of him—which he found at the same time fascinating and intensely aggravating.

He was taking immense risks for these men. They should be treating him more like a partner if they wanted his loyalty. Money was one thing; trust was another.

On the flip side, he'd gleaned two fascinating data bytes from the furious back-and-forth.

This situation was personal. They were going to fix the jury on this case so the CEO wouldn't face criminal charges if CEP was found guilty in the civil action. This situation had nothing to do with financial gain or protection of an industry on a large scale, as the oil case in Los Angeles did. This had to do with a direct family relationship.

The second piece here was that Rockwell could now finally figure out the identity of one of the Grays—at least find the family name if there were more than two brothers. Now he *really* couldn't wait to get on the road. As soon as he got back to Connecticut, he would go on the Internet and find out the CEO's name.

"The real problem," one of the men spoke up, "is that this case will be tried by a jury behind the walls of the old Archer Prison. This will be one of the first cases Victoria Lewis gets her hands on."

"Christ," the man whose brother was CEO hissed. "That's just great."

"How do we know?" someone asked.

"My contact down in Virginia got me that information. His contact inside the Supreme Court got a list of those initial cases directly from Judge Eldridge's office. And this was one of them."

"Damn it."

"That man in Virginia has been quite helpful. He was also the one who found out that the professional jurors will be paid two million dollars a year."

"Two million?"

"That's incredible."

"It's ridiculous."

"Would you completely cut yourself off from the world for two years for four million dollars?" Rockwell asked.

A hush fell over the room.

"I thought I read last night that one of the primary motivations for establishing this facility was to seat objective juries." Rockwell spoke up nervously, uncertain of whether he should have blurted that question out—based on the stony silence and the stern warning of before. "So if Archer is just starting tomorrow, won't all the people going inside the walls have already heard about the Commonwealth Electric case?"

"Not necessarily. It hasn't gotten a lot of press. It's in a remote part of the state."

"Mark my words, they'll find twelve people who haven't heard of the case, people from the eastern part of the state like Virginia Beach and Norfolk."

"Speaking of Virginia Beach and Norfolk, let's get back to Angela Gaynor and her senate campaign against Chuck Lehman."

"Wait a minute. What about the Commonwealth Electric issue? What are we going to do there?"

The room fell silent again.

"We must find a way to manipulate the jury even though they're inside Archer."

"And that makes your associate's mission in Virginia this afternoon even more crucial. Does he understand how important his success is, Mr. Rockwell? And, by extension, how crucial it is for you?"

"Yes," Rockwell answered deliberately. He hadn't heard that threatening tone from any of these men before, and it sent a shiver all the way down his spine, past that bad disc. "He understands."

"Do you?"

"Yes," Rockwell answered after a few moments, "I definitely do." Finding out who these men were had suddenly become even more critical. It could help protect him from that threatening tone—and make him more of an equal in all this. He'd have a very important bargaining chip if he ever needed it.

"Let's get back to Angela Gaynor," one of the Grays suggested.

"As you may or may not know, Mr. Rockwell," another of them said, "the United States Senate Majority Leader is a man named Chuck Lehman."

"Of course I know that," Rockwell retorted sharply from beneath the blindfold. For the Grays to even consider the possibility of him not knowing the name of the senate majority leader was insulting. "Senator Lehman is from Virginia. He's nearing the end of his third term after serving two terms as a US congressman."

"Yes, that's right."

"I believe," Rockwell went on, "he's been mentioned as a potential presidential candidate when the time comes."

"And we want to make certain he maintains that good momentum toward the White House. All of us in this room have certain political and business interests that need to be protected. Senator Lehman will make certain to do so."

"Therefore," another man added, "we must make sure he's reelected to the Senate. Unfortunately, it looks as though we may have to get involved."

Interesting, Rockwell thought to himself, this was the first time the Grays had ever mentioned targeting the political system for manipulation.

"From everything I've read and heard, Senator Lehman is fine," Rockwell spoke up. "I thought he was a lock to be reelected."

"Nothing is ever a lock these days. Social media can destroy a lifetime of loyalties in seconds."

"Does the name Eric Cantor ring a bell?" one of them asked.

An excellent example, Rockwell was forced to admit. Cantor had been the House Majority Leader one day, and the next been defeated by an unknown economics professor *in his own party's primary*. So, of course, Cantor had gone to Wall Street to lick his wounds and feel better by making ridiculous amounts of money. He wondered if the Grays had manipulated that move and that reward.

"That's true," Rockwell agreed. "These days allegiances turn on needle points instead of dimes."

"And the Cantor disaster occurred in Virginia. For some reason that state is ripe for these kinds of crazy situations. We cannot have that happen to Chuck Lehman. The House is one thing. The Senate is quite another."

"That's where Angela Gaynor comes in. Apparently, you haven't heard of her."

The name sounded familiar, but Rockwell couldn't quite place it. "Um . . ." After sounding so sure of himself concerning Senator Lehman, it was embarrassing not to know this one. "No."

"Angela Gaynor is a state senator from Virginia Beach, Virginia. She's a rising star, and leaders on that side of the aisle are talking about her taking on Chuck Lehman. We need to make certain we're prepared for her if that happens. Angela Gaynor cannot unseat Chuck Lehman."

"What do you want from me?" Rockwell asked despite their warnings about his posing the questions. "You always provide me with the information that exerts the influence."

"Ms. Gaynor is a self-made millionaire. She comes from a Norfolk ghetto. But she pulled herself out by the bootstraps by founding Gaynor Construction and growing it into one of the largest and most successful building contractors in the region. We want you to find out *everything* about her life, both business and personal. Find out all about her connections in the business and political worlds. Find her skeletons as well. We're too close to the political world to get too deeply involved in this project ourselves," the man explained. "And, ultimately, if we think Ms.

Gaynor is gathering too much momentum or we can't find any meaningful sound bites with which to blackmail her, we may want to go in a different direction."

"You mean, plant something?"

"And, if that doesn't work, avail ourselves of JD's sniper skills."

CHAPTER 12

SKYLINE DRIVE OF VIRGINIA

Victoria sprinted along the flat rock of the overlook, five feet from the edge of the cliff, five feet from that straight-down plunge. Any closer and the sight of and proximity to the drop would paralyze her, cause her to suffer a living rigor mortis, and then she'd be defenseless against this beast who was chasing her.

As she dashed ahead, she glanced over her left shoulder. He was gaining.

When the overlook ended abruptly, she darted left onto a narrow path, which ran just in front of the tree line. The trail dipped down and up suddenly, then snaked in and out from between several massive boulders. She muted a scream when it swerved to the right of another rocky outcrop, and the world fell away on her right again. The sheer edge was still several feet from the path, but *seemed* only inches, and dizziness attacked from all angles as her legs wobbled beneath her like stilts. Paralysis was only seconds away, she knew.

When the path swerved left and away from the cliff, the phobia retreated, relief surged through her, and her legs went strong again as the trail entered the forest a few feet inside the tree line.

For an instant she considered going off trail and into the trees. She could try to forge her own path off the mountain to the parking area. She might be able to beat her pursuer down the wooded slope, make it to her car, and escape on Skyline Drive. Perhaps even find a ranger to protect her.

But if she chose that option, she might suddenly find herself at the edge of a minicliff. Even a drop of fifteen feet would be too much to jump without breaking a bone, and she'd be forced to turn around—right into him.

She stayed on the trail, veering left at a fork in the trail. She'd never been this way, had no idea where it would lead as she sprinted ahead, panic-stricken. So she was shocked when it plunged down so steeply she nearly pitched forward and tumbled. Then, just as suddenly, it narrowed to little more than shoulder width when it split into a thin crevice between boulders, which soared fifty feet above her on either side.

She was tempted to dart into one of the small caves lining both walls like doorways. But none of them appeared to extend very far back into the rock. If he saw her duck into one, she'd be trapped.

The echo of his pounding footsteps reached her ears as she raced deeper into the narrow canyon. They seemed to be growing ever closer with each stride.

Out of nowhere the trail veered left, the right side of the canyon fell away to nothing, and the ledge on which she was running narrowed to what seemed tightwire thin.

The rock wall to her left rose straight up. The cliff to her right dropped straight down. And the world below spread out before her for miles and miles. Farmhouses and barns were barely distinguishable dots; roads just tiny lines on a massive grid, and a buzzard circled lazily *below* her. The view was gorgeously terrifying, and, the instant she took it in, the world began to spin.

The slender shelf on which she was suddenly perched continued around the bend of the sheer rock face—but she could not. She stopped short, pressed her chest tightly against the cliff as she gasped for air, and clutched at anything protruding from the escarpment to keep her from falling a thousand feet down. She shut her eyes, but the dizziness continued its brutal assault on her psyche despite the lack of the horrifying view. The damage had already been done. Victoria's brain would not be fooled into believing the danger had passed simply because she'd closed her eyes.

The rock she squeezed with her left hand seemed solid, but the jagged stone within the fingers of her right hand did not. Could she stay on this cliff if it gave way? Did it matter? He had to be close.

"You hate heights," he whispered, his lips only inches from her ear.

She shrieked at the sound of his voice so close, and her terror spiraled even higher. She'd never felt panic like this.

"Don't you, Ms. Lewis?"

"Who are you?" she managed through her labored breathing. "Why are you doing this to me?"

"They told me you hated heights. They told me this would paralyze you."

She managed to pry her eyelids open slightly to peek at him, but shut them again tightly right away. "Who told you?"

"It will look like an accident. A thousand feet down. No way for investigators to know I threw you from this cliff."

"Please," she begged as his fingers snaked onto her left arm, "please don't do this."

"It won't take long. Just don't open your eyes on the way down. Then you won't know how close death is. It's better not to know. It's better not to see him coming closer and closer. That's the only way we humans can survive, by not knowing. If we knew all along when we were going to die, it would drive us insane."

Against his advice she opened her eyes again—and found herself staring straight into his again. She glanced down slightly at his fingers and sobbed as they curled tighter and tighter around her upper arm. There would be no sympathy from this monster.

At any moment, she would be tumbling through the air.

VIRGINIA BEACH, VIRGINIA

"Quiet, *quiet!*" Angela yelled, holding her hands in the air and waving. Trying, but failing, to get control of a hundred second-graders. They were racing around one end of the huge school gymnasium. Some were playing dodgeball, others tag, still others a disorganized game of basketball. It was all mixing together into one, big, uncontrollable mass, like someone was tossing a huge salad.

"*Hey!*"

She glanced over her shoulder at the parents who'd just finished helping her set fifteen long tables for the delicious dinner she and Gaynor Construction were providing free of charge tonight for the underprivileged families. Several of them shrugged back sheepishly.

"I've got a surprise for you!" Angela shouted, turning back toward the chaos. "And it's a really good one!"

No response.

She was about to take her chances and wade into the middle of the melee when a shrill, earsplitting whistle pierced the shouting and screaming, and brought the gym to a standstill. She whipped around to see who'd finally taken control.

Trent stood on a sturdy folding chair near the door to the locker rooms where he'd been hiding, smiling down at her with that ear-to-ear grin, pinkie fingers still between his teeth.

She smiled back and mouthed a quick, "thank you." He seemed twenty feet tall standing on the chair, like a statue in the middle of a town square.

"All right," he called out in his deep, booming voice. "It's dinnertime. Let's go, find a seat right now."

Once more the gym burst into chaos as Trent hopped down from the chair. Instead of finding seats, the kids raced toward him.

Angela burst into laughter when he gave her a helpless expression as the kids closed in, and the mothers and fathers dug through their purses and pockets, frantically searching for pens and paper for autographs. They'd all recognized him immediately.

She watched as he was mobbed by the kids and the parents. Oh yeah, he was going to be a huge addition to her campaign. Chuck Lehman better watch out now that she had Trent Tucker in her corner.

SKYLINE DRIVE OF VIRGINIA

"It's time for you to die," her predator whispered, "and Project Archer along with you. Good-bye, Ms. Lewis."

As he pulled her left arm, her phone pinged loudly—an incoming text.

His eyes flashed down, away from hers, for a split second.

It was the instant Victoria needed, the momentary distraction that gave her a chance at survival.

From the cliff, she wrenched a softball-sized rock—the one that was loosely attached to the escarpment—and struck the young man in the forehead. As he tumbled backward, the momentum of her action sent her teetering toward the abyss. She flailed and grasped wildly in the air for anything to cling to after dropping her weapon.

At the last moment, just as she was going over the edge, her fingers wrapped tightly around a sturdy vine, and she swung herself back.

Somehow her attacker had remained on the ledge, too. He lay on his back, one ankle dangling precariously over the cliff, bleeding profusely from a deep cut above one eye, apparently unconscious.

As Victoria stared down at him, two searing revelations flashed through her mind simultaneously.

She'd conquered her fear of heights.

And she wanted to push this monster off the cliff and watch him fall a thousand feet down until his body shattered on the stones at the bottom of the gorge.

CHAPTER 13

RICHMOND, VIRGINIA

Mitch limped as quickly as possible on his prosthesis toward the waiting limousine, constantly swiveling his head as he moved through the darkness of the deserted warehouse district, seeking any signs that someone who shouldn't be watching . . . was. He took one more look around, and then slipped into the back of the sleek black vehicle through the door, which the driver was holding open for him—after being thoroughly frisked by the swarthy man.

"What the hell happened?" Mitch demanded of the imposing figure who reclined on the wide, comfortable seat facing his, calmly smoking a cigarette. "I just wanted you to get that envelope from Acosta. That was all. God damn it, Salvatore, I did not want you to kill Raul Acosta."

Salvatore Celino ran all southeastern operations for the Gaggi crime family of Brooklyn, New York. Mitch had checked out Celino and the Gaggi family through contacts in the Manhattan DA's office and on the Internet. While most other New York mafia families were suffering a decade-long decline, the Gaggis were decidedly not hurting, according to his sources.

They were headquartered in Brooklyn and still doing "business" in all five boroughs. But in the last ten years, they'd expanded their operations to smaller, less obvious cities like Charlotte and Raleigh, North Carolina; Charleston, South Carolina; Savannah, Georgia; and Richmond, Virginia. They'd taken over gambling, prostitution, and retail intimidation in these smaller southern cities in which law enforcement was unaccustomed to their organization and harsh enforcement techniques.

Salvatore lived near Richmond so he could run the southeastern operations but be as close to Brooklyn as possible. He'd always told Mitch he hated living in a city that didn't have delis and had to get back to New York for real pastrami as often as possible.

The New York DA's office had informed Mitch that Salvatore was as cold and calculating as they came. Worse, he was sophisticated.

"Careful how you speak to me, Mr. Mitchell," Salvatore answered calmly, after taking a long drag from the Camel no-filter. He was a big man with strapping arms and shoulders who worked out constantly. "You may be a war hero, but that's history. You will quickly become *part of* history"—the mafia boss growled as he patted his suit coat above the 9 mm he always carried in the shoulder holster hanging against his chest—"if you don't watch your tone."

Cigarette smoke swirled thickly inside the limousine. Why anyone ever picked up this nasty habit was beyond Mitch. It seemed ironic to him that Salvatore exercised and lifted weights like a madman . . . but smoked like a chimney when he wasn't working out.

"I'm sorry, Salvatore." He'd lost his temper and that was stupid. Salvatore was not a man to trifle with. "What happened?"

"Acosta must have spotted the tail. He took evasive action. They found his truck, but he was gone. When he got back, he surprised them."

Mitch coughed twice into his elbow. "Tracking people down is your business, sport."

"Well," Salvatore said with a thin smile as he took another heavy puff from the Camel, "*one* of my businesses, anyway. Why were you so worried about that envelope, anyway?"

"It doesn't matter." Judge Eldridge had seemed so distant lately. Mitch was terrified that his uncle had somehow found out about these clandestine, late-night meetings. And there would go his life.

"Acosta proved to be resourceful," Salvatore said as if it didn't really matter to him. "What can I say? He's originally from Brooklyn, from my family's neighborhood." The Mafioso chuckled as the limousine moved ahead. Salvatore never stayed in one place for long. "I understand why he's so good."

"He's not from your neighborhood anymore . . . or good. He's dead. And I have to go to his funeral and face his wife."

"Poor boy."

"Can't you have a *little* compassion?"

"Compassion is for pussies, mothers, and priests. Besides, his wife doesn't know who the hell killed him."

"Yeah, but I do," Mitch countered softly, grimacing as he thought about Sofia's lovely face contorted by sobs. He'd only met her a few times, but her beauty and gentleness had made a lasting impression. "And they have kids."

"Too many people have kids. If you ask me, we could do with a lot fewer carpet rats running around."

"Jesus," Mitch whispered, ruing the web he'd woven more now than ever.

He hated money. He hated how much he needed money. He hated how much his wife wanted what it provided, and that he'd gone to such lengths to get those things for her. He'd never thought he'd stoop so low.

A year ago he'd started getting the feeling that his wife's sympathy for a husband with a prosthetic leg and grotesque facial scars was running low. She'd made a nasty comment during sex one night. She'd denied making it the next morning when he'd asked, but he'd heard it all right.

And then there was her obsession with moving into Richmond society, which, Mitch knew, was almost impossible if you weren't from the right circles—which his wife wasn't. It was a long shot at best, but he wasn't going to tell her that. They'd gotten the kids into the right schools, but they needed to move to the West End to make it into the right clubs. And Mitch needed even more money for all that—much more than being his uncle's chief of staff could possibly provide.

So when Salvatore's messenger had quietly approached him six months ago with a proposition involving a significant amount of money in exchange for information from Judge Eldridge's desk regarding Project Archer, Mitch had listened—and then taken a meeting with the mobster. Hindsight was always twenty-twenty, and now he wished he'd never agreed to that first meeting. But hindsight was no help at this point in his relationship with Salvatore Celino. Mitch was in deep. Getting out of this clean—and alive—would be dicey.

"You've put me in a terrible situation, sport."

"What's put you in a terrible situation, *sport*," Salvatore repeated tersely, "is three kids and a wife who's obsessed with a spot in Richmond society. A big house with a mortgage to match, nice cars, the private school tuitions, country club memberships, and vacations to the Caribbean every winter are what has you feeding me all that confidential information from the Supreme Court." Salvatore pointed the cigarette's burning ember at Mitch. "Yeah, I checked your wife out. Don't look so surprised. She's a redneck, and she's—"

"She's not a redneck."

"She's not from society, either."

Mitch couldn't argue that. He could barely argue the redneck part.

"And she's spending all your money to buy herself a seat inside that Richmond society circle." Salvatore chuckled. "And maybe she doesn't like getting in bed every night with a scarred cripple."

Mitch started to bark back, but what would be the point? The mobster had his wife pegged better than an FBI wanted sign on a post office wall. And pissing the man off made no sense.

"Salvatore, if anyone ever connects me to—"

"Relax," Salvatore cut in. "No one's ever going to connect you to Acosta's death. I can assure you of that."

"The same way you assured me you could handle this one favor I asked of you in return for everything I've gotten you, for all the advance information I've gotten you regarding Project Archer? On which you must have made millions." Mitch had no idea how Salvatore could be profiting from having the reams of data on Victoria Lewis' project. But he assumed it *had* to involve money. In the end, that was why the mafia did *everything*—for profit. "Right?"

"You've made your money, too, kid." Salvatore picked up an envelope stuffed with cash off the seat beside him and tossed it to Mitch. "Don't get all high and mighty on me, hero boy. I could get you in a lot of trouble if I wanted to, if the mood strikes." He laughed meanly. "Now give me what you got."

Mitch handed him the folder.

"Does this contain all the names?"

"Yes. Eldridge kept that one close, very close, but I found it." Salvatore laughed loudly. "Good boy. Now get the hell out of here."

A moment later, Mitch was out of the limousine. As it moved off, he realized he had no idea where he was or how to get back to his car.

He was about to pull his phone from his pocket to check GPS, when his fingers stopped a fraction of an inch from the device. Acosta had once asked how Mitch could afford all the expensive items Salvatore had just ticked off in the back of the limousine. Mitch had deflected Acosta's question with a quick change of topic.

But Acosta had been suspicious enough last night to avoid Salvatore's men. Not smart enough to avoid being killed, but suspicious enough to temporarily avoid the tail. What if Acosta had been suspicious enough of Mitch's lifestyle to do some of his own checking, like Salvatore had? And what if he'd mentioned those suspicions to Sofia?

CULPEPER, VIRGINIA

"You were right," Victoria murmured from the passenger seat as Cameron slipped behind the wheel of his BMW after shutting her door.

He'd just picked her up after driving seventy miles from Richmond, after receiving her SOS call.

After half running, half tumbling off Stony Man Mountain, she'd managed to make it to this small town. But she'd barely been able to keep her car on the road, she was so upset. So she'd pulled off and called Cameron. He'd dropped everything and come to her aid immediately.

"You were right, Cam. I need bodyguards . . . as soon as possible."

"Why?" His mouth dropped slowly open as she related the story of her harrowing escape.

"You saved my life," she whispered.

"How?"

"The text you sent—checking up on me. It distracted him. It gave me the second I needed. I owe you everything." She put her head back on the seat as she flexed her hands into tight fists and ground her teeth. "Please. Get me a security detail."

Cameron picked up his cell from the console. "Okay. But you have to promise me one thing."

She knew exactly what he was going to say. He'd seen her making fists and grinding her teeth. "Look, I—"

"I'm not putting up with this anymore. You have to stop."

"You know I can't—"

"*Right now* . . . or I'll leave you. I love you, but I'm not dealing with this one more day."

INTERSTATE 95, CONNECTICUT

"Hello."

Rockwell grimaced when his call was answered on the first ring. He wasn't supposed to dial this number often, as infrequently as possible, he'd been instructed from the beginning. But he felt he needed to convey the disappointing news immediately. He wasn't looking forward to the reaction.

"Do you know who this is?" he asked hesitantly.

"Of course," the Gray answered in a measured tone. "You are the only other individual who has this number. The process of elimination didn't take long."

This one always seemed aggravated, Rockwell thought to himself, even more than the others. Perhaps, he realized, because the man had a brother who was CEO of Commonwealth Electric Power, a brother who would be in serious trouble if they could not influence the trial. And that was going to be exponentially more challenging now that the case would be heard by the jurors going behind the walls of Archer Prison tomorrow night.

"I have some bad news," he spoke up as he drove.

"Be careful the way you say it."

"I just heard from my messenger. The mission was not executed today."

"You're right. That is bad."

Rockwell grimaced again. "I'm sorry."

"What happened?"

"According to my messenger, the target suddenly has a huge security force. He wasn't able to move in on her."

He'd been halfway back to Connecticut when he received the call from JD. His first thought was that the Grays couldn't blame him for Victoria Lewis' security force. *Who was he kidding?* he thought now. They'd blame him for whatever they wanted to.

"The same messenger who was going after the target this afternoon was also involved with the trial that didn't go so well, correct?"

"Yes."

"Do you still have faith in him?"

"Absolutely." He had to say that. He couldn't show any loss of faith in his messenger. That would be as bad for him as it would be for JD. "He's the real deal."

"All right," the Gray agreed after a few moments. "Well then your man should keep trying."

"Even with the pris . . . facility opening tomorrow?"

"Yes, but he should still not attempt the mission using long-range options. You understand what I'm saying?"

"Of course. I've been thinking about ways to get to the people we need to get to inside the place," he said.

"We already have."

"You've already gotten to people who are going inside?" Rockwell asked incredulously.

"Yes. Our source provided us with names, and we have already made contact. Even if they aren't chosen for that proceeding we discussed, they will approach those who are with data we will inject. I'll be in touch."

CHAPTER 14

JURY TOWN

Victoria gazed out from the podium that had been erected in the massive Central Zone of the brand-new facility, where the jurors would take meals and socialize. Many of the same people who'd attended her announcement in the Supreme Court building were here tonight. Governor Falkner, Lieutenant Governor Paulson, nearly all the General Assembly senators and delegates, Richmond Mayor Eleanor Bush, as well as a huge gathering of the press corps including reporters from all the major national news organizations.

The only notables missing were Chief Justice Eldridge and General Assembly Majority Leader Barney Franz. She'd anticipated Eldridge's absence—he'd committed to only that one appearance at the Supreme Court building, and she understood why. He had to keep a low profile for multiple reasons.

She'd not anticipated Franz's absence. By avoiding tonight's historic beginning, the Majority Leader was making an obvious statement, hurling down the gauntlet in a very public way on top of walking out of the announcement. Cameron was convinced that they hadn't heard the last of Franz, and he'd been in close contact with his best sources in the GA all day to get the jump on anything Franz might have up his sleeve. But they'd heard nothing so far.

She had no time to worry about a senior official's childish tantrum. Also gazing back at her from the audience were 196 new arrivals. The men and women had spent this morning and early afternoon being processed and indoctrinated at an old armory outside Richmond. They had then taken those four buses up here. These were the individuals who deserved her focus at this moment.

Victoria had forced herself to tour one wing of rooms this evening before taking the podium a few moments ago. As Clint Wolf had predicted, personal touches now intact, the facility looked much better, almost homey. It reminded her of her first day of her first year at the University of Virginia—as opposed to the reopening of a prison. She and Wolf had received hearty congratulations and compliment after compliment from everyone so far this evening—including the press.

And the demons hadn't haunted her too badly as she'd looked at the rooms. She'd taken the liberty of convincing herself that her father's room at Archer Prison hadn't been on the wing she'd toured . . . which had helped her internal struggle immensely.

She tapped the microphone three times, glanced at the three pennies on her bracelet, and then nodded to the crowd. By the time she and Cameron had reached Richmond last night, a security force was in place and waiting at her house. Cameron had made good on that promise, and, after what had happened at Stony Man Mountain, she was very glad he had. She'd gotten a decent night's sleep, and spent today relaxing at home in anticipation of this moment.

"Well," she began with the same smile that had decorated her face the night she'd been elected governor, "after so much hard work on the part of so many people, our vision is finally becoming reality." She consciously avoided even a glance into the many television cameras, which were focused on her at this moment. Tonight wasn't about her. "Before I go any further, I want a standing ovation for the man who brought this facility to life." She pointed to her right. "Mr. Clint Wolf."

As people rose, clapped, and cheered for Wolf, Victoria thought about how many dedicated and talented people it had taken to get the project to this precipice. And about that one potential juror she wanted so badly but hadn't quite been able to convince yet. She'd been depending on having Acosta inside the corps of guards as her eyes and ears—but that strategy had died in the West End hospital. Convincing a man named David Racine to become a juror was now absolutely *crucial*.

When the ovation for Wolf finally faded, Victoria signaled with her hands for quiet. "This is it," she said, raising her arms in triumph when all had gone silent. "Let's get started, jurors. Welcome to Jury Town!"

This second standing ovation lasted seven minutes.

GORDONSVILLE, VIRGINIA

Wayne Bennett's eyes went wide when Victoria slid into the back of the state police car beside him. "Aw, Jesus," he muttered nervously, glancing out his window into the dead of night on this lonely country road. "What's going on here? Is the Keystone trial still haunting me? Is that what this is about?"

"Obviously you know who I am," she said. She'd left Jury Town thirty minutes ago to make this meeting. She needed to turn around and go right back as soon as it was finished.

"Obviously."

"I have a few questions, Mr. Bennett."

She could tell by his expression that he knew exactly where this was going. For all intents and purposes, she already had her answers. But she would ask the questions anyway. She wanted to hear Bennett say these things.

"You were the foreman on the Keystone trial?"

"Yes."

"You acquitted the CFO, the man whom the state accused of paying bribes to a Pentagon official." She hesitated. "Were you approached by someone who wanted to influence the verdict?"

Bennett leaned slowly forward and sunk his face into his hands.

"Tell me," Victoria pushed.

"I can't talk about it," he muttered.

"I don't want to know if you actually changed your vote because you were approached. And I don't care what they had on you. All I want to know is whether or not you were approached. You will not be prosecuted for anything you say here. This is strictly off the record."

Bennett grimaced. "Yeah, yeah, I was approached. So were at least two other jurors I know about."

"I have one more question, Mr. Bennett. Was Mr. Tolbert guilty?"

"He was guilty as sin."

She patted Bennett on the shoulder, then climbed out of the patrol car. Bennett was guilty of something terrible, too—and he'd clearly betrayed the judicial system and his conscience because of it. But she could have compassion for him. Life wasn't always black-and-white. Shades of gray followed everyone. She knew that oh so well.

"Well?" the officer standing outside asked.

Victoria nodded. "Thank you for bringing Mr. Bennett down from northern Virginia, officer. I'm finished with him. You can take him back now."

As the patrol car took off, an overwhelming sense of pride surged through her. Wayne Bennett had just confirmed everything she and Eldridge had suspected for the last year. Everything Attorney General Delgado had believed as well. Someone very powerful was tampering with high-profile juries. But it was all about to stop—at least in Virginia.

She sighed heavily as two of her new bodyguards ushered her into the back of a black SUV. Now the real work began.

"Take me to Charlottesville," she ordered as the driver pulled away from the side of the country road.

"I thought it was back to Goochland."

"Not yet," she answered. "I've got one more thing I need to finish tonight at Jury Town."

———————

Bus after bus roared through the gates of Jury Town and into the midnight darkness veiling the facility. When the legitimate jurors had disembarked and began heading inside, the long line of stand-ins began to board.

Victoria and Cameron stood side by side, watching the process.

"Incredible," Cameron murmured as the last of the stand-ins boarded the last bus. "Everyone at the ceremony tonight actually thought those were the real jurors. No stories on the Internet, either. Nobody broke. You did it, Victoria."

"Best two million dollars we spent. They got ten thousand each to be stand-ins, to make everyone think they were the real jurors."

"An insurance policy," he added. "I'll give you credit. You think of everything."

"I don't know about that, Cameron. I don't think I'm *that* smart." She smiled wanly as the door on the last bus shut, and the convoy roared away toward Richmond with 196 stand-ins aboard. "But based on the number of bribe attempts the stand-ins reported to us in the last few weeks, I'm betting someone somewhere is going to be pretty upset when they hear about this."

PART TWO

CHAPTER 15

JURY TOWN

Until eight thirty yesterday morning, Kate Wang had been a history teacher in Leesburg, Virginia, which was forty-two miles west of Washington, DC, and not far from the West Virginia line. At eight thirty, after being notified by phone that she had officially been selected as a professional juror, she'd walked into the assistant principal's office at Loudoun County High School and resigned.

She hadn't given a reason for her resignation to the stunned older man, hadn't given him a chance to negotiate, and hadn't hung around to bid anyone good-bye. She'd exited his office, walked straight to her car, and driven to Richmond. To a staging area at an old armory in the city where last evening, after a long day of completing paperwork, she'd boarded one of four buses waiting to take her and 195 others to their new lives for the next two years.

Kate had been almost certain she'd receive the call. But Victoria Lewis had left a seed of doubt in her mind throughout the eight-month process. Kate had thought it strange last week when she'd started hearing and reading about others who had *definitely* been chosen as jurors. She'd thought it strange until last night when she realized in the Jury Town parking lot, as she was getting off the bus from Richmond, that the "definites" she'd heard and read about in the press were just stand-ins, running cover for her and the rest of the legitimate jurors. The stand-ins were waiting to get on the same buses that had just dropped her and the other legitimate jurors off—to go back to Richmond.

That switch was also the reason Cameron and Victoria had warned her to keep everything about the selection process completely confidential. The reason they'd told her that if they found out she'd communicated *anything* to *anyone*—even to her immediate family, she would be dropped from the program immediately, and there would go four million dollars up in a devastating puff of smoke.

Kate grinned as she applied mascara to her thin line of lower lashes in the mirror above the sink in Room Nine of Floor Two, Wing Three. She'd been passed over for promotion at the high school last year and received only a cost-of-living bump to her meager thirty-one-thousand-dollar salary. She and the assistant principal had disliked each other intensely from her first day at Loudoun High School three years ago, though Kate was never certain why. However, she was certain that the mutual animosity was the cause of her being passed over.

Her grin widened. She'd wanted so badly yesterday morning to tell that horrible little man who'd screwed her why she was resigning and that she was about to become a multimillionaire. But that had to wait until after her two-year commitment was over, and she was a free woman again. Hopefully, he'd still be there in the same dead-end job so she could wave her success in his face—which she definitely planned on doing.

Kate put the mascara down on the sink as she rose up and gazed at herself in the mirror. Twenty-seven and single, she was a mix of Chinese, German, and Brazilian ancestry. An exotic potion, for sure, but if she was going to be honest with herself, the result was resoundingly plain. She had short, jet-black hair, teardrop-shaped brown eyes, a square jaw, and a bit of a pug nose—which was the feature she disliked most about herself.

Twenty-seven, single, and earning thirty-one thousand dollars in Leesburg, Virginia, she'd been on the highway to nowhere—in the fast lane, to boot. She'd been on the verge of deep depression, especially after her cat had died in her arms of a stomach tumor.

Now she was in the fast lane to becoming a multimillionaire. When her two years at Jury Town were finished, she would get plastic surgery, travel the world, and find a husband.

"Can't think about all that right now," she murmured to herself as she picked up the knee-length dress she'd laid out on the bed and slipped it over her head, then headed to the desk and glanced at the message on the small screen one more time. "I have to be in Jury Room Seven in five minutes."

She scrolled down to the inspirational quote at the bottom. A different one every day, chosen by Victoria Lewis.

"Perfection is unattainable. But if we chase it, we catch excellence."

Kate laughed softly. "I like that," she murmured.

———

Harold "Hal" Wilson finished the last bite of a delicious breakfast, which had included three scrambled eggs, crisp bacon, hash browns, freshly squeezed orange juice, and great coffee. Since graduating from William & Mary in 1981, he'd been an insurance salesman, saving 327,000 dollars in his 401(k). He was fifty-six, twenty pounds overweight, and nearly bald. His wife of thirty-three years had died of heart disease last year; his two grown children lived in Seattle and San Diego, and his two closest friends had moved to Florida. He had nothing tying him to his modest three-bedroom house in a quiet neighborhood of Williamsburg, Virginia—except memories. And he wasn't ready to throw in the age towel yet.

So he'd jumped at the chance to be a juror, even though Cameron Moore hadn't told him what his compensation would be until a week ago. When he'd heard two million dollars a year, he'd burst out laughing. It was the heartiest laugh he'd enjoyed in quite some time. When he'd realized a few moments later that Cameron was absolutely serious about the money, he'd literally fallen from his chair.

Wilson put his fork down on the empty plate. One of his resolutions, after receiving final confirmation of his selection as a professional juror at nine o'clock yesterday morning, was that he would use his time here to get back into shape. He told himself that over and over on the bus trip up from Richmond last night. And the workout facilities here were incredible. He'd even intended on eating healthy this morning. But at the last minute ordered the full breakfast just to see how the food was. The answer: delicious.

He glanced quickly around the facility's cavernous Central Zone as he stood up to head to Jury Room Seven. There were about fifty people in the massive room, eating breakfast. He'd thought about joining a group of five people at one of the larger tables after getting his tray through the slot, but he was naturally shy, so he'd kept to himself. Besides, he had two years to meet everyone. There was no need to rush anything.

Including getting back into shape: the lunch menu looked delicious as well.

———

Felicity West walked briskly down the administrative corridor, headed for Jury Room Seven. For a decade, she'd been an engineer for the CSX Railway—until yesterday morning at six thirty.

She'd grown tired of driving the huge locomotives, which hardly needed driving anymore because they were so automated and computerized. Being constantly away from home on trips up and down the east coast had caused both of her marriages to end—badly—which was the way most things ended, of course.

So when she'd been quietly approached nine months ago about becoming a professional juror, she'd submitted an application and endured the difficult process—then shouted for joy three days ago when she found out she'd be making four *million* dollars in two years.

She'd been on pins and needles about winning a juror spot until Cameron Moore had called yesterday morning—even though they'd told her she was almost a lock to get the job right after they'd told her about the pay. So she'd shouted for joy again after hanging up with him this morning.

Now Felicity was nervous that somehow the powers that be would find out she'd run a one-woman dominatrix business on the side for the last two years—when she wasn't guiding those huge diesel locomotives all over the east coast. The contract she'd signed at the armory in Richmond clearly stated in Section Fourteen that she had told them about *every* job she'd ever had since college. It had also stated that if she hadn't disclosed everything, she would forfeit the money and could be criminally prosecuted for lying. So this was a be-careful-what-you-wish-for situation.

She didn't care about prison. The four million dollars was all that mattered. Jury Town was an all-or-nothing proposition . . . for her.

She caught a glance of herself in the glass of a painting hanging from the admin corridor wall as she headed toward Jury Room Seven. She was tall and naturally blond, which the men—and women—who'd paid her excellent money to be chained and whipped loved.

The odds were tiny that anyone at Jury Town would have ever used her services, but as a precaution, she'd started dying her hair auburn and keeping it very short in the back, above her shoulders, as opposed to the tresses that had fallen all the way to her ass in the back before.

Felicity had brought a good deal of auburn-colored dye with her—but it wouldn't last two years. Hopefully, her color would be available in the commissary.

CHAPTER 16

RICHMOND, VIRGINIA (WEST END)

David Racine sat at the head of the antique table in the breakfast nook, palms pressed together before his mouth as if praying. Two months ago his wife, Tess, had decided to remodel and expand the kitchen of their big, five-bedroom home.

He'd gone along with everything, hadn't said a word. He was too busy at work to object—and he loved her that much. He'd never been able to turn Tess down for anything, not since they'd been high school sweethearts twenty years ago.

When the remodeling was complete, he had to admit this kitchen looked stunning, as it should have for forty-seven thousand dollars.

A week later, Tess was gone.

She was having an affair with the tennis pro at the Country Club of Virginia, which was only a nine iron from where he was sitting right now, and the two-timing pair had finally come out of hiding to make it official. The bum with the long, stringy, dirty-blond hair and the annoying accent had been offered a new gig at a club in Beverly Hills, and Tess was moving to the earthquake coast to be with him. She'd explained it all in a brief, hand-scrawled note she'd left on this shiny new six-thousand-dollar table where he now sat. He'd discovered the note one awful night two weeks ago, when he'd finally gotten home from the office a few minutes after midnight.

He hadn't started divorce proceedings yet. He didn't have the bandwidth. And, down deep, he was still holding out hope she'd come to her senses and come home.

The e-mail hit his laptop with a resounding ping that seemed louder than normal. He confirmed the sender's address and then closed his eyes. He'd been waiting all day for this message and anticipation surged through him. He wasn't a hard-practicing Episcopalian—as if any Episcopalian really was, in his opinion—but it seemed an appropriate time to ask for divine intervention. And his hands were already in position.

"Give me something," he whispered. There hadn't been much good news lately, but this e-mail could quickly right a dangerously listing ship. "I haven't asked you for much in my life. I've tried to stay out of your way as much as possible. But I need this one."

Racine was cofounder and chief executive officer of Excel Games, an online sports-fantasy-league company he'd cofounded in Richmond with his best friend, Bart Stevens. Racine and Stevens were seeking five million dollars of equity from a wealthy Chinese investor. In return for the cash, they were offering the man a fifty percent equity stake in Excel Games. With that cash and a little luck, EG could be worth a hundred million dollars inside a year. And the man from China had been making all the right noises for the last week.

Racine opened his eyes and then the e-mail.

The message was short and sour. The man from China was intrigued with the opportunity to purchase ten million shares of Excel Games at fifty cents per, but he wanted more time to think.

Being "intrigued" and "wanting more time to think" were the words all sophisticated investors used to nix a deal. Racine had read enough of these rejections in the last few months to decipher the code.

Even on the remote chance this man was sincere about being intrigued, EG would be out of cash in a few days, and then Racine wouldn't be able to pay his all-important programmers. The last-gasp flame of saving his company had just been snuffed out.

He leaned back, rubbed his eyes, and then ran his fingers through his long, dark hair as he stared at the ceiling fan twirling slowly around and around ten feet above him. As he gazed up, a gut-wrenching wave of panic squeezed his chest. He'd always worked hard for his success, but it had always come. Failure was new and terrifying.

Maybe he should have kept that marketing job at Proctor & Gamble. And maybe he would have if he'd known how brutally tough this entrepreneurial path was going to be. The P&G job had been about as stimulating as watching hay grow, but he'd been outstanding at it. And you never worried about a Fortune 50 company running out of cash.

Being CEO was a ruthlessly lonely place at times like these.

He checked the name flashing on his phone's tiny screen, and for a moment, considered not answering. But that wouldn't be fair. At least it wasn't a bill collector.

"Hello, Bart."

Bart Stevens wasn't just the cofounder of Excel Games. He was also its chief financial officer and a man Racine leaned on twenty times a day. They'd known each other for over a decade, ever since their first day of Harvard Business School. Since then they'd become best friends.

After Harvard, Bart had gone to Wall Street to be an investment banker at Morgan Stanley, beating out scores of classmates to win the coveted job. Stevens had been on the fast track to making millions when Racine had convinced him to be CFO of Excel Games in return for twenty percent of the company. In return for the prospect of making even more money than he could at Morgan Stanley.

But the prospect light of that had just faded from dim to out. What was he supposed to tell Bart now?

"Hello there, Bart," he said in an enthusiastically confident way, making certain his tone gave away no hint of the panic attack he was battling. "Why the heck are you calling? I'll be at the office in a few minutes, as soon as Claire gets off to school."

"You know why I'm calling," Stevens replied matter-of-factly. "So?"

"So . . . what?"

"Come on, David. Don't play me. Did you get the damn e-mail? Did you hear from the man in China?"

"Nope, nothing yet."

Bart groaned.

But not like he would have if he'd known the truth, Racine figured. "Stop worrying so much. It'll be all right, Bart."

"Are you sure?"

"Absolutely," Racine replied convincingly. "Mao Xilai is going to invest. He'll jerk us around on terms a bit, but we'll get the money."

"I hope so. I believe in you, David. Everyone at the company does."

"I'll bring this home."

"Are you okay?" Bart asked as Racine was about to hang up.

"Sure. Why?"

"Amy and I have been thinking a lot about you lately. What Tess did, well . . ." Bart's voice trailed off momentarily. "Why don't you and Claire come over for dinner this weekend? We'll grill out."

"That's nice, Bart. We'd love to. I'll see you at the office in a few."

After ending the call, Racine pushed the laptop aside and allowed his head to sink slowly down onto the table.

"Dad."

He rose back off the table quickly, jolted by the soft voice. Claire, his fourteen-year-old daughter, stood on the other side of the new kitchen, clad in her school uniform. God, she was growing up fast. Why did she have to look so much like Tess? At least she didn't act like her mother. Claire had a wonderful heart.

"Hi, honey."

"Are you okay, Dad?"

"Of course, Claire, I'm fine, just fine."

"You don't look fine."

"Thanks a lot." He regretted his sarcasm instantly. She was just worried about him. "Really, I'm doing great." He gestured at the laptop. "Just getting a jump on the day, that's all."

As she gazed at him her lower lip began to tremble. "I love you, Dad," she murmured. "And I hate Mom."

"No, no," Racine murmured. "You can't hate her, honey. You have to love her no matter what because—"

"She's a bitch."

The word shocked Racine. He wasn't naïve enough to think that fourteen-year-olds didn't already know everything there was to know in this day and age of impossible-to-block information highways. What shocked him was that Claire would say it. He'd never heard anything remotely offensive come from her mouth.

It was definitely something Tess would say, and he hated that she was still influencing their daughter from three thousand miles away. On Monday morning, despite what he'd have to deal with at the company, he'd start the divorce process. He had to face facts. Tess wasn't coming back.

"Your mother's going through a hard time."

"*What?* We're the ones going through a hard time. She's off in California, partying. She's sent me pictures."

"It'll all work out, Claire. I promise." There he went again, promising things he had little hope of delivering on. But that was life as a CEO and a parent. He found the roles similar in that way.

"How can you be so nice about this, Dad?" Claire asked in a frustrated tone. "I mean, she ditched us."

Racine gazed into her beautiful bright eyes for a few moments and then looked away when he couldn't meet the glare any longer. His life was imploding. But that wasn't the tragedy. As his life went, so did Claire's. That was the disaster.

She was an eighth grader at St. Catherine's School, the most prestigious girl's prep school in Richmond. She was making straight As, her teachers loved her, and she had tons of friends. She had the world in front of her for the taking.

But tuition at St. Catherine's, even for an eighth grader, was over twenty grand. And Racine had put every penny he could get his hands on into Excel Games—including the proceeds from a second mortgage he'd taken out a few months ago. At this point he had no way to pay for her second semester.

Hell, a week from now, he wouldn't have a buck for a burger at McDonald's.

"Get going to school and I'll see you tonight," he said, just as the doorbell rang. He rose and headed down the hall toward the foyer.

"Hello," Racine said politely to the middle-aged man waiting on the stoop when he opened the front door. The man wore a paint-smeared jacket and jeans, along with scuffed construction boots. His leathery face looked vaguely familiar. "Can I help you?"

"Don't you remember me, Mr. Racine?" the man asked as two younger men emerged from behind the big oak tree in the front yard.

Racine glanced at the two younger men apprehensively as they moved to where the middle-aged man stood. "No. Should I?"

"My sons and I remodeled your kitchen."

"Oh, *that's* right. My wife was the one who worked with you mostly. But now I remember."

"You owe me forty-seven thousand dollars."

"I'm sorry, but I—"

"I've been calling you a lot. I must have left you fifteen messages."

Racine winced and nodded. "I've been very busy at work. No excuses, but I'm very sorry."

"You need to pay me."

"I'll write you a check as soon as I get to the office." He couldn't come close to covering a forty-seven-thousand-dollar bill, but what was he supposed to say? "I'd do it right now, but my checkbook's at the office."

"Okay," the older man agreed in a friendly tone. "I really appreciate that, Mr. Racine. I'm glad this was easy."

Relief coursed through Racine. The sons seemed relieved, too. This could have gotten nasty.

"And just so I'm sure you'll remember to write that check, my sons are going to leave you a little reminder."

Racine tried to slam the door shut as the man's sons lunged for the door. But one of the young men wedged his boot into the doorway, and then both of them quickly forced the door wide open. One of them grabbed Racine from behind, while the other struck him three times in the gut with wicked punches.

As they took off, Racine collapsed to the foyer floor in a tight fetal position. Eyes shut tightly, he tried desperately to suck air into his lungs as he groaned loudly.

When he was finally able to pry his eyes open, Claire stood in front of him, tears streaming down her face.

CHAPTER 17
JURY TOWN

"Good morning, Ms. Wang."

"Good morning."

Kate sat alone in Jury Room Seven. As the previous candidate had instructed, she sat in the middle seat of the jury box's front row, staring up at the camera, which was affixed to the wall above the stack of electronics equipment in the corner to her left. The four huge screens hanging from the opposite wall were all turned on, which was distracting. The movements on the massive screens kept catching her peripheral vision. But she managed to stay focused on the camera so the attorneys who were sitting in an intimate-looking courtroom in the tiny town of Abingdon in far southwestern Virginia could see her face as she answered. She *really* wanted to be part of this jury. Then she could always say she was a member of the first jury to ever hear a case at Jury Town.

But that wasn't the extent of her agenda—far from it.

"Where is your home?"

"Leesburg, Virginia."

"Where is that located?"

"About forty miles west of Washington." She glanced to her right so she could see the screens and the two lawyers at the defense table leaning together to confer.

"What was your living arrangement?" one of the men asked as he came back to the microphone.

"Excuse me?" That seemed like a strange question.

"Did you live in an apartment or a house?"

"Oh, I lived in an apartment." She laughed nervously and tugged on her necklace. "I thought you meant something else."

"Did you pay the bills?"

"Yes, I lived there by myself."

"Who provided your electric service?"

"Um, Commonwealth Electric Power."

"And you paid that bill yourself?"

"Yes. I just said that, didn't I?"

"Ever have any problems with Commonwealth?"

"What do you mean?" she asked.

"Ever have any complaints about CEP's service or had any problems with the bill?"

She shrugged. "No. Everything was always fine. Sometimes we lost power in the summer because of thunderstorms. But they were always real good about getting the lights back on."

"Okay." The defense attorney nodded to the prosecutor.

"Are you familiar with any legal problems Commonwealth has?" the prosecutor asked. "Any idea why you're here?"

Kate raised both eyebrows and shook her head. "No."

The prosecutor nodded to the defense attorney, then leaned back to the microphone. "Thank you for your time, Ms. Wang. We'd like you to be a member of this jury."

"Okay," she said calmly, giving away no hint of the thrill racing through her. She'd been worried that they might have detected her lie in her reaction and her response to the last question. She knew all about CEP's coal-ash problem in southwestern Virginia outside Abingdon—which, she assumed, was what this case would be about. "Can I go?"

"Yes. Please tell the next prospective juror to come in. His name is Harold Wilson. And could you tell him to sit in the same seat you were sitting in?"

"Sure," she called back as she headed for the big snack table to the left, which was covered with all kinds of goodies. She was going to grab a few 3 Musketeers Bars. They were her favorite.

GREENWICH, CONNECTICUT

"Did you hear what she did now?" the Gray yelled.

Rockwell held the phone away from his ear. He'd barely said, "hello" before the man blurted out his vitriol. "No, what?"

"She switched out the damn jurors, every damn one of them."

"What?" Rockwell asked incredulously as he gazed at the computer screen in his Rockwell & Company office. He'd just pulled up the senior management section of the Commonwealth Electric Power website, and he was staring at the confidently smiling picture of the CEO—the brother of the man he was on the phone with right now. "What do you mean?"

"Late last night four buses pulled up to Archer Prison with a hundred and ninety-six people aboard. They got off and went inside. Then the hundred and ninety-six people who'd been bused up there from Richmond yesterday afternoon, the ones who'd attended the opening ceremony, got on the four buses, went back to Richmond and back to their boring lives. We thought the first group was the real juror pool, but obviously it wasn't. Our contacts were all in that first group, but they were just part of an elaborate hoax Victoria Lewis was playing. That *bitch*!"

It occurred to Rockwell that the Gray who had called used the words "Archer Prison." Rockwell had been warned over and over *never* to use actual names for *anything* during these telephone conversations. He wondered if the Gray even realized what he'd done.

"Wow."

It also occurred to Rockwell that Victoria Lewis was turning out to be a formidable enemy.

"The good thing," the Gray spoke up, "is that we've identified three of the people who are in there now, one of whom will be on the jury that I care very deeply about."

Rockwell glanced at the picture of this man's brother on the computer screen, wondering how in the world the Grays could have already identified one of the jurors on the Commonwealth Electric trial. At least the Gray hadn't identified the case by name.

"I want you to check her out," the Gray continued. "Her name is Felicity West, and she worked for CSX before going inside Archer."

Rockwell cringed as the man used more names.

"Did you get that?"

"I got it," Rockwell answered quickly. Suddenly, he wasn't sure he wanted to be part of this anymore. For the first time since he'd joined he was hearing desperation in one of the Gray's voices. People tended to do very stupid things when they were desperate.

"Get back to me as soon as you have anything on her."

"I will," Rockwell assured the man.

"What about the woman in Virginia Beach? Have you—"

"I'm already working on that," Rockwell interrupted loudly. He definitely did not want the Gray mentioning Angela Gaynor's name on the phone. Some woman named Felicity who'd worked for CSX was one thing. A Virginia state senator was quite another. "I'll be back to you on both of them by COB today."

"Good. I look forward to hearing from you ASAP. What about our young friend? Is he going to finish what we—"

"He's been tasked. Believe me."

"Fine. Call me as soon as you know anything."

Rockwell exhaled heavily when the call was over, and for several seconds gazed ahead, suddenly ruing what he'd gotten himself into.

When he'd calmed down, Rockwell searched the Commonwealth CEO's name on the Internet. It didn't take him long to find out that the CEO had only one brother. It didn't take him long to find out what that brother did, either. And it didn't make him feel any better about the Grays and his situation with them when he saw what the man he'd just been speaking to did for a living when he wasn't in northern Maine.

"Phil."

Rockwell's eyes raced to his office doorway and Shane Harmon, the man who headed the mergers-and-acquisitions department at Rockwell & Company. Fortunately, Rockwell's screen was positioned such that Harmon couldn't see it from the door.

"Yes?"

Harmon shook his head, as if he wasn't sure he actually believed what he was about to say.

"What is it?" Rockwell pushed, a bad feeling coming over him. "What's wrong, Shane?"

"Nothing. In fact, everything's awesome."

"What do you mean?"

"I just got a call from the CEO over at Hydra Corporation. They want us to advise them on the hostile takeover bid they got yesterday. They're in play, so they know they're going to be acquired by someone now. But the CEO doesn't like the outfit that made the hostile tender offer. So he wants us to find him a white knight, or at least goose the hostile offer higher." Harmon shook his head again. "One way or the other, we stand to make fifty million dollars on this deal, Phil." Harmon laughed like his ship had just sailed into port with all flags flying. "Fifty million on one deal, Phil, and the publicity we get for being the investment bank on this deal will get me a lot more high-profile deals like this one. It's unbelievable. I'd like to tell you I expected it, but I really didn't."

When Harmon was gone, Rockwell glanced at the computer screen again. The man he'd just been speaking to on the phone before Harmon had interrupted with his incredible news was the number-two official at the National Security Administration. No wonder the Grays could get information on anyone they wanted, whenever they wanted to get it.

He glanced at the doorway again. He was going to earn fifty million dollars on one transaction. As Harmon had candidly admitted, he hadn't expected it. The Grays had sent another huge fee his way. Now he could buy that chalet high in the Swiss Alps he'd been drooling over for the last five years.

Rockwell clicked away from the Internet, unaware that he was leaving a trail leading from his computer directly to the Grays.

CHAPTER 18

VIRGINIA BEACH, VIRGINIA

Angela Gaynor closed her eyes as a refreshing breeze blew gently across her face. Like soft bristles of a child's paintbrush, it tickled her cheeks. She hadn't always appreciated the sea, not when she was a little, fat girl. But she could now.

"It feels so good to be here," she murmured, aware of how much more acute the sounds and smells of the sea were with her eyes shut. They were twenty floors above the beach, leaning side by side on the balcony railing of Trent's oceanfront condominium, elbows touching as they gazed out into a gorgeous day. "It's beautiful, Trent."

"So was that dinner you put on for those kids and their parents the other night," he said, "very beautiful."

"Thanks."

"Know what I was most impressed about, Angie?"

She glanced up at him. "What?"

"You invited as many white kids as blacks."

"I invited the whole second grade. The neighborhood's fifty-fifty. It's that simple. Don't overanalyze."

"Still."

"Still . . . what?"

"You could have been selective."

"Why would I?"

"You didn't like white people when we were kids."

"Neither did you."

"*I'm* not denying it."

"We lived in an all-black ghetto," she said deliberately. "All we saw on TV were white people living the good life. Now I know better. Poverty plays no favorites. Many more poor white kids live in this country than poor black kids. I didn't know that back then."

"Innocent little white kids grow up to be prejudiced adults."

"When did you get so cynical?"

"All I'm saying, Angie, is that you've got to keep fighting the fight. *We* have to keep fighting the fight. Too many before us sacrificed too much to ease up on the accelerator now, too many brothers and sisters felt the whip. Worse, they died inside a noose or at the wrong end of a gun. I don't want you going soft."

"No one's going soft," she snapped. "But I'm going to fight for everyone if I get elected to the United States Senate. I'm going to fight for what's right, without regard for the color bar."

"That sounds a lot like going soft to me."

"I can't be biased."

"You *have* to be biased."

Angela shook her head, exasperated. "You are amazing."

"Well, thank you."

"I didn't mean it as a compliment."

"Yeah," Trent muttered, "somehow I didn't think so."

"How much did you make your last season in the NBA?" she asked.

"That's getting a little personal."

"Really?" she asked, digging her phone from her jeans and holding it up in front of him. "I bet I could get a pretty good idea in about four seconds."

"Okay, eleven million."

"Wow."

Trent spread his arms. "*Wow?* You're one to talk. I read an article in one of the local business rags last month that put your net worth at fifty million and climbing. My career's over. Your company can go on forever."

"Thanks for making my point."

"Which is?"

"Everyone in this country has the opportunity to be successful."

"That's because a lot of people before us made the ultimate sacrifice." Trent turned to face her. "I'm talking about a lot of *black* people."

"No doubt about it, and I say a prayer for them every night. From Martin Luther King all the way to every black boy in Mississippi who got dragged into the woods and lynched for looking at a white girl the wrong way. But let me ask you a question," she continued before he could break in and get on one of his rolls. "Don't you think some white people had to be involved for us to have all these opportunities now? Do you really think we could have done it without having some of them on our side? If every white person wanted to keep us down, we'd still be down. I can assure you of that. Don't you at least have some respect for the white soldiers in the northern armies who fought in the Civil War to free us?"

"Don't kid yourself. Those men weren't fighting to free slaves. They were fighting because they were ordered to fight. And they were ordered to fight because the fat cats wanted to keep the country together. They knew that this nation was stronger united. The north had factories. The south had raw materials. It wasn't about freeing slaves. It was about the money, for most of them, anyway. Read your history books. It's always been about the money and always will be about the money."

"Spoken like a true fat cat."

"Hey, I—"

"Sorry," she said, holding up one hand, "that wasn't fair. But answer me this. Who do you think sold our ancestors into slavery? Yeah, yeah, whites bought us, but who sold us? Don't tell *me* about the history books. And who's got you reading so much lately? I know damn well it can't be one of those twenty-year-old floozies I see with you in *People*."

"All I'm saying is that the fight isn't done," Trent answered. "There are still plenty of places where black people don't have an equal shot."

"Like the NBA?"

"Well . . ."

"Which is seventy-six percent black, and the NFL, which is sixty-five percent black. I looked it up."

"It's not like that in the owner's box."

"It will be."

"Only if we keep fighting."

Their faces were inches apart now, and her urge to be with him was powerful as they gazed intently into each other's eyes, both of their angers boiling over. Anger was such an aphrodisiac.

She shocked herself as she slipped her hands to his face and then pulled him to her gently. As their lips met for the first time in their lives, a thrill coursed through her body, along with a wave of relief. She'd been terrified he'd resist.

She must have wanted it, she figured as their kiss went deep and passionate. She never did anything she didn't want to do anymore. At this point in her life, she had that luxury, and she'd worked damn hard to get it.

"I want to be a United States senator," she whispered as she finally pulled back. "And I need your help to do it, Trent. Will you help me?"

"I already told you. I'll give you everything I have, Angie, every damn thing."

"I'm going to announce my campaign very soon, and I want you to be there with me on stage when I do. I want you there right from the start."

"I'll be there every step of the way. Right up through election night. I can't wait to hold your hand up in victory after Chuck Lehman calls to concede defeat. That will be one of the best moments of my life."

Angela smiled up at him. "Mine, too." She hesitated. "This one isn't bad, either."

CHAPTER 19

SANDSTON, VIRGINIA

"Raul was a good man," Mitch said quietly from behind Sofia Acosta. The service was over, and they were the only two people remaining in the small chapel. Everyone else had filed out solemnly a few minutes ago. "I miss the old sport very much."

"My husband was a *great* man," Sofia murmured, touching the coffin as she fought her emotions. "I don't know what I'll do without him."

"You'll pull yourself together and keep going." Mitch limped up beside her. "You're a strong person. I sense that about you, Sofia."

"How?" she snapped. "How do you sense that about me? How do you know *anything* about me?"

She was grieving so he took no offense at the tone or question. "I'm good at sizing people up," he answered. "When I was in the military, I knew in the first few minutes of meeting a man if I'd have confidence fighting beside him in combat, if I could count on him to back me up, not to run even if we were getting pounded by the enemy. I was always right, too. And, let me tell you. I would have fought beside you with supreme confidence." Mitch reached down and took her soft hand in his. "The way you stayed strong while you gave the eulogy was absolutely inspiring. There were no dry eyes in the chapel, including mine." He squeezed her slender fingers gently. "It's a survival spirit. Some have it, some don't. I've seen tiny men who've been blown apart make it back from the edge because they have that spirit. I've seen big, strapping guys who weren't hurt that badly changed forever because they don't have it." Mitch tapped his hip and then pointed down at the prosthetic hidden beneath his suit pants. "*I've* been wounded pretty badly. I know what that survival spirit's all about. You have that same spirit, Sofia."

"That's nice," she whispered, muting a sob. "Thanks, Mitch."

"Of course, I—" Mitch interrupted himself as Sofia's son Daniel came back into the chapel, head down, shoulders slumped. He was a tall, strapping boy for his age—and the spitting image of Acosta.

Sofia whispered something to him in Spanish, and he turned around and walked back out.

"I have to stay strong," she spoke up when Daniel was gone. "I don't have any choice. I must have that survival spirit because I must survive. I have two children. They're depending on me, completely, *just me* now."

"What will you do?"

"What do you mean?"

"Will you stay in Richmond? Will you go back to New York City?"

"I . . . I don't know yet. Why?"

"Just wondered."

Mitch reached out and turned her so they were facing each other. "If you stay here and you ever need anything, you call me." He put a finger beneath her chin and lifted gently. "I mean it, too. I'm not just saying it. It's the least I can do for you and the old sport."

Her chin trembled on his finger, and she moved away a little. "I'm sorry I snapped at you."

"No worries."

Mitch didn't like the way Sofia wouldn't look him in the eye when he'd lifted her chin—she'd been obvious in her effort to avoid his gaze—and he was a man who drew important conclusions from things others might find insignificant. He'd learned that from his uncle. Judge Eldridge was always scouring the details for clues.

And, at this point, Mitch was turning very paranoid, especially after his interaction with Raul the other night. He recognized his paranoia, but he couldn't fight it. He knew Raul had been more than a little suspicious of the big house, the cars, and everything else and how that could all be funded on a government salary. Maybe Raul had followed him into the warehouse district to Salvatore Celino's long black limousine. Raul had been meeting with Judge Eldridge behind closed doors lately. Maybe he'd told Eldridge what he suspected.

Mitch's gaze stayed on Sofia. Maybe Raul had told his wife what he suspected, too. That possibility was even more likely. He knew full well how close Raul and Sofia were—much more than most couples.

He intended on finding out exactly what she knew. If it was too much, he'd make another request of Salvatore—this time it would involve murder. "Will you be home tonight?"

This time Sofia's eyes raced to his, then flickered away just as fast. "Why?"

"I figured I'd give you a call. You know, just to see how you are."

RICHMOND, VIRGINIA (WEST END)

Racine raised the full glass of vodka to his lips as he sat in the 750, listening to the Grateful Dead on the BMW's stereo. He loved this old music almost as much as he loved this car. He and Tess had listened to the Dead all the time in high school, this song in particular. So why was he torturing himself by bringing back all those memories?

He took another healthy swallow of Grey Goose as he gazed ahead into the dimly lit garage, at the ghostly silhouettes of bikes, yard tools, and patio furniture.

Claire was right. Tess *was* a damn bitch, and he *was* being too nice about everything. She'd been screwing the tennis pro for almost a year.

And she'd told him in the most cowardly way of all—with a note. She hadn't the courage or the courtesy to face him.

"Christ," he hissed as he eased back onto the leather headrest. "How did I get myself into this?"

Two mortgages, fifteen hundred dollars a month for the 750, twelve hundred a month for Tess' Escalade, tuition payments, what he owed on the kitchen, and a Niagara Falls cascade of everyday expenses were crushing him. But he hadn't taken salary in three months so he could pay his programmers. He had a thousand dollars to his name. And the bill collectors were calling constantly. Personal bankruptcy was a week away—at most.

He'd been living the life while Excel Games exploded on an early-stage rocket ride. Everyone in Richmond wanted his time—bankers, politicians, reporters. But suddenly there'd been an issue with EG's software—as well as the ominous appearance of a Silicon Valley competitor with huge backing from several major venture capital firms. Excel Games had dominated a specific sector of the lucrative online fantasy-league gaming space, but was suddenly being muscled out. That quickly he and Bart had gone from hanging onto the reins as their thoroughbred galloped around the track with no other horses even in the race, to barely making payroll every two weeks.

He loved the way this car smelled of rich leather, and he hated thinking about a flatbed truck pulling into his driveway to repossess it. Almost as much as he hated thinking about his beautiful West End home being sold at auction—and Claire having to leave it.

He'd actually called his old boss at Proctor & Gamble yesterday, just to see what was what. The prick was in the same old boring job, doing the same old boring crap, and he'd laughed aloud when Racine had brought up the subject of job availability. Then the line had gone dead. The same old job and the same old crap—the lucky bastard.

Racine finished what was left of the Grey Goose, as his phone chimed with an incoming text.

His pulse raced when he saw the sender: Tess. Maybe she was flying back to Richmond tomorrow, and everything would be all right again. Maybe she'd come to her senses.

"Please, God," he whispered. "Please."

Words on a screen betrayed him—as they had when the man from China had sent his message.

Racine clenched his jaw as he read her message.

I'm starting divorce proceedings. I'll be asking the court for full custody, and I'll get it. Claire will be better off with me in California. I'm sorry, David, but this is for the best. Claire loves me more. That's just the way it is with a mother and daughter.

Racine dropped the phone, put his head back, and shut his eyes tightly—trying desperately to fight back the tears.

There was still one alternative, one chance to save everything. But it would involve a *huge* sacrifice. He would be forced to say good-bye to Claire completely for two years.

SANDSTON, VIRGINIA

Sofia stood still behind the floor-length drapes in the darkened living room of her three-bedroom ranch house. She couldn't hear Mitch's steps moving across the room's thick carpet, but she could hear his breathing.

He'd knocked twice on the front door, then, shockingly, let himself in when she hadn't answered.

After the first knock, she'd glanced out her bedroom window and recognized him standing on the stoop in the dim rays of the closest streetlight. She'd had a bad feeling about their conversation in the chapel after Raul's funeral service, especially when he'd asked if she was going to be here tonight. It was as if Mitch knew Raul was suspicious of him, as if Mitch knew Raul had followed him on several occasions into downtown Richmond to that limousine.

So when she'd seen Mitch on the stoop, she'd panicked.

She'd torn down the stairs, intending to race out the back. But then she'd heard the front door open and been terrified he'd catch her before she could get to the kitchen. So she'd hidden here, behind the drapes in the pitch-dark living room.

Mitch's breath was getting louder and louder. He was coming closer. It felt as if he was just on the other side of the drapes now.

She clenched her jaw, waiting in terror for him to rip the drapes back and expose her hiding place—prepared to fight if she had to.

Would she have any chance?

The ring of a cell phone and now Sofia could hear Mitch's footsteps—hurrying away. He'd forgotten to mute the ring, and it must have startled him, worried him that she might call the police if she'd heard that ring from upstairs.

A moment later, the front door opened and closed loudly, and Sofia rushed from her hiding place to a front window. The lights of a car were already speeding away.

Finally she exhaled. It felt as if she'd been holding her breath forever. Thank God Daniel and his sister, Maria, had already left this afternoon for New York with her mother.

Her eyes narrowed. She needed to visit Judge Eldridge—at a time when she was certain Mitch was nowhere around. She didn't trust him at all.

CHAPTER 20

RICHMOND, VIRGINIA

As Racine turned after closing the corridor door, he nearly ran into a young woman coming out of Victoria Lewis' office on the twenty-seventh floor of the skyscraper just across the street from the courthouse. The woman had long, dark hair; honey-hued skin; green, almond-shaped eyes; and gorgeous, delicate features.

"I'm sorry," he said politely as they both stepped back from their near collision. So he'd finally met a woman more beautiful than Tess.

"I'm fine. No problem."

He found her Spanish accent exotic—along with everything else. She had an intense, almost blinding natural charisma. But there was sadness about her, too, a dark halo he noticed as he looked again, harder. And fear.

"I'm David Racine."

She hesitated—as if unsure of whether or not to introduce herself, as if she were carrying some crucial national secret, and she figured he might be a foreign agent.

"I'm Sofia," she finally answered.

"Are you part of this," he asked, "of Project Archer?"

"I'm not sure yet."

"Oh, well I—"

"It was nice meeting you, David," she interrupted, moving past him.

Racine glanced over his shoulder at the closing corridor door as the pleasing scent of her tropical-scented bodywash drifted to his nostrils. He hadn't coaxed a single smile from Sofia.

He turned back toward the young man sitting behind the desk of the reception area. A trace of pity seemed to be rippling through the kid's bright-eyed expression. "I'm here to see Victoria—"

"Hello, David."

Victoria Lewis stood in her office doorway. "Hello, there," Racine said. "It's nice seeing you again."

"Come on." Victoria waved for him to follow as she stepped back into her office. She closed the office door behind him, then headed for her desk. "I trust you haven't mentioned to anyone that you and I are still talking about your potential participation. If you have, tell me now. Remember, if I find out later, after you go in, you forfeit everything. Maybe even your freedom."

"Not a word."

"Good."

"Quite the security crew outside your office," Racine said. "I was frisked twice. They weren't here last time."

"Apparently there are people who very much want to see Jury Town fail." She pointed at a row of captain's chairs in front of her desk as she sat behind it. "Please."

"Nice painting." He pointed at the watercolor hanging on the wall behind her. "It's the Corps of Discovery, I assume."

"Meriwether Lewis has always been a tremendous inspiration."

"As well he should be. I've been through Montana and Idaho. I've seen the mountains those men dragged their boats up to go from river to river. It's incredibly impressive."

"As is your résumé, Mr. Racine."

She wasn't wasting time. Well, given his financial situation, he was all for efficiency.

"Tell me about Excel. Online gaming, but what does that really mean?"

"We manage fantasy leagues in all different sports. We offer season-long, month-long, and even as little as day-long sessions for our clients to play."

"And bet on?"

"Define bet."

She rolled her eyes. "There are other companies doing that. It's nothing new, correct?"

"Our sizzle," Racine answered, "is that, in addition to regular in-season fantasy leagues, we also run simulation leagues. So people can play baseball in the winter and football in the summer, basketball and hockey in the off-seasons as well. We don't need actual games to be played on the field, court, or ice to give fans the ability to field a team in a certain sport. We simulate the games and the seasons and catalogue all the simulated stats. We do the traditional stuff as well, but the simulation option has been the key differentiator for us. We need incredibly powerful software to do all that. We can't have anyone getting behind our firewalls to manipulate the simulations, either. We have every minute of every simulated game audited by one of the big-four accounting firms. But we must be intensely careful about any intrusions to the random generation of plays and results."

"Fascinating."

"We think so. Apparently, lots of fans do, too."

"How's the company doing these days? Financially speaking, I mean."

"We're fine, just fine."

Bart Stevens wouldn't agree with that, far from it. Excel was dripping dry of cash, and Bart was going crazy. He hadn't been able to pay himself this month, and the bank was about to foreclose on his house. He'd been warned that he had three days before the sheriff would show up to evict him and his family.

It wouldn't be long after that before the sheriff showed up at Racine's house to take the same action.

The only potential saving grace: the man from China was in Washington, DC, on business as of last night, and his people had made an appointment for him to meet with them at Excel headquarters tonight in Richmond. His people claimed that if the meeting went well, he would invest the entire five million they were seeking—immediately.

Racine was praying . . . again.

"I remember you guys doing very well," Victoria spoke up, "and then there was a competitor on the west coast who was doing the same thing you were. And then there was a software problem."

"We're fine," Racine repeated.

"If that's true, why are you here?"

"Excuse me?"

"Why deal with the aggravation you've had to go through to get to this point in the process if Excel Games is doing so well?"

"The road here hasn't been that bad."

"Really, David?" she asked, mystified. "If that's true, you're the most patient man I've ever met. To get to this meeting with me, you've been through four ninety-minute interviews, you've completed three rounds of psychological tests, and you've had your entire life since kindergarten dissected by two background-check companies. If Excel Games is doing so well, why bother with all that?"

"Well, I—"

"Is this a dive for cover? For a man with a first and second mortgage, huge car payments, forty-seven grand to pay off on his new kitchen, and a nasty divorce settlement looming on the horizon, this would be a nice alternative if his company's going into the toilet."

Racine smiled stiffly. "I'm getting a front-row seat on why you got so many programs established as governor."

"Answer the question."

"Okay, I'm hedging my bets."

"That's better. I need you to be candid with me going forward, David. I must know I can trust you completely."

It was time to go on offense. He hated backpedaling. "I haven't decided to do this yet."

"And I haven't offered you the opportunity."

Victoria Lewis was a formidable woman. "So what's this really about?" he asked. "Of course, I know the general idea. The whole state does since you made that announcement at the Supreme Court Building. Heck, the whole *country* knows." He paused. "And you're exactly right. It's been an *incredible* grind getting through all the interviews, tests, and background checks. I want details. I deserve them."

"All right, so let's get to the gorilla in the corner first. Let's get to the detail I know you're *most* interested in."

Racine held his breath.

"You'll make two million dollars a year for two years as a juror."

His mouth fell slowly open. "Two million?" he gasped.

"That's right. Four million in total."

"Of course, I'll be sequestered from the outside world for those two years."

"That's correct. You won't even be able to contact Claire, not even send her letters or receive hers. If you do, even if you just try, it will be a felony punishable by five years in prison."

He hadn't missed her passing reference to Claire. She even knew the name of his daughter. "What if a family member becomes terminally ill or has a bad accident?"

"There will be exceptions in the case of immediate family members. The same will apply to the jury members themselves, of course. If you become seriously ill or hurt, you will be excused."

"What about the money in that case?"

"If a juror is forced to leave because of illness or injury, the money will be prorated based on how many days of the two years were served. But if you voluntarily leave the program without a viable excuse, you'll get nothing, even if you only have a few days left in your commitment. And you'll go to prison if we prove you were talking to people on the outside."

"So I'll be an inmate at Archer Prison for two years."

"I don't know of many inmates who are handed four million dollars the day they're released from prison. And please refer to it as Jury Town. No more Archer Prison."

"Are you running the program now that it's operational? Are you staying with this?"

"I am." She leaned forward over the desk. "And I'm going to need strong personalities inside the walls. Strong personalities like yours. I want you to be part of this project, David. I see you as one of our most important cogs, definitely a foreman type. You're a CEO. You know how to motivate and lead." She grinned. "And you're tall, dark, and handsome. All the predictive data suggests you'll be perfect. As does my instinct."

He laughed self-consciously. "I'll give you the tall and dark."

"Fine, but don't give me false modesty. You're a charismatic, good-looking man, and that helps me. Whatever helps me, I'm all for. I believe this program could completely revamp the judicial system for the better, but it's going to take a Herculean effort from a lot of people to achieve what I'm seeking to achieve. People like you." She hesitated. "And there's one more thing specific to you."

"Oh? What's that?"

"I'm going to need someone inside the facility who can keep me informed."

Racine looked at her like she was crazy. "You want me to be a snitch?"

"Not a snitch, an informant."

"What's the difference?"

"Informant sounds better."

He eased back into his chair as she leaned even farther over her desk. "Why would I do that?"

"Because I sense that you'll have something you'll need from me." She held up her hand before he could respond. "And I'll make it worth your while. I'll solve your liquidity problem."

He gazed at her, his heart beginning to beat harder.

"I still have three open spots," Victoria said quietly. "It's an incredible opportunity, David. A lot to consider, but I need your answer quickly."

Two years without seeing Claire, Racine thought to himself ruefully as he stared back at Victoria. Two uninterrupted years for that prick tennis pro to become the father figure. Was four million dollars worth that risk?

"How *exactly* are you going to solve my money problems?"

She couldn't lose this one—Victoria's father was whispering that to her from the grave. David Racine was one of the stars who could make Project Archer a tremendous success. One of those rare individuals everyone wanted to be around, who could lead simply on the strength of his natural charisma—*and* had the analytical mind to process data, to see problems and opportunities that others didn't.

Victoria desperately needed an informant who would be completely loyal—Racine fit that bill perfectly. Once he committed, he committed. The psychological tests had shown that. Out of all the candidates they'd interviewed, he was the one.

In fact, she even liked that he had money problems. Without those challenges, she wouldn't stand a chance of him sacrificing two years with his daughter. He loved Claire far too much, according to their intelligence.

"This evening," Victoria answered, "I'm sending you a contract that will bind you very tightly to Project Archer. Show it to your attorney, but no one else. You have two days to think through your commitment, and then you're signing on the bottom line . . . or not. If you sign you'll receive five hundred thousand dollars immediately, as well as my undying appreciation."

"Five hundred—"

"Yes."

Racine had tried hard to mask his shock and awe at this new sound bite. But, as cool a customer as he was, she'd seen the emotion break his expression. For a few moments, he'd looked like a man who was about to be served a thick T-bone—after not eating for a week. "It's a down payment on the four million, and it will be in your account a few hours after I get the executed contract." Her eyes narrowed. "But if you turn on me after signing that contract, it'll cost you a million dollars to get back out of it. And I'll make certain the state of Virginia files against you in court if you don't come up with the money immediately."

"You're quite the negotiator, Ms. Lewis."

"This is for keeps, Mr. Racine."

"So I see, Ms. Lewis."

She stood and walked to the door, where they shook hands. Racine stepped into the hallway. He glanced at the four security people guarding the door, then turned back toward Victoria. "There was a young woman coming out of your office when I got here," he said. "Her name was Sofia. Is she going to Jury Town?"

Victoria wasn't surprised that Racine had been immediately attracted to Sofia Acosta. Sofia was as beautiful a woman as Victoria had ever seen. And if politics had taught her anything, it had taught her to exploit situations that presented themselves out of nowhere.

"Yes, David," she answered, "Sofia will be going to Jury Town. And she'll need a strong shoulder to cry on when she gets there."

———

Mitch tapped out a text on his phone as he limped up Ninth Street along the crowded sidewalk, nearly running into several people hurrying the other way, muttering a curt apology to their wake. He was late for a meeting with his uncle, and he was going against the early rush-hour traffic to get back to the Supreme Court Building.

Not many people were aware, but Chief Justice Eldridge had a fiery temper behind closed doors. He never screamed or yelled, so no one ever heard his wrath. He carefully safeguarded his reputation as the eternally calm voice of reason. But he could be scathingly spiteful to subordinates, sometimes over seemingly minor issues, even to his chief of staff.

Mitch stopped behind a huddle of people, waiting for the light at Franklin to change, then trailed along when they began to move. There was no way to get around the pack. He'd just have to face his uncle's wrath for being late.

Halfway across the street, Mitch glanced up from his phone, and for a moment, came face-to-face with a young woman hurrying the other way. She seemed *so* familiar, despite the sunglasses and baseball cap pulled low over her eyes.

Then she was past him.

Mitch whipped around, wincing as a bolt of pain knifed though his bad hip. "Sofia!" he yelled. The woman's shoulders seemed to hunch when he called out. But she didn't look back. *"Sofia!"*

As he took a step to go after her, his phone pinged. Eldridge was already grilling him by *anticipating* his lateness.

When Mitch glanced back up from his phone, the woman was gone.

CHAPTER 21

RICHMOND, VIRGINIA

"Close that door, Mitch," Judge Eldridge ordered sternly from behind the ornate desk of his Supreme Court office.

"Yes, Your Honor."

Mitch addressed Eldridge as "Your Honor" at all times these days, even at family functions. It had always been Uncle Dan before, here in the office as well—at least privately—but their relationship had cooled in the last few months.

Mitch had no idea why.

In fact, he wondered if he'd still have a job in a few minutes, or if this meeting had to do with something more ominous. Perhaps his uncle's command to close the door had been given to cover law-enforcement people who were massing outside the office, about to arrest him for accepting bribes from Salvatore Celino in exchange for Supreme Court documents, perhaps even charge him as an accessory to Raul Acosta's murder.

Mitch didn't like that drab, dark-blue bow tie his uncle was wearing. Whenever Eldridge delivered bad news, he wore ties like that one. Every lawyer in the city who argued before the Supreme Court recognized that signal. But today's courtroom proceedings had been routine. There had to be another reason for the sad tie—at least, not in the courtroom.

"Sit," Eldridge ordered gruffly as he eased into his leather chair, still wearing his long black robe even though court was over for the day.

Eldridge always wore his robe at the office, even on days he wasn't going to court. The other six justices did as well, though Eldridge had never asked them to. They did it out of respect.

"Is something wrong, Your Honor?"

His uncle's forehead creased, and he raised a hand to smooth the divot of stress between his brows. "I'm very sad about Raul. He was a good man."

Mitch nodded. "Of course you are. I am, too. He was a *very* good man."

"Have you found out anything more about the shooting?"

Well, at least it didn't sound as though this meeting had anything to do with an accessory-to-murder charge. "I've been in touch with city detectives several times, but they have no leads."

"Do you think it had anything to do with that letter he was carrying for me?"

"I don't know, Your Honor." Now he was lying directly to his dead father's brother. If it all came out, he'd go from war hero to villain in no time. Of course, it wouldn't really matter at that point because he'd be behind bars. "I don't even know what was in the letter. You never told me. I delivered it to Raul, as you requested. That was all."

Eldridge shook his head. "Even if it was a random shooting, Raul was out late because of me. His death is on my shoulders."

Mitch began to relax. He wasn't out of the woods, but the conversation didn't appear to be heading in the direction of him being fired, either.

"Raul had a wife and children," Eldridge said softly.

"A boy named Daniel who's ten, and a girl, Maria," Mitch answered. "His wife's name was Sofia."

The Acosta house had been dark and empty last night when Mitch had gone there to find out what Sofia knew. He'd assumed she'd already gone back to New York with the children. In fact, he'd intended on asking Salvatore to find her in Brooklyn. But he could have sworn he'd just passed her on the street a few minutes ago. Maybe she'd heard his cell phone go off after all. Maybe that's why she'd ignored him on the street.

"I know. Sofia was here a little while ago," Eldridge said. "I spoke to her."

Mitch's eyes raced to his uncle's, then quickly away for fear Eldridge might see his shock. "Oh?"

"She invited me to Raul's funeral, but I couldn't go. I asked her to come in here and talk."

"What did she say?" Mitch asked hesitantly. Perhaps he shouldn't have started feeling better after all.

"It's what I said to her. I gave her the opportunity to become part of Project Archer. I gave her the opportunity to go to Jury Town. Then I sent her over to see Victoria."

"Why did you do that?"

"Money."

"Money?"

"She's a single mother now. She'll need a big income."

"And she'll get that from being a juror inside Archer?"

"I haven't told you everything about Project Archer, Mitch. I've had to keep things very secret." Eldridge winced apologetically. "I'm afraid I've been short with you the last few months. I'm sorry. It hasn't been you; it's been me. Project Archer has been quite a challenge. I've gone back and forth many times about bringing you in on everything. But Victoria Lewis and I had to maintain the utmost security level around the project. We still do, but I feel it's time to bring you in, especially now that Jury Town has gone live."

Mitch leaned forward in his chair. He had to *appear* as if he had no idea what was really going on, even though he'd read everything he'd given to Salvatore. "What things have you not told me, Uncle Dan?" he asked, feeling *very* good now about going back to the old habits.

Eldridge was accepting blame for them not being so close the last few months. It was nothing he had done.

"For starters, the jurors are earning two million dollars a year."

"My God," Mitch whispered. Had that sounded genuine? "That's incredible. Where do I sign up?"

"Yes," Eldridge said expectantly, "that's everyone's first reaction. But would you really give up two years with your children? No contact with them *at all* for two years? Honestly, Mitch."

He eased slowly back into the chair and, after a few moments, shook his head. "No, I wouldn't. Not at the ages they are right now."

"Even though I know you could use the money."

Again Mitch's eyes raced for his uncle's. "What do you mean?"

"To buy all the things your wife has cajoled you into buying, you must have run up a mountain of debt. It's no secret in the family that we think she's a very pushy woman. No offense, Mitch."

Relief eased through him—again. His uncle knew about his wife's extravagances, but assumed it had been funded with loans. "None taken."

"She's a social climber, too, though I think we both know she has no chance of ever piercing the society circles she's trying to invade. You know this city. I'm sorry, but a woman like that, especially one who isn't from Richmond, doesn't have a chance. They'll string her along and make her think she does, because that's the kind of people they are. But she doesn't." Eldridge winced. "Glad my wife never got caught up in all that."

"Yeah, well—"

"I feel bad. You've taken extraordinary care of me as my chief of staff for the last few years, but you've been doing it on a state salary. You need to start earning some real money, Mitch. So I've taken the liberty of arranging a position for you at Knowles & Williams."

Knowles & Williams was the largest and most prestigious Richmond law firm.

As active as Eldridge was, it was easy to forget he was seventy-six. Today, he looked it. "But—"

Eldridge held up a hand. "I'm retiring, Mitch, in ninety days. I need to take care of you before I do. So the managing partner at Knowles and I have agreed on a package for you. When I retire, you'll go into the firm as a senior associate, two years away from partner. You'll make two hundred thousand a year to start. He's going to give you a decent signing bonus as well, so you can pay off some of that debt your wife's pushed you into."

Immense relief flooded Mitch. "I don't know what to say except *thank you*." After the initial shock, a stunning realization hit him head-on. He had to disengage from Salvatore Celino. As long as Salvatore was alive, he'd be in the mobster's debt—and no lawyer's salary could pay that off.

"But you'll stay here with me until I retire." Eldridge leaned over the desk. "And we have a problem you need to take care of immediately, a *serious* problem." Eldridge pursed his lips. "Someone's been going through my office."

For the third time during this meeting, Mitch's eyes raced to his uncle's.

"I'm certain some of my files have been moved overnight several times in the last few weeks. Very slightly, but I noticed in the morning as soon as I got here."

"I'll have the lock changed on your office door immediately."

Eldridge shook his head. "We need to take it a step further than that. After hours and as soon as possible, I want you to have a hidden camera installed. You must find out who's been going through my office."

"I'll get to it tonight." He'd been the one going through his uncle's office, of course, so there wasn't really any need to follow through here. But if he didn't, Eldridge might become suspicious. "We'll find out who's been in here," he assured his uncle confidently, feeling emboldened.

He'd had nothing to fear after all. He'd just been paranoid all along. "What else haven't you told me about Project Archer?"

Eldridge exhaled heavily. "You must keep this absolutely confidential."

"When have I ever violated that?"

"Never. It's just one of those things I have to say to everyone. You know that, Mitch."

Mitch nodded. "What's the big secret?"

Eldridge's pause stretched out long enough that Mitch thought he'd changed his mind. "Project Archer didn't start with Victoria Lewis," Eldridge said finally. "It started with the United States attorney general."

Mitch caught his breath. "With Michael Delgado?"

Eldridge nodded. "Delgado and I believe a growing list of high-profile cases are being manipulated through jury tampering. Whoever is behind this is using very personal information against jurors to blackmail them into voting certain ways. These cases aren't just civil matters or isolated crimes. They're cases that affect the very ability of state and federal governments to enforce laws. And, to the extent these bad verdicts keep coming down, they set precedents for other cases. We must stop these people." The judge grimaced. "Even if we can't figure out who 'these people' are."

"So you put jurors behind walls and guards where they can't be manipulated."

"Exactly."

Mitch shook his head. "And one of them is going to be Sofia?"

Eldridge nodded. "Victoria still had a few spots left to fill. Sofia's struggling with that same question I asked you earlier. She won't be able to see or even speak to her children for two years. But she's in a different place than you are. She can't earn what you will in private practice, not even close. She wants to see her kids go to college. What she earns at Jury Town will enable her to secure a very nice future for her kids and herself."

"She's a very—"

"Strange thing about her," Eldridge interrupted.

"Oh?"

"She doesn't like you very much."

An uncomfortable expression clouded Mitch's face. He shrugged. "I barely even know her."

"She wouldn't come up here until she was convinced you were gone. And when she first arrived, it seemed she had something important she wanted to say about you. After I asked her about the possibility of joining Project Archer, she didn't want to discuss it anymore." Eldridge held his gaze. "Any idea what was on her mind?"

CHAPTER 22

GOOCHLAND, VIRGINIA

"Do we get David Racine or not?" Cameron asked as he sat down at the small wrought-iron table on the intimate slate patio. A small yard extended in a semicircle out from the slate. Otherwise, the quaint Cape Codder was an oasis in a desert of dense forest.

"We'll know tomorrow," she answered, taking three sips of her favorite Merlot. She'd offered Cam a glass of wine, too, as soon as they'd arrived. But he'd declined.

"Why are you so laser focused on David Racine joining Project Archer?" Cameron asked. "Why is he—"

"Ms. Lewis."

She and Cameron glanced up simultaneously at the sharply dressed, African-American who'd just walked up to them from around one corner of the house. Tall and impressively fit, Dez Braxton was the man Cameron had hired to lead Victoria's security detail after the attack on Stony Man Mountain. He was a highly decorated ex–Navy SEAL.

"Yes, Dez?"

"You need to move inside," he answered as he held one long forefinger to the earpiece of his communication device. "I've got a number of my people here, but we can't possibly cover the forest in front of you as well as everything else with any degree of confidence," he said, pointing to the tree line at the edge of the grass. "You are vulnerable to sniper fire."

"I'll be fine," she answered politely, "but thank you, Dez."

"Victoria, you need to listen to him."

"I'm not going to let my life be dictated by—"

"Ms. Lewis," Braxton cut in, "I need you to go inside *right* now. A pickup truck is parked on the side of the main road less than half a mile away. No one's in it, and we have no idea how long it's been there. We're running plates as we speak. Please, Ms. Lewis," he said politely but persistently when she didn't react, pointing over her shoulder at the patio door. "Let's go."

She picked up the glass of wine off the iron table and stalked toward the door. As she was about to go inside, she stopped and turned back. "Dez."

He glanced up from a text. "Yes?"

"I know you're just doing your job. I'll try to be better about listening."

"Good. Now *go*."

"This is already getting to be a major problem." She eased into the chair behind her study desk—tapping the desk three times gently—as Cameron relaxed into the chair in front. "Now I can't go out on my patio and enjoy a nice evening?" As she glanced at the broken column inside the gold frame, she slipped the bracelet from her wrist and put it down in the only open spot amidst the clutter. "And my driveway looks like a Beverly Hills Cadillac dealership with all those black Escalades out there."

"Dez Braxton is the best," Cameron countered. "He doesn't usually work outside DC, but I leaned on an old friend up in the District to help get him down here for you. You must listen to him." Cameron pointed at the bracelet she'd just taken off, the plain silver band from which three pennies hung. "You've been wearing that a lot lately."

"It's a charm bracelet my mother made me," she answered. "What's the update from Jury Town?"

"We have four trials in progress, including the Commonwealth Electric Power case. Two more should start tomorrow, and no one's reporting any issues. I spoke to Clint Wolf and George Garrison, the head of the guards. I also spoke to the judge in the CEP case. Everybody's feeling good. Everything's running very smoothly."

"Good," she murmured, picking up the bracelet as the Merlot began taking the edge off.

"Why did your mother take that particular lode of legal tender out of circulation?" Cameron asked. "There must be a story."

Victoria smiled nostalgically. "I found these three pennies one day while I was hiking up Stony Man Mountain with my father. In fact, I found them right on the overlook. I was six." She shook her head. "I know you'll laugh because you aren't superstitious at all, but ever since that day, three's been my lucky number."

"Yeah, that's so hard to tell."

"What do you mean?"

"You always tap the microphone three times before you start a speech. You tap a desk or table three times when you sit down. Sometimes you sip your drink three times in a row. And, of course, you never step on a crack anywhere."

"That last one's just the OCD kicking in."

"If you were OCD, your desk wouldn't look like a battle zone," Cameron argued, nodding at the chaos.

"I gave these three pennies to my father the day he went to prison," she said softly as she gazed at them. "Right before I said good-bye to him."

Cameron's eyes fell to his lap. "Oh."

"He said he'd give them back to me as soon as he was released, which he did. Know what his cell number was at Archer Prison?"

"I'm guessing it wasn't two or four."

She took a long swallow of wine. "It was 333."

"Wow," Cameron whispered.

He'd shivered, Victoria noticed, as if her answer had sent an eerie chill up his spine. "And listen to this. With a year to go in his sentence, my mother was running out of money." She took another guzzle of wine. She was finally starting to relax from the stress of the day. "The bank was about to take our farm, and she was a mess."

"Understandably."

"One night I had a dream about my mother playing the lottery using his prison cell's number. So I convinced her to do it. I made her go to the store the next day, and I made sure she played 333. She won a hundred thousand dollars, and we saved the farm. That's a true story."

"Seriously?"

"Absolutely. My father gave these pennies back to me after he got out, just like he promised. Said they really helped him, and that they really were lucky. So my mother made the bracelet for me after he died two years later."

They were silent for a few moments.

"You better stay off the cocaine," Cameron said somberly. "Like I said the other night, I don't want to experience that again."

Victoria's eyes flashed to his. He figured she was vulnerable after telling the story, so he'd attacked. For her own good, but still. "I know."

"I'm just glad I never saw it while you were governor."

"I never did it while I was governor," she said sharply.

"Okay."

She hadn't liked his tone. *"Well, I didn't."*

"So when did you—"

"About six months ago, I met up with an old friend from college, and she had some. We went out to dinner and when we got back to her house, we did it." Victoria took a deep breath. "I'd done it with her at UVA all those years ago." She sighed heavily. "She gets me some every once in a while. I don't know, Cameron. I guess it was the pressure of getting Project Archer executed and, like you said, the ghosts and the demons from the prison. It's not an excuse; it's an explanation. I get that I'm weak, and I hate myself for it. And I'm not going to do it ever—"

Victoria was interrupted by the sound of the patio door bursting open and footsteps sprinting toward the study.

"Yes?" Victoria asked in a relieved voice as Dez rushed into the room. She had no idea who'd been coming at her. And, after what had happened on Stony Man, she found her heart suddenly beating a million miles an hour. "What is it?"

"I need to get you out of here right now, Ms. Lewis. We have a situation."

CHAPTER 23

JURY TOWN

The front-end loader roared into the massive pile of gray ash towering over it, scooped up a huge bucket full of the toxic material, then
backed off, turned right, and moved away from the cameraperson who
was obviously filming from a stand of heavy brush.

A moment later the front-end loader was roaring toward another
camera in the grainy video, toward a second individual who was filming
from inside a grove of trees. The vehicle headed past the cameraperson and
then out onto a short dock, where it dumped its load onto a small barge.

When the video finished and the lights in Jury Room Seven came
up, Kate glanced first at Hal Wilson and then at Felicity West, who
glanced back with raised eyebrows. It seemed obvious that both of
them felt the same way she did: it was going to be very difficult for the
Commonwealth Electric Power lawyers to convince them that coal ash
had not been deliberately dumped into the river that ran beside the
generating plant outside Abingdon, Virginia.

Kate had played pool many times with her four older brothers, two of
whom were very good.

But not like Felicity. The tall redhead had just destroyed Hal Wilson in three straight games of eight ball. Wilson hadn't been able to drop a single shot in. Now Kate felt like the next shark victim.

A dozen players in the large poolroom had stopped their games on the four other tables to watch, which wasn't helping Kate's nerves. They, too, had noticed Felicity's skill as she'd wiped the floor with Wilson three times in a row.

"You break," Felicity called as she chalked her cue.

"You beat Hal," Kate called back, nodding at the foreman of the Commonwealth Electric jury, who'd stuck around to watch. "You get the break, right?"

"It's okay. Go ahead."

Kate wasn't going to argue. She knew she needed all the help she could get.

She placed the cue ball on the tan felt near the left cushion, leaned down, curled her left forefinger around the smooth lacquered wood of the cue, took a deep breath, and fired.

"Excellent!" Felicity shouted as the cue ball slammed into the triangle of balls at the far end of the long table with a loud crack, sending a stripe and a solid into separate pockets as the rack dispersed. "Nice break. You got one of each. Call it."

Kate heaved a sigh of relief as she glanced around the table. She'd been worried about scratching—whiffing on the strike or sending the cue ball flying off the table after hitting it. "Solids, I guess." Neither option looked great given the way the balls had broken.

"Okay," Felicity said, "I'm stripes."

"Four in the side," Kate called.

She lined up the shot and gently rolled the cue toward the purple ball. It caromed on contact and almost dropped in the pocket, then bounced away from the cushion at the last second, to the groan of the crowd.

In short order Felicity dropped the six stripes remaining on the table and then the eight ball—in a row. The crowd shouted and clapped.

"That woman is good," Wilson said to Kate as he placed his cue back in the stand hanging from the wall. "See you tomorrow at trial."

"Wait," Kate called to him as he turned to go. "Let's get Felicity and go to dinner."

Thirty minutes later the three of them were finishing a delicious meal in the Central Zone.

"I'm going to gain twenty pounds while I'm in here," Wilson muttered as he ate the last bite of apple pie, then patted his paunch.

Felicity laughed.

"It's not funny," he went back at her as he broke into a self-conscious smile. "Maybe you're satisfied with the rabbit food," he said, pointing at the large chef's salad she'd barely touched, "but how could I possibly turn down a T-bone and baked potato with all the toppings?"

"Let's talk about the case," Kate suggested, pushing her tray to one side as she leaned over the table. The hum of conversation was loud with nearly two hundred people eating. "Commonwealth is so guilty. That video we watched today proved it. And it sure sounds like everybody up the chain knew what was going on, including the senior executives."

"We're not supposed to do this outside the jury room," Wilson warned. "You heard the judge the first day."

Kate rolled her eyes. "Give me a break, Hal. What difference does it make?"

"And the video didn't prove anything," Wilson objected, unable to hold back. "It could have been made anywhere. We've got to hear from the guy who drove the front-end loader and the other guy who drove the barge. In fact, we've got a lot more testimony to hear."

"CEP is guilty of dumping coal ash in that river," Kate said confidently. "We need to get on with it."

"What's your rush?" Felicity asked.

"I want to make history," Kate answered bluntly. "I want to be a member of the first jury to render a verdict at Jury Town. Fifty years from now, they'll write about us, especially when all the other states and the Feds do the same thing as Virginia. Think about it. It's our chance to be part of something *huge*."

"I'm out of here," Wilson said, standing up. "As foreman, I can't listen to this. I'm going to watch *Dirty Harry*. I always loved that movie."

"You think they're guilty, don't you?" Kate asked Felicity as Wilson walked off.

Felicity shrugged. "I guess. Like Hal said, we've got a lot more testimony to hear."

"Where'd you learn to play pool like that?" Kate liked Felicity. She had right from the start, since they'd eaten lunch together the first day of the trial.

She shrugged again. "Around."

"Did you ever play professionally?"

"Nah. You know, you're pretty good yourself."

"Are you kidding?" Kate asked, her expression coiled in disbelief. "You killed me."

"I saw the way you broke. You're good. Where'd you learn?"

"Four older brothers. Maybe you could teach me a few things they didn't."

"Sure."

"What did you do before you came in here?"

"I was an engineer."

"You design bridges and buildings?"

Felicity smiled. "No, I drove trains for CSX."

"Cool."

"I guess."

"Do you party?"

Felicity's eyes raced to Kate's. "What?"

"Do you party? Do you get high?"

GOOCHLAND, VIRGINIA

"I'm bringing her out," Braxton said calmly into the tiny microphone appending from the earpiece. "Get Vehicle Two as close to the front door as possible. I'm bringing the COS as well. I don't want to leave him behind. Too dangerous."

"What's going on?" Victoria demanded.

"We've got unknowns in the perimeter. I want you out of here now," Braxton answered as he stared through the narrow window beside the door, watching for the Escalade to pull up. "I don't want you coming back here, either."

"That's ridiculous. I love living here. I love my house."

"So do your enemies. You're too vulnerable here. I was afraid of this right from the start."

"I will not be a hostage, Dez. I will not be intimidated out of my—"

"Let's go," Braxton interrupted, grabbing Victoria's wrist with one hand while smoothly withdrawing a pistol from beneath his black blazer with the other. "Stay close," he called over his shoulder to Cameron as he shoved open the door and burst through it, pulling Victoria along with him. "Hurry!"

They raced a few short yards to the waiting black Escalade. The driver had already opened a back door for them.

Victoria ducked inside, followed by Cameron.

Braxton slammed the door after them, then jumped into the front. "Go, go," he ordered the driver, pointing ahead through the windshield with his weapon. "Let's get out of here."

The Escalade took off down the narrow driveway, which was lined by tall trees on both sides, followed by two more black SUVs.

JURY TOWN

"Put this along the bottom of the door," Kate instructed as she tossed a towel at Felicity, then opened a drawer of the desk in her room and grabbed an old Band-Aid box.

"Are you crazy?"

"Maybe," Kate admitted as she removed a joint from inside the box, held it up, and smiled devilishly.

"If we get caught, we're out four million dollars."

"Who's going to catch us? As long as we're quick about this, other jurors won't smell anything. The guards don't come into the living quarters unless there's an emergency. Cleaning staff comes once a week, but we know when they're coming, and, besides, they aren't going through our stuff while we're not here."

"Don't kid yourself," Felicity snapped, making certain Kate's door was locked. "I bet they will. How'd you get that in here anyway?" she asked, pointing at the joint. "They searched through everything I brought at the armory in Richmond before I got on the bus. And I mean they really searched."

"In my bra."

Felicity burst out laughing. "Seriously?"

"Yup. I brought six in, three in each cup."

"But they had dogs."

"Lots of perfume," Kate answered, handing the joint to Felicity. "And if one of those dogs had gone for my bra, I would have had a good lawsuit."

"What perfume was it?" Felicity asked as she ran the rolled white paper beneath her nostrils.

"Addicted," Kate joked as she picked up a lighter from the drawer, then waved and moved into the little bathroom. "By Dior."

"What if they do drug tests? This stuff is in your system for thirty days, right?"

"They aren't doing tests," Kate said firmly, lighting one end of the cigarette.

"How do you know?"

"I read the fine print of the contract."

When they'd both taken several long drags, Kate extinguished the ember then sprayed the room with air freshener.

"What flavor?" Felicity asked as she eased into the desk chair.

"Mediterranean Lavender."

They both laughed loudly as Kate dropped the air freshener can on the bed and then sat on the mattress herself.

"This stuff's already getting to me," Felicity admitted, putting her head back and closing her eyes. "Feels so good."

"Tell me where you learned to play pool like that."

"Around."

"Don't give me that. Come on."

"Clubs."

"What kind of clubs?"

Felicity grinned. "You're nosy."

"And stoned. Tell me where."

Felicity exhaled heavily. "Promise you won't say anything to anybody?"

"Of course."

"It doesn't really matter if you do. It was a long time ago."

"Where?"

"Strip clubs."

"I knew it."

"How did you know?"

"You've got this power, especially over men. I noticed it the first day of the trial. It's like a swagger. It's like you don't care. I love it. I always wanted to try that once. Stripping, I mean."

"Be glad you didn't."

"Anything else crazy?"

"You sure ask a lot of questions."

"Come on," Kate urged.

"You ought to find a better place to hide your stash," Felicity warned, pointing at the desk drawer. "I wouldn't trust the cleaning people."

"What else?"

Felicity shook her head. "I'm only saying this because I'm high as a kite. Promise me you won't say anything."

"I already did, and, besides, if I do, you can tell the people in charge I have pot in my room. If they found it, I would obviously get kicked out of here. So, you've got something on me. Now, tell me."

"Before I came in here I was a dominatrix in my spare time, when I wasn't driving trains."

Kate gasped. "Oh my God, that's *so* cool."

"I did a man two nights before we reported. The money's incredible. They pay you to discipline them. I could never understand that." Felicity grinned. "Of course, I never tried very hard. I was too busy beating them."

CHAPTER 24

GOOCHLAND, VIRGINIA

"We've got a challenge, people," Dez said calmly into his microphone as the Escalade skidded to a halt on the narrow, tree-lined driveway after coming around a sharp turn. "We've got a pickup blocking our progress thirty yards ahead. I see no one in or around the vehicle."

Victoria leaned toward the middle of the backseat so she could look through the windshield, and was startled when her head touched Cameron's. He was trying to see what was happening, too.

"Is it the same pickup that was out on the main road?" Dez asked. "Yes? Okay. I want two of you from V-3 to inspect, one up each side. Use the trees for cover." He touched the driver on the arm. "Can you turn around fast if we need to, Lionel?"

"No way. Trees are too tight. I can make this thing go plenty fast in reverse if we need it."

"Ten four," Dez answered as two members of the security detail passed them on either side of the Escalade, just inside the tree line, pistols drawn.

"Give me a gun."

Dez glanced over his shoulder at Victoria like she was crazy. "What?"

"Give me a gun," she repeated.

"Negative," he snapped, focusing front again.

"I know what I'm doing, Dez. My uncle taught me how to shoot when I was a teenager." From the corner of her eye, she could see Cameron looking at her the same way Dez just had. "I think he was a charter member of the NRA in a previous life," she said, following the progress of the two men as they closed in on the pickup. "Look, I don't want to be unarmed if we have a problem. I want to be able to defend myself."

"I'll defend you."

"Give me a gun."

Dez muttered something under his breath she couldn't understand.

"Dez."

"There's a Glock beneath you."

"Jesus," Cameron whispered when she reached beneath the seat and pulled out the black 9 mm pistol.

"Is the first round chambered?" she asked as she slid the top of the gun back and forth quickly, more to ease Dez's mind as to her experience than to elicit a response.

"No."

"There's an extra clip down there, too," Lionel called.

As she reached down again, the pickup blocking the road ahead of them exploded, shooting flames and pieces of steel in every direction. Both men close to the truck were engulfed by the explosion. A piece of flying debris smashed the Escalade's nonshatter windshield.

"Back, back, back," Dez ordered, pulling his phone out and pressing a single button, which immediately sent out a 911 call along with their exact location. "We go back to the house and hole up until the cavalry gets here. We'll fight from there."

The driver turned around, put his right arm over the front seat, and gunned the truck in reverse, then quickly skidded to a halt again on the gravel.

"What's wrong?" Dez demanded.

"The guys behind us aren't moving."

"Back to the house," Dez ordered into his mike again. "Move it!"

Gunfire from behind them suddenly peppered the dusk outside.

"They think she's in the last vehicle," Dez muttered, shoving his door open and then racing around the front of the SUV to Victoria. "Come on," he urged, pulling her from the back. "Stay with us, Cameron," he yelled. "Let's go, Lionel!"

Dez in the lead, the four of them sprinted for the woods as bullets angrily smacked the SUV.

As she glanced left just before making the tree line, Victoria spotted two men from her security detail crouched down beside the last SUV, firing back at several enemies dressed all in black.

"Oh, God!" Cameron shouted, tumbling to the leaves. "I'm hit!" he yelled, crawling a few yards farther into the trees, before collapsing onto his stomach with a groan.

"Cameron!"

Victoria had made it twenty yards into the woods, directly behind Dez and in front of Lionel. But now she peeled off and darted back for Cameron.

"Damn it!" Dez hissed, chasing after her.

She dropped down beside Cameron, who was writhing in pain and grabbing his left side as bullets tore through the trees around them.

"Look out!"

She scrambled left as Dez dropped down beside her, grabbed Cameron, literally tossed the small man onto his shoulders, and rose back up.

"Jesus," she whispered, awestruck by the power she'd just witnessed.

"Come on!" he yelled over his shoulder.

As they hustled ahead, Lionel fired into the woods to the left several times.

Through the trunks of trees, Victoria caught fleeting glances of people running. Behind them, shooting continued where they'd left the Escalades.

She glanced up at Cameron. His eyes were shut, and he was bleeding from his mouth and nose.

"This way," Dez growled, sprinting right toward a small ridge and the rock line at the top. "We've got to go on defense, Lionel. We'll never make it out to the road. Get her!"

Lionel grabbed Victoria's wrist, pulled her up the small slope, and pushed her behind a boulder. "Get down. Shoot anybody you see at this point," he said, pointing at the woods they'd just come through.

Her uncle had taught her how to shoot all right—and she wasn't bad when it came to firing at targets. But her lessons had never included shooting at humans—*or being shot at*. Why did anyone want to kill her this badly, especially now that Jury Town was operational?

And then it hit her as she heard the wail of sirens in the distance: Whoever was behind this was sending a message to the senior officials of other states who might want to initiate a Project Archer of their own. To the Feds, too. And a hell of a message it was.

A bullet ricocheted off the boulder before her. Instinctively, she grabbed the handle of the 9 mm with both hands and peered into the trees, leaning out as far as she dared to check the area. Someone was darting from tree to tree out there to the right, getting closer and closer. Dez and Lionel were shooting to the left as the barrage of incoming fire intensified.

"Dez!" she yelled as he popped an empty clip and reloaded. "I've got someone over here!"

"You wanted the gun!" he yelled back, aiming at someone as he fired three rounds, then two more. "Shoot him!"

Bullets ricocheted off rocks and strafed trees, echoing eerily as they screamed past Victoria.

Dez and Lionel were completely and furiously occupied with the center and left of their position, and the darkly clad enemy she'd been tracking on the right was closing in with at least one other man coming up behind him.

She had no choice. She had to engage. She had to become part of this battle—or die.

Her heart was pounding so violently it felt as if it would burst; her throat was bone-dry; her body was quaking, and it seemed as if she hadn't taken a breath in forever.

She was petrified that she was about to pass out. Or maybe passing out was what she desperately wanted. They would certainly kill her then, but at least she'd feel no pain.

The terror of the battle was ripping away her will to live, she realized.

The world began to spin, as if she were inches from the edge of the Stony Man Overlook, as if she were staring down from that sheer cliff into an abyss from which there was no escape or survival. She felt herself losing consciousness, felt herself falling over the edge even as the sights and sounds of the battle flashed all around her.

Then everything happening so frantically and furiously decelerated suddenly, and all sounds became singularly identifiable. Miraculously, she was breathing normally again, her heart rate slowed, and her hands steadied. In a microsecond, everything had changed.

Her survival instinct had crushed her mortal fear.

She glanced down at Cameron, who lay still on the ground behind Dez, then turned, checked the three pennies dangling from the silver bracelet snaring her wrist, thought of her father for an instant, and then clasped the gun with both palms, leaned slightly out from the rock she was taking cover behind, aimed, and fired.

Her target had paused behind a tree fifteen yards away, and she struck him in his shoulder, the only fraction of the man that was exposed.

As he recoiled from the wound, he howled and whirled away from the trunk, wholly exposed among the tall trees.

She fired true again, hitting him in the left thigh, and he crumpled to the ground—just as a bullet glanced off the rock immediately beside her face, splintering a shard from the boulder, which tore at her cheek as it deflected away.

She fired again and again, aware of sirens in the distance as she nailed the other attacker racing toward her position. He tumbled to the ground ten feet to the left of where she'd hit the first man—who'd dragged himself behind a tree.

"Look out!" Dez shouted.

She whirled around as a man rose up from behind a rock less than ten yards away—just in time to see the round that Dez fired tear through the man's chest and send him tumbling backward as he tossed his pistol high in the air.

Dez Braxton had just saved her life.

She spun back around in time to squeeze off four rounds at a man aiming at Lionel. One good turn always deserved another.

A helicopter thundered overhead, circling tightly in the sky immediately above their position atop the small ridge. Men leaning from the open doors on either side rained hell down on their attackers with submachine-gun fire.

The sirens blared louder, and the barking of dogs became chaotic. That quickly, the men who'd ambushed them were suppressed and scattering.

Victoria dropped to the ground beside Cameron and pressed two fingers to his neck, searching desperately for a pulse.

CHAPTER 25

VIRGINIA BEACH, VIRGINIA

Angela stood behind a curtain to the left of the stage, astounded by the crowd's size and enthusiasm.

"They love you," Trent said loudly. "This is awesome."

She leaned forward so she could see the emcee, who was dressed in a sharp blue suit. Her entire body shook with anticipation.

"Quiet!" the emcee begged. "Good people of Virginia Beach, give me some *quiet!*"

The boisterous mob was packed tightly into the main promenade of Lynnwood Mall, the area's largest indoor shopping mall.

"Please!"

But the people refused to yield to his request, cheering louder and louder as they surged toward the raised platform at one end of the mall and jammed the railings of the second and third floors overlooking the stage.

"I'm not going any further until you people pipe down," he warned.

Cheers instantly turned into a thunderous chorus of boos and then chants for his head.

"Okay, okay," he muttered nervously. "I'm just kidding. Come on."

Raucous cheering returned.

"But before we get to the main attraction, I've got a special guest to announce."

Now, without asking, he quickly received the silence he'd been seeking. Everyone in the mall was ninety-nine percent certain of what the main event was all about. Information had run rampant in the local media for a week, and today was simply confirmation of the rumors swirling through the district like so many minitornadoes.

But nothing about today had advertised a special guest. This mystery piqued their interest, and a hush rolled through the huge building.

"Should have thought of that before," he murmured.

"Get to it!" a man yelled from the crowd. "Let's go!"

"All right, all right," the emcee agreed, waving in the direction of the voice. "Before you get to see the woman you've all been waiting for, I'm handing the microphone over to a man everyone here will recognize immediately, and *he* will introduce her."

The crowd held its collective breath.

"Here we go," Trent said, leaning down to give Angela a quick kiss.

"A very *tall* man," he shouted, pointing to his right. "Four-time NBA all-star with the Washington Wizards, national champion at the University of North Carolina, and Virginia Beach's very own . . . *Trent Tucker!*"

The mall erupted into another deafening roar when the six ten hometown hero emerged from behind a curtain on stage left and hustled up the platform stairs to loud music that ignited on cue. When he reached the emcee, he grabbed the microphone and held his arms aloft in victory, as he had on the basketball court so many times during his glittering career.

Angela held both hands to her mouth. She'd been so right to ask Trent to help her.

———

JD had arrived early to get a front-row position, and he was glad he had. Rockwell—and the men Rockwell was serving—wouldn't be thrilled to see the size of the crowd that had turned out to support Senator Lehman's competition.

One of the men had contacted JD directly, though he'd been warned very firmly not to let Rockwell know. Then a hundred thousand dollars had shown up in JD's bank account an hour later. He wasn't going to tell Rockwell anything, the bastard. He wouldn't have, even without the money. But the money made it much better.

Only a string of large security guards stood between the platform and JD as the music finally faded. He'd heard of Trent Tucker before even though he wasn't much of a basketball fan, though he'd never seen the man in person. Now that he had, he was duly impressed. Tucker was a huge physical specimen with a personality to match. JD didn't know the technical side of politics the way Rockwell obviously did. But it seemed certain, based on the reaction he'd just witnessed, that the basketball star was going to get Angela Gaynor a lot of votes very quickly.

"It's time!" Tucker shouted to the crowd, which quieted instantly for him. "It's time to make the big introduction and big announcement you've all been waiting for."

Someone sneezed, and a baby cried. Those were the only sounds in the huge pavilion.

"It is my great honor and privilege to present to you the next United States senator from the great state of Virginia. Please join me in welcoming Ms. Angela Gaynor!"

Gaynor appeared from behind the curtain and quickly climbed the stairs to the stage as the crowd erupted and the music reignited.

JD watched as she took the microphone from Tucker and begged the crowd for quiet while Tucker shook his head, wagged one long finger and exhorted the people for more. No wonder Rockwell was worried about this woman. She and Tucker formed a tremendous team. That was clear even to the casual observer.

The chanting and the music faded as JD focused. Even the people right around him who were whooping and hollering evaporated to nothing as his tunnel vision took control, and his eyes bored in on Angela Gaynor's head. If Rockwell gave the word, he would blow that head apart with a single bullet. And that would be that. Her campaign for the United States Senate would be over in a fraction of a second. And not one of the screaming, cheering idiots in this huge mall had any idea what was going to happen—only him.

RICHMOND, VIRGINIA

Chuck Lehman sat in a big, leather easy chair in the study of his West End mansion, sipping his third cup of espresso. Photographs of him with celebrities, sports stars, and other high-ranking politicians littered the tables and bookshelves. The room was a shrine to him, and he didn't mind admitting how good it made him feel to see himself with all those other important souls.

He loved spending time in here. Unfortunately, he didn't love what was on the wide flat-screen hanging from the far wall. It was ruining the great vibe he usually enjoyed in here. But he felt he had no choice but to watch.

"What are you watching, dear?"

Lehman glanced away from the screen as his wife, Martha, entered the study. She was tall, slender, and blonde, and at forty-seven still retained her classic beauty without having submitted to a single incision from a nip-tuck expert. He broke into a satisfied smile as she ran her fingers gently through his salt-and-pepper hair. He marveled at how she never failed to light up a room, any room, whenever she entered it.

"We're watching this idiot from Virginia Beach announce that she's going to take on—"

"Easy, Paul," Lehman chided. His older son was home from Princeton for a few days, and they were going to spend the afternoon watching sports after Angela Gaynor was finished announcing her candidacy. "Let's have some respect."

"Sorry, Dad."

"I've read a lot about her lately," Martha said, nodding at the TV. "She's a remarkable young woman. She pulled herself out of poverty by the bootstraps and built one of the biggest construction companies in eastern Virginia. She hasn't let anything get in her way her entire life. When she was eleven, she shot a crazy man who'd broken into her mother's apartment looking for drug money."

"Guess I better wear a bulletproof vest if we have any debates."

Paul put his head back and laughed loudly. "Good one, Dad."

Martha patted Lehman's shoulder. "She's a gamer, Chuck. You better be careful."

He squeezed her hand gently. "You're right," he replied, "and I will. I always trust your instincts."

"I don't want anything getting in your way to the Oval Office."

She was the perfect political wife, Lehman thought to himself as he stared up at Martha. She'd told him on their wedding night that he would be president one day, and that she would do everything in her power to help him achieve that goal. He was convinced he was one of the few fortunate men in the world when it came to wedlock.

"I'm going downtown for a while," she announced, running her fingers through his hair again. "We're opening another home for runaway girls tomorrow, and I want to make sure everything is ready."

"You're too good," he called after her as he refocused on the television. "I love you."

"Love to both of you," she called as she headed off.

"Do you really think this woman can beat you, Dad?" Paul asked when his mother was out of earshot.

"Not a chance," Lehman answered confidently. "She thinks she's God's gift to the universe because she got lucky with her construction company. People in her district like her, but she has no idea what she's up against now," he said, grabbing the remote off the ottoman in front of the chair. "Let's watch something else."

CHAPTER 26

JURY TOWN

The guard jogged up to the young kitchen worker just as she reached her car in the parking lot. She'd been opening her door, but he slammed it shut again and stepped close.

"What are you doing?" she demanded angrily. It had been a long shift, she had a thirty-minute drive back to her dive apartment in Charlottesville, and she wanted to get on the road. She assumed he was about to ask her out—they'd made eye contact twice out here in the last few days—but that nasty look in his expression confused her. "I don't have time to—"

"There's money in this for you."

She'd been about to start screaming when he blocked her hand from the car door, but the scent of cash distracted her. "What do you mean?"

The guard glanced around furtively. "I need to get a message to one of the jurors."

"Are you *insane?*"

"There's *a lot* of money in this for you."

"I could get fired. Worse, they could bring me up on charges. Clint Wolf sends us memos and e-mails all the time warning us about this. Don't you get those?"

"I'm talking ten thousand dollars."

The guard's image blurred before her as she gazed up at him, thinking about the things ten thousand dollars would do for two small children and her mother. "Ten grand?" she whispered incredulously.

"In cash."

"My God."

"I told you."

She stared up at him for several moments more, then finally shook her head. "You could pay me a hundred grand, and I wouldn't do it. We've got cameras on us constantly, and my boss is always watching for things like that. He tells us he's watching; he doesn't make any secret of it. And he's got people watching him. He tells us that, too." She shrugged. "Besides, the trays go through slots on conveyors. We never see the jurors. I'd have no way of knowing if I was getting a message to the right person. They've got them roped off good. You're going to have to find another way to get to them."

He reached for her, and she jerked back, seeing that nasty look flare in his eyes. But he only touched her arm.

"We never had this conversation. You understand me?"

RICHMOND, VIRGINIA

"How's he doing?" Dez asked, nodding at Cameron, who lay unconscious on the bed, hooked up to a multitude of tubes and machines.

"The bullet went through his left lung," Victoria answered, rising from the chair she'd been sitting in for the last fifteen minutes. She'd been thinking long and hard about that gun battle as she'd stared at Cameron's ashen face. "It's bad, but the doctors think he'll make it." It occurred to her that the surgeons might be painting a rosier picture than reality. "It's seventy-thirty at this point. That's what I was told, anyway."

"What about you, Ms. Lewis?" Dez touched her cheek, and the dried blood just below the spot where the rock shard had torn her skin. "You got a nice battle scar there."

"Yeah," she whispered.

"It hit you, didn't it?"

She glanced up at him, still awed by the image of him tossing Cameron onto his shoulders like a rag doll. "What? The piece of rock?"

"No. The will to live. I saw it happen. You were about to give up; the panic was crushing you. But then everything cleared in a moment. You decided you weren't going to die, not without one hell of a fight. I saw it happen."

"Yes," she said softly, goose bumps suddenly covering her arms. "Everything went to slow motion, and I could hear all sounds individually but all at the same time. It was bizarre."

"That's it," Dez confirmed. "It's a hell of a thing. Some people freeze at that crisis moment in their first real combat. I've seen men who've trained for battle for years and years still go cold at that moment. Some people can't handle the chaos and the fact that other people are trying to kill them. You've never trained at all, but you handled it." He hesitated. "I was impressed. I don't say that often."

"Thank you. I wouldn't want to make my living at it," she said lightly. "Thanks for saving my life, Dez."

"Thanks for saving Lionel's." He shook his head sharply. "Besides, it's my fault you got caught in that. I didn't anticipate that kind of ferocity. You told me the attack on the mountain was made by one man."

"That's right."

"I'm glad I clued in the local people as soon as I got down here. I'm not sure how much longer we could have held out. That won't happen again. I can assure you of that."

An hour ago she'd found a dark, secluded corner of the hospital and sobbed uncontrollably, overcome by the terror of coming so close to death and her fear that Cameron would die on the operating table. Dez didn't seem fazed at all by what had happened.

"Who's trying to kill you, Ms. Lewis?"

"People who don't want Jury Town to succeed. People who want to send a message to other states that are thinking about doing the same thing." She glanced up at him. "Did we catch any of the men involved in the attack?"

"Several. And the ones who weren't wounded went to jail."

"Anything?"

"We never had a chance to interrogate them. They've all made bail and disappeared. Even the ones who were shot are long gone from the hospital." Dez shook his head. "They were turned loose like nothing happened. I've never seen anything like it." His tone was grim. "Those people that you just mentioned, the ones who are trying to kill you to send a message. They are very powerful, Ms. Lewis."

He was so right, she knew. The proof was lying on the hospital bed beside her.

"I want you by my side all the time from now on, Dez." She could feel the deep furrows tightening her brow. "I don't care what it costs. I don't care what it takes to get your time like that. I need you with me constantly."

He broke the tension with a smile. "So is that a promotion or a marriage proposal?"

CHAPTER 27

NORTH WOODS OF MAINE

Philip Rockwell sat in the same secluded north-woods cabin, in the same hard wooden chair, beneath the same heavy blindfold, which reeked of furniture polish. The primary difference this time being that the Grays had engineered two massive merger-and-acquisitions deals directly into the glad hands of Shane Harmon, Rockwell & Company's Managing Director and Head of M&A—on top of the equity underwriting transactions they'd already manipulated to the previously struggling investment bank.

Harmon had called to tell Rockwell about the second M&A deal just as he'd crossed over the Maine state line in his Mercedes a few hours ago, just as he was starting to become incensed by the long drive. Harmon had been as giddy as a kid on Christmas Eve as he'd described the sixty-million-dollar fee. And the rest of the drive had seemed to fly by for Rockwell.

Rockwell & Company was suddenly the hottest I-bank on Wall Street, and, in a matter of months, Rockwell's personal net worth had soared to over a hundred million dollars.

So he sat dutifully in the uncomfortable chair, hands folded in his lap, as the meeting went on and the pain in his back intensified.

"Angela Gaynor has declared her candidacy against Chuck Lehman. It's official."

That was the Gray whose brother was CEO of Commonwealth Electric—Rockwell quickly recognized the voice—the Gray who was second in command at the National Security Administration. The Gray he'd tracked down on the Internet.

"She was introduced on stage when she made her announcement in Virginia Beach by a man named Trent Tucker."

"Who's Trent Tucker?"

"A pro basketball player who grew up with Ms. Gaynor. They've been friends for years. He's a star with the Washington Wizards."

"Was," Rockwell spoke up. "He retired last year."

"Yes, well, apparently people haven't forgotten about him. The early poll results are staggering. Gaynor's just twelve points behind Senator Lehman."

"Twelve? *That's all?*"

"And climbing."

"She should be fifty points behind him and *falling*."

"The place went ballistic when Tucker went on stage," the NSA official spoke up. "Even crazier than when she did. This guy is a force. He could win her an election. It was an incredibly shrewd move on her part. You should have heard JD describe it."

Rockwell caught his breath, resisting the urge to rip off the blindfold and run for his Mercedes. *He* had ordered JD to Virginia Beach to witness the Gaynor announcement in person, and he'd spoken to JD afterward. The kid had mentioned the crazy reception for Trent Tucker—but not a conversation with one of the Grays. The Grays were talking directly to JD?

The first pang of mortal fear rippled through Rockwell's body. When intermediaries became expendable, they were terminated. But then why would the Grays pay him so much? Why would they navigate so much investment banking business to Rockwell & Company?

"Ms. Gaynor is a force. There is no denying that."

"We may actually have to take extreme measures if her momentum continues. Chuck Lehman must win this election. We must protect our interests. If Chuck was defeated, and the balance of power in the Senate shifted, our use of all the information we have would very likely be curtailed."

"Laws would be enacted. Watchdogs would appear everywhere."

"Our ability to manipulate would be severely inhibited, perhaps ended."

"Not to mention what would happen to income and inheritance taxes."

"And the defense budget. God help us."

"It's the nightmare scenario."

"Did you hear all that, Mr. Rockwell?"

He'd been hearing it for a year. And he understood and agreed with everything. They seemed to think that what was over his eyes paralyzed his ears. Perhaps they simply took a perverse pleasure in reminding him of the blindfold. "I heard it," he answered in a distracted tone. He was still stunned by the fact that they were talking to JD directly.

"We may need JD's sniper skills at that point."

"Easy, easy," someone spoke up loudly, "let's not be hasty. Assassinations ignite serious investigations. While I think we're insulated, there's no need to jump into the deep end of that pool."

"We're already in that end of the pool in terms of terminating Victoria Lewis."

"All the more reason not to possibly point *two* investigations in our direction. No need for that kind of cross fire." The man paused. "Have you been looking into Angela Gaynor's affairs as we requested, Mr. Rockwell? Have you been digging?"

"I have."

"And?"

Rockwell shook his head. "She's clean as a whistle. Gaynor Construction has never had any major problems. Minor things any business runs into from time to time, but nothing of any consequence. Personally, she's never had an issue, either, never even been stopped for speeding, as far as I can tell. But you are the ones who seem able to get anything on anyone."

"Lucky we anticipated her honesty," one of the men spoke up.

The other men chuckled loudly and stomped their feet.

Rockwell had no idea what that few seconds of stomping was all about, but his nerves could suddenly use a dose of something soothing. Every time they did it, it nearly gave him a heart attack.

"What about the Commonwealth trial, Mr. Rockwell? Have we gotten to Felicity West?"

"We've . . . tried," Rockwell answered carefully. He was about to disappoint them again. "We made a first attempt . . . but it didn't go well."

"What do you mean?" the NSA official snapped.

"Through our senior contact at Jury Town, we had one of the junior guards approach a kitchen employee. We were going to slip Felicity West a note when she was getting a meal, telling her we knew about her felony conviction for running a prostitution ring as well as her arrest for running a dominatrix service, both under an alias, of course. Both of which would certainly disqualify her from further service at Jury Town."

"And from four million dollars."

"If she didn't do exactly as we ordered."

"And that is to find Commonwealth Electric not guilty of all charges at the end of the trial."

"Yes," Rockwell confirmed.

"We *must* find a way to get to her," one of the men said.

"Mr. Rockwell?"

"I'm trying."

"No trying, Mr. Rockwell. You *must* succeed. Rockwell & Company won two huge M&A deals this week."

"Yes, yes we did." Rockwell hadn't liked that ominous tone, the same one he'd heard last time. "I'll figure it out. I'll get to Felicity somehow."

"You do that."

"What about Keystone Systems?" the man from NSA asked. "Now that the trial has concluded favorably, what's going on with that contract?"

"I spoke to the CEO yesterday," another man answered. "The helicopter contract is back on track thanks to the work of Mr. Rockwell and JD."

"As are the profits of those two oil companies in California," another man added, "thanks again to JD and Mr. Rockwell."

"Hear, hear!"

The men stomped the floor in unison, sending Rockwell's nerves flying—again. At least this time they were extolling his work.

"We're tough with you, Mr. Rockwell," the NSA man said when the sharp echo of hard soles to wooden floor had faded. "But we appreciate what you and your messengers do."

"Thank you." He made certain not to exhale too obviously in relief. He'd needed that confidence builder. "What about Victoria Lewis?" he asked. "Do you want me to have JD go after her again?"

"It turns out JD was quite right about her having bodyguards," one of the men answered coyly.

"We'll take care of Ms. Lewis from now on," another assured him.

That seemed strange to Rockwell. They'd taken something else away from him.

Another prolonged silence filled the room, and Rockwell prepared himself for one of the Grays to escort him to the porch and then tell him they were done with him until the next time.

"Stand up, Mr. Rockwell."

Just as he'd assumed, they were kicking him to the curb.

"You may take off your blindfold, Mr. Rockwell. You are one of us now. You are a Gray."

CHAPTER 28
RICHMOND, VIRGINIA

"I like Excel Games very much." Mao Xilai pointed first at Racine and then at Bart Stevens with a perfectly manicured finger. "You and you have done very good jobs. In the end, there could be great value here."

"Thank you, Mr. Xilai," Racine answered respectfully from across the polished sheen of the long conference-room table. He and Stevens had buffed it hard before Xilai arrived. "We appreciate you coming all the way from China to visit us in Richmond."

Xilai grinned as he tugged on his dress shirt's perfectly pressed French cuffs, clasped together by links of onyx and gold, and then adjusted the sharp lapels of his navy-blue suit. "I had other business in Washington, Mr. Racine. Yes, there is great value to Excel Games. But you two aren't that important."

The three men shared their first laugh. Until this moment, Xilai had been unfailingly formal, maintaining a poker face the entire time. This sincere display of relaxed emotion was a positive sign, Racine figured. Xilai was going to make an offer. That seemed clear.

But what would it be? And it wouldn't be just the amount that mattered. The terms would be vitally important—one in particular.

The man from China had spent the last three hours touring Excel Games, interviewing programmers and salespeople in depth, and scouring the financial statements for ninety minutes one-on-one with Bart

Stevens. A driver was waiting outside in a limousine to take Xilai back up to Dulles Airport. But that was it. Xilai hadn't brought the legion of assistants they'd been expecting.

According to the investment bankers, Xilai was worth six billion dollars, depending on the day and the exchange rate. The stocky, dark-haired man stood barely over five feet tall. But, now that they'd met in person, Racine fully understood how the man had generated his huge wealth. He was relentless in his pursuit of answers, and nothing slipped past him. It might seem to momentarily, but he always circled back to the open issue and corralled it.

Xilai leaned over the table as the laughter faded. "Gentlemen, it is look-each-other-in-the-eye time. Now that we are on the doorstep of partnership, I must have something that is much more important to me than all the due diligence and all the background checks in the world. I must have your word. I must know that as long as I am an investor in this company, you will treat it as you would treat your child." He gestured to Stevens. "Do I have your word, Mr. Stevens?"

"Yes, sir," Stevens answered immediately.

Xilai shifted his attention to Racine. "Mr. Racine?"

"Absolutely," Racine replied evenly, staring straight back at Xilai. "You have my word."

"All of your attention, Mr. Racine, every second?"

"Yes." Racine added a touch of defiance to his tone. He needed this man's money—desperately—but he wasn't going to beg.

Xilai picked up a white porcelain cup and sipped a special tea he'd brought all the way from China. "There is, of course, one other thing I demand. And that is your honesty." He placed the cup back down on its saucer. "And let me tell you about my definition of honesty just so we are all perfectly clear. I assume that you both will give me one hundred percent truthful and reliable answers to all my direct questions. That is a given. But I don't want to have to dig, either. I don't want to hear later from either of you that I didn't ask a question specifically enough.

"Please forgive my forwardness on this matter," he continued, "but I detest this American phenomenon of using situational ethics when it is convenient. I am very black-and-white when it comes to honesty. I expect full transparency at all times. No hiding behind technicalities. You will both sign employment contracts next week. But my opinion of contracts and laws is that they were invented for criminals and stupid people. My attorneys demand these contracts be put in place. But, for me, your word will be your real bond." Once again Xilai gestured at Stevens. "Am I making myself clear on this? Do you fully understand me?"

"Yes, sir."

Xilai pointed at Racine.

"Absolutely."

Out of the corner of his eye, Racine caught Bart flinching. The reaction had been slight, ever so slight, but Racine had seen it. He just prayed Xilai hadn't—which he realized was naïve given how Xilai seemed to notice everything.

"I completely understand, Mr. Xilai."

The investment bankers had told Racine and Stevens on a conference call that the Chinese venture capitalist was a reasonable man—as long as he believed you were honest with him. But, the I-bankers had also warned them that Xilai could be ruthless in exacting revenge if he believed he'd been lied to or defrauded in *any* way.

Bart was terrified—he was aware of one of Racine's options, which would put both of them in direct conflict with Xilai's transparency demand.

"Before we close our meeting and begin our partnership, is there anything either of you want to tell me?" Xilai's eyes narrowed. "Anything at all?"

"No, I think we're—"

"One of our major software applications still has a bug," Stevens interrupted. "You need to understand that before you make this investment.

It's almost stamped out, it's almost gone, but the last tail of it is still avoiding our programmers. I don't want you to think otherwise."

"Thank you for your honesty, Mr. Stevens. Actually, I was aware of that," Xilai said, casting a deliberate glance in Racine's direction. "I didn't tell you this, but my technical people identified that bug during our technical due diligence. The good news is they believe they can fix it relatively quickly. You see, I don't just bring money to the table. I bring everything I have. And I ask the same of you two." His focus returned to Stevens. "I appreciate you making me aware, Mr. Stevens."

"You're welcome."

"Here's the even better news," Racine spoke up with another trace of CEO defiance. "A week ago I hired an ace from Silicon Valley to fix that software roach. His name is Frankie Federov."

"I think I have heard of him," Xilai said quietly, nodding. "He is one of the best out there at debugging systems. He goes by the name of—"

"The White Russian," Racine interrupted. "As of this morning, our software is fixed."

"You didn't tell—"

"I didn't want to bother you, Bart."

"How did you pay for him?" Stevens asked.

"Yes," Xilai seconded, "now that I've seen your books, how did you pay him?"

"I gave Federov some of my company shares so there was no dilution to any of the existing shareholders. I took it as a major positive that he would take shares as compensation instead of cash. He told me this morning we have a tremendous engine here."

Xilai considered this, then nodded again, seemingly with approval. "We have discussed offer terms prior to today via e-mail, but here is my final proposal." Xilai stood. "I will invest four million dollars in Excel Games equity for fifty percent. It isn't the five-for-fifty you wanted, Mr. Racine, but it is fair."

Racine kept his expression neutral, but his mind was going a million miles an hour. If Xilai would personally advance him just a small percentage of that four million, maybe, just maybe he could . . .

"I want to say one more thing," Xilai continued, "before I take a short restroom break and give you both a chance to consider my offer in privacy. I am worth almost nine billion dollars. I am sure your investment bankers gave you some sort of estimate as to that figure, but they really have no idea.

"I don't give you that figure to brag or be arrogant. I give you that figure simply so you truly understand what I think of the upside for Excel Games. I believe this company can revolutionize the online-gaming industry with what you have here, along with what you will build onto it with the help of my investment." He chuckled. "And Mr. Federov, of course. Based on my meetings in Washington the past few days and certain gratuities I have extended to states around the country, I believe the overall online-gaming market will expand dramatically in the near future, making this company even more valuable.

"Here is the bottom line with respect to what I am saying. When a man who is worth nine billion dollars wants to invest four million dollars in your company, you should sit up and take notice. It means he thinks his four million will be worth enough someday to matter to him. That logic has excellent implications for both of your personal fortunes as well." He shook his head. "But, remember, I hate lies." He smiled for the second time in four hours. "I believe in both the stick and the carrot, as you like to say here in this country."

He nodded respectfully to both of them and then headed for the conference-room door.

"One more thing," Xilai spoke up as he turned back.

Racine's eyes raced toward the door. "Yes?"

"If we do agree on a deal and I put four million dollars into this company, there will be no sly moves with the money."

"Sly . . . moves?"

"I saw on the books that you haven't paid yourself in a while, Mr. Racine, and I am sure that has been difficult. When my money is here, you will certainly begin taking your salary again." Xilai pointed at Bart. "As will you, Mr. Stevens."

"Thank you."

"But neither of you will take loans or advances from that money."

Xilai had just put a stake in the ground as far as that one vital term went.

"Of course not," Stevens answered. "You have my word on it."

"All the same," Xilai spoke up, "my people will be watching your corporate bank account *very* carefully."

"I don't blame you," Stevens agreed. "We need to earn your trust."

"Exactly. I'll be back in a few minutes. I hope to have a deal done when I return."

Claire's beautiful face rippled through Racine's mind as he watched Xilai disappear through the doorway. Every risk he took from now on would be for her, even if she didn't understand what was going on, even if she were disillusioned with him, even hated him for a time. He had to act in her best interest, even if that meant bearing the brunt of her tears and her anger.

The thing was, just having his salary spigot turned back on wouldn't cut it. He had an angry contractor with two large sons after him—and that was only scratching the surface of his money problems.

———

"Hello, Salvatore."

"Mitch."

Mitch swatted a hand in front of his face as he eased onto the limousine seat. The cigarette smoke was unbearably thick tonight.

Salvatore gestured at the package Mitch had set beside him. "You got some good stuff on Jury Town for me tonight?"

"All the latest." Mitch coughed. "You got my cash?"

"Of course."

"What exactly do you do with this information, anyway? How are you profiting?"

Salvatore shook his head. "No questions like that, son. You should know that."

"Sure, sure, but if I knew how you were profiting, maybe I could get you even better data. Maybe you'd even cut me in on it a little."

He cringed as he said it. His number-one priority was transitioning from the Supreme Court to the law firm of Knowles & Williams, and reaping the benefits from the amazing parachute package Eldridge had arranged for him there. The key to that transition was getting away clean from the mobster he was sitting across from.

Salvatore chuckled loudly. "So the war hero wants to get his fingers even deeper into the crime pie."

But it wasn't *just* getting away clean from Salvatore. Even Salvatore would have to understand that once Mitch left the court and his uncle retired, he'd have no more access to the information. Before that time came, he needed to know exactly what Salvatore was doing with the Jury Town files. He couldn't risk somehow being tied later to what he'd been sneaking out.

"Why hold back? I'm already in, and I could use the juice. My wife's pushing for a bigger diamond, and I don't know how I'm gonna pay for that. She claims the women in her 'high tea club,'" he continued with a snobby accent, "are laughing at it behind her back."

"All right," the mobster said, "so what can you offer me?"

Salvatore was so predictable. He was always open to a moneymaking scheme. That was the way to get to him. That was his ultimate vulnerability.

"I can think of one opportunity in particular. But I'd have to know there would be reciprocity."

Mitch had considered asking Salvatore to go after Sofia, but she was insulated now—there was no way to get to her at this point without being blatantly obvious. Besides, apparently, Sofia hadn't said anything specific about her suspicions—probably because she had no real evidence from Raul. She'd acted strangely enough when she'd met with Eldridge that his uncle had noticed *and* said something, but nothing had come of it. And it didn't seem as if anything would. His uncle was too preoccupied with guilt over Raul's death.

"What is the opportunity?" Salvatore demanded.

"It's real estate, and it's big. The possibility of making millions very quickly. A case the high court will decide in the next month, and I know how they're going to come down. You can get the land on the cheap now. After the case is decided, the land's value will instantly skyrocket."

Mitch was careful not to react when Salvatore's eyes went greedy wide. "Go on."

"Like I said, I need reciprocity."

"I'll cut you in a little."

Mitch grabbed the package lying beside him and held it up. "I need to know what you're doing with this, too."

And then it hit Mitch—exactly what Salvatore had been doing with the information. Of course. Why hadn't he thought of that before?

———

"You *cannot* become a professional juror," Stevens seethed through clenched teeth when Xilai had exited the conference room. "You cannot be away from this place for two years."

Racine had been under strict orders from Victoria and Cameron to tell no one about potentially joining the ranks at Jury Town. But Bart Stevens was his business partner and best friend. He had to tell Bart.

"Relax, Bart."

"Relax? *Relax?* Did you hear what Xilai said about honesty and transparency, David? Or did I just imagine him saying all that?"

"Of course, I heard it."

"Not being here for two years is the worst fraud you could play on him," Stevens said, shaking his head. "Xilai's investing in you personally as much as he is in this company. He said that very specifically a few minutes ago. You are the face of Excel Games. You are the man who makes this place go. Xilai expects you to be here every day. You told him you would be."

"I know."

"And did you hear what the investment bankers said this afternoon about what Xilai does to people who lie to him?"

"They were exaggerating."

"Really?" Stevens asked sarcastically as he dug into his pocket, pulled out a folded piece of paper, and slammed it down on the conference-room table. "I printed that off the Internet this afternoon, after our call with the I-bankers. Read it."

Racine unfolded the paper and began to read, but stopped abruptly two sentences in. He'd spotted the words "the body showed signs of torture prior to death" a few sentences ahead. "This happened in China, and the article is very clear that there was never a direct link to Xilai."

"There were other articles about corporate executives of his portfolio companies dying suspiciously. The one you just read wasn't the only one by a long shot. Several others in China, two in Europe, and then there was a guy in Illinois six months ago. Xilai is vindictive as hell, David. I'm not going to be a part of this. I'm not risking my life for this."

Racine shrugged. "What do you want me to do?"

"Forget about Jury Town."

"I can't do that, Bart. I *need* the money."

"If we accept Xilai's offer, he said he'd have his people wire us the money tomorrow. We'll be able to catch ourselves up on salaries immediately. And I'll be able to keep a roof over my family's head. I won't have to give the keys to my front door to a sheriff."

"Just catching up on salary doesn't do it for me, Bart. I'd need a loan out of that money, but he was very clear that he'll be watching every dime we spend. Just getting my salary reinstated won't work." But the five-hundred-grand prepayment Victoria was offering him when he signed the Jury Town contract absolutely would. Racine had told Stevens about the two million a year, but not about the advance Victoria was offering. "I need more than that. I owe a contractor fifty grand for my kitchen thanks to Tess. And that's just the start of my debt problems. I'm behind on the mortgage, I've got tuition payments, car—"

"You can't leave me here by myself."

"I don't have a choice, Bart."

"This is crazy. Xilai's offering us four million dollars. With that kind of money, we could make this company worth hundreds of millions. Your stake will be worth way more than the money you'll earn at—"

"Is there a problem, gentlemen?"

Racine and Stevens' eyes raced to the conference-room door.

"No problem at all," Racine answered smoothly as he stood and walked toward Xilai. "I was trying to convince my CFO that we should stick to our five-million-dollar premoney value, but he won't budge. And in the end, I always listen to him."

"Do we have a deal then?" Xilai asked as Racine reached him.

Racine held out his hand. "We have a deal," he confirmed as he glanced over his shoulder. "Right, Bart?"

Stevens stared back without answering.

"He's overcome with joy," Racine said smoothly. "He can't believe this is finally happening, and he's finally going to have money in the till again."

INTERSTATE 95, NEW HAMPSHIRE

Rockwell sped through the night, feeling untouchable for the first time in his life.

"I'm a Gray," he whispered, still shocked by what had happened, by the twist they'd thrown at him in the middle of the meeting when they'd told him—with no ceremony—that he could remove his blindfold.

They'd had a big easy chair waiting for him—no more of that uncomfortable wooden chair. And, from now on, they were going to chopper him to and from meetings using a helipad that lay a quarter mile deeper into the forest—as he'd always suspected. He'd proven himself worthy, and now there were five when there had once been four.

"I'm one of them."

Rockwell had many things to do when he got home—in addition to running one of the hottest firms on Wall Street.

He *had* to make sure his contact got to Felicity West.

He had six more trials around the country he needed to send his messengers out to influence.

And he needed to start focusing on Angela Gaynor. It turned out the Grays had already begun implementing a plan to frame her if her campaign gained too much momentum too quickly. It turned out they weren't all prepared to shoot Ms. Gaynor down in cold blood—not yet, anyway.

Though that wasn't the case with Victoria Lewis—just the opposite, in fact. Apparently, they were doing everything in their power to murder her in order to send a clear message to the rest of the states around the country—particularly New York and California—about setting up their own Jury Towns. However, she was proving incredibly difficult to kill, thanks to her bodyguards. The other Grays had asked him to do background work on Dęz Braxton as well. If they couldn't kill him, maybe they could influence him.

He had all of those critically important tasks to focus on when he arrived home. But none of those things would be first on the list.

Before anything else and as soon as he was in his office, no matter how tired he was from this final drive, Rockwell intended to try to match the faces he'd met in that cabin to pictures on websites. He wanted to know exactly who he'd just become partners with. He'd start with the employee websites of the CIA and the Department of Homeland Security.

RICHMOND, VIRGINIA (WEST END)

"Good night, Claire," Racine called softly from the bedroom doorway.

"Night, Dad," she called back through a yawn, pulling the covers up over her shoulder and turning on her side, away from the door. "See you in the morning."

He was about to flip off her bedroom light, but stopped with his finger on the switch. "There's something I need to say, honey." He'd been dreading this moment ever since the meeting with Xilai had ended. But he couldn't wait any longer to tell her.

"What is it?" she asked, sitting up in bed, suddenly wide-awake.

He took a labored breath as he moved a few steps back into her room. She'd always looked at him like he was her hero—and now he was going to risk all that. "You have to go live with your mother in California for a while."

"*What?* No way! I'm staying here with you."

"And I want you to stay, believe me, Claire."

"They can't make me go. I'm fourteen. I can make my own choices. And I'm not going to live with that tennis guy Mom's shacked up with. I hate him. I don't care about a court order. I'll talk to the judge myself," she said defiantly.

"It's not about a court order or talking to a judge."

"Well, what is it?"

"It's something I have to do. It's on me this time." Telling Stevens about Jury Town was one thing, but he couldn't burden Claire with it. "I have to work on a project for two years."

"A project?"

"I have to go away."

Her blank stare slowly morphed into suspicion. "What do you mean, 'go away'?"

"Well, I—"

"You mean you won't even be here at the house?"

"No, I won't." He grimaced. "In fact, we won't even be able to talk to each other while I'm working on this."

She gazed at him for a long time, until tears rose in her eyes. "Is it jail?"

"What? No, I—"

"Are you going to jail, Dad?" She sobbed loudly. "Is that what's *really* happening?"

CHAPTER 29
JURY TOWN

"Talk to me, Billy," George Garrison demanded quietly but firmly as he shut his office door and headed back behind his desk.

Billy Batts came from the less privileged side of the tracks, as most of the guards at Jury Town did—education requirements weren't rigid. Billy had also been in a bit of trouble, which most of the others hadn't— and *that* made him the perfect accomplice. Garrison had done Billy a huge favor by hiring him—he'd kept the misdemeanor scratch on his record hidden from Wolf and Victoria's keen eyes, so Billy was deeply indebted. These days that misdemeanor could have kept him in the unemployment line for a long time.

Garrison liked having a subordinate who was a little on edge exactly for this reason, always had—which Wolf didn't know. In this business, earning some shady money was always a possibility. And the IRS didn't need to know *everything*. Neither did Clint Wolf.

In fact, there was a lot Wolf didn't know.

"Why wouldn't the woman in the kitchen pass the note to Felicity West?"

"She's terrified of being caught," Billy answered, glancing at the nameplate staring him down from the front of the desk. It read, in gold letters, highlighted by black: George Garrison, Head of Guards. "It's that simple."

This was the first time they'd had a chance to meet face-to-face about the problem. Billy had called Garrison immediately to let him know what had happened in the parking lot when he'd approached the woman. But Garrison hadn't wanted to stay on the phone a moment longer after getting the bad news. You never knew who was listening to cell conversations, Garrison knew.

"Really?" Garrison's bushy eyebrows creased tightly together as he eased into the chair behind the desk. He was a big-boned man with thick, hairy forearms who always wore his shirtsleeves rolled up above his elbows: it made him look no-nonsense. "That scared?"

"Oh, yeah. All of Wolf's e-mails and speeches about being brought up on criminal charges for trying to contact jurors have *everybody's* attention. And the woman said she can't see through the slots when they put the trays of food on the conveyors. She said she wouldn't have any idea if she was getting a note to the right person."

"She's lying. They can see out through the slots if they try hard enough."

"Then that's her point," Billy said, "she has to *try* to see what's going on. She's worried she'll be spotted if she's obvious."

"Did you offer the money?"

"Ten grand, like you told me."

"And she *still* wouldn't do it?"

"She thought about it for maybe three seconds, and then turned me down flat."

"Didn't you tell me you saw where she lives in Charlottesville?"

"Yeah," Billy answered. "It's not a great neighborhood."

"And she has two little kids?"

"Her mother takes care of them when she's working. I don't know how the four of them make ends meet because the mother doesn't work."

"And she wouldn't take ten thousand dollars in cash," Garrison muttered. The young woman turning her back on the money was almost inconceivable to him.

"She was all about people watching people and Wolf's warnings. Let me tell you, Wolf did it right." Billy shook his head. "Hey, he brought you in, didn't he? You worked for him at the Federal Bureau of Prisons, didn't you?"

"Yup."

"Well then you knew how thorough he was before he got here."

At this point Garrison had been contacted by a second individual about influencing the Commonwealth Electric trial. An older, more experienced man this time, judging by the voice. Not just the blond punk who'd surprised him in a Charlottesville strip mall near his home. This second man was offering a hundred thousand dollars—fifty more than the kid had offered—so Garrison had a significant amount more to give and still keep most of the bribe for himself.

These were serious people trying to influence the Commonwealth Electric trial, Garrison figured. There would be more trials that would need manipulation; the older man had made that very clear, so there could be a great deal more money in this for Garrison if he could prove himself.

Garrison winced. But there might be problems for him if he couldn't. The man hadn't made any overt threats, but that was Garrison's gut. It only made sense.

"We'll try the cleaning people next," he said.

"Am I offering ten grand again?" Billy asked.

"Yes."

"Am I still *getting* ten grand?"

"Yes," Garrison confirmed—which meant, if this worked, he could pocket seventy thousand. "I'll get the schedule for the cleaning people from the admin assistant." He was paying the admin assistant ten grand, too. "Be back here in thirty minutes, Billy. We'll go over the list of cleaning people going into Wing Three this afternoon and figure out which one you'll approach."

"Got it."

Garrison's eyes narrowed as he watched Billy Batts disappear through the doorway. The rumor was that Victoria Lewis had been attacked in the driveway of her home by some very serious people—though she was trying to keep it all quiet. She'd not been injured in the chaos, but Cameron Moore had taken a bullet. Good if it was true. That should keep Victoria distracted.

―――――――――――

Kate sat with Felicity and Wilson at a table in the Central Zone, eating lunch after a morning of testimony.

"*Now* do you believe me, Mr. Foreman?"

"Believe you about what?" Wilson asked, just before pushing the last bite of a delicious cheeseburger into his mouth.

"We heard the testimony of the guy driving the front-end loader this morning. He swore he got his orders to dump the coal ash into the river directly from the plant manager who reports directly to corporate headquarters in Richmond."

Wilson shrugged as he finished the bite, as if he was losing the will to fight her. "I hear you," he said, chuckling as he stood up. "You really want to be on the first jury to reach a verdict, don't you?"

"You're damn right I do."

"Well, here's what *I* want," he said, pointing at Felicity, "I want a rematch tonight in pool."

Felicity smiled. "Okay."

"We'll have a round-robin tournament," Kate suggested.

"Sounds good," Wilson called as he walked off. "See you back in the jury room in an hour. I'm taking a walk outside."

"What's your real angle?" Felicity asked, once Wilson had left.

"What do you mean?"

Felicity rolled her eyes. "You want to be on the first jury to reach a verdict blah blah blah. What's the real reason you want to find Commonwealth guilty?"

Kate stared intently at her for several moments. "Do you believe they're guilty?"

"There's no doubt. They dumped the ash in the river on purpose, and a lot of people inside Commonwealth knew about it. Just to save a little bit of money. It's disgusting. It's evil."

Kate nodded. "Okay, well I guess we're keeping each other's secrets, so here it goes. I have a close friend from college whose family is from that little town, from Abingdon. They live right on the river, and that ash has ruined their property for years and years to come."

"Oh." Felicity shrugged. "Well, if Commonwealth wasn't so obviously guilty, I guess I'd care."

"What do you mean?"

"You shouldn't be on this case if you're biased."

Kate waved. "Like you said, they're guilty. What's the big deal?"

Felicity leaned toward her. "You know, you should do a better job of hiding that stash of yours. Our wing is being cleaned this afternoon. You're risking four million bucks if somebody finds that."

———————

Sofia Acosta slipped a spoonful of peach yogurt into her mouth as she sat alone eating lunch in the Central Zone. She couldn't believe what she'd just overheard. The one named Kate had a friend in Abingdon who had been wronged by Commonwealth Electric. She wasn't objective at all.

"My God," Sofia whispered to herself, "the woman lied to get on that jury."

CHAPTER 30

RICHMOND, VIRGINIA

"Okay, Victoria, you got me."

Victoria glanced up from behind her desk as David Racine entered her office in downtown Richmond. "Good," she answered, gesturing for him to bring her the contract he was holding. "Let me see it."

"Don't you trust me?" he asked as he handed her the document.

"I just want to make sure you got it notarized," she answered as she thumbed quickly to the back. "Perfect," she murmured, glancing up at him. "So, what did you end up telling Bart Stevens? I know you got a four-million-dollar offer from Mao Xilai. My investment banking contacts, remember?"

"What was I supposed to tell Bart?"

"The truth, I'm assuming."

Racine nodded. "I didn't have a choice. Look, if you want to shut this down right—"

"No, I don't. I want you inside . . . and you know why. But I'm betting Bart wasn't very happy."

"He wasn't, but what was my alternative?" Racine said stoically. "Xilai made it clear we couldn't raise our salaries or take advances from the money he invested. I have debts, *big* debts."

"I'll have half a million dollars in your account by this afternoon. That better take care of your debts."

"I need one more favor," Racine said, his voice going soft. "It's personal."

"I'll do that for you," she answered, when she'd heard the request. She rose to shake his hand. "Welcome to Jury Town. And remember our deal."

"How could I forget?"

JURY TOWN

Billy Batts approached the cleaning woman as she emerged from her car in the satellite parking lot. He'd been prepared for the same reaction he'd gotten from the kitchen worker. But this older woman shrieked at the opportunity of cashing in on ten thousand dollars for simply placing a note under Felicity West's pillow. So loudly, Billy had hissed at her to quiet down.

When the arrangement was complete and they'd split, Billy smiled to himself as he thought about giving George Garrison the good news— and making ten grand for himself.

Billy wouldn't have smiled if he'd known he was being watched.

RICHMOND, VIRGINIA (WEST END)

Victoria knocked on the open bedroom door. "Claire?"

Claire had been staring out her bedroom window. "Oh, my!" she exclaimed as she turned toward the voice.

"Do you know who I am?"

"Of course, you're Victoria Lewis. You were the governor of Virginia."

Victoria nodded, impressed. According to Racine, he hadn't given Claire any advance warning. "You're a very informed young woman."

"What are *you* doing here?"

"Your father and I are friends." Victoria touched Racine's arm. "Can you keep a secret, Claire? You must promise me you can."

"Yes, ma'am."

"Your father isn't going to jail," she said, crouching down to eye level. "That's not why he's going away. In fact, your father's a hero. He's working with me on a very important project that will help many, many people."

Claire raced through the bedroom and threw her arms around him as he knelt down to catch her. "I'll miss you, Dad."

Racine hugged her back tightly. "I'll miss you too, honey."

Victoria watched them embracing, thinking how she'd clutched her father the same way the day he'd reported for prison. She was glad she'd agreed to do this. Not just to secure Racine's help. But for Claire.

CHAPTER 31

BLACKSBURG, VIRGINIA

"If you elect me to the United States Senate in November, I promise to give you everything I have every day of my term!" Angela shouted above the applause that was hurtling up into the rafters of Cassell Coliseum, Virginia Tech's cavernous basketball arena, and then echoing back down, creating a continuous, deafening roar. "I will never, never stop working for you!" she yelled into the microphone affixed to the dais in the middle of the huge stage. "I promise you I won't!"

Kanye West was appearing tonight on this stage, and Trent had arranged the rally through Kanye's people and the Virginia Tech athletic department's senior staff, all of whom Trent knew from his days as an NBA star. Somehow he'd also filled the coliseum with more than ten thousand screaming fans who seemed obsessed with a changing of the guard in Washington, DC.

She'd assumed when she walked onstage forty minutes ago that she'd be met by a polite, low-key crowd half filling the arena, which would dutifully listen to her explain her major initiatives. She'd assumed wrong. Trent had filled the place to capacity, arranged for network coverage, all prior to raising significant money for the campaign from influential people in the Blacksburg area at an intimate downtown breakfast this morning. He seemed to know everyone everywhere. He seemed able to achieve anything for her campaign—including quickly shaving points from Chuck Lehman's lead.

"When we announced our candidacy, no one gave us a chance," she said, signaling for quiet. "The reporters, the political pundits, even most people on the street shook their heads and said I had no chance to defeat Chuck Lehman." Cassell Coliseum had gone pin-drop silent in an instant. "They said he was an institution in Washington, destined for greater glory when he finished his third term as senator. That I was crazy, even arrogant, to believe I could beat him. After all, he is the senate majority leader. Well, let me tell you all something," she said defiantly, pushing her chin out, "as far as I'm concerned, there is no greater glory than serving the people of the Commonwealth of Virginia as a United States senator. That's all I want. That's all I'll ever want. I don't need anything more than that. I want to serve you. I have no other agenda."

Trent exhorted the crowd from stage left—to which they responded immediately.

"We started out so far back, I couldn't even see Chuck Lehman ahead of me," she said, raising her voice along with the crowd noise. "He laughed at our campaign when we announced it. He called it 'cute.'"

The roar intensified.

"Senator Lehman isn't calling it cute anymore."

When Trent waved to the crowd with both arms, the applause quickly turned wild, the loudest yet.

"Lehman needed binoculars when he snuck that first peek over his shoulder in our direction. Oh, yeah, I saw him do it."

The crowd rose to their feet, and the building shook as people began to jump up and down.

"Well he doesn't need those binoculars anymore. He doesn't even need to look over his shoulder. All he has to do is look over. I'm right there with him now, and it won't be long before we'll need binoculars to see him in our rearview mirror!"

As Angela's last few words evaporated into the thunder, Trent trotted to where she stood in the middle of the stage and raised her hand in his.

She smiled up at him, in awe. The polls didn't show her drawing even with Chuck Lehman. She'd exaggerated that for effect, taken a little political liberty with the numbers to help her corner. But she wasn't that far behind, either. Only yesterday, one of Lehman's aides had admitted to a Washington reporter that the Gaynor campaign was far more potent than anyone had foreseen.

Her smile widened as she gazed out over the cheering crowd. All of this was thanks to Trent Tucker. As they leaned against each other, she broke her hand from his and slipped her arm around him. She wanted him . . . desperately.

DARIEN, CONNECTICUT

"Jesus," Rockwell muttered to himself as he watched the raucous video clip of Angela Gaynor's rally, which had just concluded. "Chuck Lehman better be worried."

The message attached to the clip read: *some polls have her down by just six points.*

Rockwell shook his head as he moved away from the clip and began roaming the Internet again. His instincts had been exactly right. He'd found one of the Grays on the Department of Homeland Security website. Again, the man was a senior staffer, just like the man at NSA who Rockwell had found by doing this same thing.

Now he was looking for the third man—and it didn't take long to find him. The third Gray was CIA—at the very top of the pyramid there—exactly as Rockwell had anticipated. Rockwell was doing this just from memory, but the face on the screen was too familiar to mistake. It was the same man whose hand Rockwell had shaken immediately after the blindfold had come off in the Maine cabin.

He reached for his small, black, leather-bound datebook, which was lying beside the computer, and wrote down the man's name beneath the name of the man from DHS, whose name was immediately below the name of the man from the NSA.

Now he needed to find that fourth man.

As he began to search, his phone rang. "Yes?"

"We believe we have success," the voice spoke up quietly. "The message you wished to convey should be conveyed later this afternoon. All has been arranged."

"Excellent," Rockwell whispered, "excellent."

"What about the money?"

"I'll have all hundred thousand to you by COB today. And by the way," Rockwell spoke up as he thought about how ecstatic the other Grays, one in particular, would be when he related the news, "there will be more, much more."

"Better be."

WASHINGTON, DC (GEORGETOWN)

"Can she beat you?"

Chuck Lehman glanced over at Martha. He'd been gazing into the full-length mirror of their bedroom in the four-story Georgetown town house in which they stayed while the Senate was in session. They were attending a reception this afternoon at the French Embassy. Then it was on to a formal White House dinner for the president of France later tonight.

He'd been admiring himself in his tuxedo. Now he was admiring Martha. She looked delicious in her lacy, short slip and high heels.

Lehman had wandered into the adultery swamp a few times in the early days. He and Martha had been married when they were both twenty-two, only a few months after they'd both graduated from the University of Virginia, but before he'd finished sowing his oats.

But he hadn't strayed since those early days, and not once in Washington despite the almost daily invitations from younger women who were drawn to his undeniably dashing good looks and immense power. He was almost as proud of his record of being faithful as he was of being senate majority leader.

Martha had delivered two perfect sons to him. Both were handsome, spitting images of him. Paul would graduate from Princeton in May and go to Wall Street, while Peter was a sophomore at Harvard. She worked tirelessly at several charities, in Washington and Richmond. She only ever had one drink at any function and spoke four languages, so foreign dignitaries were routinely enthralled with her. Through the years she could have had her own affairs with powerful people from around the world. But, according to the CIA and the FBI, she never had. She had classic beauty, the gentleness of an angel, the poise of a president, and the heart of a lioness.

She was the perfect political wife.

"What did you say?" he finally asked in a distracted tone so she understood how much he was still attracted to her.

"Can Angela Gaynor beat you?"

"Don't be ridiculous."

"I saw a poll today that claimed she'd cut your lead to single digits."

"She's getting a bang out of something new. We've seen it before. We'll see it again. It won't last."

"The basketball player seems to be helping her quite a bit."

Lehman glanced back into the mirror. Looking in the mirror pleased him. Hearing about Angela Gaynor and Trent Tucker did not. "This country's obsessed with sports," he muttered. "It'll end up being our downfall."

"Maybe you should counter Trent Tucker with a sports celebrity of your own."

Lehman straightened his black bow tie, then moved to where she stood and slipped his arms around her slender frame. "Then I'd look like I was imitating her. I'd give her credibility by doing that. As the senate majority leader, I shouldn't be derivative of anyone."

"I don't like this woman gaining on you," Martha admitted. "It makes me nervous. You've worked hard to get where you are. I don't want to see a fickle and mostly uninformed public make a big mistake."

He kissed her gently on the forehead. "I love you."

"I love you, too, Chuck."

"Don't worry. I've got this all taken care of."

"Do you? Do you *really*?"

He grinned as he stared into her flashing eyes. "I've never seen you like this before."

"I've never felt like this before. If she beats you, well, that would be unthinkable. It would ruin your chances for the White House, and I want you to be president, Chuck. More importantly, you deserve to be president. Even more importantly, the *country* deserves it."

"Thank you, sweetheart."

This time she kissed him. "I like being a guest at White House parties." She smiled. "But at some point in the near future I want to host them."

Oh, yes, she was the perfect political wife.

BLACKSBURG, VIRGINIA

Angela tumbled down onto the mattress from atop Trent and eased back onto the pillows. Her heart was still going a million miles an hour. She'd never felt anything like that in her life.

"That was incredible." She could barely breathe. "Where am I?"

He chuckled as he pulled her onto his broad chest, then pulled the covers up over both of them.

"I'm assuming from your reaction you've heard that before."

"Once or twice," he admitted, caressing her shoulder.

"I've been waiting twenty-five years for that," she admitted in a dreamy tone.

"I know."

"Well, you don't have to be so smug about—"

"So have I."

"Really? You're not just saying that, Trent?"

"I don't think I really knew it until that day we met on the beach. But I realized it then for sure. And I really did want to wait until the campaign was over. But after I saw you onstage today whipping ten thousand people into a frenzy, well I couldn't resist anymore. I had to have you." He glanced down at her as he caressed her shoulder. "You had every person in that arena in the palm of your hand, including me."

"I've never experienced anything like it," she admitted, then laughed when she realized what she'd just said. "Not until two minutes ago, anyway." She shook her head as she ran her fingernails across his chest. "I had the two most incredible experiences of my life in the same afternoon. That shouldn't happen to a girl. It's all downhill from here."

"No way. The day you're elected a United States senator and you take down Chuck Lehman will be even better. I guarantee it."

JURY TOWN

The cleaning woman glanced over her shoulder to make certain she was alone in Felicity West's room. All of Wing Three was closed off to jurors while they changed beds, vacuumed floors, and dusted—but at least ten other members of the cleaning staff were on the wing, and she couldn't chance being surprised by one of them. That could mean being fired, facing criminal charges, and, worst of all, losing out on ten thousand tax-free dollars.

Her fingers shook as she reached into her pocket, lifted the pillow of the freshly changed bed, and slipped the note between the mattress and the pillow.

Then she headed out, glad that they were keeping no official register of who had cleaned which room.

As she emerged from the room, she nearly ran into the guard who had been in charge of watching this cleaning shift. He seemed to take an extra-long, suspicious look at her.

Hopefully, she was just imagining things. Her heart was pounding so hard she could barely breathe.

CHAPTER 32

RICHMOND, VIRGINIA

Victoria sprinted down the long hospital corridor—past gurneys, wheelchairs, doctors, and nurses, with Dez on her heels.

She'd gotten the jarring call fifteen minutes ago out of the blue and bolted from her office in downtown Richmond immediately, without even grabbing her pocketbook, shrieking for Dez to get her to the hospital. Cameron's vital signs were quickly deteriorating.

Dez had driven the lead Escalade himself, with two subordinates inside and two more bulletproof black SUVs trailing.

Victoria raced into the hospital room, dodging a young nurse who tried to restrain her, and rushed to Cameron's side, sinking into the chair beside the bed and slipping her hand into his as he lay there on his back.

She was too late. His fingers were already cold. The bullet through his lung had ultimately killed him. The surgeons had been wrong.

"I'm sorry, Cam," she whispered as the first heavy sob wracked her body. "I owe you everything." Tears spilled down her cheeks in rivers. "I'll call your mom. I'll tell her . . . what a good son . . . what a *great* man you are . . . were."

Dez grimaced as he glanced away, then ushered the young nurse out and closed the door when sobs overwhelmed Victoria, and her forehead fell slowly to Cameron's pale hand.

After a few moments she rose up and hurried straight for him.

"Hold me, Dez," she begged, overwhelmed by how alone in the world—and scared—she was.

His strong arms comforted her, and she was reminded of how her father had held her in the parking lot the day he'd been released from Archer Prison.

"I'm getting your shirt wet," she murmured, pulling away. Dez's shirt smelled so good, unlike her father's. "I'm sorry."

"Stop it," he said sympathetically, easing her face gently back against his chest.

"I need to go somewhere," she whispered.

"Where?"

"Anywhere but here. Take me . . . please."

WASHINGTON, DC

"Rockwell's running all over the Internet to find us."

"Do you have track-and-trace on him?"

"I'm watching him as we speak. He's found three of us. His virtual fingerprints are everywhere."

"He cannot be allowed to find Walter Morgan."

"That would be very difficult for him to do . . . but, unfortunately . . . not impossible."

"I'm disappointed in Mr. Rockwell. I was hoping he'd be more satisfied to stay in his place and not go digging for things we cannot have him find. I was hoping the money would be enough and that we'd found a permanent solution in him."

"As we all were hoping. That's the reason I've gone straight to JD. Mr. Rockwell cannot be trusted. He's trying to insulate himself, trying to find ways to protect himself. I'm glad we decided to keep watching him."

"Yes, you were right. Time left?"

"A minute. I'll let you know as we close in. What do you have?"

"The information has been passed to Felicity West. It details what we know about her and, in no uncertain terms, what we'll do unless she votes to acquit Commonwealth Electric Power."

"How did it happen?"

"I'll give Rockwell this. He did a nice job of recruiting George Garrison, the head of the guards at Jury Town. Garrison had one of his thugs get to a cleaning woman. Of course, now that Garrison's taken a bribe, he's ours for good. We'll feed him a little along the way, for insurance, but he's in our pocket."

"Everyone has a price."

"Felicity West is still in the jury room; court's still in session. But she's in for a nasty surprise when she gets to her room."

"Angela Gaynor has a nasty surprise of her own approaching."

"If we can't manipulate juries, we'll manipulate the evidence."

"Exactly. Although, thanks to Garrison, it looks like we're back in business in Virginia."

"It didn't take long, and it's so much more dependable in the long run."

"Money talks, bullshit walks. That's the mantra."

"That's *always* the mantra."

They shared a harsh laugh.

"And Victoria Lewis?"

"She remains a top priority."

"Fifteen seconds."

"That's all I have. Good timing."

"Fight on."

"Yes, fight on, my brother."

JURY TOWN

"Hi, David."

Someone tapped Racine gently on the shoulder, and he glanced up from a delicious dinner of roasted chicken and dumplings—straight into Sofia Acosta's dazzling green eyes.

"May I sit with you?"

"Of course," he answered—a little too loudly, he chastised himself—and stood up to hold her chair out.

He'd arrived this afternoon and hadn't finished arranging his room on Wing Four when dinner was served. Tantalizing aromas had seeped into his room, and he was famished, so he'd left the rest of settling in for later. It felt surreal—and lonely—being locked inside these walls. It was only the first day, the first few *hours*, but he wasn't certain he'd ever become accustomed to it. Two years was going to seem like ten.

He'd been agonizing over whether Claire had made it to Los Angeles all right—she had a connecting flight. He'd dropped her off at the Richmond airport and then reported directly to Jury Town—and not knowing if she was okay was killing him. He wouldn't know if she'd arrived all right for two years. He was definitely hungry; however, he'd also been hoping dinner would distract him from her trip. But it hadn't.

Seeing Sofia did.

"It's nice to see a familiar face."

"You're telling me," she agreed. "I've been walking around like a zombie, not knowing anyone." She gestured toward the middle of the room as she put her tray down and sat in the chair he was holding. "Thank you." A hundred people or so were eating. "They all came to Jury Town together. It's been hard breaking in."

Racine grinned as he sat back down. "I don't imagine it's too hard for you to meet the men. The women I get, but not the men." He regretted the remark when a self-conscious expression clouded her face. "I meant that in a nice way. I meant no disrespect."

"I know," she said quietly. "It didn't occur to me when I ran into you that day that you'd be heading here, too."

"Well, here I am."

"Yes . . . here you are."

"Are you on a jury yet?" he asked.

"No. But we're starting a selection process tomorrow morning."

"Jury Room Nine?"

"Yes."

"I've been called to that one, too. That's an interesting little monitor on the desk, lots of information."

"Including Victoria's quote of the day and one thing at the bottom of the screen that I don't—"

"Hopefully, we'll be on that jury together," Racine interrupted gently.

"I'd like that."

Their relationship was in its infancy, but he could always tell when he'd made a connection with someone. He definitely had with Sofia. It was all in those glistening eyes.

She still had that dark halo of sadness to her, though the fear he'd noticed that day outside Victoria's office seemed to have eased. Maybe she still needed a strong shoulder. Victoria had offered him no details as to what she'd meant by the remark.

"It is difficult coming in after everyone else. I had a hard time making up my mind if I would. You?"

"Mine was a last-minute thing," Sofia answered. "I didn't go through quite the same process you did."

She seemed to be struggling with how much to say. Was her sadness connected to whatever personal reason had led her in here? "Look, um, you don't . . . you don't have to—"

Before he could fumble anymore, she cut in, her voice a whisper just loud enough for him to hear.

"See those two?" She nodded at a pair of women who'd just passed by, holding their dinner trays. "They're both on a jury involving Commonwealth Electric Power. I overheard one of them say that she can't wait to find CEP guilty because she's got a personal vendetta."

Racine glanced at the women who'd sat down a few tables away, his pulse ticking up. Victoria was savvy, obviously, but he hadn't expected to find the sorts of flaws in the system she was looking for so quickly. "Which one?"

Felicity smiled as she breezed into her room to change for the marathon round-robin pool tournament she, Kate, and Wilson were waging tonight. The room smelled fresh and clean. She loved it.

So far she loved everything about Jury Town. And then there was that four million dollars at the end of the rainbow. That would be the best thing of all.

Her smile widened as she headed for the bureau. She loved playing pool. She kept her arrogance controlled in front of others. But, deep down, she thrived on the attention she won for putting ball after ball into those pockets.

She laughed softly. She was going to start taking a dive tonight—a big one—to let Wilson win a chain of games and make him think he was better than he was, and that she wasn't nearly as good as she'd played the other night. She wanted to walk out of Jury Town in two years with more than four million dollars.

And Hal Wilson was the mark.

He was quiet, but intensely competitive beneath his unassuming surface. He thought men were naturally superior to women, though he would never say so, of course. And he believed himself a much better pool player than he really was.

He wasn't the type to ever have shown up at her door to be dominated, just the opposite, in fact—which made him the perfect kind of man to take money from on the pool table. She'd play this out for two years, but in the end work Wilson for at least ten grand.

She was about to pull the flashy top she'd chosen out of the drawer when she noticed what looked like the corner of a piece of paper sticking out from beneath her pillow.

She moved slowly to the bed, slid the paper out from its hiding place, and read. Halfway through it she eased onto the bed as the words on the page blurred before her.

Suddenly she hated Jury Town.

DARIEN, CONNECTICUT

Rockwell glanced away from the computer monitor in his Connecticut study to his phone when it rang shrilly. "Hello."

"Hello, Mr. Rockwell."

"Jesus," he hissed, "why are you using names?"

"What's the problem?" the Gray asked calmly. "Are you worried someone might be trying to find you?"

That sounded strange, Rockwell thought. Maybe it was because he'd been hard at work on the Internet again, trying to find the fourth Gray, when the call had interrupted him.

"No."

"Don't worry," the man said confidently. "For the next ninety seconds, we're on a secure line."

"Oh," Rockwell muttered, relieved. Of course, it made sense given that this man was so senior at NSA. Still, the remark had unnerved him.

"Is the intruder ready?" the Gray asked.

"Yes."

"Everything prepared?"

"Yes."

"Then she may fire at will."

As Rockwell hung up, he heard a shuffling sound in the hallway outside his study—strange because he was the only one there.

He stood up quickly, grabbed his pistol from a credenza drawer, and hurried for the door. He hesitated a moment, then burst into the hallway, swinging the gun quickly in both directions.

"Good Lord," he whispered as he lowered the gun, and his shoulders sagged when he spotted his black Lab. "I thought you were outside, Drexel."

JURY TOWN

Racine remained in the hallway after Sofia unlocked the door to her room and moved inside. He'd enjoyed her company so much at dinner, he wasn't looking forward to being alone again, but he didn't want to push this. "It was great seeing you," he called.

"Are you leaving?" she asked, disappointed. She tossed her keys on the desk and turned back to face him.

"I guess."

"You don't have to be anywhere until nine o'clock tomorrow morning. Why are you leaving me?"

"Well, I—"

"Don't be rude. Come in."

"I like what you've done with the place," he offered, sitting in the desk chair.

"You're funny, too. I like that."

"Funny?"

"It's a refurbished prison cell," she said, sitting on the bed after closing the door. "There's only so much a girl can do with it."

"Well, it looks a lot better than mine."

"So . . . I'm sorry I dodged your question while we were eating."

He wanted to ask Sofia what she meant by funny, *too*, but held back. "Which question?"

"How I got here."

"I didn't mean to pry."

She took a deep breath, then put a hand on her chest, emotion catching up. "Sorry."

"Are you okay?"

She took several seconds to answer. "My husband was murdered. That's why I'm here."

"My God," Racine murmured.

"Raul was head of security for the Virginia Supreme Court."

"I read about that, about him. It happened close to where I live. That was *your* husband?"

She nodded. "Chief Justice Eldridge felt very guilty about it. He arranged for me to come here so I could . . ."

"Earn the money," Racine finished. "I get it."

"It's a lot of money, but now I won't see my kids for two years."

"I get that, too," he said quietly. "I'm in the same boat with my daughter. I put her on a plane to Los Angeles earlier today. I don't even know if she got there safely."

"Los Angeles?"

"Her mother and I are separated. Tess moved to Los Angeles, so Claire will live with her."

"How old is Claire?"

"Fourteen. How old are your children?" he asked.

"Daniel is ten and . . . Maria, my baby, is eight." Sofia shook her head hard. "This conversation's too real. Let's talk about something else, okay?"

Racine nodded. "Sure."

"What should we—"

"What's the name of the woman who's on the Commonwealth trial? The woman with the vendetta you pointed out earlier."

PYONGYANG, NORTH KOREA

The young woman had been probing the company's firewall all night from her laptop, testing spots that would be easy to penetrate. And, equally important, spots that would leave no trace of her crime after she'd dropped her bomb on the network, no electronic footprints that would be discernible.

A smug smile creased her face when she finally located what she'd been searching for. In a few seconds, she'd be into the network, able to travel around—and leave—like a ghost through an old castle. With no one ever knowing she'd been there.

This castle was Gaynor Construction, Inc.

Her eyes narrowed as she finished her work. Leaving *zero* footprints was impossible. But, like tracks in old snow covered by a fresh blizzard, the electronic trail she'd just created was all but invisible. Only a handful of people in the world were skilled enough to detect her work at this point.

The woman who'd just been hacked would have no idea who those people were—nor would the lawyers she was about to need.

RICHMOND, VIRGINIA

Dez sat down on the edge of the bed beside Victoria. He'd nixed her return to her secluded house in the country and was having her stay in a guest bedroom of the place he'd rented in Richmond. This house was surrounded by his crew 24/7. If someone tried to kill her here, they'd need an army.

"You okay?" he asked softly.

"I'm responsible for Cameron's death," she murmured. "I might as well have killed him myself."

"That's ridiculous," Dez said firmly, shaking his head, "you are not responsible."

"He was my best friend."

"We all lose good friends in fights like these. That's just the way it goes." He pulled her gently to her feet, drew the covers down, guided her back down onto the mattress, and then pulled the covers up over her. "Get some sleep. I'll see you in the morning."

"Dez," she called when he reached the door.

"Yeah?"

"Will you stay with me a little longer? Just talk to me."

"What about?"

"I really don't care. I don't want to cry alone."

CHAPTER 33

RICHMOND, VIRGINIA

"Mitch?"

Mitch froze at the sound of Eldridge's voice. He'd scoured his uncle's Supreme Court office for several minutes—desktop, cabinets, and credenzas—before finally locating the file he'd been seeking. The file covering the real estate case he intended on seducing Salvatore Celino with.

"What are you doing?"

Mitch glanced up calmly. "I wanted to review that wetlands appeal," he answered in his most convincing, all-business tone, "the one involving the thousand acres beside the James, a few miles downriver from here. I want to make sure I've studied it thoroughly so the staff can prepare the best brief possible."

The chief justice glanced at his watch. "I appreciate your commitment, Mitch, but it's almost nine o'clock, and the date for that case is still a ways off." He moved to the desk, opened the top drawer with a key, and removed an envelope. "I was having dinner in the city tonight, and I almost forgot this," he said, holding up the envelope as he relocked the drawer. He pointed at the file Mitch was reviewing. "Make sure you put that back in the credenza where you found it, and make certain it's locked. Anybody gets a look at that thing, they could make a lot of money fast, based on the notes I've made." The old man put his hand on Mitch's shoulder and smiled wanly. "I implore you to take time for your children, son, even if you aren't so fond of your wife. Life goes by very, very fast. Not giving enough attention to my children is my one regret."

"Uncle Dan," Mitch spoke up as Eldridge turned away. He just wished not spending more time with his kids was his only regret in life.

"Yes?"

Speaking of life, it would never be the same after this—not for him. For a moment he considered making another lame excuse. He could still turn back. There was still time. "I didn't stay late tonight to study this file."

Eldridge's brows knitted together suspiciously. "What are you saying, Mitch?"

The guilt was too much. He couldn't live with it anymore. "I stayed late to copy it." There was no going back now.

"What? Why?"

"We need to talk."

JURY TOWN

Racine eased down into the desk chair in his room and stared at the screen embedded into the desktop. Dinner tomorrow night would be New York strip steaks and baked potatoes with green beans—or a baked-in-butter halibut. And, of course, there was always an option for the health nuts: a Caesar salad with grilled chicken, even some anchovies if you really wanted them.

His upper lip curled at the thought of anchovies, then he broke into a grin as he scrolled down to Victoria's quote of the day: "Everything you can imagine is real."

"Thank you, Pablo Picasso," Racine murmured as he continued down to the bottom of the day's data—the small, seemingly innocuous string of numbers and letters he assumed Sofia had been referring to when she'd mentioned the one thing at the bottom of the screen she didn't get.

He pulled out a small piece of paper from his shirt pocket and matched the string to what was on the paper. "I just hope I'm in time," he muttered, glancing at the red emergency button every room also had.

The button blurred before Racine as he leaned back in the chair. He wondered what Sofia was doing. He smiled. She'd asked him to knock on her door anytime. He was tempted to take her up on that, even though they'd only said good-bye a few minutes ago.

His smile faded. He wondered if Claire was okay. This was hell.

RICHMOND, VIRGINIA

"I've been doing a bad thing," Mitch spoke up, taking a deep breath. He wondered if his uncle would have him arrested immediately. There might be an alternative that would enable him to right a great wrong—at least start to. "I've been providing confidential information about the Supreme Court to a man I know is a member of a New York City crime family operating in the southeast. Information related to Project Archer, to Jury Town."

"Mitch."

Eldridge's voice sounded as though he'd just received news he had cancer—and two weeks to live.

Mitch's lower lip trembled. "This is not an excuse, Uncle Dan. It's an explanation."

"I'd wondered why you hadn't installed the camera."

"I'm in debt up to my neck, Uncle Dan, even with the money the mob's paid me for the information. I'm . . . I'm sorry."

"You'll turn yourself in."

There was his answer. "I think I know what the mob's doing with the information. It was something you said the other day, Your Honor."

"What?"

"I think they're turning around and selling it to someone or some group, for a profit, of course. Potentially the people who've been—"

"Manipulating my juries."

Mitch hadn't heard that southern drawl of his uncle's so animated in years. The white whale had been sighted off the starboard bow. "I've reviewed a number of the cases you identified as having strange verdicts. I can't see how the mob would have benefitted directly, in some for sure, but not many." He hesitated. "I have a plan."

"Talk to me," Eldridge demanded breathlessly.

When Mitch was finished, Eldridge stared at him for a long time. "There's a man you need to speak to. His name is Dez Braxton. But I need to speak to Victoria Lewis first."

CHAPTER 34

JURY TOWN

"Are you ready for this?" Kate asked. "I know *I am*," she spoke up again quickly when Felicity didn't say anything. "I can't wait to nail these people."

Felicity looked away as Kate sat down beside her at the table in the Central Zone with her breakfast tray full of scrambled eggs, bacon, hash browns, and toast. She'd already grown tired of Kate. The woman smacked her lips obnoxiously the whole time she ate. And she *never* stopped talking about screwing Commonwealth Electric.

"I guess," Felicity answered, pushing her half-finished bowl of grapes and strawberries away. As soon as she'd finished reading the note hidden beneath her pillow—which detailed all the sins that would have her excommunicated from Jury Town . . . if she voted guilty—she'd ripped it up and flushed it down the toilet.

"I'm thinking the defense will rest at some point this afternoon," Kate said, "and, when they do, we're going to take ten seconds to convict Commonwealth. Then we'll take another ten seconds to set damages at a billion dollars, at *least*. Then we'll celebrate. We'll be the first jury to render a decision. And we'll nail these executive suits to the wall while we do it. Two birds with one big stone, and it's gonna be awesome."

"Uh-huh."

"What's wrong?" Kate demanded, munching on a strip of crisp bacon. "You actually lost a few games of pool last night, you didn't want to party afterwards, and you're grumpy this morning. What's up?"

"Nothing."

"Come on, tell me."

"Stop."

"Are you switching sides on me?" Kate asked suspiciously.

"What are you talking about?"

"You told me you had no doubt about Commonwealth being guilty of dumping that coal ash in the river. You told me you had no doubt the senior executives knew all about it, even the CEO. You told me they were all guilty." Kate pointed at Felicity with what remained of the bacon. "But all of a sudden, I'm not getting the warm and fuzzies."

Felicity shook her head. "It's almost like you're getting a kickback if there is a big settlement."

"What's that supposed to mean?" Kate snapped.

"Take it however you want to take it," Felicity retorted as she stood up. She was voting innocent no matter what. She had no choice after reading that note. Kate might as well get an inkling of what was on the way. Commonwealth Electric would not be found guilty—not on this go-round, anyway. "See you in the jury room," Felicity muttered as she stalked off.

"Hey. *Hey!*"

———————

Fifty seconds after Racine pressed the emergency button on the desk, three guards burst into his room.

"What is it?" one of the uniformed men demanded gruffly as he knelt down. "What hurts?"

"My stomach," Racine gasped, glancing up from his coiled-tight, fetal position on the small Oriental rug he'd brought from home. One of the other two guards was filming everything. "My gut feels like it's gonna burst."

Three minutes later they eased Racine gently down on a small, uncomfortable infirmary bed.

"The doctor will be right in," the guard who'd knelt down next to him in the room advised.

"Tell him to hurry," Racine groaned.

When the guards were gone, he kept the act going, kept his knees to his chest, concerned he might be on camera.

"David."

Racine's gaze shot toward a closing door and a silhouette standing before it. "Victoria?" he asked, sitting up. The string at the bottom of the jurors' screens was a code detailing when she would physically be present in her office at Jury Town—so she could meet him this way when he ignited his emergency button, which she was immediately alerted to. Apparently, he wasn't too bad at deciphering.

She moved out of the shadows. "What do you have for me?"

"Are you all right?" A deep sadness was etched into Victoria's expression. It reminded him of the dark halo he'd noticed about Sofia that day outside Victoria's office.

"Cameron died."

"I'm sorry," he said as he rose from the mattress. "What happened?"

"What do you have for me, David?" she asked deliberately. "We don't have much time. The doctor will be in here momentarily."

"But—"

"We must keep up appearances. Tell him you think you ate something bad. Now, *what* do you have?"

"A woman named Kate Wang on the Commonwealth Electric Power jury has an agenda. Apparently, she knows people in Abingdon. She'll vote guilty no matter what."

Victoria shook her head. "I was afraid of this on the first few cases.

Thank you, David," she called over her shoulder, moving back toward the door through which she'd just emerged. "Don't hesitate to do this again."

"Hey," he called back, "we still have our deal, *right*?"

———————

Dez leaned into Victoria's office at Jury Town. She'd just made it back from seeing Racine. "Yes?"

"Rex Conrad to see you. He's one of the guards."

Her eyes narrowed. The name didn't ring a bell. The guards were George Garrison's purview. Why was this man coming to her? "Okay."

"I'll be right outside if you need me."

"Thanks, Dez." She nodded at the clean-cut young man who entered her office wearing his Jury Town uniform. "Good morning, Mr. Conrad. Please sit down."

Conrad placed his guard hat down on her desk but didn't sit. "Good morning, Ms. Lewis."

"What can I do for you, Mr. Conrad? She was exhausted. She'd finally fallen asleep at two o'clock this morning with her head on Dez's shoulder. But it had been a fitful rest, punctuated by a sequence of nightmares in which she couldn't save Cameron's life. "Why me? Why not George Garrison?"

"I'm not sure I trust Mr. Garrison with this. I felt it was necessary to go outside the chain of command. It occurred to me Mr. Garrison might have . . . an interest."

Victoria's eyes raced to Conrad's. Suddenly she was wide-awake. "What are you talking about?"

"I observed another one of the guards approach a member of the cleaning staff in one of the satellite parking lots," Conrad explained. "That guard is a guy named Billy Batts. I also observed him approach a kitchen worker. I thought you should know. I admire you very much, Ms. Lewis. Even when you were governor, I always thought you were honest."

WASHINGTON, DC (GEORGETOWN)

"I just heard a very disturbing sound bite." Martha pointed at a small TV on the opposite counter as Chuck strode into the kitchen of their Georgetown home.

"What was that?" he asked, opening the refrigerator.

"Angela Gaynor has pulled even with you."

"I heard that, too," he said, reaching for the orange juice.

As if, Martha mused, she was telling him about tomorrow's weather, but he had no plans to go outside. As if he couldn't care less about what should have been shocking data.

"And it doesn't bother you, Chuck?" She watched as he pulled a glass from the cupboard and poured.

"We'll be fine." He smiled and nodded at the now-full glass of OJ. "Want some?"

She shook her head in amazement. He never lost his cool, even under immense pressure. She loved that about him. But was he misguided in this case?

"I hope you're right about being fine. I want to live in the White House."

He chuckled. "I know you do, Martha. Don't—"

"I'm not sure you really do," she snapped. "I haven't waited all this time to see you end up being beaten by some upstart." She didn't care that he was suddenly looking at her like someone he'd never met. All she cared about was that he understood how she wanted this as badly as he did. If he lost this election, there would go the White House. *"Do you understand me?"*

"Don't worry," he assured her, still gazing at her with uncertainty. "Someday you'll be sending out Christmas cards with a return address of 1600 Pennsylvania Avenue. I promise."

As if he knew something he wasn't telling her. He'd better.

JURY TOWN

As Victoria hurried out of her office, she nearly ran headlong into George Garrison coming out of his. "Good morning, George."

"What was Rex Conrad doing in your office?" Garrison demanded, glancing at Dez before blocking Victoria's path down the admin wing.

"I'm sorry?"

"I just saw Rex Conrad exit your office. What was he doing in there?"

"Speaking to me."

"Well, I'm head of the guards—"

"I'm aware of that, George," she said, moving past him.

"Wait just a minute," he hissed, catching her by the elbow. "We need to have a chain of command here. We need to—"

"Get your hand off her," Dez ordered, stepping between Garrison and Victoria so Garrison had to relinquish his grip, "and don't ever do that again."

"Or *what*, you—"

An instant later, Garrison was flat against the cinder-block wall outside his office, both feet dangling a foot off the tile floor, gasping for air as Dez held him up with one arm and pressed the other to Garrison's throat.

"Or *that*, Mr. Garrison."

CHAPTER 35
JURY TOWN

"Watch yourselves in the back row," Hal Wilson called loudly to the other thirteen jurors—including the two alternates—as he reached for the button on the wall. "I'm going to lower you. You people in the front row, watch your heels and toes."

The defense team in the Commonwealth Electric trial had rested ten minutes ago, and after receiving instructions from the judge, Wilson wanted to get started. They could have taken a break, even waited until tomorrow morning to initiate deliberations. But, last night, as he'd been lying in bed tossing and turning, he'd finally bought into Kate Wang's hype about being the first jury to reach a decision at Jury Town.

One of the other trials going on inside the old Archer Prison walls was close to being completed, according to something he'd overheard at dinner last night. And he didn't want to give that jury a chance to catch up. Suddenly he wanted to be the first foreman to reach a verdict here. He'd never been noted as a leader for anything in his life, never even been close to being famous. This would be a nice middle-aged change.

"The first order of business," he said, returning to his seat in the back row, which had now descended so that it was level with the front, "is to find out where we stand. Let's do a quick anonymous vote with this scrap paper I'm going to pass—"

"They're guilty," Kate blurted before Wilson could finish. "We all know it. The only question is how much CEP has to pay. There's no need for a straw vote."

Wilson grinned nervously and held his hands out. He'd been anticipating this from Kate. But, no matter how accurately he'd anticipated, he still hated confrontation. "Easy, easy, Ms. Wang, let's just take the vote. Let's follow procedure."

"They're *not* guilty," Felicity called loudly from the far end of the jury box. "I say the executives are being framed. I say it's all the work of one disgruntled employee. It's the guy driving the front-end loader. And nothing's gonna change my mind."

"Ms. West," Wilson begged, "please let's not jump the gun here." He'd *not* been anticipating this from Felicity. "You and Ms. Wang will both have plenty of time to—"

"What's wrong with you?" Kate snapped at Felicity. "You were rock solid on them being guilty until yesterday. We certainly didn't see or hear any evidence yesterday or this morning that would have changed that. To think one guy dumped that ash on his own is *ridiculous*. Did someone get to you, Felicity?"

"Hey, hey!" Wilson shouted, shooting out of his chair. "That's enough of that, Ms. Wang. We'll have no accusations of that kind of—"

"No, Kate," Felicity shot back, "no one got to me. But I think that pot you smuggled in here to Jury Town must have gotten to you."

"You bitch!" Kate yelled shrilly.

"You're the bitch!" Felicity screamed back. "You're probably stoned right now!"

As Jury Room Seven turned chaotic, and other jurors scrambled to get between the two women, Wilson hustled for the emergency button on the wall beside the button he'd just pushed to lower the back row of the jury box.

Garrison hit redial again, trying desperately to reach Billy Batts. He had a very bad feeling about what Victoria and Rex Conrad had been discussing in her office. He hadn't liked her tone or that accusatory gleam in her eye when they'd nearly run into each other out in the corridor. Maybe he was just being paranoid, but he couldn't take the chance. He had to do *something*.

"*Damn it!*"

For the eighth time in the last thirty-five minutes, Garrison's call went directly to Batts' voice mail. The kid wasn't working today. He should have picked up immediately.

Garrison ran a hand through his thinning hair. If Victoria or Conrad or both somehow suspected Billy Batts of being involved in getting that note to Felicity West's room, and they could get Batts to confess what he'd done, Victoria wouldn't give a damn about bringing Batts up on charges. In fact, the first thing she'd do would be to give Batts full immunity so Batts would start singing about where everything had started.

Garrison took a deep, troubled breath. Then he'd be the next one to have immunity offered up. But that immunity might as well be a death sentence.

———

Clint Wolf grabbed the landline receiver of his office phone as soon as he saw the number of the extension flash on the screen. He'd been deep into writing the speech Victoria had asked him to give to the Virginia General Assembly in two weeks, and the last thing he needed was a distraction. He wasn't much of a writer, and he'd hated public speaking ever since he could remember.

But this was the control room calling. He had to pick up.

"What?" he growled.

"One of my guys was monitoring Jury Room Seven through the camera, and there was an incident."

Wolf checked the slate of trials on his computer. According to the screen, the foreman of the Commonwealth Electric trial in JR7 was a man named Hal Wilson. "Did Mr. Wilson push the emergency button?"

"Almost."

"But he didn't push it, did he?"

"No."

"Then what's the problem?"

"They just went to the deliberation phase, and two of the jurors got into it over the verdict right away."

"So?"

"While they were yelling at each other, one of the two jurors screamed at the other about smuggling marijuana into her room here at JT."

"Christ," Wolf hissed to himself. Prisons would be such wonderful places without prisoners. "Which one supposedly has the stash?"

"Kate Wang."

Wolf tapped his keyboard and brought her file up on his screen, topped by her smiling-sweetly photograph. "I'll take care of it," Wolf muttered.

"Yes, sir."

"And no word of this to *anyone*."

"No, sir."

Wolf hung up and speed-dialed Garrison, whose office was three doors down the corridor.

"What's up, Clint?" Garrison asked.

"I need a dog."

"Why?"

"Just get one," Wolf ordered sternly, checking Kate Wang's room number on her file. "Organize a camera crew, too. You and I are going to Wing Three in five minutes. And I want it documented so there are no questions later about what happened while we were inside juror quarters. Five minutes, George."

CHARLOTTESVILLE, VIRGINIA

"Open up!" Dez called loudly as he banged hard on the front door of the run-down little house with brown clapboard siding. He had one of his security team watching the back door so no one could get out that way. "Open up!"

"Break the door down," Victoria called from the backseat window of the second Escalade. "Hurry."

"You sure?"

"This is the address," she answered, checking a piece of paper she was holding. "This is where the woman on the Jury Town cleaning staff lives. We have to get to her *now,* before someone else does."

He pulled his pistol from the holster at the small of his back, took one step away from the door, kicked the lock in, and headed inside with his gun leading the way.

Moments later he found the older woman sprawled on the floor of the upstairs bathroom, a deep, bloody gash across her forehead. He pressed two fingers to her neck as he crouched down over her. Dead.

He glanced into the tub. It was full of water. And there was blood on one corner of the sink. "Must have slipped getting out of the tub and smashed her head," he muttered to himself.

Dez smiled sadly at the silver fawn pug, which had been sitting beside the woman's body when he'd entered the bathroom. "Sorry, pal, but it looks like you're coming with me."

He rushed back down to the front door, and waved to Victoria, who, accompanied by three others of the crew, sprinted inside and up the stairs to the bathroom.

She winced. Another dead body.

"Looks like she slipped getting out of the tub," Dez said.

Victoria shook her head. "Don't bet on it. Let's go."

CHARLOTTESVILLE, VIRGINIA

Conrad's first clue to something amiss was the slightly ajar front door of Billy Batts' fifth-floor apartment. The second was the shattered window at the far end of the short, carpeted hallway leading away from the door.

Gun drawn, Conrad entered the apartment cautiously, followed by a state policeman who also had his gun out.

Conrad had not met Batts, only observed through binoculars the young guard approach the kitchen worker and then the cleaning lady in the Jury Town parking lot.

"Stay by the door," Conrad called over his shoulder quietly to the state trooper before moving slowly down the hallway. He glanced into the kitchen and the apartment's lone bedroom—which was a wreck—before reaching the broken window.

Sprawled out on the pavement five stories below was a twisted body, blood trails seeping in several different directions out and away from the man's mangled face.

———

JD drank a Coke from a large cup as he watched a guard and a state trooper enter Billy Batts' apartment. All was perfect in his world, he thought happily.

An hour ago, he'd surprised the cleaning woman in the living room of the little house her late husband had left her when he'd died two years ago. In a strange way, the cheap furnishings and decorations had reminded JD of the trailer he'd grown up in outside Macon, Georgia.

He'd smashed the old woman's head with a crowbar and then created the scene in the bathroom after cleaning up the blood in the living room. The crime scene investigators would probably determine, in the end, that it hadn't been an accident, but it didn't really matter.

One down and one to go, JD had driven here, smashed Billy Batts' head in with the same crowbar after surprising him, and then tossed him out the window.

Again, the CSI experts would probably determine that not all of Batts' wounds were a result of his impact with the pavement five stories below the window. But, again, it didn't really matter. He hadn't shot either of them, and he'd left no fingerprints. There was nothing that could link him to the murders if, in the unlikely event, the cases ever went to trial.

He slipped the silver Charger into gear and pulled away down the street.

CHAPTER 36
JURY TOWN

"What's the meaning of this?" Kate demanded angrily as two large guards escorted her down the administration corridor. She yanked her arm away defiantly when one of them tried grabbing her by the elbow.

"In there," the other one muttered, pointing at the open conference-room door, then to the lone chair on the opposite side of the table from Victoria Lewis and Clint Wolf.

"Why in the hell am I here?" Kate asked, hoping the utter desperation she was feeling didn't show on her face. Goddamn Felicity. "What's this all about?" she demanded defiantly.

When the guard was gone and the door closed, Wolf reached into his jacket pocket and tossed a small cellophane bag onto the table between them. It contained the joints Kate had been hiding in the Band-Aid box.

"That was found in your room, Ms. Wang," Victoria explained, pointing at the bag, "hidden in your closet."

"It's not mine," Kate protested. "I don't know anything about it."

"We videoed the search of your room," Wolf explained. "The dog is trained to smell drugs, and it scented to the marijuana very quickly. We took fingerprints from that bag and the box it was hidden in. We have your fingerprints on file, and I'm sure we'll find the ones on the bag and the box match to the ones on file . . . if we really need to."

"You went in my room," Kate said in a hushed voice, *"without my permission?"*

"Don't even try that," Victoria volleyed back, leaning over the table. "The contract you signed with me empowers me to search your room at any time. You know that."

"The weed was obviously planted in my closet by someone."

"The contract also empowers me to go after you criminally if I determine that you lied to me in any way during the application process or during juror interviews."

"I never lied," Kate retorted.

"I'm betting if I dug deep enough, I'd find you to have a very personal connection to Abingdon, Virginia. And that you are *not* objective when it comes to Commonwealth Electric Power. I've got a witness who will testify to that, too."

"Yeah, well, she's—"

"It isn't Felicity. You have no idea who it is."

"You're bluffing."

"Try me."

Kate's lower lip trembled. "Please don't kick me out of here."

"You've given me no choice."

Kate's chin fell as the outcome turned inevitable. As the possibility of earning four million dollars and traveling the world to find a husband evaporated. "Are you going to—"

"I want your signature," Victoria interrupted, sliding a single piece of paper and a pen across the table. "It states that you permanently and irrevocably forfeit and forego any and all claims to financial compensation from Project Archer. It states that you will never take any legal action against Project Archer or any of its directors or employees. Finally, it states that you will never speak to anyone, including members of the media, regarding your time inside these walls. If you do, I can throw the book at you in criminal and civil court. In exchange for your signature on that piece of paper, I won't turn you over to local authorities to face prosecution on a marijuana-possession charge. And I won't charge you with breaking several sections of your contract with me. No harm, no foul, and we're even. That's how I'm looking at this, Ms. Wang."

Kate stared at Victoria intently for several moments, then reached for the pen and signed on the bottom line, without bothering to read the language. What was she going to do now? Go back to teaching high school, this time in an even more remote location?

"Print your name beneath your signature," Victoria ordered.

When Kate was finished, she put the pen down, hung her head, and sobbed. Her world had just disintegrated.

"Do you think Felicity West was influenced?" Victoria asked as she reached for the executed agreement. "Do you think someone got to her regarding the Commonwealth Electric trial?"

"What, is this a goddamn test?" Kate murmured as tears trickled down her cheeks and onto her blouse. "I can't talk, remember?"

Victoria exhaled a frustrated breath. "Get out of here. Someone will take you back to Richmond. We'll have the contents of your room shipped to you in a few days. Good-bye, Ms. Wang."

Wolf eased back in his chair when Kate was gone. "That young woman just lost four million dollars so she could smoke a few sticks of marijuana. I'll never understand the human race."

Victoria gazed at the doorway Kate Wang had just exited through. What would Clint Wolf think of the human race if he knew everything about the woman sitting immediately to his right . . . and her cocaine habit? Not everything was as black-and-white as Wolf wanted. Maybe that many years in the Federal Bureau of Prisons had completely polarized him. Live long enough and shades of gray haunted every moment. That was more the reality, Victoria believed—for everyone.

She shook her head. She still couldn't fathom that Cameron was gone. It hurt so badly. Thank God for Dez. She'd been so wildly tempted to seek refuge in a cocaine haze, but Dez had short-circuited that awful possibility—though he had no idea.

At least, she assumed he had no idea. Knowing her as well as he did now, maybe she shouldn't be so sure.

Wolf chuckled. "You did a nice job bluffing Ms. Wang on your supposed witness."

"I wasn't bluffing, Clint."

She knew she shouldn't enjoy the look of shock on his face, but she did.

"Oh," he spoke up. "Well, maybe it's time I ask you about David Racine's emergency."

Now it was Wolf who seemed to be enjoying himself.

"What's happening?" Felicity demanded as the two guards escorted her down the administration corridor toward the executive offices.

"In there." One of the guards pointed at the open conference-room door, then to the lone chair on the opposite side of the table from Victoria Lewis and Clint Wolf.

"This is ridiculous," she muttered as she sat.

"Were you approached about voting a certain way on the Commonwealth Electric trial?" Victoria asked.

Felicity hadn't liked Victoria when she was governor, and she liked her even less now. "Approached?"

"Don't do that, Ms. West. This is as serious as it gets."

Felicity crossed her arms over her chest. "I don't know *what* you're talking about."

Victoria's eyes narrowed. "I'm *now* aware of certain matters you didn't tell me about yourself when you were offered the opportunity to participate in Jury Town, matters that would have precluded your involvement here, matters that could land you in some very deep trouble if I choose to follow through."

Felicity started to argue, but that seemed pointless. They obviously had her dead to rights. "What do you want?" she whispered.

Victoria slid a one-page agreement across the table. "Read that, print your name beneath the signature line, and sign it."

Felicity grimaced when she got to the middle of the page. "I have to give up *everything?*"

"You lied to me." Victoria paused, then smiled.

Felicity did not find that smile at all reassuring.

"But here's what I will do," Victoria continued. "I'll give you ten thousand dollars as a going-away present, if you tell me the truth. Were you approached on how to vote in the Commonwealth trial?" She wagged a finger. "Don't tempt me to prosecute you."

Felicity stared sullenly back for several moments, then finally nodded. "Yes," she admitted, almost inaudibly.

"How did they get to you?"

"The tooth fairy left a note under the pillow in my room."

Victoria shot a glance at Wolf, then looked back at Felicity. "Whoever it was wanted you to vote innocent?"

"Yes."

"Or they'd splay your skeletons all over Jury Town for me to see."

"Yes."

"All right. I'm going to add something to your going-away package, Felicity, because, in my humble opinion, you're going to need it very badly."

"What?"

Victoria gestured at Wolf. "For a number of years this man ran the Correctional Programs Division of the Federal Bureau of Prisons. In addition to managing over two hundred thousand federal inmates, he also ran something within CPD called the Federal Witness Security Program, aka WITSEC, aka the Federal Witness Protection Program." She leaned over the conference-room table. "I'm going to ask Mr. Wolf to help get you into that program because I don't want to read about you turning up dead somewhere on a lonely country road the victim of a hit-and-run. If my hunch is correct, without the program, you almost assuredly will."

The bottom suddenly dropped out of Felicity's world. Witness Protection? "Okay," she agreed hesitantly.

"Get out of here. And remember, that piece of paper you just signed absolutely prohibits you from discussing anything about your time inside these walls with anyone, including members of the media. Are we clear on that?"

"Yes, ma'am."

———

"Why do I feel like there's something very important going on here that I'm not privy to?" Wolf asked, when Felicity was gone.

Victoria was impressed—he hadn't asked her who her informant as to Kate's bias was or how she'd found out about Felicity's background. Maybe he was beginning to trust her, and not just because she paid him to.

"Because you're a smart man, Clint," she said, "and there is."

———

"I don't have time for this," George Garrison growled as he sat down on the opposite side of the conference-room table from Victoria and Wolf. "I've got way too much going on to waste time like this." He glanced at Wolf. "Come on, Clint. What is this?"

"I wouldn't worry about what else you have going on, George," Victoria said calmly. "What you need to worry about is the following. Billy Batts is dead."

Garrison's mouth fell slowly open. "What?" he whispered.

"Someone threw Billy out the window of his fifth-floor apartment in Charlottesville. We haven't actually proven that he was thrown yet. But I doubt it'll take the CSI people long to confirm that."

"My God."

"A woman named Melinda Jones has also died under very suspicious circumstances," Victoria continued. "It looked like she'd slipped in her bathroom while she was getting out of the tub. But we think she was slammed on the head with a blunt object, and her death was made to look like an accident."

"Who's Melinda Jones?"

"Ms. Jones *was* a member of the cleaning staff here at Jury Town . . . until she turned up dead."

Garrison's face went pale.

"You want to tell me anything about those two deaths?" Wolf spoke up angrily.

"Why would I know anything?" Garrison asked, running his hand nervously through his thinning hair as he stared at the floor between his feet.

"Because—"

"For starters," Victoria cut in, "you called Billy Batts eleven times in less than an hour. But he never answered."

"That doesn't mean I know anything about him being pushed out a window, for Christ's sake."

"Five minutes ago," Victoria continued, "I fired one of our jurors. Her name is Felicity West. Ring a bell?"

"No."

"She told me a very interesting story, George."

"Oh?"

"She found a note under her pillow in her room. That note threatened to reveal very personal and damaging information about her to me unless she voted 'not guilty' in the Commonwealth Electric trial currently being heard in Jury Room Seven. Ms. West was being extorted,

George. You know, do what we want, or lose four million dollars. Obviously, whoever was responsible for that note assumed I'd fire Ms. West as soon as I found out about her past."

"That's despicable on several counts, but what does it all have to do with me?"

"Melinda Jones was one of the cleaning staff on Wing Three the day Felicity West's room was cleaned. I think Ms. Jones was working for whoever was ultimately responsible for that note. I think Ms. Jones was the one who physically put that note under Felicity West's pillow, probably for a lot of cash, which she'll never get to use, if she ever actually even got it. And I think Billy Batts was the one who approached Ms. Jones about planting the note."

"Why Billy?"

"Billy was observed approaching a woman on the kitchen staff, and, later, approaching Ms. Jones."

"I still don't understand what any of this has to do with me."

"Billy Batts reported to you," Wolf hissed.

Garrison shrugged. "Still, I don't know how—"

"I trolled you," Victoria interrupted as Wolf grimaced and looked away, obviously frustrated at the man he'd personally hired to be head of the guards. "I wanted to see if you were loyal. And I wanted to see how fast someone might try to influence a jury."

"What do you mean, 'trolled' me?"

"I allowed eight people into Jury Town who could be vulnerable to influence," Victoria answered, "who I believed had backgrounds that potentially made them targets to those who would seek to manipulate verdicts inside these walls. But I didn't let on to those jurors that I knew about their pasts." She paused. "You aren't supposed to know the names of any of the jurors, George. Only Clint and I are to know the names of the people inside Jury Town. But I made certain you saw eight juror names in a folder I had someone 'accidentally' leave in your office. I wanted you to see those eight names. One of the juror names in that folder was Felicity West. Are you connecting the dots here?"

"No."

She leaned over the table toward Garrison as his eyes finally rose to meet hers. "You and I are the only ones inside these walls who saw the names on that list, the *only* ones. Let me translate, George." She forged ahead before Garrison or Wolf could say anything. "You are obviously part of the influence chain when it comes to Ms. West. I don't think it starts with you, but you're undoubtedly a crucial link." She pointed at him. "I want to know everything you know. And every second you hesitate to tell me, I'm going to have Judge Eldridge add another month to your sentence." Victoria tapped the table three times with her forefinger, jingling the pennies on her bracelet, as she glanced over at Wolf, who was looking at her the same way Judge Eldridge had been looking at her that day onstage at the Supreme Court Building—transfixed. Her gaze moved smoothly back to Garrison as the three pennies touched the table. "Let's go, George. You've already bought yourself another year. Pretty soon, I'll have you in there for life."

Garrison winced as he glanced at Wolf. "Help me, Clint, for old time's sake."

"Not on your life," Wolf replied firmly, "or mine."

CHAPTER 37

VIRGINIA BEACH, VIRGINIA

"Trent."

He opened his eyes slowly to a dark bedroom, so dark he wasn't convinced at first that he'd really opened them, that he was even actually awake. Perhaps Angela's far-off call had been part of a pleasant dream he'd been drifting through.

"Trent!"

The bedroom door burst open and light from the hallway streamed in. Not a dream.

"What's wrong, Angie?" he mumbled, lifting a hand to his face to keep from being temporarily blinded.

"I expected this at some point," she answered, seething. "I told myself it would probably happen. But it's still tough to take when you actually see it on the screen, when you see the words right there in front of you."

"What words?"

"Come and I'll show you," she said breathlessly. "Hurry."

"What time is it?"

"Ten after five." She stepped to the bed and grabbed his hand. "Come on."

"Easy, easy," he pleaded as she pulled.

After so many seasons of running up and down basketball courts a hundred times a game and banging for rebounds against other huge men, he needed time to get out of his specially made, eight-foot-long bed. He'd escaped the NBA without major injury. But his knees and back ached constantly from years of sprinting, jumping, and changing directions on a dime, and they always required a good stretch to limber up—especially at five in the morning.

"Sorry," Angela apologized. "It's just . . . I can't believe it."

He heard the tremble in her voice. "What's going on?" He swung his size-nineteen feet to the carpet. "And why are you always up so early? Don't you need sleep like the rest of us?"

She wasn't swayed by his attempt at levity. "This is serious, Trent. My name is all over the Internet. So is Gaynor Construction's. Not in good ways, either. I need you to look at this. I need my baby's help. *Now.*"

WASHINGTON, DC (GEORGETOWN)

"Is it in there?" her husband asked as he hustled into the kitchen of their Georgetown home, an expectant expression riding shotgun.

Martha glanced up at him over her reading glasses and nodded. "A major piece right on the front page of the *Washington Post.*" She tapped the headline. "Angela Gaynor's company allegedly bribed government officials in order to win projects all over the Tidewater. It says Gaynor Construction is accused of paying councilmen and women in Virginia Beach, Norfolk, and Hampton Roads hundreds of thousands of dollars to influence decisions on huge construction deals over the past two years." She shook her head incredulously. "It's one thing to see it on TMZ, but this is the *Washington Post.*"

Lehman squeezed her shoulder. He was more buoyant than he usually was before he'd had his OJ—but he wasn't surprised. He'd known something like this was going to happen. "It must be true if it's on the front page of the *Post,*" he agreed. "They want Angela Gaynor to beat me. You know they would have endorsed her outright now that we're a month off from the election." He smiled ear to ear. "Not now. Not even they could justify that now. It must have been so hard for them to print this story."

"The article doesn't link Gaynor directly to payoffs."

"Does it matter? In this day and age, she's guilty by association. There will be no stopping the social media express train at this point."

Martha raised a considering eyebrow. "The article goes to great lengths to explain that she hasn't been linked to any wrongdoing yet." She pointed at a paragraph halfway down the page. "It says here she stepped away from the day-to-day operation of the corporation when she entered local politics. They don't even say who at Gaynor Construction was responsible. They don't even name the people who were paid off."

Lehman sat down beside her. "Is anyone going to believe she didn't know exactly what was going on at the company she built from the ground up? I mean, her entire reputation is wrapped around her being Miss Hands On with everything she does." He looked over her shoulder. "Does the article reference who actually broke the story?"

"A local newspaper in Norfolk, I think," she said. She glanced over at him. "I'm still amazed at you, Chuck, even after all these years."

"Why?"

"Your confidence. That's what drew me to you the first time I saw you, even from across the room."

"You mean it wasn't just my fabulous looks?" he teased.

"You seemed to know something like this would happen to Gaynor. You kept telling me to wait and see. It's eerie how clairvoyant you are sometimes." She kissed him on the cheek. "I love you."

"Love you too, honey," he said, then pulled the paper across the table so it was in front of him. "She's finished," he muttered ecstatically as he focused on the article, "at least in this town. And she's getting what she deserved. Thinking she could challenge me."

"It's like you knew something," Martha whispered as she slipped her arm through his. "Did you?"

"Did I what?" he asked.

"Did you know something like this was going to happen to Angela Gaynor?"

VIRGINIA BEACH, VIRGINIA

"How could this twenty-three-year-old, wet-behind-the-ears punk reporter from the *Daily Press* get this kind of information?" Trent snapped angrily. He scanned the story on his laptop for the hundredth time today. He'd refused to let Angela leave his place and risk being mobbed by the press.

"Does it really matter?" Angela asked.

"You're damn right."

"Why?"

"It smells bad to me, *really* bad."

"What do you mean?"

"This kid had to get records somehow, right? Even some small-town editor isn't going to print a story like this without some kind of evidence. Somebody hacked into your system or broke into your offices."

She perched on the edge of the desk next to him, her restless hands revealing a nervousness he'd rarely seen her fall prey to. "I already told you. There's no record of anything like that. No alarms were triggered at the office. No video of anything. No firewalls breached as far as the company network is concerned. The reporter is claiming someone sent him the data anonymously."

"A whistleblower?"

"Yes."

"I don't believe it," Trent snapped, leaning forward to grab his phone off the coffee table. "It doesn't sit right. It's too coincidental."

"What do you mean?"

"It's too easy to connect the dots from this to your campaign."

"Who are you calling?"

"A guy I know at that paper."

"Trent, I don't think—"

"We're not rolling over on this, Angie. We've worked too hard to get where we have. We're too close to something very good to roll over. If there's one thing I learned playing all those basketball games, sometimes you have to attack. Offense starts with defense, but defense can't win games. I'm on it. The counterattack starts now."

"Social media will destroy me."

"Angie, you need to pick yourself up, dust yourself off, and get back at your campaign."

"What campaign?" she asked despondently.

JURY TOWN

"Have you reached a decision, Mr. Foreman?"

Hal Wilson rose from his seat in the jury box's back row—which he'd raised again for the verdict's announcement—then stepped down to the floor, and moved out in front of the rest of the jurors so he was directly in front of the camera. In his peripheral vision, he caught a quick view of himself on one of the four giant screens on the front wall, and glanced away immediately. He'd already gained five pounds inside these walls, and he hated how his paunch was becoming even more obvious.

"We have, Your Honor."

"What say you?"

Kate Wang and Felicity West had been removed from the jury. Wilson had gotten that message on the screen on the desk in his room. Apparently, they'd been removed from the facility altogether because neither he nor any of the other jurors had seen the women around at all, though no general announcement had been made. However, rumors were flying through Jury Town.

The only thing that mattered to Wilson right now was that their removal from the jury had made his job a great deal easier. He was disappointed that he wouldn't be able to take Felicity for money in pool, but this outcome was definitely for the best. And, thanks to the alternates who had been present every step of the way, the verdict had not been delayed nor a mistrial declared.

"In the first decision to be made here at Jury Town, we find Commonwealth Electric Power guilty as charged."

Through the speakers, Wilson could hear wild jubilation explode in the courtroom, and the judge hammering for silence with his gavel. He hoped Victoria Lewis was watching or would at least hear about his preamble to the verdict. He'd missed a movie last night to draft the little speech and then practiced it in front of the mirror in his room.

"All right," the judge called out loudly as the courtroom finally began to settle down, "now we go to the damages phase of the trial."

"We already have, Your Honor," Wilson spoke up. "We award the town of Abingdon, Virginia as well as Washington County one point two billion dollars."

Once again the courtroom erupted. This time the judge could do nothing to control the elation.

CHAPTER 38

VIRGINIA BEACH, VIRGINIA

"Stay strong, Angie, stay strong."

She let loose an exasperated sigh. "I'm trying. But it isn't easy."

She and Trent stood on the balcony of his condominium, overlooking the Atlantic. The day was crystal clear, and the sun's rays sparkled beautifully across the ocean's surface. She wished her mood matched the weather.

Trent shook his head. "Your CEO is really doing a number on you."

"I don't understand why Jack's saying these things. How can he possibly accuse me of knowing anything about bribes at Gaynor Construction?"

"The whole situation is insane," Trent agreed as he looked down, reading from the article he'd pulled up on his phone. "He's saying you ordered the payments. How can anyone believe him?"

"I had *no idea* Gaynor Construction was doing any of this. The criminal conduct stops with Jack Hoffman. I haven't been active in the business since I went into politics, since well before any of these alleged payments were made."

"This is a case of a CEO trying to cut his losses by implicating someone at the next level. And, since you're the only owner, you're the only one he can implicate. Hoffman's got a hungry young prosecutor all over him who's looking to make a name. Taking down a prominent local politician who's about to go big-time would do wonders for his career. So Hoffman figures if he can pull you into the conspiracy and testify against you for the prosecutor, maybe he can steer clear of prison."

She refused to give in to the tears lurking in her eyes. This whole thing was surreal. "How can they say they have e-mails showing I ordered the bribes? That's absurd. I'm being railroaded here," she said angrily. She snatched Trent's phone.

"Don't keep looking at the numbers," Trent advised, slowly letting his forehead fall to the railing.

"I can't help it. I can't stop myself." She held the phone up. "The latest *USA Today* poll has me down twelve points to Chuck Lehman. We were even with him, and now we're twelve points behind. *That fast.*"

Trent groaned. "All that work and all those possibilities, and now everything is destroyed."

"Hey," she said, touching his arm. "Hey!"

Trent lifted his head slightly off the railing and gazed up at her. "What?"

"Nothing's destroyed yet. Get your head up. *Right now!*"

He smiled grimly as he straightened to his full height. "*That's* the Angela Gaynor I know."

"I'm not gonna roll over and just take this thing, Trent. I'm not giving up this election, either. You're right. We've come too far."

Trent slipped his arms around her. "That's what I wanted to hear."

"Are you still with me?"

"Absolutely. I'll tell you what. I've got a—" A knock at the door interrupted him. "Who can that be?"

Angela followed him inside but peeled off toward the kitchen to get a drink when he headed for the door. As she reached for the refrigerator, she heard raised voices and hurried for the front door.

"There she is!" a young man wearing a plain, gray suit and a solid-blue tie called over his shoulder to someone Angela couldn't see. "I told you she was here!"

"What's going on, Trent?"

"Get back, Angie!"

"Stop right there, Ms. Gaynor!" the man in the gray suit yelled. "You're under arrest on suspicion of bribing multiple public officials."

"Don't come in here!" Trent warned the young man, who was trying to push his way past. He was a foot shorter and a hundred pounds lighter, and making no progress. "I'm warning you, son!"

Suddenly the doorway filled with uniformed policemen.

"On your knees!" one of the cops shouted. *"Now."*

As three policemen slammed Trent up against the wall, the man in the gray suit finally barged past. "Turn around and get your hands behind your back, Ms. Gaynor," he ordered, producing a pair of silver handcuffs from beneath his coat. "You have the right to remain silent. Anything you say can and will be used against you in a court of law."

"They're doing this just to ruin you in the election, Angie!" Trent yelled as the cops forced his arms behind his back. "That's all this is! You're innocent!"

"I know!" she called back. "I'm gonna get this to court right away. *Right away!*"

CHAPTER 39
JURY TOWN

"You got 'em, didn't you, Victoria?"

She glanced up at Wolf as he moved into her office. "Who do you mean?"

"George Garrison, Billy Batts, the cleaning woman, Felicity West. You tracked them all down. And in the nick of time, so you could pull Felicity from Jury Room Seven and get the verdict I'm sure you wanted in the Commonwealth Electric case."

Victoria put down the file she'd been reviewing. "I don't want any particular verdict here," she replied deliberately. "I want the *right* verdict, Clint. And it's bittersweet for me that two people died, even if they were involved in the conspiracy. It makes me hate whoever's at the end of the chain that right now stops at George Garrison. Powerful people are pulling strings, and I hate that I can't get my hands on them yet. But I'm trying."

"Yeah, well one of the people I brought in here for our team turned out to be a bad guy. If you want my resignation, I'll understand. I'll have it for you first thing in the—"

"Stop," she interrupted, glad that he'd offered his job to her. Now she could be sure that he was innocent of any complicity. "You're a loyal man, Clint. And I want you here at Jury Town for as long as you'll stay."

"Thanks," he mumbled gratefully, pushing back the brim of his white Stetson. "Garrison still isn't talking?"

Garrison was sitting in a jail cell outside Washington, DC, where Victoria felt more confident about her prospects of keeping him alive. So far, he'd steadfastly refused to say anything—even as much as to proclaim his innocence. But she remained hopeful.

"No," she answered, "he's not saying a word." It was imperative to her that Wolf truly believed he still had her full support. "By the way, I need your recommendation on who should replace Garrison."

Wolf nodded. "For now it's me, but I'll get working on it right away. I hate to say it, but I think it's best if I work from a candidate pool with which I'm not familiar."

Victoria picked up her phone when it alerted her to an incoming text. Her eyes raced through the message, which had been written by one of her friends inside the Virginia General Assembly. Barney Franz, the majority leader, was quietly stirring up trouble for Jury Town within the ranks of his party. She'd heard the rumblings for a while, and now Franz was close to putting his plan into motion, according to her source.

Cameron's prediction was coming true. Franz was furious that she hadn't kissed his ring, and he intended to make her pay.

Well, Franz better make sure he knew what he was doing. She'd always considered him a colleague. Not one who typically saw eye to eye with her, but that was all right. That was government.

At this point, he was quickly becoming an enemy.

NORTH WOODS, MAINE

"It's a bad news, good news night," said the Gray who was easing into the big chair to Rockwell's left.

That was the senior official at CIA, Rockwell remembered from the picture of the man he'd found on the Internet.

Rockwell took his seat in the semicircle of easy chairs positioned before the cabin's big stone fireplace. These meetings were much better now that he was being ferried to and from the cabin by helicopter. He didn't miss that hard wooden chair or the blindfold, either.

"My brother is looking at prison because of what we failed to accomplish at Jury Town," the man from the NSA growled. "Commonwealth was found guilty."

Rockwell winced. Hopefully, he wouldn't end up shouldering the blame for the verdict. It wasn't his fault Garrison had been foiled. But they might not see it that way.

"Let's not jump to conclusions," the Gray from DHS cautioned. "That was a civil case. The guilt bar in criminal trials is much higher. And don't forget, we can hide your brother if it comes to that."

"Nice life that would be."

"The really bad news about what happened," said the fourth man, "is that it seems obvious we're going to have a very difficult time influencing verdicts inside Jury Town."

"Should we take care of Mr. Garrison? The way we took care of Billy Batts and that old woman."

Rockwell made certain not to look up from the floor at what he took to be more confirmation that someone else in this room was communicating with JD. He'd read about Batts' death on the Internet. The only conclusion he could draw was that JD had carried out that murder. Or maybe it wasn't JD, he realized. Maybe they had other assassins on the payroll—which made him feel even more nervous about his usefulness to them.

"Perhaps."

"Let me look into that one."

Rockwell hadn't been able to locate the fourth man anywhere on the Internet—at any of the "usual suspect" agencies—the way he'd found the other three Grays.

"Where's the good news tonight?" the man from the NSA wanted to know.

"Angela Gaynor now has an arrest record. So does the basketball player."

"And the Gaynor Construction CEO, Jack Hoffman, is deep in our pocket, *and* Ms. Gaynor has no idea."

"Plus she'll never find out how we penetrated the company network from across the Pacific. It's beautiful."

"Even more beautiful," the fourth man spoke up, "Ms. Gaynor is fifteen points behind Chuck Lehman and falling like a stone." He pointed at everyone in turn. "Let's make tonight even better. Let's go 'no limit' on Victoria Lewis."

"Hear, hear!" the men shouted in unison as they stamped the floor hard.

Rockwell tried to keep up, but he was late on both the vocal and the stamp.

"Mr. Rockwell?"

"Yes?"

"It's time to let JD loose with his sniper rifle. It's time to put Victoria Lewis six feet in the ground. We're going 'no limit' on this."

He hated to ask a question, but there was no choice. "What does—"

"Tell JD to use any and all means necessary. She thinks she can get in our way? Well, no, *hell no!* Tell JD to blow her goddamn head into a thousand pieces."

"Hear, hear!" the men shouted again, stamping their feet on the floor in unison. *"Hear, hear!"*

RICHMOND, VIRGINIA

"How we doing?" Dez asked cheerfully as he looked up from cleaning a Glock 17. Parts of the pistol lay spread out on the table in front of him, surrounding a rag and a can of solvent. "Better?"

Victoria sat at the other end of the couch, clad in jeans and a baggy, UVA sweatshirt, watching him. It was almost midnight, and neither of them could sleep. She'd never needed much sleep, even as a kid. Dez never seemed to need *any.*

"I'm fine."

"Was it a good day or a bad day?"

She shrugged. "It was fine."

"Fine and fine. Good to know. Glad I'm on the inside here, Victoria."

"Sorry, I'm just—"

"You're frustrated," Dez preempted. "You feel like a prisoner here at my house because I won't let you go anywhere or do anything unless it involves Jury Town, including go back to your little house in the woods you love so much."

"Exactly."

It was Dez's turn to shrug. "Now you understand how celebrities feel."

"I don't think it's this bad for them."

"Not quite, but close. I've protected a few, and they get frustrated, too."

She was longing for the white powder, for just a line or two. But she'd made a pact with herself today—at Jury Town. She was giving it up forever, in Cameron's honor.

She pictured a mirror on the table beside the pistol parts, with a pile of it on there. Could she resist? That would be the struggle for a long time, but she had to do it—for Cam, but even more, for herself.

"Yeah, well, I bet they wouldn't switch with me."

"Maybe not," he agreed. "I can't believe I'm asking you this, but how about something to take the edge off?"

"Like what?"

"I've got a bottle of Absolut you can hit."

"How'd you know I was a vodka girl?"

He made a face. "Come on. What, are you gonna drink . . . bourbon?"

"Right. So that sounds good. A little vodka. You know, to help me sleep."

"You don't have to rationalize anything for me. Bottle's inside there," he said, pointing at a small cabinet in a far corner of the room. "Need a mixer?"

"No."

"Wow," he muttered, raising one eyebrow as he began reassembling the gun, "hard-core. Well, get yourself a glass and some ice from the kitchen, and have at it."

Moments later she was back and filling her glass to the lip with vodka. "How many people are guarding the house tonight?" she asked, going through the pile of discs beside the CD player on top of the cabinet.

"Fifteen, and all armed with Heckler & Koch MG5 submachine guns."

"Jesus," she whispered, "submachine guns?"

"And we've got a few more tricks up our sleeves if that's not enough. A few of them are even packing—"

"*Frank Sinatra?*" she shrieked, grabbing the CD when she saw the name. "You listen to Frank Sinatra?"

Dez spread his arms wide. "Just because I'm black, I can't listen to the Chairman of the Board?"

"I love Ol' Blue Eyes," she said, holding up the disc. "Can I put this on?"

"Sure."

She moved back to the couch as "*The Way You Look Tonight*" began playing. "Do you want a drink?"

"Nope."

"Come on."

"Not while I'm taking care of you."

Victoria sat down on the sofa, aware that she was a little closer to him than before. *Watch it*, she told herself. The first few sips were already affecting her. "So we'll never be able to have a drink together?"

"Never say never, but not anytime soon."

"I love this song," she murmured, watching him finish putting the Glock back together. "You ever get scared, Dez? I've wanted to ask you that question ever since we met."

"Why?"

"Because I don't think you do. It's like you have no fear of anything. I've only known one other person like that."

"Your father?"

She smiled at him. "How'd you guess?"

"It wasn't hard." He took a deep breath. "Sure, I get scared sometimes. Just like your dad did."

"Were you scared when we were attacked on the driveway at my house?"

He shook his head as he eased back onto the couch. "I know how this'll sound, but I didn't have time to be scared. I was afterward. I always get scared after when I think about what just happened, how close I came to dying. It was the same for me when I was a SEAL. I never got scared during a mission, but always after."

She bit her lower lip gently. "I miss Cam."

"I know."

"It's my fault he's gone."

"No," Dez countered deliberately and firmly, "it's not. It's the fault of the people who are trying to kill you. You've got to get off that road."

"Do you ever get lonely?"

"You're full of interesting questions tonight."

"Do you?"

"I love what I do."

"That doesn't mean you don't get lonely. Is there a future Mrs. Dez Braxton up in Washington?"

"Maybe . . . but I haven't met her yet." He gestured to Victoria. "Are you lonely?"

As the song faded, she felt for a moment like an ordinary person, not Virginia Lewis, former governor. It usually took cocaine to make her feel this way. "You know I am, Dez," she finally whispered, "very lonely. It seems like I've never had time to get really close to anyone."

"Make time."

She shook her head. "I can't. Not yet."

"Why?"

"There's still too much to do," she said as *My One and Only Love* began to play. "Oh Lord," she murmured as the slow song drifted through the room. "This is my *favorite* Sinatra. It gives me goose bumps every time I hear it." She held her forearm out so he could see.

He glanced at her arm, then into her eyes. "Dance?" he asked, standing up and holding out his hand.

"Yeah," she answered taking his hand, "I'd love to dance with you, Dez."

She laughed softly as she blended into his body perfectly, and they began to move as one.

"Am I that bad?" he asked.

"You're awesome."

"Why'd you laugh?"

"I don't even know where you're from, and I'm living in your house and dancing slow with you."

"But why'd you laugh?"

She pressed her face to his chest. "I guess I always figured you Special Forces crazies all come from the same tough-as-nails small town in Texas or Montana or someplace wild like that."

Dez leaned back with a confused expression. "What?"

"Where are you from?"

"I could tell you, but then I'd have to kill you."

"Blah, blah, come on."

He shook his head as she pressed her face back to his chest. "I'm serious. There're some nasties around the world who'd love to find that out, so they could get to my family and get their revenge. I was involved in some very classified stuff."

She looked up at him again. "You're kidding, right?"

He shook his head.

"So is your name really Dez Braxton?"

He smiled widely. "What do you think?"

PART THREE

CHAPTER 40

VIRGINIA BEACH, VIRGINIA

"Please state your name, sir," the prosecutor requested in a friendly tone as he walked out from behind the long table.

He paced across the courtroom toward the witness stand, soles clicking purposefully on the buffed hardwood. His steps broke the breathless silence, which filled every corner of the courtroom. A courtroom packed to capacity, save for the jury box . . . which was a ghost town.

The prosecutor couldn't keep himself from glancing in that empty direction. It was odd not to have a jury sitting to his left as he approached the witness stand; unsettling not to have them follow his every move and hang on his every word as he constructed his case; eerie to realize they were all watching him through a lens from two hundred miles away, like so many voyeurs.

He cleared his throat twice to erase any nerves that might be loitering in his voice. "For the record, sir."

"My name is Jack Hoffman."

"What is your occupation?"

Hoffman gave a curious, uncertain look. "Um . . . I'm unemployed."

The prosecutor winced. A terrible gaffe and he'd practiced this opening many times at home before the bathroom mirror. He had to relax and let things flow naturally. But the stage had never been this daunting. There was so much riding on this trial. It would make or break his career. That had been made very clear.

The fundamental challenge for him was that Angela Gaynor's high-powered attorney team had steamrolled this case into court very quickly—because of the election. He hadn't been allowed anywhere near the normal time to prepare, and he was a painfully deliberate man, always had been. So he wasn't confident in his facts or his witnesses. The doubts were fueling his nerves.

He inhaled deeply to calm himself. "What was your most recent occupation?"

"I was the chief executive officer of Gaynor Construction Incorporated before I was terminated."

"Where is Gaynor Construction headquartered?"

"Virginia Beach, Virginia."

"Who owns that corporation, Mr. Hoffman?"

"Angela Gaynor. One hundred percent."

"Is she in this courtroom?" Now he was finding his rhythm. His breathing was becoming normal; his chest was relaxing; his thoughts were coming quickly.

"Yes."

"Could you please identify her?"

Hoffman pointed to the defense table, arm and forefinger fully extended. "She's right there," he said loudly, without hesitation, as Angela Gaynor's eyes narrowed to slits.

Out of habit, the prosecutor glanced at the jury box, but he quickly redirected his gaze to the camera aimed at the defense table. He hoped the jury had gotten a clear view of Gaynor's angry reaction to her former CEO's demonstrative and committed identification. He hated them not being in the courtroom.

"Let the record show that Mr. Hoffman has identified the defendant as the owner of Gaynor Construction Corporation," he said loudly.

Twenty-nine years old, the prosecutor was a child of the technology era, unlike his middle-aged associates in the DA's office. He should have been more comfortable with the new arrangement. But he was still having trouble transitioning to the jurors' invisibility. He liked seeing their faces. More importantly, he liked seeing that they liked him—as most juries apparently did, based on his outstanding won-lost record. Would he have that same winning effect through a screen?

"Mr. Hoffman, please give the court a brief description of Gaynor Construction's activities."

"The company builds a variety of large commercial structures including office buildings, high-rise apartment complexes, warehouses, and sports venues."

"In fact, during your tenure as CEO, didn't the company begin construction of the new Hampton Roads Sports Arena?"

"We did."

"What is the cost of that facility, Mr. Hoffman?"

"When it's finished, the total cost will exceed two hundred and fifty million dollars."

A gasp raced around the courtroom.

Even the judge seemed impressed, the prosecutor noticed. "So, Ms. Gaynor will make a quarter of a billion dollars on that—"

"Objection!" the lead defense attorney shouted. "The prosecutor knows full well that what something costs has nothing to do with what Gaynor Construction will actually make on a project. What the company makes on that project, if anything, will be far less than the amount he's citing."

"Sustained. The jury will disregard."

"Mr. Hoffman," the prosecutor continued—certain he'd deftly made his point despite the objection—"did Ms. Gaynor direct you to make cash payments to three Hampton city council members and the mayor in order to ensure that Gaynor Construction would be named the prime contractor on the project?"

"No."

The prosecutor's gaze raced from the camera aimed at the witness stand to the witness. "Excuse me?" he asked, doing a horrible job of masking his shock. They'd been over and over Hoffman's testimony. This one wasn't his fault. Had someone gotten to Hoffman? Was he recanting?

"She directed me to make *three* payments. She made the fourth payment herself."

"Objection! Hearsay!"

"Sustained. The witness will—"

"Ms. Gaynor made that bribe personally to the mayor of Hampton," Hoffman continued loudly over the judge's warning. "It was for fifty thousand dollars."

"Objection!"

"The other three I made were for twenty-five thousand each. Twenty-five thousand so we could make two hundred fifty million," Hoffman kept going.

"Objection!"

"She forced me to make the payments, or she told me she'd fire me!" Hoffman yelled bitterly as the judge hammered the bench with his gavel. "I had to do it. I have a family. I have e-mails that prove everything! Who to bribe, how much to pay, and that she'd can me if I didn't!"

"He's lying!" Angela screamed over her lawyer and the gavel, shooting up from her chair so fast it tumbled over backwards. "He's lying about everything! Not just about the mayor's payment. I knew nothing about *any* of this."

The defense team pulled Angela back down after righting her chair. But the damage had been done.

"Don't do that again," her lead counsel begged. "It only makes you look guiltier," he whispered . . . just as the courtroom went silent.

"Guilti*er*?" she asked loudly, her words echoing around and around the room.

The prosecutor muted a grin as he watched the scene playing out at the defense table. Jackpot.

That testimony about Angela delivering the mayor's bribe herself was strong, incredibly strong, even if it was technically hearsay. But where had it come from? This was the first he'd ever heard of it.

He'd find out later.

Now all he had to do was introduce the stack of incriminating e-mails Angela Gaynor had sent to Hoffman—and this case was over. Gaynor would be heading to a state penitentiary—not to Washington, DC.

And his career was about to take off.

JURY TOWN

Racine shifted in his chair at the back right of the jury box as the testimony continued.

He glanced at the defense table, which was on the upper right-hand screen affixed to the opposite wall. Angela Gaynor was so compelling. She seemed smart, hardworking, and honest. And he related easily and completely to the struggles she'd endured and conquered on her way to making Gaynor Construction a force. He hoped Excel Games would ultimately perform as well as Gaynor Construction had.

He liked Angela Gaynor. He wanted her to be innocent.

But the evidence was piling up against her. As jury foreman, Racine would maintain his neutrality until the bitter end. He would show no bias either way, unlike several of the most outspoken jurors who were already muttering about her "obvious guilt." But he couldn't help starting to believe she'd end up serving prison time. That perhaps the outspoken jurors were correct. Key people were testifying against her. And the jury was about to see the e-mails the prosecutor kept alluding to. E-mails Gaynor had allegedly sent to Hoffman, which proved her complicity in the conspiracy beyond a shadow of a doubt. If the e-mails were as damaging as the prosecutor claimed, that would clinch her guilt.

Racine's thoughts wandered as Jack Hoffman stepped down from the witness stand. He wondered how Excel Games was performing with the money from Mao Xilai—and how Bart Stevens was coping with everything by himself. It was horrible, being unable to speak to Bart, even worse being cut off from Claire. He had to keep reminding himself he was doing the right thing, that it was all for her even if she hated him when he came out.

As he refocused on the proceedings, Racine realized that Sofia had just glanced over her shoulder at him from the front row of the jury box. They'd been spending a great deal of time together since they'd arrived at Jury Town, eating most meals together. She was teaching him how to play pool—she was surprisingly good—and he had to admit he was having feelings for her. But she was still in mourning for her murdered husband, and he didn't want to push.

He smiled at her when she glanced over her shoulder again—and she smiled back.

WASHINGTON, DC

"We got to the mayor as well," the man from the NSA explained from the other end of the phone. "He'll plead to a three-year sentence, but we'll get him out in less than two months."

"Excellent. About the same time we get Hoffman out."

"Hoffman testified today that Angela Gaynor had physically made the payoff to the mayor herself. We got to him just before he went on the stand to let him know about the mayor, and it was beautiful. Gaynor started screaming and yelling in the courtroom. It made her look very guilty."

"Nice."

"In return for getting him out of prison so fast, the mayor will testify tomorrow that Gaynor paid him directly, even though she's never been anywhere near him in her life, much less with fifty grand."

"Even though she never even knew any bribes were being made," the man from Homeland Security said, chuckling. "She thought she'd hired a loyal man as her CEO."

"Money has a way of disrupting loyalty."

"Money has a way of disrupting everything, and thank the Lord. If it didn't, we'd be hurting."

"Jack Hoffman will have eight million dollars waiting for him when he gets out. *Twice* what the jurors will get. I thought that was appropriate."

"And he'll make it in much less time. Love it. Victoria Lewis can't beat us."

"The mayor's testimony and the e-mails we planted on the company network will put Angela Gaynor away for at least a decade. She'll learn her lesson sitting in that cell."

"As long as the jury sees everything the same way we do."

"It's a done deal. Chuck Lehman will be running unopposed when this trial is over." The man from the NSA laughed. "I guess we have a new plan. If we can't rig juries, we manipulate witnesses." His voice turned somber then. "One more thing. From what I understand, George Garrison may have had a change of heart since he's been sitting in jail."

"Oh?"

"It sounds as though he may be willing to be more forthcoming about whose orders he was acting on when he instructed Billy Batts to influence Felicity West."

"No way to get to Garrison?"

"Victoria Lewis has effectively insulated him from us by having him incarcerated in Northern Virginia as he awaits trial on violating his contract with her."

"Are you concerned that Rockwell wasn't as careful as he should have been about contacting Garrison?"

"Yes. If Garrison can lead Ms. Lewis to Rockwell, Rockwell could lead them to us, especially if he's looking at serious time. He hasn't found Walter Morgan yet, but we know he's found the rest of us."

VIRGINIA BEACH, VIRGINIA

"How many years have you been building and securing corporate computer networks, Mr. Abrams?" the prosecutor asked.

"Seventeen."

"And that would include all facets of interfacing, including construction of Intranets as well as, obviously, linking networks to the outside world."

"Of course," Abrams answered.

"You've also been intimately involved in building and maintaining network security."

"Yes, as I stated before."

"You're an independent consultant?"

"Yes."

"You aren't employed by one company because you can make so much more money on your own. Many, many companies request your services."

A self-conscious expression rose to Abrams' face.

"It's okay," the prosecutor prodded. "Take credit where credit is due."

"Well, yes, that's right. I'm very fortunate."

"Please name some of the corporations that have engaged you to help them with their networks."

"Bank of America, Home Depot, Proctor & Gamble, Royal Dutch—"

"An impressive list, for sure."

"Thank you."

"Would you please read the printout of the e-mail I handed you a few moments ago?"

Abrams slipped on his reading glasses. "Jack, we need to get twenty-five thousand dollars to Councilman Weber immediately. See to it."

"In your professional opinion," the prosecutor spoke up when Abrams was finished, "did that e-mail come from Angela Gaynor's laptop?"

"It did."

The prosecutor glanced smugly at the stony faces behind the defense table. "Your witness."

RICHMOND, VIRGINIA

Bart Stevens cringed when he saw the number of the inbound caller flash on his cell phone. It was Mao Xilai, the man who'd invested four million dollars into Excel Games, the man making it possible for Stevens to pay his mortgage again and keep a roof over his family's head. This was the call Stevens had been dreading ever since David Racine had disappeared inside Jury Town.

"Hello," Stevens said hesitantly.

"Mr. Stevens?"

"Yes. Oh, hello, Mr. Xilai," Stevens said enthusiastically this time—too enthusiastically. He'd sounded very nervous. "How are you, sir?"

"Fine, thank you. I have left several messages with Mr. Racine, but he has not returned my calls. In fact, my calls go straight to his voice mail every time."

Stevens cringed again as he thought about the investment banker's warning and about the news articles describing the gruesome fates of executives who'd fallen out of favor with Xilai.

"Do you know where he is?"

Stevens took deep breath. "He had a doctor's appointment, I believe."

"That's quite an appointment. I've been trying for three hours to get him."

"Yes, well—"

"I am going to be in Washington, DC, on business, Mr. Stevens. When I'm finished in your capital, I will come to Richmond to see how our company is doing. I will send details of my visit later. Please make certain Mr. Racine has no appointments that day. Do you understand?"

"Of course, Mr. Xilai."

This was the nightmare scenario.

When Xilai was gone, Stevens dialed the private number he'd been given and held his breath as the phone began to ring. "She better keep her end of the deal."

CHAPTER 41
JURY TOWN

"What's up?" Dez asked, closing the door to Victoria's office behind him.

"Thanks for coming so fast."

"No problem."

"Have a seat." She pointed at the chair in front of her desk. "I need to give you a heads-up. I have to go before the General Assembly. The majority leader, Barney Franz, is making trouble for me."

"How so?"

She liked that Dez was becoming more interested in things affecting her life beyond her security. "Franz is angry that I didn't consult him while I was organizing Jury Town."

"I thought you didn't have to. I thought the Supreme Court had total jurisdiction over everything related to Project Archer."

Victoria liked that he was listening, too. She'd told him a great deal about Jury Town while they were hanging out together at night, listening to music in his rented house, and he'd clearly absorbed what she'd told him. He was a very bright man, she was coming to find. He wasn't outspoken. But, when asked, he had an opinion that was always deliberately conceived with the application of unbending logic.

"Technically," she answered, "that's right. But Franz is a powerful man. He's throwing rocks at the proverbial hornet's nest, and I'm starting to get worried calls, especially as things seem to be going well here." She gestured around. "So I'm going to appear before the General Assembly to answer questions and nip this in the bud."

"You're going to kiss the ring."

"Okay, let's call it that."

"When?"

"Tomorrow."

He grimaced. "Doesn't give me much time to secure things, and I hate the idea of you being exposed in downtown Richmond like that."

"You'll figure it out; you always do. Dance tonight?" she asked as he stood up.

He grinned. "Sure. And I've already got an idea for how to make your assembly visit foolproof."

"Get to it, then. And one more thing before you go." Victoria picked up a small piece of paper from her desk and held it out for him. "I need you to call this man immediately. The number's there below his name."

"Ryan Mitchell?" Dez read from the paper.

"Yes, but he goes by Mitch."

BELLWOOD, VIRGINIA

Mitch stood beside his wife's Denali in the darkness of the secluded dirt road. She hadn't been happy about him taking it—but he couldn't have gotten the SLK down here. The road down the long hill was rutted and muddy.

The James—the wide river that flowed past downtown Richmond—was only fifty yards away through the dense trees. He couldn't see its black waters, but he could hear them gurgling past.

Would Salvatore show?

Mitch checked his phone for the third time. The mafia boss was forty-five minutes late. Whenever they'd met before—in the warehouse district—Salvatore's driver had called just before the appointed time with the meeting place, making the mobster effectively a moving target with multiple escape routes.

Mitch had chosen this destination. Despite the lure of a big, quick payoff, perhaps Salvatore had developed a bad case of cold feet. He'd never been more than five minutes late before.

At one hour past the appointed time, Mitch kicked at a pebble on the road and turned toward the Denali's door—just as he heard a vehicle approaching.

The SUV stopped fifty feet away. Two large men climbed out and hustled to where he stood.

"We got six people here," one of the men explained as the other patted Mitch down. "Not including the boss and the driver. Four of them are out in the woods around here. And they've been here for a while checkin' things out. Nothin' better happen."

"Don't worry, sport."

"He's clean."

"Go get Salvatore."

Moments later another figure climbed out of the SUV and ambled down the dirt road to where Mitch stood. "Okay, kid," Salvatore said, "what you got for me?"

"In three months a significant amount of land along the river in this area will, in the time it takes a gavel to fall, go from protected wetlands to zoned commercial. It's taken the developer who owns a lot of this land three years to get it all the way through to the Supreme Court. Obviously, that man has some significant pull in this state. Still, most people are betting against him. They think my uncle will rule against him."

"But you know differently."

"Yes. And, given that we're only a few miles downstream from Richmond, when Judge Eldridge votes for him, the value of this land will skyrocket."

"Is there land available?"

Mitch nodded. "I know of about three hundred acres you could get very cheap." He lifted the folder he was carrying. "You'll get about a ten-times value blast *overnight*. The whole thing's detailed in here."

"What do you want out of this?"

"Half."

Salvatore sneered. "Including me, I got eight guys here. You're alone. What's to keep me from just taking it from you?"

Mitch put his head back and gazed up into the night sky, forcing an aggravated expression to his face. "You don't know I'm alone."

"My guys have been all over this place for hours. You're definitely alone."

"I've got more deals coming," Mitch warned. "Don't screw this up. We can all make money."

"Ten percent, kid, and appreciate that I'm being so generous. Give me the folder."

"Where's my cash? There's Jury Town stuff in there, too."

Salvatore reached into his jacket pocket for an envelope.

As they exchanged folder for cash, ten figures dropped silently from the night sky onto the road, cutting their parachutes away even as they opened fire with automatic weapons.

Fifteen seconds later, three mobsters were dead and Mitch and Salvatore were side by side, eating the Denali door, hands cuffed tightly behind their backs.

CHAPTER 42

RICHMOND, VIRGINIA

"In a very short time, Jury Town has proven to be an outstanding success, a truly invaluable asset to Virginia's judicial system. While the sample size is still relatively small in terms of trials concluded, everyone involved agrees that juries inside the walls are making extraordinarily strong decisions in an extremely efficient manner, much faster than they do on the outside. The mathematicians caution me that it's early yet to draw iron-clad statistical conclusions from the data, but I can tell you this. If we keep moving in this direction, very soon the statistical results will be absolutely meaningful and will prove overwhelmingly positive. Many jurors are into their third and fourth trials at this point, and are becoming quite familiar with the process and the laws. We have more and more instances of jurors correcting lawyers in terms of procedure and application of the law, and, in one rather embarrassing case, even correcting a judge. I have every reason to believe these trends and results will continue."

Victoria paused to swing her gaze deliberately from left to right, catching as many eyes as possible of the one hundred and forty senators and delegates sitting before her, and currently representing the longest continuously operating legislative body in the country. "Officials from New York and California have been calling constantly, trying to arrange interviews and fact-finding trips, to catch up with what we're doing. So far, I've had no time to meet with them. But I promise you I will. Virginia will forever be regarded as the leader of this groundbreaking change to our nation's judicial system, and we must never forget the Supreme Court's support of Project Archer. The foresight and steadfast commitment of Chief Justice Eldridge and the other six justices on the high court have made the difference for Jury Town." She nodded respectfully down from the podium at Majority Leader Barney Franz, who was sitting in the front row, frowning with his arms crossed tightly over his chest. "In conclusion, I want to thank Majority Leader Franz for the opportunity to speak here today. I'm always willing to answer any questions you may have."

After a few moments, Franz rose slowly from his seat with a sharply pained look on his face. "You must give us more than that, Ms. Lewis. I mean, *really*."

Victoria maintained her passive expression even as Franz's deep voice boomed his accusatory tone out into the Virginia General Assembly.

"While I appreciate that these people in Jury Town may be making good decisions quickly," Franz went on, "I hardly think that justifies an annual price tag, which, according to my aides, appears to be nearing half a billion dollars. With all due respect to you and Judge Eldridge, I have a problem with that kind of irresponsible spending."

A murmur of assent rolled through the chamber like far-off thunder.

Victoria stared down at Franz, literally biting her tongue. She could not admit to these legislators—to *anyone*—that the impetus behind Jury Town had originated with the United States Attorney General because of his suspicions of nationwide jury tampering. She could not communicate that she'd already experienced and defeated an attempt to manipulate the Commonwealth Electric Power trial—proof, for her, of the tampering conspiracy. That later today she would personally interrogate George Garrison to try to determine who was sitting on the next rung up of the influence ladder with respect to the CEP trial. She couldn't tell them that she'd almost been killed on the driveway of her home—and that Cameron Moore had effectively given his life for Project Archer. All of that had to remain confidential.

For the first time in her political career, Victoria understood how the President of the United States felt in election debates with the opposing party's candidate when the subject of national security arose. The president knew so much more than the other candidate but could say nothing on top-secret matters, even when he or she knew the other candidate was wrong, even lying.

"A cynical man," Franz bellowed in his heavy southern drawl, turning to face his fellow lawmakers who were sitting in a large semicircle behind him, "might have a very dim view of spending five hundred million dollars of taxpayer money so freely."

"The efficiencies we will achieve from this program," Victoria responded, "will ultimately *more than* pay for the expenditures. That new hundred-million-dollar judicial complex on the South Side of Richmond has been put on hold thanks to Jury Town. And I'm drawing up—"

"A cynical man," Franz interrupted rudely, "might call that money you're spending so freely nothing but campaign funds."

"Excuse me?"

"Ms. Lewis," Franz chuckled in a sarcastic way, "we all know of your aspirations for higher office."

"That's ridiculous. I've never once made mention of any—"

"Jury Town has proven to be a fabulous way for you to gain national attention with all the publicity it's drawn in the press. And you've funded all that publicity and selfish acclaim with taxpayer money." He turned back to Victoria and wagged an accusing finger. "I've heard all about how the Supreme Court and Chief Justice Eldridge have unilateral purview over the jury system in our commonwealth, but I don't care. I think it's high time for the legislative body to become involved."

As a group of legislators loudly cheered Franz's assertion, Victoria stared down at him, wishing she could fire him. Finally she headed down the short flight of stairs leading from the podium down to the chamber floor.

"I need to see you in private," she hissed as she swept past Franz toward the anteroom, where she'd waited before coming out on the floor. "Right now, Barney."

JURY TOWN

"She's innocent."

Racine glanced across the table at Sofia, then around furtively. They were sitting at the table where he always sat, the small table for two at the periphery of the Central Zone. "I can't talk about—"

"Angela Gaynor is being framed. I'm convinced of it."

"I'm foreman, Sofia. I—*we* can't talk like this."

"I'm talking to you as my friend, David, not as the foreman. I can't stand seeing this poor woman railroaded so badly."

Against his better judgment, Racine leaned over the table. Perhaps it was simply to get a better look at those emerald eyes he was so captivated by. But then he opened his mouth. "What makes you so sure she's being railroaded?" he whispered. This wasn't the first time she'd confidently made the assertion. They'd been talking in her room until two in the morning last night.

"A lot of it is feeling, I'm happy to admit."

"We can't go on feelings inside these walls, Sofia. We must follow evidence. And the evidence is strong. The witnesses, the e-mails."

"Anyone could have sent those e-mails from her computer."

"One or two, yes, but *that* many and at that many different times?"

"That CEO Jack Hoffman is a snake. I don't like him. I could just strangle him with my bare hands. He's so smug. *Liar.*"

"Maybe we shouldn't use the term 'strangle' in—"

"She's innocent, David."

He couldn't get enough of that Spanish accent, or those eyes, or the way she twirled that long, raven hair when she was being demonstrative—which was often. She was an intensely passionate woman, which she freely admitted. He'd wanted to kiss her so badly last night as they'd said good night at her door and explore her passion. But he hadn't tried—out of respect for her and her murdered husband. Though, he wasn't sure how much longer he could control himself.

And what a bad scene it would be if she turned him down. There would be an intense period of discomfort between them. And it wasn't as if they'd be able to avoid each other.

"You can express those sentiments during deliberations," he said as she reached across the table and grabbed his arm. Her touch was electric.

"Do me a favor, David."

"Why do I feel like I'm setting myself up here?"

"Think about the moment the prosecutor asked Jack Hoffman if Angela had directed him to pay bribes to three councilmen and the mayor."

"Okay."

"Hoffman answered 'no.' He testified that Angela had paid the mayor herself."

"So?"

"So the prosecutor looked like he'd stuck his fingers in a live electric socket as soon as Hoffman gave that answer."

"So?" But Racine understood where Sofia was headed with this. "You're saying a prosecutor should never be surprised by the testimony of his own witness."

"*Exactly*. He should have known what Hoffman would say. But then Hoffman said Angela had paid the mayor herself. The prosecutor looked shocked, like he'd just won Powerball."

"Keep going."

"Look at the video of that moment with me, when the prosecutor asks Hoffman the question. Please. If we request it, they will play the video for us. Will you do that for me?"

He gazed over the table at her, struck by her intuition, her ability to instantly and expertly recognize and interpret human emotions. "Yes,

I will." He caught his breath as she blew him a kiss and gave him that sultry look that made him melt.

RICHMOND, VIRGINIA

"What is the meaning of this sketchy backroom maneuver?" Franz demanded as he followed Victoria into the small anteroom. "I was tempted not to honor your request to come in here. But, after all, you are our former governor. Out of respect, I will give you one minute of my time, Ms. Lewis, and not one second more."

"I won't need that long," she assured him, nodding for Dez to close the door behind Franz.

"Nothing you say will change my mind," Franz assured her. "I will not support you on Jury Town," he said as he brushed a piece of lint from his dark gray suit coat. "You thought you could do this project without me. You thought wrong. I intend to start an investigation into this charade," he promised, glancing at Dez. "Is he on the payroll, too?"

"Dez Braxton is my head of security."

Franz sneered as he rolled his eyes. "Security. What do you need security for?" He shook his head. "Oh yes, I'm starting an investigation this very afternoon." He waved behind himself at the door leading to the General Assembly chamber. "And I have tremendous support for that course of action out on the floor. How does that sound to you, Ms. Lewis?"

"It sounds fine," she replied calmly, moving to the anteroom door opposite the one leading to the chamber.

"Are you taunting me?" Franz demanded. "Are you daring me to do it?"

"I'm telling you to go ahead," she said defiantly. "But I think it's important for you to understand what my response will be before you initiate your investigation." She tapped the knob three times, then opened the door Franz was facing, and nodded to the figure standing there. "Barney, I believe you know Rex Conrad. He's a guard at Jury Town."

Franz's mouth dropped slowly open at the sight of Conrad.

"Dez," she said, nodding at the door to the chamber, "could you give us a moment."

"Certainly."

When he was gone, she turned to Conrad. "Thanks, Rex." And she closed that door. Now it was just Franz and she inside the anteroom. "So now you know what I have on you personally. Right?"

Franz nodded, his face ashen.

"Here's the more important point. You're right. Jury Town is costing the state quite a bit of money at this point. In the long run, it will more than pay for itself; I'm convinced and confident of that. But I can't deny those fiscal accusations you're hurling at me out in the chamber." She hesitated. "I'm taking you into my confidence, Barney. This must remain absolutely confidential between us."

"All right," Franz agreed quietly.

"There is another reason I'm certain Jury Town will not cost the taxpayers of Virginia anything."

"What?"

"The federal government is prepared to write us a check every year to pay for Jury Town. And that comes straight from Michael Delgado, the United States attorney general. No matter what the deficit is, they'll make it up to us. It will probably come from the Energy Department labeled as something else, but it will come."

"Why is Delgado willing to do that?"

"Now do you understand?" she asked when she'd finished her explanation of the nationwide jury tampering.

"My God," he whispered, nodding. "No wonder."

"Remember, you can't tell the hounds out there what's really going on. You must figure out another way to explain it to them." She pointed at him. "Be a good politician. Don't make me use what I have on you personally."

CHAPTER 43

RICHMOND, VIRGINIA

"What happened back there?" Dez turned to look back at Victoria from the front passenger seat of the third Escalade in the convoy, which was rolling through downtown Richmond. "Why was Barney Franz so scared when he saw who was standing behind the door of the anteroom?"

Victoria glanced to her left at the woman sitting beside her, then back at Dez with a raised eyebrow.

"She's okay," Dez assured Victoria, nodding at the woman. "I mean, look at her. How can you not have faith in her, given how she's dressed?"

Victoria trusted Dez completely at this point. If he claimed the member of the security team sitting to her left was okay, then she was okay.

And then there was his other point on top of all that.

"I do like your outfit," Victoria joked as she gave the woman an apologetic smile. "It makes you look even more like me."

"Thanks."

"I'm just being careful, as your boss has taught me," Victoria said, gesturing at Dez. "No offense meant."

"None taken."

"What about Rex?" Dez asked.

"Rex was a state trooper before he came on board at Jury Town. In his off-hours from the state force, he ran security for a few high-ranking members of the General Assembly when they needed it. One of those individuals was Barney Franz." Victoria leaned forward as the Escalade pulled to a stop in front of the Virginia Supreme Court Building. "Mr. Franz has a wife and three children. But, apparently, he's having an affair, or at least he was. And it was with a young man. Quite by accident, Rex Conrad discovered that affair one night."

"Jesus," Dez whispered. "People."

"That's why Mr. Franz was so shocked when he saw Rex. He knew what was up immediately."

"And you knew he would."

"I don't believe Mr. Franz will be stirring up any more problems for Jury Town in the General Assembly."

"Nice."

She shook her head and grinned wryly. Jury Town had been organized to defend against exactly the sort of blackmail Franz had just been a victim of—and he'd been trying to destroy it. The irony was almost too perfect for her to accept.

"Arriving at the Supreme Court," Dez muttered into his microphone. "Everyone ready."

"Thank goodness," Victoria said quietly to herself, glancing at her watch as the car pulled to a stop at the curb. "Judge Eldridge despises being kept waiting." She reached for the handle of the door.

JD had not been left with a great deal of time to make arrangements. Still, he was quite satisfied with his impromptu sniper nest.

Two hours ago, he'd trailed an elderly woman back to her apartment in downtown Richmond, forced his way inside when she'd answered his knock, strangled her, and then hidden her body on the floor of her bedroom closet.

The old woman's ninth-floor apartment had a small balcony with a beautiful view of the Virginia Supreme Court Building.

As the convoy of four black SUVs came into view, he began to breathe deliberately, consciously controlling his heartbeat. God, he loved these moments just before a kill.

He quickly checked right and left, at the balconies on either side of him, then raised his M40A5, rested the rifle's black barrel on the patio's banister, pressed his eye to the near end of the scope, and grinned slightly as those old familiar crosshairs came into view.

As soon as the blond woman wearing the red suit appeared from the back of the convoy's third SUV, JD acquired her, held his breath, and squeezed his gloved finger. Through the scope, he saw the woman fall.

"What the hell are you doing out here?"

JD rose up quickly and pivoted right. A man had appeared on the balcony next door. Well, this would be an even simpler shot.

He hit the man squarely in the forehead, sending him over the banister and down nine stories.

JD set the rifle down. He hated to leave it, but he couldn't be seen carrying it. Besides, he had nine more exactly like it at home.

Now he had to meet Salvatore Celino—and then get to Maine.

JURY TOWN

Racine and Sofia stood side by side in her room, watching a replay of the prosecutor interrogating Jack Hoffman on the screen on the desk. Court proceedings had concluded for the day an hour ago, and he'd arranged, as the foreman, to have the replay sent to Sofia's screen so they could watch it together.

"Here it comes, here it comes," Sofia murmured excitedly, clenching his arm.

"Quite a grip you've got there," he said, laughing as the wonderful tropical scent of her body lotion reached him.

"Watch, watch!"

As he gazed at the prosecutor's face, Racine realized that Sofia was right. The man did seem shocked by Hoffman's answer to his question. And why would he? Hoffman was *his* witness.

"You see?" she asked, leaning toward him so her face was close to his.

Her expression was almost childlike, and it melted him. "I do," he admitted. He wasn't just saying it, either. She was right.

"Angela Gaynor is innocent."

Racine gazed into those glittering green eyes for several moments. "I've got an idea."

"Is it to help her?"

"Yes."

"Oh, bueno!" she shouted, thrusting her arms around him and hugging him tightly. "What is the idea?" she asked, leaning back.

"I'll tell you later." He reached up and gently brushed tears from her face. "What's wrong, Sofia?"

"Nothing," she murmured, turning away.

"Tell me."

"I miss my children so much."

"I'm sorry. I know it's so hard for you to—"

Racine stopped short when he caught a look at Victoria Lewis' inspirational quote of the day, visible at the bottom of the screen now that the video they'd been watching had ended.

And a chill crawled slowly up his spine.

"Are you all right, David?"

He glanced over at her. "Yeah, I'm fine. I'm thinking maybe I can help you with how much you miss your children . . . maybe for a little while, anyway."

CHAPTER 44

NORTHERN VIRGINIA (FAIRFAX)

Dez grabbed his phone off the interrogation room table inside the Fairfax County Jail and scanned the message. "Good news."

"Melanie?"

"Yes, and she's fine. She's out of the hospital. They kept her overnight for observation, but they released her a few minutes ago."

Victoria's shoulders sagged with relief. "Thank God."

Melanie Otto had acted as Victoria's double yesterday on the trip into Richmond. She and Victoria were roughly the same height and petite build; Melanie had worn a blond wig as well as a red suit, matching the one Victoria had appeared at the General Assembly wearing, to complete the illusion.

Beneath the suit, she'd worn the latest high-tech body armor—ultrathin but ultrastrong. The assassin's bullet had been straight and true, directly on target to pass through the heart from behind. If not for the armor, Melanie would have been killed after stepping from the SUV onto the sidewalk in front of the Supreme Court Building.

"She's got a hell of a bruise on her back," Dez said, finishing the message, "but she's okay."

"What if the shot had been to her head?" Victoria asked.

"No chance," Dez answered confidently. "A sniper always goes for the chest. It gives him or her much better odds because it's a much bigger target." He placed the phone back down on the table. "It's time to take this to the FBI, Victoria. We can't hold back on this any longer. We need to find out who's after you, and we need to find out as soon as possible."

"I agree," she said quietly. "Hopefully, what you and Mitch are up to later will lead to something."

"Hopefully," Dez agreed as two jail guards escorted George Garrison into the interrogation room.

When Garrison was seated across from her and the guards were gone, Victoria leaned over the table toward him. "Are you tired of sitting in here?" she asked. "Are you ready to talk?"

"It depends," Garrison answered.

"No," she snapped, "no conditions."

"But, I—"

"We're closing in on your benefactors independently," she interrupted, gesturing at Dez. "By this time tomorrow, we may not need you, George."

"Will you put me in the Witness Protection Program?"

"If you give me a name, and that name turns out to be relevant."

Garrison exhaled heavily. "Okay."

"Who was it?" Victoria asked. "Who approached you about manipulating the Commonwealth Electric verdict?"

"A man named Philip Rockwell."

GREENWICH, CONNECTICUT

The two women behind the reception desk glanced up in shock as seven FBI agents hurried through the main entrance of Rockwell & Company, the lead agent with his badge open and displayed.

"Special Agent Holmes of the FBI," he announced to the two open-mouthed women behind the desk. Other agents had already reported in that Philip Rockwell was not at his home in Connecticut. And still others were posted at the two back exits to these offices in case Rockwell tried to escape. "I'm looking for Philip Rockwell."

"He's not here," one of the women answered in a quivering voice.

"Where is he?"

"Traveling, but we don't know where. Sometimes he doesn't tell us where he goes."

RICHMOND, VIRGINIA

Through powerful binoculars and the gathering dusk, Mitch watched Salvatore amble through the strip mall parking lot and deliver the package to a slim young man with short blond hair and buckteeth. Unbeknownst to the young man, an ex–Special Forces man was, at this moment, affixing a GPS beacon to the underside of the kid's silver Charger. Meanwhile the young man accepted what he believed was a complete list of Jury Town occupants from Salvatore, which were, in fact, bogus names.

This was the young man Salvatore had been passing Jury Town information to for the last six months—in return for a great deal more money than Salvatore was paying Mitch. Salvatore had all but admitted to this as he was being interrogated in Mitch's Denali—after being taken into "custody" on the dirt road beside the James.

The attack had been executed to perfection. Dez and nine of his people had parachuted down and subdued the mobsters in seconds, cuffing Mitch as well, so Salvatore had no idea that Mitch was involved.

Dez, who'd played the part of the detective, had promised Salvatore a "better deal" if he would cooperate. Salvatore had done exactly what Mitch had suspected. And laughed at them at first.

But Dez had persisted. Ultimately, convincing Salvatore that he'd been videoed with night-vision technology bribing a state official—which

Salvatore knew would involve significant prison time. Ultimately, the mob boss had agreed to lead them to his contact—if only, Mitch suspected, to avoid spurring a turf war among the other Mafia families if he were arrested.

Mitch shifted the binocular's aim left to the Charger. The beacon had been attached. Good thing, because the young man was already headed back to the car.

Mitch held up his phone, displaying the blinking dot on the map, and nodded to himself. The beacon was working perfectly. It was time to find out who the young man driving the silver Charger was working for.

CHAPTER 45

JURY TOWN

"I've seen enough," an overweight man in the front row of the jury box spoke up as all four screens on the opposite wall went dark, signaling an end to the week's testimony. "Angela Gaynor's guilty as sin."

Racine grimaced as he glanced down from his seat at the back right of the second row. The guy had quickly proven himself obnoxiously opinionated and unfailingly willing to deliver those opinions throughout the trial. There was always one in every crowd, Racine figured, a know-it-all who couldn't wait to speak up about anything and everything. It was the same way in business. As CEO of Excel Games, he'd made it a point to quash that obnoxious individual immediately in any meeting he attended. Here in Jury Room Thirteen, he couldn't be so aggressive.

"She had her executives paying *everybody*," the man went on, brushing Reese's Cup crumbs from the front of his scarlet golf shirt.

Racine had counted the guy making three trips to the snack table—just in this afternoon's session.

"And she paid the mayor herself on that one sports complex deal," the guy continued. "This trial's over as far as I'm concerned."

This afternoon they'd heard the ex-mayor of Hampton, Virginia, swear that Angela Gaynor had delivered fifty thousand dollars of cash to him personally.

"Over!" he added emphatically.

"Easy, easy," Racine called out, "let's not get ahead of ourselves. We've got more rebuttal testimony coming Monday morning concerning the alleged e-mails. Then we can get to the verdict. Let's all keep an open mind until then."

"And let's not forget that Ms. Gaynor had an alibi," Sofia spoke up. "Trent Tucker swore he was with her the day the CEO says she delivered money to the mayor."

Racine leaned forward so he could see.

"Big deal," the fat man snapped back at Sofia, groaning and yawning while he stretched. "Trent Tucker would probably say anything for her."

"Why?"

The fat man shrugged. "I can just tell."

"But you've got no good reason to say that."

"Do I really have to?" he asked, shooting another of the white men in the jury a knowing look. "Come on, everyone knows what I'm saying."

"Don't even go there," Sofia warned, her Spanish accent becoming more pronounced the more animated she became.

Racine grinned. Sofia never backed down.

"Why are you convinced Trent Tucker's telling the truth?" the guy asked.

"I'm not."

"Then what are you talking about?"

"Everything's packaged too neatly," Sofia explained. "The witnesses against Angela Gaynor all sound like they were in study group together."

"Give me a break."

"And I think Ms. Gaynor is way too smart to bribe people so clumsily if she were actually going to do it."

"So you're saying you wouldn't put it past her to make a bribe."

"I wouldn't put it past most people, if you want to know the truth. Everyone has a price."

"Not me," the man said arrogantly.

"You're in here, aren't you?"

Racine shook his head and grinned again. Zing.

"Yeah, well, I—"

"I think she's guilty, too," a black man sitting in the back row spoke up. "Did you hear how much she's going to make on that sports complex?" He pointed at Sofia. "Just like you said, follow the money trail and you'll find the truth."

"She's definitely guilty," a woman in the back row echoed, "and we should always send messages to fat cats when we can."

"Hear, hear," an Asian man chimed in. "I'm tired of seeing the rich get richer, especially when they cheat."

"She's not guilty!" Sofia shouted. "She's a good woman, and she's being—"

"All right, all right," Racine interrupted loudly as the situation barreled toward a brick wall. "We're officially in recess for the weekend," he said, standing up, "so boxers, back to your corners until Monday."

WASHINGTON, DC (GEORGETOWN)

"This is fantastic," Lehman said excitedly as he checked his laptop. "I'm up *twenty* points on Angela Gaynor now."

"I don't understand why her people haven't made her drop out yet." Martha gazed at the screen over her husband's shoulder. "It bothers me that she's staying in the race."

"Why? Because she's deluded herself into thinking that somehow she can still beat me from behind bars?"

"No, because she must be innocent. That's the only reason she'd stay in, Chuck. And, if she is found innocent, she'll turn it to her advantage and come roaring back at you."

Lehman slipped his arm around her. "You're reading too much into this, honey. Angela Gaynor is guilty. She's simply lost touch with reality. We see this with white-collar criminals all the time. They get swept up in the money; they can't stop themselves from continuing the scam, and then the way they rationalize what they've done when they finally get snagged is by insisting they're the victim." He pointed at Angela's picture on the screen. "She's probably been bribing public officials for years. What the authorities have uncovered now is probably just the tip of the iceberg." He pulled Martha down onto his lap and then kissed her deeply for the first time in a long time. "Don't worry," he whispered when he finally pulled back, "you're going to be the First Lady. I promise."

She smiled at him sweetly. "You're right. You're always right. I shouldn't worry so much. You've been Teflon ever since I've known you. You win at everything you do." She shook her head. "I feel sorry for Angela. She's worked very hard to get where she is. She's an American success story."

Lehman kissed her again. "Not anymore, honey, not anymore."

CHAPTER 46

NORTH WOODS OF MAINE

Rockwell and the lone Gray he hadn't identified yet moved through the north woods night, toward the helipad.

The five of them had just finished a hastily called meeting, but the other three had stayed behind in the cabin. The chopper would return for the others after taking Rockwell and this man home.

Rockwell assumed he would land first—for obvious reasons. This man wouldn't want Rockwell to know where he lived. The other Grays were still keeping a tight lid on personal information. He grinned smugly in the dark.

"Have you figured out who we are yet?" the Gray said as they passed from the trees into the clearing.

Was this guy clairvoyant? "Pardon me?"

"You've dedicated a good bit of effort trying to determine our identities. By nature, intelligent men are curious. Curiosity in any context cannot be considered a sin. It's the key to mankind's ascension to the top of the food chain. It's what sets us apart from the animals."

Rockwell laughed self-consciously. "I'm curious, sure." The chopper lights were illuminated, but the blades weren't rotating. He would have felt the breeze, heard the engine. But the forest was still and silent. "I know who some of you are."

"And?"

"NSA, Homeland, CIA," Rockwell answered. It seemed safe to admit this. He was one of them now. "The usual suspects."

"Very good," the man said as they stepped onto the concrete and neared the large chopper. "What about me?"

Rockwell hesitated, but he had yet to even form a guess. "No."

The Gray stopped a few feet from the helicopter and turned to him. "Have you ever heard of Majestic Twelve?"

Rockwell leaned away from the man, stunned. "The shadow government President Truman supposedly created in the late forties?"

"So you have."

"MJ-Twelve is *real*? I thought that was all just a hoax."

The Gray cracked a thin smile. "You're right," he said as he reached for the helicopter's door handle. "It's just a hoax. Good-bye, Mr. Rockwell."

Rockwell felt his eyes bulge as a familiar figure hopped down in front of him from the chopper. "Oh, no," he cried, throwing his arms up. "No. Wait!"

A moment later Philip Rockwell lay sprawled on the helipad, dead from a single bullet to the temple.

"Bury him somewhere in the woods up here," the Gray ordered as the chopper rotors began to turn. "Make sure it's at least twenty miles away and at least six feet down."

"Yes, sir."

"Good lad." The man gestured down at Rockwell's body. "Now get him out of here." The Gray caught JD by the shoulder as he passed. "You shot Mr. Rockwell because he asked too many questions. You get my drift?"

"Yes, sir. I'm an execution asset, and that's all."

"Good lad," the man repeated. "By the way, when you get back to Virginia, there will be two hundred thousand dollars in your account. Keep up the good work and you can expect more, much more."

CHAPTER 47

RICHMOND, VIRGINIA

"Where is Mr. Racine?"

"It's Saturday," Bart Stevens replied from the other side of the Excel Games conference-room table. "He could be anywhere."

"Well, he should be sitting in front of me, Mr. Stevens. That's where he *should* be."

"We're looking for him everywhere, Mr. Xilai. I . . . I don't know what to tell you."

"This is an outrage. You've had days to find him. I gave you plenty of warning that I was coming down here after finishing my business in Washington."

"I know and I'm very, very sorry."

"And I thought I made myself *very, very* clear."

"Everything is going so well, Mr. Xilai. Revenues and profits are going through the roof now that we've been able to advertise using the money you invested."

"Unless you locate Mr. Racine in the next five minutes, everything is definitely *not* going well."

Stevens stared across the table at Mao Xilai. He didn't like the nasty, bordering-on-evil expression he was getting. "Let me try David again," he suggested desperately, rising from his seat. Trying again was an exercise in complete futility, but he didn't know what else to say.

"Use your cell to call him," Xilai ordered angrily, pointing at the phone Stevens had just grabbed off the table. "There is no need for you to leave this room."

"I was going to see if David's assistant had heard anything."

"His assistant is here? It's Saturday."

"Oh, right. I forgot."

"Did you really?"

"I—"

"Do not leave this room, Mr. Stevens. Not until I tell you to."

As Stevens eased back down against the chair, perspiration drenched his shirt. Xilai had brought two men with him on this trip. They were outside in the parking lot, dressed in matching dark suits and sunglasses, smoking up a storm as they leaned against the limousine. He'd seen them through his office window blinds before finally getting up his nerve to walk in here. They were outside . . . but it wouldn't take them long to get inside.

"Go on," Xilai demanded, gesturing at the phone, "call Mr. Racine."

"Okay." Stevens cut the connection when the call went straight to Racine's voice mail—again. "I'm sorry, I—"

"I told you to treat this company as if it were your child."

"I am, sir. *I do.*"

"But your chief executive does not. How can he go missing like this? Would he really do this to Claire?"

Stevens grimaced. It shouldn't surprise him that Xilai knew the name of Racine's daughter. What terrified him was that it meant Xilai knew the names of his children, too. The quiet warning was coming through with deafening clarity.

"Let's start going over the numbers while we wait for David," Stevens suggested, sliding his laptop in front of him. "They're tremendous. We're on pace to do more than twenty million in revenues this year, up from five last year. If we keep pumping the ads, we might do as much as fifty million in top-line dollars next year, maybe even a *hundred.* We've got thousands of people signing up every day. It's incredible. I've got New York and San Francisco investment bankers calling me off the hook. The IPO figures they're talking about are insane. Your four million could be worth a billion in the next eighteen months. That would turn the dial even for a man as wealthy as you, Mr. Xilai."

"Why are the investment bankers calling you and not Racine?" Xilai asked coldly.

"I'm the CFO. Why wouldn't they call me?"

"I detest when people lie to me, Mr. Stevens. I told you that," Xilai hissed. "I gave you fair warning."

"Mr. Xilai, the company is doing so well."

"I do not like being disrespected!" Xilai shouted, springing up out of his seat. "I invested four million dollars in you and Mr. Racine. Not in the company. Do you not understand that?"

"I'm taking care of your money," Stevens said pleadingly as he started to stand, then hesitated, worried that he wasn't supposed to. Worried that Xilai might call his men in here. "I swear to God I am." He pointed at the laptop screen. "The proof is right here."

"Where is Racine?"

"I don't know."

"*Where* is David Racine? If you know, if you have any idea at all, you better tell me right now, Mr. Stevens!"

NORTH WOODS OF MAINE

"Mr. Rockwell is dead," the fourth Gray announced as he reentered the cabin. "JD just executed him."

The other three stamped the floor hard. "Hear, hear!" they shouted in unison.

"Good riddance," the man from DHS growled.

"He botched the Commonwealth Electric case," the CIA official hissed, "and he was a traitor for trying so hard to find us."

"Which, apparently, he did. Rockwell knew where each of you worked."

"Did he find you, Walter?"

"He said he didn't. But does it really matter now? Within the hour, his body will be six feet down in this never-ending pine forest. Maybe some future civilization will stumble on his skeleton after the next ice age. But we don't have to worry, even if George Garrison does identify Rockwell as his connection from his jail cell in northern Virginia. The connection to us is cut. I've already had a man visit his house and remove some belongings. Without his body, the FBI will think he's on the run."

"Here's another thing we don't have to worry about," the NSA official said as he tapped his phone. "Angela Gaynor is twenty points back of our man and fading fast."

"By this time next week, she ought to be in jail. Can't get any farther back than that." The man chuckled. "Unless she was dead."

"Can you imagine if she'd upset Lehman and the avalanche had started? They would have passed all kinds of legislation that would have undermined the efforts we've taken to influence juries."

"And undermined the money we make."

"Now we're safe. And we can keep the country safe. Our side of it, anyway."

"It's a great day, and we should—" Walter Morgan interrupted himself. "Does anyone else hear that?"

RICHMOND, VIRGINIA

"I've had enough of this," Xilai hissed, pounding the table. "I come all the way down here from Washington, and Mr. Racine *ignores* me? This is a terrible insult. I will not forget this, Mr. Stevens."

Stevens was terrified. Once incensed, Xilai was merciless—according to the stories—and might go after everyone. If he died, so be it. But he couldn't bear the thought of his children being murdered.

"Mr. Xilai, I'm begging you not to—"

"Hello, Mao. Hello, Bart."

Stevens' gaze raced to the conference-room door. Racine stood there, looking his usual calm, cool, collected self.

Stevens fell back into his chair at the sight of his best friend, shock and relief surging through him in wave after powerful wave.

"Sorry I'm late," Racine said with an easygoing smile, moving to where Xilai stood to shake hands. "We've got a lot of good news for you, Mao. I can't wait to tell you about it, so let's get started." His smile widened as he pointed at Stevens. "You look like you saw a ghost, Bart."

Stevens was still too relieved—and scared—to banter back a worthy response. In fact, he could think of only one thing at this moment: Victoria Lewis had made good on her promise. Racine really would be allowed out when Xilai came calling.

Stevens had insisted to Racine that Victoria would *never* come through on the deal. That, in the end, she would turn traitor on a transaction that could prove disastrous for her if she honored it, as any experienced politician would.

He couldn't remember being happier about being wrong in his entire life.

"Yes," Xilai said firmly, "I can't wait to hear all the good news."

CHAPTER 48

NORTH WOODS OF MAINE

"Chopper up!" Mitch shouted from the passenger seat as the SUV raced down the long gravel driveway through the darkness. He pointed excitedly at the running lights rising above the trees. "Got to be what that is."

"No doubt," Dez confirmed as he punched the accelerator, then punched the steering wheel, *begging* the V-8 for more speed when house lights appeared as they flew around a curve. *"Come on, baby!"*

They'd tracked the silver Charger to a secluded grove of trees just off the county road that cut a thin swath through the massive Maine forest. Finding no one in or around the car, they'd headed frantically down the nearest driveways they could locate, figuring the young man with the closely cropped blond hair had set out on foot—probably because whoever he was meeting was taking careful precautions in terms of approaching.

They'd already been down two other long driveways to dark, empty cabins—and dead ends. Suddenly, it seemed, they'd hit the jackpot. But were they in time?

"He's coming back down!" Mitch shouted, pointing again at the chopper. This felt remarkably like Afghanistan. The terrain was dramatically different, but the tension and the adrenaline were *exactly* the same. It felt surprisingly good to be back in the chaos.

"Somebody must have heard us coming and called him back," Dez replied. "We aren't gonna have much time. *Careful out there, Mitch!*"

"*I'll be fine, my man!*" He and Dez had become very close very quickly. But combat always did that.

Dez pulled the SUV to a skidding stop in front of the cabin as four men spilled out through the front door—illuminated by the truck's headlights—and scattered in different directions.

Mitch grabbed his pistol off the dash and jumped from the SUV, chasing the two men who'd headed in the helicopter's direction. A full moon cast an eerie glow on the landscape, and, despite the prosthesis, he was able to keep up, catching quick flashes of them dashing through the trees ahead.

As the roar of rotors turned deafening and the winds rose to gale force, Mitch raced across the leaves on the forest floor—despite the sharp, stinging pain knifing through his right knee with every badly limping stride. Spurred on through the torture by his intense desire to try to set things right.

Mitch understood why his uncle had allowed this to happen—Judge Eldridge was willing to compromise himself and not have Mitch arrested for the bigger picture, for the chance of destroying the men who'd tried to destroy the judicial system—successfully for a time. Mitch wanted to make his uncle proud. Thankfully the wife, and more importantly, the children, would be safe in Witness Protection—even if he didn't make it back to join them. Everything had been arranged.

One of the men tripped at the edge of the helipad. Mitch put a bullet in his back as he raced past and lunged for the chopper, which was lifting off with the second man he was chasing aboard. Out of reflex, he grabbed the landing skid, and within seconds was dangling a hundred feet above the earth.

With a Herculean effort, he lifted himself up and onto the skid, and pulled at the door handle desperately—but it was locked. After shooting it twice, he grabbed the handle again and yanked the door open—only to come face-to-face with the young blond man he and Dez had been tracking from Virginia.

Before Mitch could react, the man fired a single shot.

Mitch tumbled backward—dead before he hit the ground.

RICHMOND, VIRGINIA

Racine glanced up as the door of his Excel Games office opened, and Frankie Federov entered.

"Hello, Frankie."

"David."

"Have a seat," Racine said, gesturing at the two chairs before the desk.

Federov, aka the White Russian, was responsible for catching and killing the nasty bug that had haunted Excel Games' software for so long—a bug no else could find, though many had tried. A bug, Racine was convinced, which would have kept Xilai from investing had Federov not exerted his legendary skills on the software and the company network.

"What do you have for me?"

Federov chuckled in his deep, rolling laugh. "It was the Dragon Lady from North Korea," he answered in his heavy Russian accent. "She's very sly, but I recognized her dainty footprints. It didn't take long."

"Explain."

"As you asked me to, I hacked into the Gaynor Corporation network. I was able to determine that the Dragon Lady had planted the e-mails there." Federov grinned. "Almost impossible to tell, but I've seen her masterpieces before. It is very beautiful, as she is supposed to be. I would like to meet her in person one day," he said wistfully. "She made it look as if Ms. Gaynor had sent the e-mails. But it was her. It was the Dragon Lady."

"Can you prove that?"

"I have the proof already."

"I need you to get it to Angela Gaynor's attorneys in Virginia Beach, immediately. Your time is valuable, so Excel Games will pay you five thousand dollars for your trip down there. I've already spoken to Bart about it."

"Fine."

"I don't want anyone else delivering it but you. You will explain what you've found, but you will remain anonymous, and you will not testify. The attorney will have to find his own expert witness to explain it."

"That won't be hard with the road map I'll give the attorney."

"Good. Go."

When Federov was gone, Racine picked up the landline and dialed the number on the paper. His hand shook so hard as the phone rang he had to press it tightly to his ear.

"Hello."

"Claire?"

"Dad! Is it you?"

"Yes, Claire," he answered, almost unable to get the words out his emotion was so strong. "It's me. I love you."

"I love you, too, Dad, so much."

She was on the west coast with her mother and the tennis pro. So there was no way to see her in the little time he had outside from the walls. But at least he could hear her voice.

"Tell me everything, honey, everything about your life. I can't wait to hear."

As she began to talk, tears flooded his eyes and cascaded down his cheeks. He put the phone on mute as she kept going. He didn't want her to hear him cry.

NORTH WOODS OF MAINE

When the e-mail hit his phone, Dez scanned it quickly and then glanced up at the two handcuffed men sitting side by side on the couch in front of him. He and one of his subordinates had captured and detained the two men less than a hundred yards from here.

One of the four who had scampered from the cabin in the SUV lights had escaped on the chopper—along with the young blond guy—and Mitch was dead, which was a terrible tragedy. But three of four wasn't bad. And the fourth would probably hide for the rest of his days. The conspiracy had been shredded. Judge Eldridge—and Attorney General Delgado—were going to be very happy men tonight.

Dez shook his head. "CIA and DHS," he said, after glancing at the phone again to be sure he'd gotten the agencies correct. He'd picked their wallets from their pockets a minute ago, then called a contact in Washington with the names on each driver's licenses. The answers had come back within seconds. "Unbelievable."

The two men on the couch stared back at him impassively for several moments. Then both looked away.

"All those juries," Dez whispered, "all over the country. You bastards."

He took a deep breath and looked around—then shot both men dead through the chests. He'd been given license to kill a few years ago, and this seemed an appropriate time to use the privilege. If he'd delivered these men to authorities, they would have made bail in hours—exactly like the men who'd attacked Victoria at her home outside Richmond.

Dez chuckled as he gazed at the bodies of the two men, which were now crumpled over against each other on the couch. They weren't going to make bail now.

CHAPTER 49

JURY TOWN

"We've got to get everyone out of here!" Victoria shouted, bursting into Clint Wolf's office. *"Immediately!"*

Wolf's eyes raced up from the file he'd been studying, and his expression went mystified. "It's Sunday night. What are you doing here?"

"The hell with what I'm doing here, we've got to get everyone out."

"Why?" Wolf demanded, rising from his desk. "What's going on?"

"We've been targeted. A Delta Airlines flight bound for Atlanta was hijacked out of Dulles four minutes ago. We have credible information that they're going to fly the plane straight into us. Fighters from Andrews and Langley are jumping, but they aren't sure they can intercept in time."

For several seconds Wolf stared at her without blinking, then his eyes narrowed. "Who's the source?" he demanded. "How do you know this?"

"Michael Delgado, the United States attorney general." She raced to Wolf's desk, grabbed the landline receiver, and held it up. "You want to talk to him? I'll get him on the phone right now."

Wolf's mouth fell open. "No, I . . . uh—"

"I just hope to God you have that EVAC plan in place. You told me you did. You told me you'd thought all this through."

"I have," Wolf answered calmly. "We're fine."

Six minutes later, four buses were roaring away from Jury Town, filled with jurors.

CHARLOTTESVILLE, VIRGINIA

Racine and Sofia jogged through the forest together, through the darkness and the mist of the evening, dodging low-hanging branches, sticker bushes, and rocks.

When Racine stopped to get his bearings, Sofia leaned over, put her hands on her knees, and gasped much-needed oxygen. "I don't have much left, David."

"You'll be fine," he said encouragingly as he spotted the target through the trees. He could hear the low murmur of hundreds of voices rumbling through the woods. "We're almost there." He took her hand. "Come on."

She rose up and pulled him to her. "You gave me such a beautiful gift this weekend, David," she murmured. "You gave me the gift of seeing my children, even if it was only for a few hours."

She slipped her hand to the back of his neck and kissed him deeply.

When she pulled back, he raised both eyebrows and blinked several times. "Where am I?"

She smiled. "Taking me back to Jury Town."

"Oh, right. Come on."

Moments later they'd made it to the edge of a huge field in the middle of the forest four miles from Jury Town—where the jurors had filed off the buses to wait . . . for what, they hadn't been told.

Racine kissed her once more, then led her out of the forest and into the mass of jurors milling about in the field. They'd never been missed.

"Delta flight bound for Atlanta, huh?" Wolf muttered as the jurors filed onto the buses to head back to Jury Town. "Good one, Victoria."

She grinned as Racine and Sofia passed in front of them and climbed onto the bus they were closest to. "Just testing, Clint, just testing."

CHAPTER 50

JURY TOWN

"Have you reached a verdict, Mr. Foreman?"

Racine rose from his position at the back right of the jury box, pushed open the wooden gate of the back row, stepped down, and walked out so that he was in front of the jury box and directly before the camera.

"We have, Your Honor."

"What say you?"

"We find the defendant, Angela Gaynor, *not* guilty of all charges."

The courtroom exploded into applause, which would not be interrupted by the judge's gavel.

Armed with the White Russian's proof, the Gaynor defense team had quickly proven that the e-mails supposedly sent to Jack Hoffman by Gaynor were fraudulent. In addition, Hoffman and the mayor had been subtly notified that their benefactors were mostly dead. Understanding that they would now be looking at long sentences, they'd both offered to recant their testimony in return for reduced years behind bars. The case against Angela Gaynor had quickly disintegrated.

For a few moments, Racine watched the wild scene going on in the courtroom play out on the four screens mounted to the front wall of the jury room. Then he turned to look at Sofia.

She was standing now, too, as were all the jurors. They were all smiling now that they'd given their first verdict inside Jury Town.

But Sofia wore the widest smile of all—and she was giving it all to him.

———————

"Victoria, this jury program you've organized in Virginia has already achieved outstanding success. I wanted to be one of the first to shake your hand over the phone."

"Thank you, Senator Jordan. That's very kind of you."

Miles Jordan was a four-term United States senator from Chicago, and chairman of the influential Armed Services Committee. African-American, he was revered by Democrats and Republicans alike, and he was one of the most powerful men in Washington. Getting a call from Miles Jordan was like getting a call from Daniel Eldridge—except this involved the national stage.

"Your famous ancestor, Meriwether Lewis, would be very proud of you, Victoria. You are clearly cut from the same cloth of extraordinary achievement."

"Thank you, sir."

"Your father would be proud, too."

Some young aide to Senator Jordan had been busy. "Thank you again, Senator Jordan." Even if the aide had done the research, it was a bold and beautiful thing for Jordan to say, and it sincerely touched her heart. "That's nice to hear. I hope he would."

"Oh, he would. Listen, I'm interested in this concept for my home state of Illinois. What do you call it?"

"Jury Town."

"Yes, well, I wonder if you would have a conference call with some associates of mine in the state government back in Springfield."

This request could not be ignored or avoided. "I'd be happy to, sir."

"Great news. I can't have California and New York getting ahead of Illinois on this initiative." He chuckled in his deep, bass voice. "I'll be second in the race to Virginia, but I won't be fourth to them." He hesitated. "If you don't mind me asking, how did you come up with this concept?"

This question could easily represent a test. Jordan might already be well aware of the concept's origin. Jordan and Attorney General Delgado were close friends, she knew.

"Oh, that's confidential, sir," she said in a lighthearted way. It was the best approach to take at this level of politics. It wouldn't do her any good to drop Delgado's name right now. She'd get much more mileage out of keeping the attorney general protected. "I have to protect the guilty."

Jordan laughed heartily. "I appreciate that. One more thing before we hang up."

"Yes, sir?"

"Before you decide on your next outstanding achievement, come up to Washington and have lunch with me. I've already had some preliminary conversations about you with others of influence in this town. We think you may have something we want. More importantly, we think you may have something four hundred million people of this country want. Am I making myself clear?"

"Yes, sir," she answered firmly as a presidential thrill rushed through her.

"I'll arrange that call with my people in Springfield. And do me a favor. Go radio-silent on California and New York for a little while. Good-bye, Victoria. And congratulations again on Jury Town's tremendous success."

"Thank you, sir."

Call over, she leaned back in her desk chair and gazed up at the ceiling of her home study as that thrill surging through her grew and grew with intensity. "President Victoria Lewis," she whispered looking up at the ceiling. "What do you think, Dad?"

CHAPTER 51

VIRGINIA BEACH, VIRGINIA

Angela walked along the sun-bathed sidewalk next to Trent, the two of them attracting fascinated double and triple takes from those going the other way.

"Can I have your autograph?" a young boy asked shyly, holding up a pen and pad after scampering up to them.

Trent glanced ahead. A man who appeared to be the boy's father stood twenty feet in front of them on the sidewalk. He was waving and smiling back self-consciously.

"You don't want my autograph," Trent said, leaning down to pat the boy on the shoulder as he towered over him. "You want this lady's. She's going to be the next United States senator from Virginia."

"Trent," Angela said loudly. "He wants an all-star basketball player's autograph, not a politician's. Always give the people what they want."

"Well, he should be interested in yours," Trent said as he took the pen and pad and scribbled his name. "You're going to make history in a few days, Angie. Your signature will end up being worth way more than mine."

"We'll see about that."

With the not-guilty verdict, her campaign had quickly regained momentum. Only days to the election, and she'd pulled dead even with Chuck Lehman.

"It will be," Trent assured her, handing the autograph to the kid. "The rally tonight in northern Virginia will put you over the top."

"I hope so," she said as the boy raced away gleefully and handed the pen to his father—but not the pad.

"I'm not sure about today," Trent said, motioning ahead to the restaurant they were walking toward. "I don't like breaking bread with the enemy, especially so close to the battle."

"Martha Lehman is not the enemy."

"She's married to Chuck Lehman, isn't she?"

"Yes."

"Then she's the enemy."

"You're wrong. Martha's great. I've met her before several times, and she is wonderful. She's a tireless worker for her charities, too. She wants to talk about opening an inner-city home for runaway girls down here in Virginia Beach. I'd look pretty bad if I turned her down on that—oh, jeez."

Angela stumbled forward as her left heel momentarily caught a crack of the sidewalk.

At the same moment she pitched forward, a rifle exploded from the second floor of a parking garage three blocks away. The bullet screamed harmlessly off the pavement behind her.

But the second shot found its mark.

WASHINGTON, DC (GEORGETOWN)

When Chuck Lehman answered the loud, persistent knocking at the front door of their home, he was shocked to find no fewer than fifteen law-enforcement officials in front of him—some in uniform, some in suit and tie.

When the lead investigator had explained what was happening, Lehman, in a shaky voice, requested five minutes alone. He was given three.

After he'd raced upstairs, he turned into the master bedroom, then entered Martha's expansive walk-in closet. She was sitting in one corner of the large room, knees pulled to her chin, tears streaming down her face.

"I did it for you, Chuck," she whispered as heavy footsteps hurried across the living room downstairs and began climbing the stairs toward them. "Don't let them take me away," she begged. "Save me, Chuck."

"You set up Angela Gaynor? You wanted the White House *that* badly?" He shook his head as the pack of officers entered the bedroom behind him. "There's nothing I can do, Martha. You're going to jail . . . and then to prison."

Lehman put his face into his hands. You thought you knew a person.

VIRGINIA BEACH, VIRGINIA

"Is he going to be all right?" Angela whispered anxiously as she held Trent's huge hand. She sat beside him as he lay on the bed in the ICU.

"He'll be fine," the surgeon answered confidently. "The bullet did some damage to his right shoulder, so he won't have much of a jump shot for a while. But he'll live."

"Damn," Trent whispered, "there goes my comeback." He grinned up at her. "Kiss me, Senator Gaynor."

EPILOGUE
RICHMOND, VIRGINIA

"I'm sorry again about your nephew, Judge Eldridge."

"Thank you, Victoria," Eldridge said quietly from behind the desk of his Supreme Court office. "At least Mitch died honorably. He had a lot to make up for. He knew that. I think that's why he did what he did in Maine. He knew going up on that helicopter wasn't going to end well. He took the courageous way out. He died in battle."

"It's ironic. If he hadn't taken those payoffs from Salvatore Celino, we might never have found out who was manipulating the juries."

Eldridge shook his head. "It's still difficult to believe how high up the conspiracy went and at what agencies. CIA, DHS, NSA. It's astounding, really, and a shining example of how we must always question our leaders . . . and check on them constantly. Concentration of power is a recipe for evil."

"And we didn't get them all. One of those men is still out there."

"As is whoever tried to kill Angela Gaynor. Thank God, Trent Tucker is all right."

"I still find it hard to believe that Chuck Lehman's wife was the one who passed Angela's location on to the shooter," Victoria remarked. "She was the one who set Angela up. She seems like such a sweet soul."

"Martha wanted her husband to be president, at any cost. She was quietly but unquestionably obsessed with it. Has she said anything yet about who the shooter was?"

"Not as of yesterday. I'm not sure she knows."

"Angela came so close to being assassinated."

"So close to not becoming a United States senator and now she's on the Hill. She's quite a success story."

"As are you," Eldridge pointed out, smiling. "Jury Town is a massive success. The reason I asked you to come to my office today was to tell you that every judge I've spoken to claims it's the best thing that's ever happened to the Commonwealth's jury system. It's exactly as we hoped, Victoria. The juries are becoming incredibly efficient and incredibly knowledgeable. A couple of my old cronies say it's starting to get embarrassing because the jury members are more familiar with the law than some of the attorneys coming before them."

Victoria laughed. "Maybe someday they'll be more familiar than the judges."

"Don't hold your breath," Eldridge replied good-naturedly. "What's going on with the other states?"

"Illinois is just weeks away from bringing their project online, and California and New York won't be far behind."

"And you? What's next for you?"

She grinned as she rose from the chair in front of his desk. "I've got my eye on something big."

Eldridge winked. "So I heard from Senator Jordan. He told me you two had an excellent lunch in Washington last week."

Victoria nodded. "We did." She smiled back at him as she rose from her chair and headed for the office door. "You're a tough man. I love you, Your Honor."

He chuckled. "Just remember me when you're president, Ms. Lewis."

"That'll be pretty easy . . . because I won't ever forget you. I can't."
She moved out of the office and grinned at Dez, who was waiting for
her. "So, what are we going to do with the rest of the day?"

"Well, I thought maybe we'd finally have that drink together. And
then we'd go dancing . . . but this time in public."

"Perfect," Victoria agreed. She moved to where he stood and tapped
his arm three times so the pennies on her bracelet jingled. "Just perfect,
Mr. Braxton."

ACKNOWLEDGMENTS

To my daughters, Christina, Ashley, and Elle. The lights of my life.

To my literary agent, Cynthia Manson. A wonderful partnership that's lasted twenty years.

To my editor, Caitlin Alexander. Caitlin did a tremendous job on this book.

To all the great people at Thomas & Mercer who make these books possible . . . including Alan Turkus, Kjersti Egerdahl, Jacque Ben-Zekry, Tiffany Pokorny, and Paul Morrissey.

To Kevin "Big Sky" Erdman. I never would have known Montana without him.

To the others who've been so supportive and helpful through the years: Matt and Sarah Malone, Andy and Chris Brusman, Pat Lynch, Jack and Linda Wallace, Jeanette Follo, Lisa Sevenski, Barbara Fertig, Bart Begley, Walter Frey, Marvin Bush, Scott Andrews, and Baron Stewart. Thank you all so much.

ABOUT THE AUTHOR

 Stephen Frey has spent thirty years working in investment banking and private equity at firms including J. P. Morgan & Company in New York City and Winston Partners in Arlington, Virginia. He is the author of twenty-one novels, including the Red Cell series, *Arctic Fire*, *Red Cell Seven*, and *Kodiak Sky*. He lives in Leesburg, Virginia.